# The Musketeer's Inheritance
## Sarah D'Almeida

Goldport Press

# Contents

1.  Where the Musketeers Are Good Samaritans; Springing His Eminence's Trap; An Unwelcome Summons    1

2.  The Responsibilities of Friendship; Why an Agreed Upon Plan Is Not Always Agreed Upon; For Lack of a Horse    8

3.  How Not To Wake a Musketeer; A Little Perfidy in the Right Place    13

4.  The Many Inconveniences of Wintry Travel; Meager Purse and Rushing Mind; The Foolhardiness of Highwaymen    17

5.  Doubts and Confusion; The Improbability of Dreaming Planchet; The Difference Between a Duel and Murder    22

6.  A Close Thing; The Demands of Friendship; The Wealth of Highwaymen    29

7.  Philistines and Samaritans Again; Blood and Jewels; The Right Letter in the Wrong Place    33

8.  The Advantages of Inns and Taverns; The Languages of Monsieur Porthos; The Livers of Geese    37

9.  Where Waking Is the Best Part of Valor; The Very Odd Habits of Gascon Cutthroats; The Finer Points of Treason    43

10. The Dogs of Gascony; A Widow's Grief; Athos's Fears    51

11. D'Artagnan's Fears; The Office of Monsieur D'Artagnan    58
    Père; D'Artagnan's Secret

12. The Saints of Gascony; Feuds of Blood; Monsieur    66
    Aramis's Philosophy of Life

13. The Wisdom of the Stables; Monsieur Athos's Refusal    72
    to Suspect a Woman; Where Men Are More Than Their
    Families

14. The Lord of the Domain; Talking to Women; The Rules of    78
    Dueling

15. Porthos's Mind; Blood in the Fields; The End of the Trail    85

16. A Musketeer's Piety; Witness to Death; Where Some    91
    Truths Are Harder Than Others

17. Another Way Not to Wake a Musketeer; A Woman's Sin-    98
    gular Lack of Intuition; The Perversity of a Man's Heart

18. The Richer Branch; Nothing Is Quite as Dead as a Dead    104
    Love; The Familiar Binds

19. Religion and Fighting; Pastoral Care; A Burden to Keep    113

20. The Useful Lord; The Fine Art of Talking to Village Maid-    118
    ens; A Man in the Noonday Sun

21. Where Cousins Rarely Are Highwaymen; Surprises and    122
    Shocks; At Monsieur de Bilh's

22. A Musketeer's Conscience; Religion and the Cardinal; A    128
    Matter of Horses

23. Dead Man's Clothes; The Blood Speaks    135

24. An Unexpected Fight; The Eyes of Adulthood; What Man    140
    Knows His Own Mother

25. The Tale of the Blood; Where D'Artagnan Ponders Un-    147
    known Relatives; The Cardinal's Methods

26. Madame D'Artagnan's Confusion; Where Relatives    152
    Aren't Exactly Relatives; The Impossibility of Making
    Women Speak

27. The Impossibility of Women; Secrets and Their Keepers;    157
    An Unexpected Meeting

28. On Horses and Roads; Neighbors in Gascony; A Great    162
    Lord's Hospitality

29. The Dangers of the Gascon Countryside; Lovers and    168
    Fools

30. Four Cloaked Men Conspiring; The Many Paths of En-    172
    quiry

31. A Sacrifice of Blood; Death and Asking; The Search    174

32. Between Musketeer and Servants; Dead Man's Accounts;    178
    Letters

33. A Priest's Doubts; A Musketeer's Fears    183

34. Horses and Men; Monsieur Porthos Engages in Philoso-    186
    phy; The Odd Relationships of Provincial Gentlemen

35. A War Council; Horses and Mothers; The Dangers of    189
    Cousins

36. A Warm Reception; The Matter of a Dagger; Where Mon-    196
    sieur Porthos Loses Patience

37. Ghosts; A Musketeer's Sleeplessness; Eyes Only     201

38. Invading Bedrooms Again; A Son's Duty; Dogs and An-
gels     208

39. Old Secrets and New Grievances; Where a Father Is Lost
and a Grandfather Found; A Name Worth More Than All
Lands     212

40. The Best Laid Plans     217

41. His Eminence's Displeasure; Where a Letter Falls in the
Fire     219

42. Footnotes     221

## Where the Musketeers Are Good Samaritans; Springing His Eminence's Trap; An Unwelcome Summons

"**E**N GARDE**,**" Monsieur Henri D'Artagnan said, as he danced back to a defensive position and lifted his sword. "Unsheathe your swords."

Facing him, under the pale yellow sun of early autumn, outraging him with their presence on the outskirts of Paris, just outside the convent of the Barefoot Carmelites, three guards of Cardinal Richelieu pointedly did *not* unsheathe.

Instead, the lead one, a middle-aged blond, looked from D'Artagnan to—behind the young guard—the three musketeers who stood, staring at the scene with varying expressions of amusement.

"But, monsieur," the guard of the Cardinal said, lifting his hat and scratching at the sparse blond hair beneath. "All I did was remind you of the edicts against dueling. How would this justify *dueling* with you?"

D'Artagnan hesitated, his internal conflict visible only in a straightening of his shoulders and a sharp look up. Seventeen years old, with the lank dark hair and bright dark eyes of his native Gascony, D'Artagnan was muscular and lean like a fine horse. And as in a fine horse, every one of his thoughts was obvious in movement, in stance, in a tossing of the head or a quick glance. He knew this. He was aware of his body's betraying his impatience.

"It seems to me," a mannered, cultivated voice said from behind D'Artagnan, "that you have offered our friend a great insult, monsieur guard."

It was a voice that would have sounded very well coming out of a pulpit and explaining in rounded phrases some obscure point of theology. The gentleman who spoke, so far from looking like a priest, was a tall, well-built blond, whose hair, falling in waves to his waist, shone from brushing.

His clothes, in the last cry of fashion, boasted a doublet that was only vaguely that of the musketeer's uniform. Though blue, it was made of patterned satin and crisscrossed with enough ribbon to adorn several court dresses. More ribbons adorned his sleeves and hung in fetching knots from wrist closures. A profusion of silver buttons shone like the ice that sparkled from the ground on this cold November morning.

His name was Aramis and despite the languid speech and the intent gaze he now bent upon his perfectly manicured nails, he was known as one of the most dangerous blades in the King's Musketeers and a breaker of ladies' hearts. It was said he was pursued by princesses, courted by duchesses, and that a foreign queen had sent him the expensive jewel that dazzled from his exquisitely plumed hat.

D'Artagnan knew Aramis well enough that he did not need to turn to know that his friend's bright green eyes shone with mischief. Aramis was enjoying this. His enjoyment did not help D'Artagnan calm down.

"Indeed," another of the musketeers said. He was as tall as Aramis, but of quite a different type. His clothes were in the fashion of decades ago—a tightly laced doublet and old-fashioned knee breeches that displayed, below the knees, muscular legs encased in mended stockings.

This musketeer's curly hair—a black so dark as to appear blue in certain lights—was tightly pulled back and tied roughly with a scrap of leather. His pale skin betrayed the slight creasing around the eyes, the lines around the mouth that showed him the oldest one of those present—and as not having lived an easy life.

Looking back over his shoulder, D'Artagnan saw that his friend's smile was guarded, but that his dark blue eyes sparkled with as much mischief as those of Aramis. His name was Athos, though D'Artagnan had found that in another life—before he'd joined the musketeers to expiate what he considered his unforgivable crime—he'd been the Count de la Fere, scion of one of the oldest families in the realm.

His nobility showed now, as he advanced a foot and tossed back his head. Despite his mended clothes, he was very much the grand seigneur as he said, "I think these gentlemen owe you an apology, D'Artagnan."

"What I don't understand," the third musketeer said, his voice booming over the landscape and making the guards jump, "is why they assume we were dueling, I mean..." He paused, struggling for words.

This enmity with language was the trademark of Porthos and despite his present anger D'Artagnan couldn't help smiling slightly at hearing it. It often made people think Porthos stupid, but very few would tell it to his face, because Porthos looked like a Norse god. Much taller than his companions—or indeed than anyone else—with broad shoulders and a muscular body capable of feats of strength to rival those of mythology, Porthos could not be made more splendid by wrapping himself in finery. This didn't stop him trying.

Norsemen had dreamed of such as him in the guise of Thor, working an eternal forge. They probably had failed to imagine his gilded baldric, the rope of gold that surrounded the brim of his hat, or the multiple jewels that flashed from each of his powerful fingers. Most of them glass, if D'Artagnan knew his friend, but splendid-looking nonetheless.

Porthos shook his head, giving the impression of utter bewilderment, as he asked the guards, "*Mort Dieu*, can't four friends meet to go to a dinner without bringing you down on them with your edicts and your...your...*dents Dieu*, I know not what to say...Your regulations? The precious orders of your...Cardinal?"

"But, monsieurs..." The guard pointed out reasonably. "Surely..." He shrugged, not in a show of lack of knowledge so much as in total bewilderment. His bewilderment, his meek pose were an affront to D'Artagnan's mind and heart. "Monsieurs, surely—" He looked around at the immediate surroundings, where the scuffed ground, two broken swords, and a trail of blood leading, tellingly, to the door of the convent, all spoke of a recent fray. "Surely you see...There's been a duel here."

"Oh, and if there's been a duel, we must be to blame, eh? Very pretty reasoning that," Porthos boomed. "That's the musketeers. Always dueling. Easy thought. And wrong. We were going to dinner."

D'Artagnan, who found none of this funny, and whose bloodlust was rising at the guard's refusal to face him, spoke through clenched teeth, to repeat yet again, "En garde."

"But—" the guard said, and opened his hands in a show of desperation. His companions, two smaller, darker men, stood with hands on the hilts of their swords, but did not draw.

Aramis sighed, heavily—the sort of world-weary sigh that could be expected from a man who claimed that he was wearing the uniform of a musketeer only temporarily, until he could attain his ambition of becoming a priest. Hearing of it, no one could guess that his seminary education had been interrupted years ago when a gentleman had found Aramis reading the lives of saints—at least that was what he swore he'd been doing—to the gentleman's wellborn sister and challenged Aramis to a duel, thereby forcing Aramis to kill him.

"If you must know," he said, looking up from an intent examination of his nails and speaking in a voice that implied that no well-bred person would push the point so far. "We heard the moans of the injured and we stopped to render assistance. I am, as you have probably heard, all but in orders, and I thought perhaps I could give some comfort to the dying."

The guards looked from one to the other. "You're telling us that you came to help these other men?"

"Very good of us, it was," Porthos boomed. "In fact, we behaved like true Philistines."

The guards looked up at him with disbelief, and even D'Artagnan was forced to look over his shoulder at his giant, redheaded friend.

"I believe you mean Samaritans, Porthos," Aramis said, and coughed.

"Do I?" Porthos said, then waved airily. "All the same, I say. All those people were the same, anyway. Always giving their aunt's wife's donkey in marriage to each other." And with such a cryptic pronouncement, he said, "D'Artagnan, if they apologize, will you let them go?"

D'Artagnan shook his head. No. No and no and no. Their very apologies would only enrage him. The truth was that the guards had come—of course—just at the conclusion of a duel arranged by the musketeers the day before. They'd arrived just after the musketeers had dispatched their opponents and helped the wounded carry the dead to the convent.

And now they persisted in their nonsensical quest to arrest the musketeers—without drawing swords, without raising their voices, without, in fact, even calling attention to Porthos's blood-smeared sleeve or the noticeable tear that rent the sleeve of Athos's doublet on the right side.

They not only had found out that the musketeers were going to duel—in itself this was not a great mystery, since the duel had been called in a tavern over a handful of noblemen's refusal to drink to the King's health—but they refused to fight.

D'Artagnan's scornful gaze accessed the guards' middle-aged countenances, their pasty faces, the fact that each of them carried the sort of extra weight that a few duels a month burned off. He judged them to be nobodies. The type of nobodies given a post in the guards to appease some family connection or some powerful nobleman.

They wouldn't fight because they couldn't. And if D'Artagnan slaughtered them all, the best to be hoped for would be that he would become everywhere known as a killer of the defenseless. There was no honor in a killing such as this. There would only be shame in winning; but losing was unthinkable.

Sending these men to arrest musketeers was, in fact, not only an insult, but a cunning ploy of the Cardinal's. The sort of ploy that the snake who ruled behind the throne of France was well known for. And D'Artagnan's friends didn't even see it.

D'Artagnan stamped his foot, in hatred of the Cardinal and in fury and frustration at his friends. "Draw, or I slaughter you where you stand," he said, knowing only that to back out would be shame and to continue forward would be disaster. He was caught in the Cardinal's trap.

The sound of running feet didn't intrude into his mind. He did not look until a well known voice called, breathlessly, from the side, "Monsieur, monsieur."

D'Artagnan turned. Planchet had been left safely in D'Artagnan's lodging, at the Rue des Fossoyers. Planchet would not come here, like this, much less think of interrupting a duel without very grave reason. Reason so grave that D'Artagnan couldn't even imagine it.

All this was in his mind, not in full thoughts—not fully in words—as he turned, sword still in hand, still lifted, to see his servant—his bright red hair standing on end, his dark suit dusty and stained as if he'd run the whole way here—leaning forward, hands on knees, a respectful distance from him. "Planchet, what is it?"

And the guards attacked. D'Artagnan heard the sound of swords sliding from their sheathes and turned. He was barely in time to meet head-on the clumsy rush of the blond guard.

"Ah, coward," he said, only vaguely aware that Porthos and Aramis had joined the fray on either side of him, taking on the blond's assistants. D'Artagnan parried a thrust and made a very accurate thrust of his own, slitting the man's doublet from top to bottom and ending by flipping his hat off his head. "Would you duel with a real man?" he said.

The blond had a moment to look aghast at his torn clothing, cut with such precision as not to touch the flesh beneath, and to bend upon D'Artagnan a gaze of the purest horror. His lips worked, but no sound emerged.

And D'Artagnan, his mind viewing the man and his fear as only a move in his chess game with the Cardinal, thought he glimpsed an opening, a way out of the trap of honor in which he found himself. He lunged forward, saying, "You think you can stand up against the musketeers? Don't you think it will take more than that to face the men who have so often proved superior to his eminence's best guards?"

"That's right," Porthos said. He had, with easy bluster, inflicted a minor wound on his opponent's arm, and was grinning as he prepared to parry a counterattack that might very well never come. "That's right. We'd rather die. Be cut to pieces right here, than allow you to arrest us."

"At any rate, monsieurs," Aramis said, from D'Artagnan's right. "It would be a more merciful and quicker way to die to allow ourselves to be killed here than to face the wrath of Monsieur de Treville." There was still a tremolo of amusement to his voice, and D'Artagnan wondered if Aramis had begun to glimpse both the trap and the way out. Or if he, cunning as he was, had seen it all along, and before D'Artagnan himself had. "So we die here, monsieurs, but you cannot arrest us."

And in that second something broke in the leader's eyes. He looked down at his torn doublet that showed a dubiously clean linen shirt beneath, then he looked quickly at D'Artagnan. And then his sword clattered to the ground and, before D'Artagnan could gracefully accept his surrender, the man had taken to his heels, running fast over the ice-crusted fields, slipping and standing and slipping again.

His men, clearly treasuring following their leader over valor, dropped their swords, so fast they seemed like echoes of his, and did their best to catch up with him.

"Well played, D'Artagnan," Aramis said. "I was wondering when you'd see their surrender, or preferably their flight, was the only way out of this for us. At least the only way with honor." His lazy smile, the paternal tone of his words, implied that he'd seen this all along. D'Artagnan wondered if it was true. With Aramis it wasn't easy to say. Aramis himself might not know.

"Poor devils," Porthos said, looking after the fleeing men. "They were as set up for this as we were. And the wrath they will face from the

Cardinal makes what we'd face at Monsieur de Treville's hands seem almost gentle." He took a deep breath, straining the expanse of his broad chest. "The affront is the Cardinal's. I wish it were possible to challenge him for a duel."

"He was a good enough duelist in his youth," Aramis said, his tone deceptively light.

And D'Artagnan wondered if his mad friends, who hated the Cardinal for many good reasons as well as many foolish ones, would suddenly decide to challenge the His Emminence. Cardinal.

He opened his mouth to remind them that men such as his eminence didn't fight with their swords but with the might of the kingdom, when Athos spoke, "D'Artagnan, attend. This is grave business." He held a letter in his hand—its seal broken—and waved it slightly in D'Artagnan's direction.

"Grave?" D'Artagnan asked. He sheathed his sword and stepped towards Athos. "What is it? From whom? And for whom?"

But the words died on his lips. He'd got close enough to recognize his mother's hand, the rounded convent hand that she'd been taught as a young girl. His mother? Writing to him? Normally his father did.

And Athos was alarmed, as doubtless had been Planchet to run all the way here.

With shaking hand, D'Artagnan plucked the sheet of paper from Athos's unresisting fingers and brought it up in front of his eyes, focusing on the writing.

"Dear son," the letter started primly. "I regret the necessity of it, but I must call you back from Paris at a very short notice. You see, there is no one else to claim the name or the domain. There is no one else to take up the care of the lands, or even to look after me." D'Artagnan blinked in confusion at the words, wondering what his mother could mean, and almost had to force himself to read on. "Your father departed this world on Monday, a week ago. Today is the first time I've had the time and solitude," *solitude* was heavily underscored, "to write this letter to you. For you must know that though they say it was a duel, I cannot be easy about your father's death. He had, after all, been looking into your uncle's affairs and I think he was doing it at the behest of that great man, Cardinal Richelieu. Of course, no one else knew this, either that he was looking into things or about the Cardinal, but a woman knows these things." *Knows* was, again, deeply underscored. "You know how your father valued you and trusted you. I can't tell this to anyone else. Please, hurry home, son, and take up your rightful place in this household." It was signed in a tremulous hand with what read like Mauvais D'Aortoise but D'Artagnan could guess to be his mother's signature—Marie D'Artagnan—distorted by emotion.

But...what emotion? D'Artagnan could barely absorb the contents of the letter.

His father dead? From a duel? Impossible. Monsieur Françios Charles D'Artagnan[1] père had taught his son to such effect that even the most famous fighters in Paris could not best him.

A murder disguised as a duel? Impossible again. D'Artagnan's mind ran over the place of his childhood, those domains that he'd described often as smaller than the Cemetery des Innocents in Paris.

D'Artagnan's father had grown up there and, save for the brief time at war, lived there, in those villages and fields. There was no one there who'd raise a hand against him. It would never happen.

And yet...His father was dead. And his father had been working for the Cardinal?

Every feeling revolted, and the print seemed stark and cold upon the page. D'Artagnan felt a sob trying to tear through his throat, and fought it back with all his might, with greater strength than he'd ever had to employ against a human enemy.

He took a deep breath. His voice came out reasonably controlled. "You are right, Athos. This is grave. I'd best attend to it."

"Of course," Athos said. "When do the four of us leave for Gascony?"

# The Responsibilities of Friendship; Why an Agreed Upon Plan Is Not Always Agreed Upon; For Lack of a Horse

**"YOU** will arrange my luggage, Planchet," D'Artagnan said, as he entered his home.

It was late afternoon and the long twilight shadows of Autumn fell brownish grey into the sparsely furnished rooms. The yellowish light coming through the windows barely allowed the eye to distinguish a broad polished table with four chairs around it, and beyond, the door to D'Artagnan's bedroom.

D'Artagnan walked all the way into his bedroom, speaking, "I did not intend to be so delayed, but it is just as well. I must pack. We must leave tonight. And if we leave at night, we're less likely to be found. Porthos and Aramis are on guard at the Palais Royale tonight, are they not?"

As he entered his bedroom, he realized that Planchet hadn't followed him. He turned to see the young man standing in the middle of the entrance room, his hand on the polished table. "Leave?" he said. "Tonight? But monsieur, your friends..."

"Ah, yes, my friends. They presume they'll go with me, do they not?" Indeed they did and had consumed the best part of the afternoon in plans for how long until they could get leave to accompany their friend, how long that leave should be and how to ask Monsieur de Treville for it. D'Artagnan had listened to it all, feeling uncomfortable, but it wasn't till the way home, by Planchet's side, that he'd realized why he could never take his friends with him. And that he must leave without them. "But they don't understand, you see, Planchet. I am the only son of my father's house. Granted, my father is only a second son, and his estate, inherited from his mother, is not very big. But still I am his only heir, and as his only heir, I must stay there and look after my father's lands and tenants."

"Monsieur!" Planchet said, his tone shocked. Standing in the middle of the living room, he looked very pale, his red hair seeming to contrast unnaturally with his skin. The hand he rested on the table tightened.

D'Artagnan sighed. He couldn't begin to understand why his decision should distress his servant so. After all, what did this have to do with Planchet? It was D'Artagnan whose life had just been blighted. He'd been in Paris only six months, but in fact, between meeting Athos,

Porthos and Aramis and falling into easy friendship with them, between duels and murder investigations, he felt like his life in the capital was at least as long—and twice as rich—as his life before that, amid the drowsing fields, the bucolic landscapes of Gascony.

"I don't want to go, Planchet, but I see no other choice. Now, if you'll help me pack, we can be out of here in a couple of hours. We can stop and get some food on the way. I have some money. And we can ride through most of the night, then sleep somewhere on the wayside tomorrow. We won't need an inn during the day and that will make us harder to find. Just in case my friends..."

"Monsieur," Planchet said. "Monsieur." He was clearly in some distress and D'Artagnan could see that he was struggling for words as much as Porthos normally did. "Monsieur, only...Only think of Madame Bonacieux."

D'Artagnan groaned before Planchet had fully finished pronouncing her name. Madame Bonacieux, his Constance, was technically the wife of D'Artagnan's landlord. Technically, since hers was a marriage of convenience and she seemed extremely artful in avoiding performing those duties that the church said a wife owed a husband.

She was the goddaughter of the Queen's steward, and she served in the palace as a maid to Queen Anne of Austria. This meant, in truth, that she rarely came home and when she did it was even more rarely at such hours as might encourage propinquity. She came at noon, or in the morning, visited her husband and was gone, claiming urgent work for the Queen.

Only...only of late, for the last couple of months, she'd been coming at night, now and then. Her husband knew nothing of it. In the darkness of night, Madame Constance Bonacieux would discreetly open the door that led up the stairs and to her tenant's room.

It was D'Artagnan's first love affair, and his heart and soul had become possessed by the beguiling, blond, court-bred, cosmopolitan woman. He loved her laughter. He loved her voice, cultivated and sounding perfectly rounded, much clearer than his own enunciation, which would always owe something to his native Gascon dialect. He loved the clothes she wore—those delicate, exquisite court gowns, made of the most flawless silk, and designed to push and reveal just the right things.

But most of all he loved her without her clothes on.

He groaned again.

He didn't know when next Constance would have a night off. Those happened not at her pleasure, but at the whim of her mistress, the Queen. Like all royal caprice, such favors were erratic. Normally D'Artagnan knew about it only as he felt her slipping into bed beside him.

He supposed he would never see her again. He supposed, too, that in three months, maybe less, his mother would ask him to marry some local girl. Not too noble—no one would push high nobility at a man of D'Artagnan's possessions. In his younger days, he had conceived a desperate passion for Irene, his girl cousin—a passion that his uncle had put an end to quickly enough. Since his uncle had inherited the majority of the estate, his nephew was not nearly rich enough to aspire to a girl of the elder branch of his family.

So she would probably be a girl of the low nobility—well born but not titled. The daughter of some other small manor holder. She would speak Gascon, and she would never have been outside her native land. She would never have seen a court gown, and she would be nothing like Constance.

Of a sudden, D'Artagnan realized that the worst thing that could happen was not his leaving without seeing Constance again. No, the worst thing that could happen was his seeing her again and having to say good-bye to her, knowing it was the last time he beheld her gold and rose loveliness.

"*Mort Dieu,*" he said. "Come, Planchet. No time to lose. We must be out of here before she would come, supposing she comes tonight. We have no time to lose. We must—" He stumbled into his room, in the growing darkness, and started haphazardly throwing his clothes into a saddlebag. He didn't have many clothes. Two spare shirts and a spare uniform in the color of the guards of Monsieur des Essarts, the brother-in-law of Monsieur de Treville.

Tossing the blue grey tunics into the saddlebag, he sighed. He'd have to wear them out, of course. There was nothing for it. His family was not so wealthy that it could afford new suits of clothes on a whim. And in Gascony no one would know what these meant. Only he would. Only he would mourn that, having served his apprenticeship for musketeer amid the guards of Monsieur des Essarts, he would now have to leave without becoming a musketeer.

Frowning, he thought that he would have to write a letter, to leave here, with other letters addressed to his friends. One of his friends would have to convey D'Artagnan's formal resignation to Monsieur des Essarts. Perhaps not the best way to do it, but D'Artagnan knew he wouldn't—couldn't—be coming back, and all of a sudden couldn't bear the thought of having to take leave of any of his friends and acquaintances in person.

"We must hurry," he said.

Planchet, still looking distressed, had taken time to light a candle, which he now brought into the room. "I don't understand your determination to leave before you see your friends again," he said, in measured tones.

"Oh, them most of all I do not wish to see," D'Artagnan said. "Their circumstances are so different from mine that they'd try to convince me to return from Gascony after organizing my affairs. They'd try to convince me to leave someone else in charge and come back with them.

Only imagine Aramis's dismay at the thought that I'll go to a place where fashion doesn't penetrate. And Athos, who abandoned his own domains, won't understand that I have no convenient family to take over mine. And Porthos...Well...Porthos just won't understand. There's nothing outside of Paris for him." He shook his head. "I don't know how to explain it to them, and it's easier to present them with the fact of my departure and leave letters explaining. I will of course invite them to visit and of course they won't, but...Easier that way."

"And myself, monsieur?" Planchet asked. He set the candle down and opened his hands in a gesture of helplessness.

"You'll come with me. I'll need a servant on the way, in case I meet with some mishap. Someone to go call for help, at any rate. And besides, you'll need to bring the horses back."

"The horses?" Planchet asked, as if he'd never heard of such a creature.

"Of course." Why was the young man so slow-witted today? Normally his mind raced close enough to D'Artagnan's, or, truth be told, if it involved numbers, from the counting out of money to the planning of a leave, raced ahead of D'Artagnan's. So, why so slow today? The news of D'Artagnan's father's death could not have distressed Planchet. It must be that he didn't like the idea of that long a journey. "We'll have to borrow horses from Monsieur de Treville, and—since I won't be coming back—you'll have to bring them back to him."

"But...what about me?"

"You? What do you mean?"

"You mean to send me back to Paris," Planchet said. "How am I to make my way back to Gascony, afterwards?"

D'Artagnan frowned, suddenly understanding but still confused. He hadn't given it any thought. Planchet was just Planchet. He'd been D'Artagnan's servant from D'Artagnan's first week in Paris. He'd accompanied D'Artagnan on all his adventures. D'Artagnan hadn't thought...

Now he looked at Planchet as the horrifying realization dawned on him that he couldn't really support Planchet as a servant in Gascony. For one, the house already had servants—an elderly couple. They'd been with D'Artagnan's parents forever. In fact, the man had been D'Artagnan's father's servant in the wars.

It wasn't that the house couldn't afford one more servant—D'Artagnan cast a critical gaze over Planchet's scrawny frame—or at least it could easily afford a servant well used to starving. But D'Artagnan thought, for the first time, on what Planchet would think of Gascony. He'd worked as a clerk at an accountant's before hiring on with D'Artagnan, and he'd complained of the boredom. Surely, a rural house in Gascony could be no better.

What D'Artagnan could offer him would be a menial life working for a poor house. "I am sure," he said, not feeling sure at all, but hoping, "that Monsieur Porthos or Athos or Aramis will find you a position and—"

"Monsieur!" Planchet said. "Monsieur!" He dropped to sitting on D'Artagnan's bed. In a low voice that seemed to come from the other side of the grave, he said, "You can't mean it. You can't. I'll end up as a clerk again. Most gentlemen don't want intelligent servants. Most gentlemen would not tolerate my correcting them or...Monsieur!"

D'Artagnan could not bear it. Through his mind, still—stark—ran his mother's words. His father had been working for the Cardinal. And now his father was dead. Supposedly, he'd died in a duel. But D'Artagnan's father could not have been killed in a duel, fairly fought. So that must mean...

His heart was full of images of all he was about to lose—Athos, Porthos, Aramis. Their hours of easy camaraderie, the duels in which they all served as seconds for each other, the nights spent on guard—all would be gone, and no more than a fleeting, receding light to warm the darkness of his future years in Gascony.

Constance would be gone too. She would go back to being just Madame Bonacieux, a beautiful woman trapped in a loveless marriage. A beautiful woman he'd known all too briefly.

He managed not to sigh, but it took an effort. There was no room in his mind for Planchet. Planchet would accompany him to Gascony, and then he'd come back with the horses. And then one or the other of the musketeers would provide for the young servant. Surely, they would find him something. "I'm sure," he said, "they'll look after you. I've leave a note for Monsieur Athos."

He'd thrown all his possessions into the saddlebag, not a hard feat even if he now possessed more clothing than he had when first arriving in town. At the top he put the jar of the ointment made according to his mother's recipe, an ointment so miraculous that, by its use, every wound that had not reached vital organs would be cured in three days. After all, it was a long journey south to Gascony, and who knew what perils he'd encounter. Particularly if his father had been murdered.

"I'll write notes, now, while you go borrow two horses from Monsieur de Treville's stables. Tell them you will return them in no more than ten days. Tell them I require the horses on a matter of great urgency, but pledge my honor for their return."

As he spoke, he was heading towards the table where he kept some sheets of paper and an inkwell and quill. He must write to Athos and Porthos and Aramis. Separate letters, as his friends had very different natures. And he must write yet another note to Constance—which he'd enclose inside Aramis's note for delivery, as otherwise her husband might read it first.

He barely heard as Planchet eased his way out of the house into the evening outside.

# How Not To Wake a Musketeer; A Little Perfidy in the Right Place

**ATHOS** woke up with someone climbing in through his window. Or rather, he woke up with the window slowly creaking open and then scuffing sounds, as though someone were dragging himself up through the window.

It was so impossible, so patently impossible for anyone to be insane enough to break into a musketeer's room—much less the room of one of the most dangerous of that band of barely disciplined ruffians—that Athos knew he had to be dreaming. Asleep on the massive, curtained bed that he'd brought with him from his estate, wearing only his shirt, he turned in bed, trying to find a more comfortable position.

This turn caused the linen sheet and the blanket to slip aside. He felt a cold current of air. Cold. As if someone had opened the window prior to climbing in. The scuffing sounds were followed by two light thumps, like the sound of a not very heavy someone jumping into the room.

Athos rose. He rose before waking, tearing aside the linen sheet. His hand grabbed for the sword that he kept always by the side of the bed. By the time he opened his eyes fully, he was standing, sword in hand, bearing down on a slim figure by the window.

The figure—little more than an indistinct darker patch in the surrounding gloom—was that of a tall young man, or perhaps a woman. Tall, almost as tall as Athos himself, but much, much slimmer, with no sign of the muscles that made the musketeer a dangerous foe in combat. It made a bleating sound and pressed itself against the wall, arms splayed against it, as if it were trying to crawl into the wall.

"Ruffian," Athos said. "You thought you could come through my window and kill me while I slept. Do you go about robbing innocent men in their sleep?"

And to scare the creature—whom Athos could tell wasn't armed, and whom he merely wished to terrify away from a criminal life—Athos thrust his sword forward, stopping a hair's breadth from the intruder's chest.

"Monsieur," the creature bleated. And, on a deep breath, drawn in with force, like that of a drowning man, he added, "Monsieur Athos, it is I."

Athos blinked. That someone would break into his room was impossible enough. That it was someone who knew him—not only by reputation but by name—was unbelievable. No one, not a single one of his friends would presume that far upon their friendship as to startle Athos out of a sound sleep and count on escaping unscathed before the musketeer even regained his senses.

This was not one of his friends. Athos blinked again. "Who—"

"Monsieur, it is Planchet. You must help me with my master."

"D'Artagnan," Athos said, his voice filled with alarm. The young guard, almost young enough to be his child, had become somewhat Athos's adopted son in these last six months. By virtue of being the oldest of the musketeers, the erstwhile Count de la Fere had made it his business to keep the youngest of his friends out of trouble. Which, given D'Artagnan's nature, often proved a fraught and slippery business. "What has happened to D'Artagnan? Speak. Is he wounded?"

But Planchet only bleated again, "Monsieur," and Athos realized that he was still holding his blade in close proximity to Planchet's heart, and that there was a good chance the youth was scared.

He withdrew the blade and, by touch, made his way to the mantel in his room, from which he grabbed a candle in its pewter candlestick. He lit it from an ember in the banked fire in his hearth.

The wick, flaring to life, revealed a very pale Planchet still knit with the wall, as though fearing another bout of homicidal madness from Athos.

"Don't be a fool," Athos said, and setting the candle on the mantel, started casting about for his breeches and doublet. "What of your master? With what do you need my help? Is he wounded? Surely not. We left him hale. Did he—"

"He's mad," Planchet said.

Athos looked over his shoulder, as the young servant took a step away from the window. "If by mad you mean wandering in his wits, I doubt it. D'Artagnan is one of the shrewdest men I know. Granted, the shock and grief over his father's death," Athos said, remembering the contents of the letter he'd taken from Planchet's hand and read before passing it on to D'Artagnan, "might cause him to act a little distraught. But...mad?"

Planchet leaned against the wall again, this time as if he needed support. His skin was ashen grey, in shocking contrast with his hair. "He's getting ready to leave for Gascony now," he said. "Even as we speak, there are two horses tied at your door. They belong to Monsieur de Treville, and they will be used to carry my master and myself to Gascony. From whence I am to come back and return the horses."

"You are to come back?" Athos asked. "But we'd said—We'd agreed—" He controlled himself and pressed his lips together, as though grimly accepting the inevitable. "I see," he said. "And your master?"

"He stays in Gascony, monsieur. He says he's his father's only son and that he must fulfill his duty. He says—"

"Doubtless a great deal of nonsense," Athos said, pulling his doublet laces so tight that they were just short of impeding respiration. "His father was killed, and we don't know why, so he would go and brave Gascony on his own?"

"Yes," Planchet said. "He says he doesn't want to drag you into this, since he can never return with you to Paris, and that—"

"As you say," Athos said, strapping on his sword belt. "Mad. You did well to come to me, even if you could have used a more orthodox way of gaining entry."

"I knocked," Planchet said. "And knocked. But I can't delay too long or my master will suspect..."

"Indeed. So you took your life in your hands. A brave man, Planchet."

Planchet didn't look particularly brave. He looked like he might lose consciousness at any minute, after the shocks of the last few moments.

"Perhaps you can leave through the front door this time, though," Athos said. "I told Grimaud not to open to anyone, you see, which is why you had no answer. I thought we'd be traveling in the morning. I see D'Artagnan has changed this."

"Monsieur, you can't let him go alone. He—"

"Wouldn't dream of it. You go to your master. I will go to Porthos and Aramis at the Palais Royale."

"But Monsieur, you'll never catch up with us."

"Don't worry about that. I know shortcuts. Trust me. We would not let your master face possible murder alone."

"But I don't know which road we're taking, and I..."

"Worry not. We'll find out. Your master is not the first man we've followed." He allowed a small smile to tug on his lips remembering all the mad adventures they'd engaged in, even just since D'Artagnan had joined them. The people they'd followed. The mysteries they'd solved. "But you see, I must get Aramis and Porthos and then I must speak to Monsieur de Treville, or at least leave a note. And find someone else to take our places in the guard roster. It is a duty we can't simply walk away from."

"Monsieur, monsieur," Planchet said, alarmed by this long list of things to do. "But my master will leave as soon as I arrive. I know it. It will be hard to ever find us."

"Don't worry," Athos said. "Don't worry. We will catch you before you're too far gone."

He followed the boy down the stairs to the street, his mind efficiently organizing things and listing what he must do like any general marshaling troops for a difficult campaign. He had no doubts they'd catch D'Artagnan. Though the Gascon was as cunning and twisty minded as Aramis at his worst, he was not likely to be using his cunning fully to escape his friends. He was more likely—being modest and placing a low value on his own company and friendship—to think as soon as he was gone they would utterly forget him. The fool.

They would follow him and they would go to Gascony with him. But what madness had the boy's father got into? What could he have been doing for the Cardinal? What tangle would they find in Gascony?

# The Many Inconveniences of Wintry Travel; Meager Purse and Rushing Mind; The Foolhardiness of Highwaymen

**D'ARTAGNAN'S** face felt frozen from galloping against the cold air of fall. Though he wasn't galloping anymore. For a long time, he'd kept up a fast pace.

He thought of the letters he'd left in his lodging, neatly lined up. One for Athos, which explained everything and made it clear he must leave and that there was no other choice. The letter for Constance was within it, and beside it were the letters to Monsieur des Essarts and Monsieur de Treville. He hadn't left letters for the other two. He trusted Athos to explain it to them. Besides, had he left a letter for Porthos, Porthos would have made Athos explain it to him all the same and Aramis. Aramis...

D'Artagnan made a face. He couldn't avoid the thought of Aramis reading his farewell letter with one of those unnerving little smiles that seemed to say he saw through you and he didn't believe a word you said. Did D'Artagnan believe a word he said? Was it then so necessary that he left Paris and all behind? Was it so necessary that he bury himself in Gascony, just because his father was dead?

His father...In his mind, his father's features formed, laughing with the excitement of a mock duel with D'Artagnan. His father. Ever since D'Artagnan was very small, his father had been the man to imitate, the man whose footsteps he wished to follow.

He remembered being barely a toddler and walking behind his father, trying to imitate his father's limp because—ignorant of the causes of it—he assumed this was how a man walked. Or at least a man anyone would admire.

Then, in early childhood he'd heard his father's tales of his adventures in Paris, and he'd known he would have to go there as a young man and have those too, before coming home to live in Gascony. *Before coming home...*

Why did the words feel like the lid of a coffin shutting off all light? Hadn't he always wanted to return to Gascony after he was done with his wild years in Paris?

But some part of him protested that he hadn't wanted to return now. Not just yet. Not while he was still barely a man. When he'd imagined going back, he'd been a thirty-year-old veteran of the musketeers, with an abundant moustache and a scar or two like his father's, and his own supply of jokes and stories and battle memories.

He'd go back, then, and marry one of the buxom local beauties and set about siring little D'Artagnans. And in the evening his father and he would sit by the fire and sip at their drinks, and trade stories.

And there was the rub; and this he kept coming back to. His father wouldn't be there. And because his father wouldn't be there, D'Artagnan must be. Now. There would be no time to save money, no time to establish a reputation. No time to be young.

He rode his horse silently on a deserted road amid denuded fields. The harvest had been taken in and all that remained behind were stubbly stalks, covered in frost, sparkling in the moonlight. In the horizon there was as yet no sun or color, but rather that dishwater-dingy light that precedes the breaking of dawn.

"Monsieur," Planchet shouted from the side. "Monsieur."

He turned to look at his servant. He was, like D'Artagnan, wrapped in a cloak, his somewhat thinner than D'Artagnan's, having been D'Artagnan's before the guard's pay had allowed the young man to replace it with a thicker and better one. But the cloak's hood had fallen down a little, revealing Planchet's tuft of red hair, his very pale face. The tip of his nose was angry red, and dripped a little.

Planchet shouted at D'Artagnan, "We have to stop and rest the horses, monsieur. We can't keep them up like this without rest. They'll burst."

D'Artagnan realized his horse had slowed considerably and faltered once or twice. He'd pressed horses fast before this, of course. There had been cross-country races in great urgency. But then he'd been with his friends, and they'd had changes of mounts arranged at hostelries. Or had arranged for changes of mounts on the spot and paid more.

D'Artagnan could do neither. And beyond the natural reluctance at injuring a fine animal, he couldn't in conscience hurt this horse, since it was Monsieur de Treville's.

No. He must stop, that much was true. In fact, thinking of it, he slowed down to almost a walk.

The thing was, he knew exactly how much was in his purse, and how long he and Planchet could be on the road, before he got to his paternal abode, and the two totals didn't match. He could not buy lodging at any hostelry—much less lodging and care for his horse—and manage to get to Gascony.

A spurt of anger surged up that he'd never thought of the cold, before. He'd assumed he could stop and sleep by the roadside. He'd traveled this road six months ago, in the opposite direction, mounted on his old, orange horse, a gift from his father. But stopping hadn't been a problem before. It had been spring, and, the weather being mild, he'd pastured his horse by the roadside while he himself slept in a nearby thicket and ate whatever fruit offered from roadside trees. He'd stopped at an inn only once, in Meung.

But now, in this weather, stopping just by the roadside was not an option. Not unless he wished to catch his death in the cold and damp. And barring foraging for fallen wheat grains amid the harvested fields or the last shrunken and dried cluster of grapes accidentally left behind on some vine, there would be no food. And no food for the horses either.

Just as his mind had reached this melancholy place and he was again weighing the travel he must accomplish against his meager purse, he saw as if a shadow among the trees. It was stone and half-ruined, but it sparked a memory.

When he'd traveled in the other direction and been this far from Paris, he'd seen, near to where he'd paused for a rest, the ruin of an old building. Very old. It looked like what remained of some defensive tower, perhaps going back so far as the Romans.

As his horse pastured and rested, after D'Artagnan had rubbed him down, D'Artagnan, with a surfeit of youthful spirits, had explored the surroundings, including the remains of the tower. And he'd found, as was often common with such ancient ruins in rural locales, that the place smelled strongly of sheep and had within it a feeding through and such arrangements as indicated that it was used for lodging a flock through the winter months.

Of course the floor had been thick with muck and, it being spring, the place had been deserted, the flock probably in the fields with their shepherd. Now, in winter, it would probably be occupied and there was a good chance the shepherd slept within it, with the sheep. He would have to bribe the shepherd for oats for the horses and for lodging for himself and his servant. On the other hand, mucky and all, it would at least be warm and relatively safe. And the shepherd's bribe would probably cost much less than a night at an inn. And there was always, after all, the chance that the shepherd wouldn't be there. Sometimes such buildings were merely left locked, and not with an on-site guard. Well enough.

D'Artagnan dismounted from his horse with a leap, then motioned to Planchet. But Planchet—amid his many admirable qualities—was a trained horseman, raised in his father's horse farm in Picardy. More than that, he was accomplished at following his master's actions and guessing what they must do without asking any questions. Only Grimaud, whom Athos had trained to the task, excelled more than the young former accountant in obeying unspoken orders.

Before the thought of Athos could bring gloom to his mind anew, D'Artagnan motioned with his hand and spoke, in a controlled shout, to be heard through the cloak and the hoofbeats of the horses they led by the rein, "There's a stable there. With sheep. Well, a ruin where someone keeps sheep. I say we try to lodge there for a few hours."

Another admirable trait of Planchet's was that he never argued without need but often thought of things even D'Artagnan overlooked. He started following D'Artagnan's path but turned. "You know, monsieur, there's a good chance there will be a guard—"

"I know. We'll bribe him."

"Monsieur!" this was said with dismay. "I meant a guard dog. I doubt there will be a human guard this far out of Paris. They probably all know each other and sheep and cattle thieves tend to have a short life in this region. But a guard dog, they'll have. The same sheep dog that accompanies the creatures in the summer."

"Oh," D'Artagnan said, at a loss. And stopped, because he didn't know what else to say. His family had dogs, shaggy, shambling brutes that served equally to guard the sheep and to accompany his father on his hunts, and who were dreadful at both tasks, but nonetheless very cheerful in their incompetence. Always ready with lolling tongues and panting goodwill to welcome the son of the house and fetch a stick for him, or, when he was older, to follow him on a mad run through the fields.

He had an idea a strange sheep dog would not be anywhere near so friendly. And he had no experience of unfriendly dogs. His family being the most important in their small hamlet, it was respected enough that dogs were taught not to attack young D'Artagnan.

He frowned at Planchet. "Well...All the same, we have to try to stay there overnight, because..."

Planchet shook his head again, as though D'Artagnan had completely misunderstood him. "I don't mean we shouldn't. What I meant to ask was...well...I saved some of the sausage from yesterday's dinner. I thought we might get hungry on the way and...not have much time to dine by sleeping. And I thought...If you'd give me your permission, I could use it as another sort of bribe for the dog. In my father's farm...well...I have experience of dogs."

D'Artagnan couldn't help laughing a little—just a chuckle in his throat. "Of course you may bribe the dog with the sausage. I didn't even know we had any left. I supposed you had eaten it."

Planchet nodded. He wiped his dripping nose on the back of his hand. "If monsieur wouldn't mind, then, I'll go ahead of you, and calm the dog. If the door is locked, I'll open the padlock. It is not a problem."

"You are truly a jewel among servants," D'Artagnan said, without irony.

They had turned into a narrow path amid sparse pine trees, which wound to take them to the clearing D'Artagnan remembered. It was irregular and large and looked as a natural clearing.

The *natural* part might be pushing a point, as, beneath his scuffing boots and a very thin layer of dirt, he could feel the rounded edges of ancient paving stones. So likely, the trees couldn't get hold because of tightly laid paving.

However it was, the irregular clearing held only the one building. D'Artagnan waited with the horses while Planchet approached the padlocked door, calling out reassurances that he came in peace. Those changed to a tone of greeting and delight. D'Artagnan knew his servant was greeting a dog. It was a voice range Planchet used for horses and dogs and children and cats, no one else. He could barely see the motions as his servant reached into his pouch and gave something to the creature, all the while saying, "Who's a good puppy, then? Who is?"

The mass of fur hobbling and bobbing just past Planchet did not look so much like a puppy as like an overgrown, shaggy horse who—judging from the sounds—had learned to bark and yip. Smiling, D'Artagnan watched as Planchet turned, the dog's head playfully clasped in his arm, saying, "Monsieur, you may come. The sheep are confined within. There's room—"

Planchet froze. His gaze was turned just slightly over D'Artagnan's shoulder. D'Artagnan had lived in quite close quarters with Planchet and he knew his servant's expressions like he knew his own. There was no alarm on the boy's face, just a slow, puzzled frown.

And D'Artagnan had heard steps behind him, just a second before Planchet froze. Or not quite steps. The sound of a branch snapping, a leaf rustling.

The only reason for no alarm in Planchet's face was that the person approaching, from behind, was one of the shepherds or a rough villager.

"Ah, good man," D'Artagnan said, turning around, an ingratiating smile on his lips. "I see you think—"

His words stopped. His smile vanished. The men he'd turned to face were six and not dressed like rustics. They wore heavy, dark cloaks of at least as good quality as D'Artagnan's, and their faces were hidden in the folds of their hoods.

As D'Artagnan watched, astounded, the leader threw his cloak open and unsheathed his sword.

# Doubts and Confusion; The Improbability of Dreaming Planchet; The Difference Between a Duel and Murder

"I don't think we'll find them now," Porthos said, dolefully, for per-haps the third time in the last few minutes, since they'd dismounted and started looking about the roadside for signs of the young Gascon's passage or for a sign of him.

Athos gritted his teeth and said nothing. Aramis, both Porthos's best friend and his most constant critic, would have answered with some quip that would have ignited a never-ending exchange between the two and probably alerted the whole countryside—and D'Artagnan, were he within earshot—to their approach.

But Aramis, impatient and the youngest of the three as well as ac-knowledged as the most cunning and observant, was riding ahead, then back again, in little looping forward sorties. Porthos and Athos followed behind, slower, scanning the sides of the road for any signs of the boy.

Athos didn't answer Porthos's comment because it echoed too well with his own internal complaint. It had sounded, over and again, for some time now. *We should have seen him by now. We should have seen him or Planchet. He can't have ridden farther than this. Where can he be hiding?*

He had been so sure when they left Paris, so sure this was the road D'Artagnan would take back to the paternal abode—now devoid of his father. It was the road he had followed into town, so many months ago. Oh, there were others, less and more direct, but D'Artagnan hadn't been in Paris long enough—hadn't exploited its surroundings long enough—to know the shortcuts. And he wouldn't have any reason to take a less direct road. Not even fear his friends would follow him. He didn't know of Planchet's treason.

And yet, Athos looked at the desolate fields, sparkling with ice under the dishwater grey light of dawn, and shrugged deeper into his cloak and sighed.

"Where can they be?" Porthos asked, his voice rumbling deep and seemingly so strong as to shake the frost from the trees and bring whatever inhabitants lived hereabouts running to see the giant. Or to kill him. "What can he have done? Perhaps you got it all wrong, Athos."

"I didn't get it wrong," Athos said, quietly. Behind them, walking their horses also, their servants followed. Athos could hear the sound of their discussion and he would bet it mirrored his and Porthos's. Pious Bazin was saying something that sounded much like his endless decrying of folly. Mousqueton was arguing for a return to the city and a checking of D'Artagnan's quarters in a voice almost as loud and voluble as his master's. And Grimaud's monosyllabic answers echoed the same annoyance Athos felt.

He hadn't got it wrong. Planchet had told him that D'Artagnan meant to leave in the night and to make his way to Gascony alone. He didn't think he'd be able to return, and he didn't trust himself to be able to resist his friends' entreaties, should they ask him to come back to Paris with them.

*But where in the Devil can the boy be?* The sense of being the oldest of them all rested heavily upon Athos's shoulders, all of a sudden. He shouldn't have left the boy such free reign. He should have...

"Perhaps he changed his mind," Porthos boomed. "Perhaps he realized that going without us was madness and perhaps he—"

"Ah!" Athos said. "He's a Gascon. He lives, breathes madness."

Porthos looked at him, but before he could speak came the gallop of Aramis's approaching horse. Perhaps Aramis had found D'Artagnan.

"That he is, a Gascon," Porthos said, and sighed, not attempting to argue the madness of Gascons or the high unlikelihood of any of them—D'Artagnan most of all—coming to his senses.

He sighed again, clearly oblivious to the approaching hoofbeats. Was Athos imagining the hoofbeats? Were they only a mirage born of his imagination, of his desire for Aramis to return with news of D'Artagnan? He realized suddenly Aramis had been gone a very long time. Had he found a hostelry ahead? Or had he perhaps—

"Are you sure you didn't dream Planchet?" Porthos asked. "I mean his visit. In the night."

"What?" Athos asked, startled out of his own thoughts. "Porthos. I did not."

"But are you absolutely sure? Because just last week, after that banquet at the tavern, remember, the one that de Pignon gave to celebrate his having inherited his aunt's fortune, I dreamed I had an uncle who was a Chinese Mandarin, in a bell-surrounded tower, and he'd died and left me his tower, and his harem of fifty-five maidens. And I'd swear on the Divine Body and Blood it was true, you know? I woke up wondering what I would tell Athenais. And what she would have said to the maidens, and all."

Athos stared, at a loss for what to say about such a dream. Surely Porthos wasn't suggesting that an uncle who was a Chinese Mandarin with a harem was about as likely as Planchet's breaking into Athos's room via the window and...

Athos stopped, floundering. Indeed, the idea of a Mandarin uncle and maidens who would upset Athenais, Porthos's long-time mistress, might be less insane than the idea that anyone would break into a musketeer's room. And Athos' room at that.

"Of course," Porthos said. "I doubt she would have said anything to the maidens, for undoubtedly they would have spoken Chinese or some other heathen language, but you know what I mean."

In that moment, in the cold light of dawn, Athos stopped, as if he'd been run through by an unexpected bolt. How many times was Porthos right? How many times had the giant, with his slow words pierced through the pretty words and the pretty illusions of his more fluent friends? How many times did Athos have to remind himself that just because Porthos was slow of words it didn't mean he was slow of mind?

He touched his forehead with the tips of his long, aristocratic fingers and sighed. Had he dreamed Planchet? Planchet was not one of the ghosts that normally visited Athos' dreams. No, not *ghosts*, for there was only one. Charlotte, who'd been all too briefly Countess de la Fere and Athos' wife. And whom he'd killed. Was his guilt now driving him mad at last?

"Are you well, Athos?" Porthos asked, stopping and looking at his friend. "Only you've gone the color of the Cardinal when Monsieur de Treville tells him we've wounded three of his best fighters."

Athos struggled for words. As a child he'd been verbose; as a young man he'd been gifted with poetic speech. But his words had been left behind on the day he'd killed Charlotte. Unable to wrap his words around the thing he'd done, he'd shed the words—as he'd shed honors and title and nobility—and mutely gone to live amid rough musketeers as though they were quiet monks. He'd even trained Grimaud, who'd known him from a child, to keep silent and to obey Athos's silent commands.

"You know, Porthos," he said. And was about to confess it might all have been a dream, when he was interrupted by Aramis's voice shouting, "To me, musketeers. To me."

There was no time for thinking. This scream, which echoed around Paris a dozen times a day—often followed by "to me of the king" or "to me of the Cardinal"—usually meant that a musketeer was under attack. Often enough by the guards of Cardinal Richelieu.

A call of brotherhood and duty, a call of honor, a sacred request that must be obeyed.

Athos gave his reins to Grimaud who—well trained and ever obedient—was there, stretching his hand for them. He was aware of Porthos doing the same beside him. They ran side by side up a rise of the road, then down again on the other side.

"To me, musketeers," Aramis's voice sounded again, this time imperative. And in a lower voice, "Ah, canaille."

Athos could tell it came from within a wooded stretch, and, as he followed the imprecations of close combat, the sound of sword hitting sword, he could see a path amid the trees. He ran through it, headlong, not caring about the branches that stretched onto the path and caught at his clothes. It mattered not. None of it mattered.

Closer, and closer—his feet slipping on round paving stones beneath a loose covering of soil—he tried to count the men and managed no more than a thought that there were many of them and that D'Artagnan—if D'Artagnan were there—was unusually silent and not letting his usual gasconades be heard.

And then he erupted into a clearing around the ruined tower of a donjon. There were people fighting—many people. He recognized Aramis immediately—the younger musketeer had discarded his cloak, and fought in his well-cut, fashionable blue tunic and venetians. His long blond hair had worked free of its ties and flowed down his back like a living thing, twisting and writhing—like a bit of ice come alive in the wintry landscape.

But the fight was hardly a proper duel. For one, no one was fighting Aramis. Or everyone was. There was a group of men, right enough—a lot of them—all of them no taller than D'Artagnan. But only two of them were turned towards Aramis. And those—for all that—didn't seem to be giving him their full attention. They kept looking over their shoulders at the larger group of them, who attacked...another cloaked man who...

For just a moment Athos stopped, breathing heavily, frowning. Had Aramis picked a quarrel with strangers? Had villagers set upon him? But if so, why was he fighting only two of them?

And then in the doorway of the donjon, he saw Planchet. It was unmistakably the boy who'd once been an accountant and who was now D'Artagnan's servant. For all that Porthos seemed to think Athos was capable of hallucinating Planchet out of whole cloth, the mind boggled at the idea of creating that vivid red hair, the sharp features or the freckles that competed with blemishes on the boy's too-young countenance. He stared gape mouthed at the fight while holding back what appeared to be a massive dog of uncertain parentage.

Right. If Planchet was here, then so must D'Artagnan be. A look at the man defending himself in the melee, and Athos realized that it was none other than his young friend.

The cloak might disguise all else, but the dancing steps back and forward, the lightness of the turning and twisting, was all D'Artagnan, all over.

He was being attacked by...six men, only two of whom condescended to even defend themselves from Aramis's attack. And those two keeping Aramis at bay, the other four attempted to...murder the boy. For nothing less than murder could operate when there were four against one.

Porthos—apparently having sized the situation faster than Athos, had pushed forward to stand beside the besieged Gascon, calling out, "Deal with me, you villains. Deal with me."

And now Athos's mind went dark—with the darkness of rage and blood. It was a state obtained all too often when Athos took sword in hand—and a state he strived to avoid.

There was inside the urbane, polished count turned musketeer—behind the well-thought classical quotations, the ironical smile and the careful observation of etiquette and tradition—something raging and feral biding its time, waiting only to strike. Wanting to strike in revenge for his despoiled life, his destroyed heritage.

Most of the time Athos managed to keep the darkness at bay—locked inside him. But now watching these cowards attempting to murder his friend, he could hold back no longer. He surged forward, making a sound like a growl at the back of his throat.

Had the villain in front of him not turned at that sound, Athos—who'd raised his sword like an ax—would have stricken him down where he stood. Instead, the man turned and, sword hastily upraised, parried the formidable blow.

He was a short man and dark, like D'Artagnan was dark—olive skin tanned by an open-air life. In the effort of defending himself from Athos's fury, he threw back his cloak, and the hood fell, revealing that he looked, in fact much like D'Artagnan.

And he fought like a Gascon, even if not with D'Artagnan's imaginative quickness. He fought well enough to parry Athos's thrusts and to attack often enough that Athos was kept wholly occupied by him—incapable of helping D'Artagnan more, incapable even of seeing how D'Artagnan was doing in the fray or if any of his other friends had succeeded in freeing the young Gascon from his attackers.

With each parried thrust, each time he pressed Athos close, the adversary made Athos more and more furious, till a cold fury possessed him and drove him. In the grasp of it, he pressed forward and forward and forward, till he had the man backed against a tree. He was physically pressing close to the man, so close there was almost no room for their swords, pressed together between them, and no room at all for any maneuvering. So close to the man that he could smell the man's fear, and hear his quickened, shortened breathing.

And at that moment, from behind him, where the others were, he heard a cry of surprise and pain. It was the cry of a man pierced through. And the voice was D'Artagnan's.

"D'Artagnan," Athos said, and—coming to himself as quickly as he'd abandoned himself to the fight—he wheeled around to see his young friend fall to his knees as his opponent withdrew a red-stained sword.

"D'Artagnan," he said again, and took a step towards the youth, who was still besieged by three men in black cloaks.

A step, a broken twig, a quickened breath—something made Athos turn. Blindly, he turned and swept back with his sword.

The part of his mind that could still think registered that he'd driven his sword halfway through the throat of the man he'd been dueling. The other part of him—the part that thirsted for blood and cared for nothing else—withdrew the sword just as quickly, and swept forward, on the crest of his fury.

He felt his sword pierce a man's body from the back before he even realized he intended to do it, and he pulled back, with a rapid movement, before the falling man could pull his sword down. He lifted it again.

The two men remaining between him and D'Artagnan, who was on his knees still and pale as death, glanced over their shoulders. Whatever they saw in Athos's countenance put them to flight, running madly through the trees. Athos started after them, but a voice called him back—Aramis's voice, very even, very calm. "Leave them, Athos. Help me or the Gascon dies."

Like cold water upon a raging dog, the words stopped Athos's fury. He turned back, to see that, in the clearing, Aramis and Porthos only remained standing, amid four fallen men. And D'Artagnan. D'Artagnan, whose cloak Aramis was removing, was being supported by Porthos.

Athos retraced his steps. Barely stopping, he wiped his sword on the cloak of a fallen man, and hastened to help Aramis.

The boy wore his guard's doublet beneath the cloak, and it was stained with blood, blossoming with such exuberance across the dark fabric that one could not tell exactly where the wound lay.

They freed him of his doublet and plain shirt. The boy's teeth were knocking together, and Athos thought it wasn't good, it couldn't be good, till he remembered they were as good as undressing him to the cold winter air.

Aramis was saying something under his breath, which sounded like a lot of Latin words strung together. Praying. He was praying, and Athos hoped it was that the sword hadn't found a vital organ and that the boy would live. Athos would have prayed too, had he still thought his prayers worthy of being answered.

It was all Athos's fault—his ridiculous pride again. His pride had once caused him to kill his wife rather than admit he might have been fooled into marrying a marked woman. And now...and now his pride had told him to dismiss Planchet, and to send him ahead with D'Artagnan, instead of going with him right then, and then sending for his friends to follow.

With the clarity of hindsight, he realized that was what he should have done. He should have gone ahead, to protect the foolhardy Gascon, while sending Grimaud for his other friends. He shouldn't have allowed a young man who was little more than a child to brave the road to Gascony alone.

"Mea culpa, mea maxima culpa," he whispered.

Porthos looked at him like he had grown a second head. "Leave off the Latin, Athos. Get the famous Gascon ointment from Planchet. The sword missed the heart. The boy will live."

Blinking, through sweat that threatened to blind him, Athos saw that it was indeed so. Though the wound still bled profusely, it had pierced in a way that had to have avoided both lung and heart.

"*Hola*, Planchet," he called, his voice shaking too much for his own taste. "Did your master pack any of that ointment that will heal in three days any wound that falls short of fatal?"

The boy bobbed his head, but he was still holding the massive dog. "In his pack, monsieur. His saddlebag. The chestnut."

Athos crossed over to the chestnut horse. The boy's saddlebag had been overturned onto the grass of the clearing—doublets and shirts and all were spread around. Doubtless the men had done this before Aramis caught up with them.

Amid the clothes flapping in the wintry breeze was D'Artagnan's purse, curiously untouched. Next to it was the pot of ointment. Shattered. It had fallen against one of the stones insufficiently cushioned by dirt.

# A Close Thing; The Demands of Friendship; The Wealth of Highwaymen

**"IT** was a close thing," Aramis said. As he spoke, he heard his own voice, tight and small, as it hadn't sounded in many years. And it came to him there had been several close things. As he went on with his sentence as he'd first meant it, "I might very well have ridden past without noticing it," he realized several other things might have happened.

His friends might not have heard him, in which case all he would have achieved would have been to get himself killed alongside D'Artagnan. Alternately, Athos might have gone, finally, over the edge of that precipice of darkness that forever peeked from behind his dark blue eyes.

Porthos and Aramis had never discussed it, but Aramis was sure—as he was sure there was life after death—that Porthos too, in the back of his mind, had long ago decided someday Athos would lose all control and his civility would slip. In a moment of drinking, in a night of profound despair, Athos's veneer of civility would slip. Then would he give vent to the darkest part of his nature and he would kill and kill and kill, unable to stop—locked inside a body possessed only by a longing for blood and death.

On that day Aramis was sure, as he was sure of his hope of heaven and of the bonds of friendship, it would fall to himself and Porthos to stop Athos. And it was only by sheer luck—by a miracle—that the day hadn't arrived today.

He looked sideways at Athos's, again controlled, again civilized face, and he said again, "It was a very close thing. I heard the sound of the dog." He gestured with his head towards the ruined tower where Planchet, with Grimaud's aid, was relocking the door. "Planchet was having trouble holding him, but did not dare let him go for fear that in the confusion he would turn on D'Artagnan. The dog let a bark escape, and I looked at the sound of the bark, and I heard the swords. So I called out and I followed." He took the ligature that Planchet was offering him, and wrapped it around D'Artagnan's chest. The younger man flinched and started, as if to say something, but Aramis glared at him. "Don't speak. Let us bind this." And took from Athos the end of the ligature to tighten it around the wound. That and lacing D'Artagnan's doublet tight should keep the wound from bleeding too much, at least overnight. In the morning, on horseback...

Aramis frowned. He doubted he could convince the Gascon to stay his journey. As well to convince the sun not to rise in the morning. And on that again, no. Arguing with celestial bodies would be far more fruitful than trying to keep a Gascon from endangering his life.

He pulled the binding tighter than he had meant to and heard D'Artagnan draw in sharp breath.

"We have to keep it from bleeding on horseback," Aramis said both to D'Artagnan and to Athos. They both nodded and Athos joined in, holding one end of the strip of cloth, allowing Aramis to pull it tighter than he'd otherwise have managed. D'Artagnan went very pale and flinched twice, but—to his credit—neither cried out nor protested at the rough treatment.

Soon enough they had the wound bound—an art at which, as musketeers, they had more practice than practically anyone else alive.

D'Artagnan, still pale, allowed them to pull on his shirt and tighten his doublet more than was, doubtless, comfortable. Again, he made no sound of protest.

"Wait. We shall talk," Athos said. "But you lost far too much blood." As he spoke, he stepped towards his horse, which their servants had tethered to a nearby tree. "Here," he said, returning with a bottle. "I have brought some excellent burgundy, which you'll do me the honor of drinking before you speak."

Athos handed the bottle to D'Artagnan, and ignored Aramis's distracted frown at him. That Athos had a bottle about his person did not surprise Aramis, but it worried him. Athos drank too much. It was a sure thing that his drinking would only encourage his attacks of cold fury.

But the wine put color back into D'Artagnan's cheeks. Enough for the boy to say, in a confused tone, "How come you here?"

"By providence," Aramis said. "And you'd best thank providence on your knees. Else you'd be dead, you young fool."

He helped D'Artagnan rise, and the boy stood, swaying slightly. Only six months ago, when D'Artagnan had first arrived in town, Aramis had viewed him with the deepest suspicion, both because he wasn't sure the boy wasn't working for the Cardinal and because Aramis could easily recognize in D'Artagnan's mind a cunning to rival his own.

But blood shed together and murder avenged had brought him around to feel...brotherhood with the Gascon, a feeling very close to that which linked him to Athos and Porthos. "You fool—what did you want to go stealing off in the night alone for?" he asked, sternly.

D'Artagnan shook his head. "It is my business," he said. "My family business and not yours."

"If blood shed together does not amount to brotherhood, I don't know what does," Aramis said. "What did you expect?" He cast a look at Athos to find the older musketeer staring his solidarity at him. "That we'd stay calmly in Paris and allow you to face untold dangers alone? What did you think of us? What of the oath sworn, one for all and all for one?"

D'Artagnan shook his head, feebly. "It's not that," he said. "It's not that. Only, you see...The letter said my father had been working for the Cardinal...and then...and then there was everything else."

"Everything else?" Athos asked, his voice dangerously soft and even.

"Well, I am the only son of my father's house. Oh, I know, it is a small house, the patrimony ridiculous. You see, my father was a second son and had to rely on the army to make his fortune, only somehow he never did. Make his fortune. Instead, he spent some time in Paris and was a comrade at arms of Monsieur de Treville in his youth—which is why my father's letter to the captain was my most prized possession, but you see..."

Aramis shook his head. He did not see. D'Artagnan seemed to find Aramis's confusion funny, and he shook his head slightly. "No. I didn't expect you to understand. But my father's house is a small one, but small though it is, it is the manor house of a village, and the village and villagers depend on us for direction and on our protection should things turn violent as they often do in Gascony. So, with my father dead, I must take his place, and I must stay there: I cannot return to Paris."

He looked from one to the other of them and seemed quite wild. "I will have to stay behind there, and how could I explain it to you?" He took a quick swig from the bottle, and said, in a rush, "How could I explain to you, Aramis, that I must leave Paris and fashion behind? How could I explain to Porthos that I must leave the court and ambition behind? And how could I explain to Athos..." Here he floundered, but recovered. "...that I must give up all ambition of the honor of defending king and country, that which you"—he looked at Athos—"so often told me is the essential duty of every gentleman worthy of the name. You left estate and name behind—You—"

Athos laughed, though the sound was closer to a bark, coming as it did from a throat wholly unaccustomed to mirth. "D'Artagnan! Because I left house and name behind it doesn't follow that I don't understand the dictates of honor, and that which a gentleman might owe to his subordinates, beyond what he owes to the Crown. You could say I left to preserve my name and my honor, just as you...just as you might be required to stay to preserve yours." He shook his head. "We'll understand if you must stay behind in Gascony. We'll understand if you find that you must instead return with us. Only trust us. We are all your friends and all gentlemen. You shouldn't try to steal away from us and avoid us, like a thief in the night. Trust that we understand your best interests and will look out for them."

"But..." D'Artagnan said. "If my father was working for the Cardinal!"

Aramis realized that laughter had bubbled from his throat only as he heard it echo in the brittle air of early morning. "D'Artagnan, remember that my mother too has worked for the Cardinal."[2]

It was a jest he would not make to anyone else, but it brought a surprised smile to D'Artagnan's features. "You would not despise me?" he asked.

"We are neither of us responsible for our parents' sins," Aramis said, shrugging. "Now you see how foolish you were in attempting to leave without us."

"I would have acquitted myself well enough," D'Artagnan said.

Aramis opened his mouth to retort but was saved from offending D'Artagnan—who, being a Gascon, might very well believe that he could indeed have defended himself against six enemies and escaped death—by the sound of Porthos's voice from behind them.

"By the Mass. These are the richest highwaymen I've ever met yet."

# *Philistines and Samaritans Again; Blood and Jewels; The Right Letter in the Wrong Place*

**"PORTHOS,"** Aramis said.

Porthos looked up at the call, glancing away from the four money pouches and several jeweled rings he was holding. "Yes?" he asked.

Aramis pressed his lips together and shook his head slightly. "One does not rob the dead."

Porthos frowned at his friend. Oh, he was well aware that Aramis had gone to seminary and studied theology and all that. He spoke very easily of such things as sin and absolution and exactly what food was permitted at Lent and in what circumstances drunken revelry could be pardoned and when not.

Which was all very well, but the thing was this—that these men had tried to attack D'Artagnan, and they'd been killed for it. And it seemed to Porthos that, having died while trying to murder someone, the men were outside the rule of the church. They were probably in hell and being spit roasted by grinning demons. At least if the priest who'd taught Porthos his religion had been right—and Porthos saw no reason to doubt a man who knew Greek and Latin and the refinements of grammar.

He tried to explain himself. "Listen, Aramis—these are not dead. Or rather they are, but not dead as if we'd found them by the wayside, you know, when we might be required to be Philistines or Samaritans or Sardinians or whatever the devil the creature is that doesn't pass by on the other side. If we'd passed by on the other side, they'd have killed D'Artagnan. Since we didn't, they didn't, but died for it. And having died for it, they were...murderers. What happens to the wealth of convicted murderers?"

"It goes to the Crown," Aramis said. "But—"

"Well, the Crown isn't here, but we are, and we are the King's Musketeers, and, as such..." He shrugged. "Almost the King himself. Or at least the closest thing we are likely to find in this corner of the world. And besides, if we leave the corpses here, with all their wealth upon them, what is likely to happen? That the villagers hereabouts will take the money and the jewels. And what do the villagers have to do with these men I ask? It is not as if it was them that the men tried to kill."

"Well, it was probably them who were subjected to these malefactor's depredations for years, Porthos."

"Well, then...it wasn't," Porthos said, triumphantly. He shoved his hand, filled with coin pouches and jewels, towards them. "Because if it were, the highwaymen wouldn't have all these jewels and coin. Villagers aren't that wealthy."

This stopped Aramis right enough. He opened his mouth, then closed it, then opened it again.

"What jewels and coin?" Athos asked from the other side.

"Well..." Porthos said. "While you were tending to D'Artagnan I counted the money in these pouches and they have ten pistoles apiece. And more, there are seven jeweled rings between the four of them, and none of it is glass. And trust me, I would know glass." He frowned slightly, expecting his friends to contest that, but none did.

Instead, Athos looked at D'Artagnan in silence, and D'Artagnan frowned a little. Aramis seemed to be trying to formulate the theological argument against counting the money of the dead, and not being able to find the right words.

D'Artagnan let a soft word escape. It might have been a curse. Aloud, he said, "We're going to have to search them, then."

"Why?" Porthos said. "I'm sure I got the money and the jewels."

"We shouldn't—" Aramis started.

"We're not looking for money or jewels," Athos said, interrupting Aramis. "Porthos, did you search them else?"

"No, I—"

"Well, I will do it," Athos said. And to D'Artagnan, who made as if to start forward towards the corpses, "Not you, D'Artagnan. You are not fit." He stepped forward, leaving the boy standing, holding on to the bottle.

Porthos realized what Athos was doing as the older musketeer started searching the men's cloaks and clothes. He was looking for hidden pouches, and at this too Porthos had as much practice as Athos and more practice than practically anyone else. Or at least than those who had never joined the musketeers. He stuffed the jewels and money into his own travel pouch, then knelt on the other side of Athos, silently helping him.

While he was feeling his way inside the blood-soaked sleeve of a rapidly cooling body, his fingers struck a folded sheet of paper that rustled at his touch. "Hallo," he said. "What have we here?"

With careful fingers, he extracted the paper, which proved to be of finer manufacture than the normal letterhead, and opened it gingerly.

It was written in brown ink in an angular handwriting that Porthos knew all too well. "'It is by my order and for the good of the kingdom that the bearer of this has done what he has done,'" Porthos read. And stared, gape mouthed at the signature beneath, a single letter, boldly formed—R. Indeed...regally formed. By the man who was the power behind the throne in France.

He passed the letter onto Athos, feeling as though his mind had gone foggy with confusion. He heard Athos gasp.

"Richelieu," Athos said, passing the letter to Aramis and D'Artagnan in turn.

"It can't be," Aramis said as he read the letter.

"I told you," D'Artagnan said. "I told you his hand is in all this. I do not want to expose you to danger. You should never have come. How did you know that I had tried to leave?"

Porthos saw the look of fear in Planchet's face and did not trust Athos with the answer. The older musketeer, with his nobility, sometimes had a veritable infatuation with telling the unnecessary truth.

"Well," Porthos said briskly, "I thought you might do something foolish and I checked at Monsieur de Treville's, where I was told you'd borrowed horses."

Since he had actually checked, after Athos had spoken to him, and while *they* borrowed horses, Porthos felt in the clear with his conscience.

He saw the relief in Planchet's features and just managed not to smile reassuringly at the boy.

Instead he frowned at D'Artagnan. "Only listen. It is not because of you that we are in danger. The Cardinal hated some of us before you were ever born, or at least before you were out of your swaddling clothes. No. Listen. It is because of us that the Cardinal hates you. Did not your father tell you to respect the Cardinal and the King alike? So you see, if you didn't do it, it was because of us, and as such, it is our fault." He looked at D'Artagnan and met with that peculiar confusion that he often saw in his friends' gazes, even when he thought he was being his most lucidly clear.

"The Cardinal learned to hate you because you were our friend," he said, trying to make the whole perfectly inescapable. "And you first went up against his guards because you were fighting by our side. So you see—it is because of us that he sent assassins after you—if he sent assassins after you. It is possible they muddled the whole affair."

Aramis made a sound of dismay. "How do you mean muddled the whole affair?" he asked. "Do you think his eminence just sent men to wait on this road to murder the first voyager that passed and D'Artagnan usurped the appointed death of another of the Cardinal's enemies? Porthos!"

"Well, it's unlikely," Porthos said, with a grunt. "But then it is possible he sent them to kill one of the inseparables and they chanced on D'Artagnan before another of us." He realized the unlikelihood of this argument and sighed. "Or something. The thing is, though, the thing is, that these"—he swept a hand around—"were definitely linked to the Cardinal and as such, I don't see why we are not to take their money and jewels. After all, we would take them of people we defeated in honorable combat."

"But this was not honorable combat," Aramis said.

"No, it wasn't," Porthos said. "On their side. Making us all the more entitled to their bounty."

"But—" Aramis started.

"He's in the right of it Aramis," Athos said. "Though perhaps not for the reasons he gives." He flashed Porthos a smile that left Porthos feeling yet more bewildered. "You see, I knew something was wrong—and that there was a possibility these were not highwaymen but paid assassins—from the moment Porthos said there were exactly ten coins in each purse. That sounds uncommonly like a fee paid to them to dispatch an enemy. And from the letter"—he waved the paper at Aramis—"and from the fact they attacked D'Artagnan, we must assume the money was paid to each of them by Richelieu, and that it was meant to compensate their trouble in killing D'Artagnan." D'Artagnan made a snorting sound at that and Athos gave him an amused look. "Which means, we should take it—we are more entitled to it than anyone else—to compensate us both for D'Artagnan's wound and suffering and the risk we ran in thwarting the plan. And besides..." Athos permitted himself one of his rare smiles, though it was at least halfway a grimace. "And besides, you must warrant that Richelieu being involved, it is our duty to thwart his plan. And what best way is there to thwart his plan than with his own coin?"

Porthos grinned at Athos. Sometimes for all his philosophy and Latin, Athos could be a very sensible man. "Indeed," he said. "And now, I wonder how far we are from a hostelry where we can let the horses rest and get a room where D'Artagnan can sleep for a few hours before we must start on our way in earnest."

"I know a hostelry," Aramis said, surrendering to their argument without ever admitting it. "Down this road another quarter league. We'll walk the horses till then." He looked around, bewildered, realizing that their number of horses had been added to by the four horses of the dead henchmen. "Only D'Artagnan must ride. We'll go to the hostelry and make our plans there."

# The Advantages of Inns and Taverns; The Languages of Monsieur Porthos; The Livers of Geese

**T**EN days later D'Artagnan had to admit to the undisputable superiority of the method of travel which involved money and the ability to command inns and taverns for one's comfort over traveling alone, on a horse of odd color and with no better patrimony than a letter.

They'd sent Monsieur de Treville's horses back at the first stop and proceeded on the well-rested attackers' horses. After that, given the sudden wealth from the attackers' purses, they'd been able to command fresh horses at every stop, and did not have to worry about injuring their mounts or themselves by riding too long on tired, stumbling animals.

In a way, that might not be the best of ideas, D'Artagnan thought, as they dismounted in the yard of a hostelry just inside the walls of Nérac.

They'd come fast indeed, climbing into the Haut Pyrenees with very little account for their rest, much less for D'Artagnan's wound, taken the rolling hills between the Lot and the Garonne at a dead gallop and finally crossed the Garonne near Barbaste.

Now they were in Nérac, the town of Henri IV, where his castle loomed over the city like some ancient temple—or at least like the memory of times past. That those times were pleasant seemed to make no difference, since they were well and truly lost. As was the memory of the Gascon King who had thought Paris to be "well worth a Mass." As was—D'Artagnan sighed heavily—the younger D'Artagnan who had cantered through Nérac last spring, alive to all the beauties of the place that was often called the Gascon Athens.

Back then, his head had been full of nothing but what the town must have looked like when Queen Marguerite made her court here. His nose had been full of nothing but the smell of flowers from the great garden by the river.

Now he returned tired and heavy with fatigue. His wound remained red, as though outraged at the treatment D'Artagnan gave it, riding these long days into the hills of Gascony. Its inflamed, suppurating depths discharged blood and pus onto the bandages that protected his shirt.

Sometimes, when they finally stopped for the night, he would find that his shirt had become glued to the dressings and he would change in silence to avoid his friends' attention to his state.

His friends suspected it or suspected that not everything was as it should be with him. Not that D'Artagnan expected otherwise. One thing it was to lace ones doublet tight and to ride all day and not complain of fatigue or pain. Another and completely different to manage the easy banter he normally exchanged with his friends. And yet another, even more difficult, to not flinch as he dismounted, and not exclaim when someone ran into him in the dark corridors of one of the inns.

These last two were entirely beyond D'Artagnan's willpower and he knew they had long since given him away. But as long as he refused to discuss it, as long as he refused to let them see the wound itself, they could not tell him he must stop. After all, his pretending to be well was the equivalent of his telling them he was well. To challenge it, they would perforce need to challenge his word. And that was reason enough for a duel.

Not that—D'Artagnan thought, as the stable boys took the horses away and he stared at the stone facade of the spacious inn—he could now win a duel against them. But perhaps because of that, and because of their friendship for him, none of them would challenge his word or ask about his health.

The stones seemed to blur together in his vision and the grapevine trunks that stood, stark, beside the inn yard, seemed to writhe like brown snakes. He blinked and wondered if he had a fever.

It wouldn't be surprising considering the pace of their travel. He should delay. He should rest. He should reveal his unhealed wound to his friends and wait a while longer.

But he couldn't. He was less than three days from his home, at the pace they'd been going, and he must hasten home.

When he'd left from Paris, in high enough spirits, though afflicted by grief and filled with filial regret, he had thought to hurry home to console his mother and take up the unwanted burden of his father's duty. In his mind, if distantly, had been the Greek and Roman poems and treatises he'd studied—the duties of the loyal son, the duties of a nobleman.

Those had been reason enough to hasten home, but not to brave this type of ride with an unhealed wound. But the wound, the wound itself and the manner of receiving it—those were reason to break with all reason and logic and to hasten to his mother's side as soon as possible. Because the fact that someone had attacked him by the roadside—whether by order of the Cardinal or not—joined to his father's sudden and violent death to make D'Artagnan fear that there was some awful plot afoot and some terrible crime in all this. It made him fear that his mother, herself, was in danger. Or else that his domain was at the center of a dispute.

A ridiculous thought, when one considered his entire domain was little more than a bastide and some fields. But yet...But yet what else could he think?

"I think we've overshot our mark, and we're in Spain," Porthos said loudly, breaking into D'Artagnan's reverie.

Startled, the young man brought his swimming vision to focus on his friends who stood before a corpulent man in a clean apron. Aramis and Athos were a little aside and seemed to be conferring, leaving Porthos to his own devices—something always a little chancy. And Porthos, staring at the man, had just expressed his opinion loudly.

"Porthos! We are not in Spain," D'Artagnan said, hastening forward. "Nérac is not Spanish. Why, it is the birthplace of Henri IV."

Porthos turned back. His red eyebrows were furrowed over his eyes which were, in turn, squinting with the effort at understanding. "But we must be," he said, "because this man does not speak French at all. And what he says sounds very much like Spanish."

D'Artagnan turned his attention to the man who spoke to him, volubly. Through D'Artagnan's swimming senses only two words struck home, but those were enough. It was *lenga* and *Gascona*.

D'Artagnan felt tears prickle behind his eyes at the words—it was enough to tell him he had come home. To the man he said, in the native Gascon dialect, "I'm sorry. My friends are strangers. We need your most spacious room and dinner sent up to it. Also water for washing."

And before the man could answer, he turned to Porthos. "He speaks the Gascon language, Porthos," he said, softly, reminding himself that Porthos barely spoke his own native French and therefore could not be held responsible for knowing or speaking any other language, or even showing respect to it. "Not Spanish. No more French."

Porthos frowned. "Ah," he said. Then frowned again. "But we've been in Gascony for some time, so how come..."

D'Artagnan shrugged. "It is just that as we go farther into Gascony we will find more people whose main language it is and who speak hardly any other. Though in my village, down in the foothills, they speak some Spanish as readily as some French. But mostly they speak Gascon. The language of my people."

Porthos frowned on him slightly, as though trying to understand what any sane man might want with more than one language, but before he could find his way through the thicket of words in his own mind, the host spoke again, in a fast dialect—so fast that D'Artagnan, away from home for many months, had to strain to follow it.

"I don't think you wish to say here, sir," he said, speaking quickly. "I don't think our inn is very healthy, and I would be loath to see something befall you."

D'Artagnan frowned. In his limited experience he had never had a tavern keeper or inn host warn him away from his own place and the idea struck strangely.

"Athos," he called to the older musketeer, who had approached. "This man says we shouldn't stay here because it isn't healthy."

"Not..." Athos said, then looked straight at D'Artagnan. "D'Artagnan, I scarce understand what he's saying, save for my knowledge of Latin which patches over some of my ignorance of the language, but...Are you sure he didn't say that you are not healthy enough to stay in his hostelry? Because, D'Artagnan, you look like you're suffering from some dread plague."

D'Artagnan nodded and swallowed. This made sense. No hostelry owner wanted someone to die of some plague in his hostelry. At worst it would cause authorities to close it. At best, it would make all other travelers avoid it, lest the vapors of the illness should linger and make them sicken in turn.

And as sick as he felt, as much as words seemed to reach him through a veil of low-level buzzing like a hundred angry bees, he might very well have misunderstood what the man said. "Look," he told the man. "I am not ill. I just have a wound that is troubling me. I must get a room here as soon as possible, and ointment for my wound, or I might die of fatigue."

The host hesitated. He looked at D'Artagnan, then from him to the three musketeers who had clustered behind him, partly in the confusion of those who do not speak the tongue, and partly waiting for a decision.

"Your friends," he said. "I reckon they are all fighters, fast and fierce with their swords, are they not?" And then, with a deep sigh, as though exhaling the troubles of his soul. "I guess there would be no harm in letting you have the lodging."

Did the man think D'Artagnan was threatening him with his and the other musketeers' prowess with the swords? Certainly even here, as far as they were from Paris, the uniform of the King's Musketeers would be known. And considering what the musketeers were capable of and the—mostly true—stories told about their roguery and violence, the man might have a reason to feel threatened.

D'Artagnan started to open his mouth to tell the man that he didn't mean him any harm and that none of his friends would raise sword towards an innocent man. But then he thought better of it.

He needed to lie down. He needed to sleep. Feeling as he felt, his brain might very well be in the grip of a fever. And if not, then he'd managed to bleed enough on horseback today for his mind to be unable to focus. In either case, leaving here, looking for a hostelry in the thick of the town and perhaps being turned away at a few others could very well mean his death.

Or, if not his death, it might well mean he would be truly ill tomorrow and unable to proceed in his journey home. And he must hurry home. Even now, who knew what perils his mother was facing and what threatened his house and family?

So instead of denying any possibility of violence, he shrugged, a movement which hurt his shoulder, and said, "We can defend ourselves well enough."

In a land of gasconades and exaggerated threats, this might very well have seemed paltry, but it was clear that the man already had, in his mind, an idea of how dangerous musketeers could be, because he only sighed again and nodded. "Very well then."

He called out and a dark-haired urchin emerged from the shadows and, upon instruction, led them up the stairs to a room, which took up most of the space over what—from the sounds and the smells emerging from it—must be busy kitchens.

D'Artagnan, taking in the broad, clean-looking room, with oak flooring, fresh rushes on the floor and the sort of beds that were little more than pallets—only four mattresses set upon the barest of frames—sent up mental thanks for the separate beds. In some of the hostelries in which they'd stayed they'd had to share the beds two and two and, in one of them, all four. Getting elbowed by Porthos's giant arms in the night probably had a lot to do with how mauled he felt.

But here—he thought, turning back to the beds to discover surprisingly clean sheets and blankets, smelling of sun and wind—here he would sleep well. And tomorrow he would be well enough to go on with the travel. He must be. His mother needed him. Of this he was sure.

He heard, as if a long way off, disconnected sounds—his friends splashing water—doubtless in the lone washstand in the room—then banging dishes about, and Porthos's surprised exclamation, "The paste is made from the livers of what? And what do they do with the rest of the goose?"

He didn't remember either the water being delivered or the food being brought in. Somehow, he'd lain down on one of the beds, and he felt as if the whole world were receding before this present comfort of being off his feet and not being bounced about by a horse.

"D'Artagnan," Athos said, as if from very far away. "Are you sure you will have no food?"

"Oh, let the boy be," Porthos said. "He's been looking like curdled milk all day. Perhaps he ate something that didn't agree with him."

"I don't think so," Aramis's voice said, calculatingly. "I don't think so. I think it's his wound paining him."

"But didn't he use the Gascon balm?" Porthos asked.

"The jar was broken. He should have rested instead of pressing on."

"He feels a duty to his house and family," Athos said.

Aramis made a sound that wasn't quite a sigh and wasn't quite a tone of exasperation. "You and your duty, Athos. What you don't understand is that such a sense of duty is really the sin of pride. You hold yourself to such a duty as if you were immortal and not cut of mortal cloth. When our Lord came to the world—"

D'Artagnan could see in his mind's eye as Aramis lectured Athos on the path of holiness, and he wished he was awake enough to laugh. But he wasn't, and therefore he let himself sink, deeper and deeper into the well of sleep, till he could hear no more.

## Where Waking Is the Best Part of Valor; The Very Odd Habits of Gascon Cutthroats; The Finer Points of Treason

**D'ARTAGNAN** woke up with the sound of a knife sliding on its sheath and a voice whispering in the Gascon language, "Which of them?"

Another voice answered, in a whisper, also in Gascon, "The dark-haired one."

"But there's two dark-haired ones."

Through D'Artagnan's still-foggy mind, the thought went that his friends had learned to speak Gascon very fast. But neither of the voices sounded like his friends' voices, and then there was that knife, the sound of it. Truth, they used knives to eat with, but there were no sounds of eating.

He opened his eyes. There were two men—

He had no time to see beyond that. Two men. Two men he didn't know, and they were standing by the table. At the table, D'Artagnan's friends sat and for a moment—for a cold, heart-stopping moment—the youth thought they were dead. But their heads were down on the table, and in front of them the remains of what seemed like a cyclopic repast. And Porthos was snoring.

The two men stood by the table hesitating.

"We could cut all their throats," one of them said.

"No," the other one said. "You know his orders very well. Only the dark-haired one and no more."

"But there are—" and in saying it, the intruder, who spoke Gascon, and who was short and dark, turned to look towards the bed and met with D'Artagnan's gaze. "*Ventre saint gris*, he looks—"

He never said what it was that D'Artagnan looked, because D'Artagnan had fortuitously realized that he'd been so tired on arriving at the inn that he'd dropped right to sleep without so much as removing his scabbard and sword. His hand, as though moved by a keener mind than his foggy brain, had already grabbed hold of the blade.

Jumping across the room, ignoring the shots of pain from his shoulder, he screamed as he moved, "Athos, Porthos, Aramis. Wake up, wake up, wake up."

Porthos opened one eye. His snore stopped. But the other man had pulled out a sword and was coming at D'Artagnan, while the one with the knife backed away towards the side of the table. This left D'Artagnan free to concentrate on the man with the sword.

The man was neither swift, nor by any means as good as the duelists D'Artagnan was used to facing in the capital. He held his sword like a cutthroat and came at D'Artagnan full of intent and malice. But he lost both when D'Artagnan retaliated and soon was backing away very quickly, while the young Gascon pressed home his advantage.

Only the intruder maneuvered towards the door and, opening it, dropped his sword and ran down the stairs. D'Artagnan ran after him. He had no more than left the room, though, than he heard the ruffian left inside say, "Come back inside and drop your sword, or I cut your friend's throat."

D'Artagnan looked over and realized that Athos was still sleeping, and that the man had his knife at Athos's throat. There was nothing for it but to back inside the room and drop his sword.

As the sword fell to the floor, the intruder pulled the knife away from Athos's throat and said, "Ah, I knew you would—"

He never said what his prescience had warned him of though, because at that moment Porthos rose, swiftly, lifting his chair above his head.

The giant redhead brought the chair down on the intruder's head, just as D'Artagnan—who had been as swift to retrieve his sword—ran the man through.

Doubly mortally wounded, the ruffian made scarcely a sound as he sank to the ground. D'Artagnan withdrew his sword and wiped it on the man's clothes, and looked up at Porthos. "Why didn't Athos and Aramis wake?" he asked.

Porthos shook his head. "I don't know," he said. "Only that I still feel sleepy, as though I had cobwebs upon my senses."

D'Artagnan—ignoring his shoulder, which was hurting him more than he was willing to admit even to himself—went to the table and swiftly checked both Aramis's and Athos's pulses. He'd no more reassured himself that both were alive, than a splash of water fell over all three of them.

Looking up, D'Artagnan saw Porthos holding the empty washbasin. He was about to protest, but Athos was stirring and so was Aramis and both, by the sound of it, in a temper. Aramis said, "Porthos? God's wounds, this is my good doublet."

Athos exclaimed something more to the point and yet more profane. Looking up at the larger musketeer, Athos looked like he was keeping his temper barely in check as he said, "Have you taken leave of your senses, Porthos?"

"No, but you see, we couldn't wake you any other way."

"Wake us? Why..." And at this moment Athos stopped, as though only then realizing that they were in a room that would be pitch dark, save for the glow of the moon coming through the two windows. Judging from the food on the table, D'Artagnan guessed that they'd gone to sleep shortly after eating, which would be at sunset.

Athos ran his hand over his face. "How long did I sleep?"

Porthos shook his head. "I don't know, as I just woke, with the man saying he had a knife to your throat."

"Man?" Aramis said, and turning around looked at D'Artagnan. "D'Artagnan, why does he speak in riddles?"

D'Artagnan pointed to the man on the floor. "That man. He and his accomplice came in...somehow. I don't know whether through the window or through the door. I woke up with them in the room discussing whether they should kill me or you, Athos. I engaged in a duel with one of them, who escaped, and then this one..."

"A duel?" Athos asked.

"A duel. And you and Aramis slept through it, though Porthos gave some indication of waking up."

"Aye," Porthos said. He was pouring water from the washing jar over his head, as he leaned over the empty washing basin. He shook his hair, like a dog coming out of a river, splashing them all liberally. "I woke up, or at least you could call it that, only I was still...I felt as though I weren't quite awake. Still do, in a way."

"The wine," Athos said. And reached for an almost empty bottle on the table, smelling it. "I don't smell anything, but it must be the wine."

"How do you come to that conclusion?" Aramis asked.

"Well," Athos said. "D'Artagnan is the only one of us who did not have the drink, and the only one of us who woke up immediately, when someone entered our room. Porthos was the second most alert one, and he would be, being the largest. The dosage of whatever the potion might be would be smallest for him. While Aramis is the lightest one, and therefore would sleep soundest, except that I..." He rubbed his forehead. "I might have drunk a little more wine than the rest of you and therefore have been equally lost to the world."

Knowing his friends' drinking habits, D'Artagnan was quite sure that by "a little more wine" Athos meant easily three or four times the amount. He didn't say anything. The reverse of Athos's nobility was his inability to take criticism from those he considered his inferiors. And to Athos everyone was inferior.

"Well," Porthos said. "I shall go and ask the host why he poisoned our wine then." He said it pleasantly and carelessly, as though this were quite a normal errand.

"Stop, Porthos," Aramis said. "You could go, except you won't understand a word he says."

Athos stood up. "I shall go," he said.

"But you my friend, you do not speak Gascon either," D'Artagnan said. "And besides it is foolish of us to go charging out into the inn like this, in the middle of the night. They might very well be lying in ambush for us and, in the dark, we'd be likely to be overcome."

"D'Artagnan is right," Aramis said. He lit one of the candles on the mantelpiece from the dying embers in the fireplace. "It would be foolhardy to charge into the night, into unknown territory."

"Then you propose we cower here, in the dark, not knowing who might be ambushing us or why?" Porthos said. "And not a drop to drink that isn't drugged?"

D'Artagnan cast about for an answer, since neither alternative seemed palatable. But his chest hurt, and he could feel the blood seeping beneath his shirt and doublet, and his head going utterly dizzy with the loss.

"Well," Athos said, phlegmatically. "I suppose I should search the corpse. It might tell us something about his purpose and why he attacked us."

"He attacked us to kill either you or me," D'Artagnan said. "He said his orders were to kill the dark-haired one. He seemed confused there were two of us."

Athos raised an eyebrow at him but said nothing. Instead, he knelt by the corpse, rapidly looking in all the likely places. At last he stood up, with the man's purse in his hand. "Five pistoles," he said. "And nothing else."

"Well, that's half what the other attackers had," Porthos said.

"Perhaps Gascon cutthroats are cheaper," Aramis said.

"Are you sure there are no other papers or letters or anything that will tell us who this man is?" D'Artagnan asked, feeling as though his head were swimming. "But this is maddening. How are we to know more about this man, then?"

"I'm quite certain. If you and Porthos wished me to find out more about him, you should not have made him so thoroughly dead."

D'Artagnan opened his mouth to say that they'd seen no other alternative, but the words never formed. Instead, he stared intently at a dagger in the man's hand. Kneeling, he pulled at the man's still lax fingers to free the dagger. It was a fine implement, the handle of which was ornamented with two lions facing each other upon a field of azure. Seeing it, he felt as though a grey mist descended before his eyes. His knees gave out under him.

"D'Artagnan," Aramis yelled, followed shortly by Porthos and Athos's shouts.

D'Artagnan felt as his friends caught him before he fell and eased him onto one of the beds. As hands unlaced his doublet, he started to protest, but the words didn't seem to be more than inarticulate sounds—protests that didn't form into words.

And then Athos said, "Porthos, go and find the host, and have him send for a physician, or our brave D'Artagnan dies. Quickly."

D'Artagnan tried to exaggerate, but there was nothing for it. Words wouldn't form, and his mind was in an agony of confusion. Time seemed to pass very fast or else very slowly. Suspended somewhere where thought made no sense, but pain was quite real enough, D'Artagnan felt hands at him, tugging and pulling, and felt as dress was packed into his wound, and it was doused with something that smelled like green grass and stung like alcohol.

Then hands tied dressings tightly around his torso and hands slipped a shirt over his head.

At long last, as though the rest were a dream and he were only now waking up, he opened his eyes to see a mug of wine in front of his face, held in Porthos's huge hand.

"Drink," Porthos said. And there was no arguing, not while Porthos forced the cup on his lips. He drank one draught, two. He fully expected to fall back asleep, this time drugged, but instead, his head cleared.

Presently he became aware that his friends were all watching him and holding the landlord in front of them.

He had changed his apron for a long, flowing, white nightshirt. And in the swimming light of the candle, he looked as white as the nightshirt.

"Speak, villain," Athos said. "Tell us why you drugged our wine."

And the man broke into French—not good French, but French at any rate. "I'm sorry," he said, volubly. "Only I have a wife and ten children, and I can never be sure with ruffians like this, that they would leave my family alone. For myself, I would have resisted all attempts to make me do such a vile thing as drug travelers' wine, but for them—how could I resist when these men might have killed my family in retaliation?"

"Stop," D'Artagnan said, his head still swimming. He leaned back against pillows someone had disposed behind his head. "How comes it that you now understand French?"

The man sniffled, as though he were fighting with all his willpower to avoid crying. "I pretended not to speak French because I hoped one of you would say, 'Oh, look, it's an ignorant fool of a Gascon who doesn't even speak our language. Surely we won't stay here, but we will go down the street to the Golden Calf or the Notre Albret.' But no, you would stay. Even though I warned you." He stared at D'Artagnan accusingly. "I warned you."

"Yes, yes," D'Artagnan said. "You warned me. Though so cryptically that I could hardly be expected to understand—but still the question is, what did you warn me about?"

"And what did you know?" Athos said.

The man shook his head. He was sweating. Thick beads of sweat rolled down his forehead. "They came by. A few hours before you arrived. And they said I was to drug your wine, and let you sleep. And

I was to ask no questions." He shook his head again. "I thought...I thought that it was something having to do with politics, or messengers. Gascony has seen so much war, and it is normal for one side to try to overcome the other by treason and to use us, locals, as cat's-paws. 'So, you see,' I told the man, 'I will not take this powder you give me. If it's a sleeping draught you want in the wine, then I will use some herbs that I know, and they'll sleep.'"

He looked from one to the other of them, halfway between pride in his own reported actions and obvious fear that they would not approve of them. "You see, I told them that, and they laughed at me, and that's what I did, because I couldn't be sure this powder of theirs, you know, that it wouldn't kill you. And I didn't want to be responsible for a murder."

"But you were willing to let them come in here, while we were in a drugged sleep," Athos said, "and cut our throats without our being able to defend ourselves. How is that less murder? And why should I not slay you for it right now?"

The man shook his head. His hair came loose in the movement, shaking itself free from a tie that held it at the back of the head. It was black hair heavily streaked with white, lank and lifeless and shoulder long. "No, no. You see, I heard them talking when they thought I wasn't listening. And what they said—what they said was that this would stop the papers ever coming to light. So I thought they just meant to come to the room and steal some paper or some letter. It wasn't till I saw one of them run out, and found the other dead, and these kind gentlemen"—he bowed slightly, first to Athos, then to Aramis—"told me that he'd tried to kill monsieur that I realized they were assassins, you see."

"I still say," Porthos rumbled, as he poured himself a fresh mug of wine from the new jar that he must have had the landlord bring in, "that if we can't prove you knew of their murderous intentions, we should, nonetheless, set fire to the inn, to punish you for drugging us."

The landlord cringed. "But I had my family to think of," he said. "Surely, you didn't want me to let them kill my family, only to keep strangers safe."

"It is difficult, in Gascony," D'Artagnan said, almost not believing what he heard come out of his own mouth. "We have been at war so long, and the war has been so fierce. It is difficult sometimes to remember that strangers are also people and deserving of your protection."

"How could I protect you, monsieur?" the landlord asked. "I tried to warn you."

"I still say he wasn't very Philistine, and we should—"

"It is Samaritan, Porthos," Aramis said, with a heavy sigh.

"I'm not sure that you didn't know they were assassins," Athos said.

"Listen," D'Artagnan put in, feeling tired and above all else not wishing to see the landlord killed. Perhaps he was lying. Perhaps he had no family. But as he was, with his hair streaked with white, he reminded D'Artagnan, forcibly, of his own father, so recently dead. For the sake of his father, he did not wish to see this other man killed. "I say he puts us up for the couple of days I will take to recover before we resume our way." He paused and allowed his comrades to protest without actually listening to their words. He registered that they thought two days insufficient for his recovery, and yet he knew he could wait no longer. "We'll see," he said. "But for however long we need to stay, he will put us up and feed us. And we'll speak no more of this, if he doesn't betray us again."

In the back of his mind was the thought that if the ruffians did come back to take revenge on the landlord, they would have to contend with himself and his friends. And that he did need to recover.

"Two days," he said. "And I hope no more. Someone is trying very hard to keep me away from my domains. That makes me all the more anxious to get there."

Later, after the landlord had gone, the four of them barred the door by pushing the table in front of it and shuttered and locked the windows.

In the impenetrable darkness, D'Artagnan lay staring at the ceiling, turning in his mind the image of that dagger. How could the man have come by it?

"D'Artagnan?" Athos's voice just barely louder than Porthos's snoring reached his ears.

"Athos. You're awake."

"I rarely sleep. D'Artagnan—why did you startle at the sight of that dagger?"

D'Artagnan drew a deep breath. Porthos snored too convincingly to be awake and from D'Artagnan's other side came the sound of steady breathing. But the breathing didn't mean Aramis was asleep. He might be awake and listening.

And then D'Artagnan realized it didn't matter at all. Aramis had doubtless already remarked the emblem on the dagger—it was the sort of thing that did not escape the cunning musketeer.

In a few days, when they arrived at D'Artagnan's home, he would know what that coat of arms was.

"D'Artagnan?" Athos said.

D'Artagnan sighed. This journey into his home would not allow him to hide any shame or confusion.

"It is the coat of arms of my cousins, the de Bigorres," he said at last. And to Athos's silence, which seemed of a sudden so absolute as to have a physical presence, "The senior branch of my family."

Athos didn't answer and as odd as it would be, D'Artagnan wondered if he'd fallen asleep.

But at long last, out of the dark, Athos said, "I'm sorry, D'Artagnan."

D'Artagnan protested, with heat he did not feel, "Perhaps it was stolen."

"It's possible," Athos said. "Very possible, considering the man was a thief. But..." Deep breath. "One thing I don't think is worth arguing anymore after these attacks..."

"What?" D'Artagnan prompted, knowing what the answer was likely to be, but hoping for any other.

"We can no longer delude ourselves that your father died a normal death in a normal duel."

"It is possible," D'Artagnan said. And then bit his lip. "But I always thought it unlikely given my father's skill with a sword."

"That and two groups of people trying to kill you before you reach your destination must perforce mean that we have to investigate your father's death. And consider it murder till proven otherwise."

"I'm very afraid," D'Artagnan said, "that you are right."

"The thing is," Athos said. "The first set had a safe-conduct from the Cardinal. This one didn't—or at least not on the dead man."

"Was it the Cardinal who sent them? Or someone using the Cardinal as a cat's-paw?"

"Whoever it was," D'Artagnan said "doesn't want me in Gascony."

# The Dogs of Gascony; A Widow's Grief; Athos's Fears

"**W**E are near your house, then?" Athos asked.

They were riding down the slopes of rolling hills that led in turn to a comparatively flat land, covered in scrubby pine forests. The road, a beaten dirt track, wound between these pines and was therefore green shaded and fragrant even in bleak late fall.

"Just around the next turn, we should be able to see my domain," D'Artagnan said, and blushed.

Athos smiled. It was a peculiar obsession of D'Artagnan's that his friends would despise him for the meager extent of his lands. As though they'd befriended him for the nobility of his line; as though they were all grand seigneurs living from their lands.

The truth was they'd developed a friendship for the young Gascon based on nothing more than his bravery, his nobility of spirit and his willingness to throw his lot in with theirs when theirs seemed wholly doomed.

That and, if Athos were honest, Athos's own forlorn wonder at finding himself past his mid-thirties and with no son to take up his name. Oh, his mind knew well enough the young Gascon was not his son. So did anyone who saw them, as the two could not be more different in appearance—Athos being tall and spare and looking as he was, the result of centuries of noble ancestry; while D'Artagnan was short and muscular and had the agile bearing of a Gascon seigneur. But Athos's emotions had attached to the young man as though he were the son that Athos had always expected to have. And in spirit, cunning, bright, fast-moving D'Artagnan was the son Athos's heart would have longed to father. A worthy heir to Athos's ancient lineage.

He now spied anxiously, with a father's eye, for signs of fatigue or a look of illness to the young man. However, since they'd taken the three days to rest in the tavern, the miraculous ointment of Gascony, provided this time by the hosteler, seemed to have taken the desired effect.

D'Artagnan was still paler than normal, to be sure. His olive skin showed an ashen grey tinge. But his eyes shone with excitement and perhaps apprehension at the approach of his paternal abode. And he sat effortlessly in the saddle.

"There, there," D'Artagnan said. As he lifted his arm to point, it was clear that the movement didn't pain him, and Athos felt free to look towards where that arm was pointing.

Though the land was relatively flat, showing only rolling hills, they were at a slightly elevated point, looking down on an array of well-ordered fields and denuded vineyards, and the tall stone walls of an enclosed city. They were high enough above the city that they could see within its well-laid streets.

"You live in a fortress," Aramis said, in a tone of surprise.

D'Artagnan laughed. "It's a bastide," he said. And turning around to look first at Athos and then at Aramis, he laughed slightly at what must have been a look of total astonishment on their faces. "I suppose it is a Gascon thing?" He laughed again, a little. "They were new towns, built centuries ago, on the land that noblemen hadn't claimed. Free towns, where the bourgeoisie could hold their own and do their trading in any way they wished, without...rulers." He laughed, as though amused at the idea. "The fishing was free, they could marry their children to whomever they wished, and they had the right to a market or fair. Oh, and they were exempt from military service."

Athos caught the tinge of irony behind D'Artagnan's voice, and he looked curiously at his friend. "This is not, then, part of your domains?" he asked. "Since I assume that whatever domains your father ruled accept D'Artagnan suzerainty?"

D'Artagnan shrugged. He looked back at Athos, his eyes dancing as though at a joke. "Ah, no, my friend. Those are my domains. Those and the surrounding fields and vineyards. You see, the bastides were also, initially, built without a wall. There was peace, you see, and the merchants and farmers did not need seigneurs. But then..." He gave a sigh that held more than a bit of the dramatic and more than a touch of humor. "But then the wars came. English and French and the wars of religion. And, you see, they found they needed a wall and seigneurs after all. And they came, hat in hand, and gave up some of their privileges, in return for my family's protection."

"Ah," Athos said, remembering the blood-soaked history of Gascony, disputed between two countries, torn between two religions. Interesting that at any time the people of this region had thought they were done with war and needed no more protection. And yet, looking at the rolling hills, he could see the attraction of the fantasy, and he almost wished he could believe it himself.

"It was inherited by my father, as second son, from his mother's family," he said. "And it is nothing to the domains of my uncle de Bigorre.[3] They are the great lords of this region. But, enfin, it is enough to support me and mine."

"You were mistaken," Porthos said, in a low rumble.

Athos turned back to look at him at the same time D'Artagnan did, and found Porthos frowning, with an intent expression in his eyes, under his unruly reddish eyebrows. "Your domains, if they include the bastide, are, perforce, much larger than the Cemetery des Innocents."

D'Artagnan laughed, a low gurgle in his throat, and instead of attempting to explain metaphors to the giant redhead—an enterprise all of Porthos's friends knew to be perilous and possibly fruitless—he said, "Perhaps they are. A little." He looked at each of them in turn. "Come, my friends. Let me lead you to my home."

But before they could move, a horseman approached at a gallop. He was singular looking, as he dressed all in black and rode a pitch-black mount. He approached at full gallop, and as he approached raised his whip, as though he meant to clear the road of them by force of his whip. Which was ridiculous, because they were not obstructing the road, but to the side of it.

At his lifting the whip, all of their hands went to their swords, and he seemed to think better of it, and rode by.

"Relative of yours?" Porthos asked, as the horseman's hoofbeats distanced themselves.

"No, *prie a Dieu*," D'Artagnan said. "It is Sever de Comminges. The de Comminges are great noblemen in this area. They own ten times more land and more wealth than I do. And I envy them not at all if they have to claim relationship to Sever."

With those words, he took his horse at a gallop down the path, which became increasingly more winding, till they left behind them the last of the scrubby pines and were hastening down the path between fields and vineyards.

Even at a gallop, Athos could pick up the signs of the approaching city—the smell of fires, the sounds of human voices.

Before the gate of the city they slowed a little. The gate was open to all and Athos wondered if it was always so—these being peaceful times—or whether it closed at night.

D'Artagnan paused just long enough to say, "Welcome to Tournon sur l'Adour."[4]

Inside the gate, the streets were paved with broad paving stones and wide enough for a carriage to pass by without crushing pedestrians. In that, it was perhaps better than most Paris streets. In fact, pedestrians walked out of their way without undue haste, as they took the streets at a moderate speed, climbing slowly as they rode, until they found themselves before another wall with gates—these also open.

The gates led directly into the expansive courtyard of what was a large house and also, clearly, a working farmhouse. There were carts in the yard, one of them loaded with barrels, another stacked high with hay. A patient ox tied to one of the carts chewed its cud wonderingly looking at them. The men working at various tasks in the yard looked too, without surprise and, for a moment, with no reaction.

Then one of them—an older man who held a pitchfork, with which he'd been loading the hay cart—gasped. "Monsieur D'Artagnan," he said, and swept his cap from his head. "Monsieur D'Artagnan, you are returned."

As though this were a signal, all the other men in the yard removed their hats, and an elderly woman came out of the shadows, hurrying towards them. "You are back, monsieur," she said. "Why I scarcely recognize you, so tall and finely dressed."

D'Artagnan laughed. In all their time in Paris, Athos had never seen him laugh so much. He thought, with a pang, that perhaps, for D'Artagnan's own sake, they should allow him—nay, encourage him—to stay in Gascony. It was clear something about his ancestral abode cheered him up. Never mind that his leaving Paris would sensibly add to Athos's loneliness and his knowledge of being on a path to nowhere, a path far removed from that he'd once thought to follow.

Vaulting off his horse, he heard D'Artagnan tell the woman, "No, Marguerite. I might be more finely dressed, but taller I am not. It is a long time since I stopped growing and, besides, I've only been gone six months."

"Ah, but you look taller to my eyes. And I think you're mistaken. It can't be only six months. Seems like years, why, with your mother crying every day for missing you and your father—" She stopped, as though only then remembering that Monsieur D'Artagnan père was no longer among the living. "Ah, monsieur, your poor father. You've heard, have you?"

It wasn't quite a question, and D'Artagnan didn't quite answer it. His features went all sober, and he nodded and swallowed, then turned to introduce the elderly woman to them. "This, gentlemen, is Marguerite, who was my nurse, once upon a time, and who is almost a second mother to me."

The woman protested, "Oh, monsieur," but blushed and her eyes shone with pride.

"And Marguerite, you've doubtless heard of the King's Musketeers and how fierce they are. And how noble. Well, these are the three fiercest and noblest of them all—Monsieur Porthos, Monsieur Athos and Monsieur Aramis."

The three removed their hats and bowed. Marguerite blushed and giggled a little, as though she were a young girl. Perhaps as a young girl she had dreamed of musketeers and, as such, she now found herself transported to that girlhood. She curtseyed towards them and said, "Any friend of Monsieur D'Artagnan will always be received with respect in this house. I am deeply honored to meet you, monsieurs." Then to D'Artagnan, "I'm afraid your mother is in the praying room. She's been in there the whole while. I'll get Rafael to see to your horses. You go inside."

At her gesture, a strapping young man came from the shadows to take charge of the horses, even as their servants hastened to help.

"Marguerite will have taken charge of our servants in no time at all," D'Artagnan said. "She'll make sure they have a place to sleep and are well fed. She is the cook for my family too, as well as supervising those of the village women who come to help with the housework. You see, her husband, Bayard, was my father's servant in the war. And they both came and settled here afterwards. Their son, who is my age, is one of the soldiers in the employ of my uncle de Bigorre."

He spoke hastily, hurriedly, as though trying to evade his own thoughts by racing ahead of them with his voice. Athos would wager that part of D'Artagnan was refusing to think of his father's death—of his father as being dead.

In fact, D'Artagnan rushed ahead, under a stone balcony, to a narrow door, calling out, *"Maman!"*

A sudden furious barking answered him, and from inside the house a small mutt came who looked like nothing on Earth. Combed, bathed and perfumed, he might have resembled those lap dogs that some ladies at court affected and which were pampered past human endurance. However, this dog's long brown hair was matted to the point of almost obscuring his eyes; his tail looked like a mat of its own, and one of its ears flopped down all on its own.

"Angel," D'Artagnan screamed, with certain joy, though the dog had stopped some steps away and started barking furiously. "Angel, you fool!"

He reached towards the snarling, barking creature and picked it up bodily. "It is I, you ridiculous creature."

The dog stopped mid snarl, and made a sound that Athos had never heard from a canine throat. He was sure it was a snarl turned mid sound into a joyous bark. However, as it emerged, it had almost the tone of a human exclamation of surprise. Little mad eyes peering amid the tangled hair regarded D'Artagnan with joy.

"Yes, yes, you fool. See. It is I," D'Artagnan said, enduring mad licking from the happy beast. "This, gentlemen, is Angel, who started out as my mother's pampered dog, and whom I wholly subverted in my wild childhood, till he followed me everywhere and often went hunting with me. He has no notion of his true size and as such he will charge a stag and bring him to ground as though he were a hound."

Athos had a sudden impulse to tell D'Artagnan that the dog was like the master, but instead, bit his tongue and said, "You know, when I was young and I read the *Odyssey*, I was moved almost to tears by Ulysses's return to his home, as a beggar, when no one recognized him, save his old and faithful dog. But I see in Gascony this is reversed. Everyone recognizes the returning master save the faithful dog."

D'Artagnan looked at him with a furtive grin. "Ah, in Gascony even dogs don't like to believe they have masters," he said. Then shrugged.

"Angel is very old. Almost blind and almost deaf. He sees mostly with his nose. He needed to catch my scent to recognize me."

He set the dog down, and the dog followed him, with wagging tail.

"*Maman,*" D'Artagnan called again, to what was a long, dark corridor that smelled faintly of grapes. Then to them, "She will be in the room at the end of this hallway, if she's still in her praying room."

"Do you wish us to leave you to meet her in privacy?" Aramis asked.

D'Artagnan shot him a puzzled look. "No. Oh, no. The sooner she learns she has guests, the better. And there is really nothing I need to tell her in private upon first meeting her."

Which was how the three of them came to follow him, down the long, cool hallway, to a small door at the end. At this door, D'Artagnan knocked and, obtaining an answer none of his friends could hear, opened the door.

And Athos received a shock. However he'd imagined Madame D'Artagnan, the mother of that fierce duelist, his friend, D'Artagnan, this was not it.

It was clear from the way D'Artagnan hugged her, shouting "*Maman,*" and the way the woman clung to him, crying a little, that she was, indeed, D'Artagnan's mother. It was, however, a puzzle how this could be since she looked scarcely older than D'Artagnan and almost certainly younger than Athos himself.

In fact, the woman looked hardly out of her childhood. Small, with a round face and honey blond hair, she had the kind of very pale, even complexion that seems to belong to a doll and not a living human. Her eyes, huge and blue and round, added to the impression of youth and guileless innocence.

Her midnight black dress—modest by court standards, since it wholly covered her bosom and revealed her girlish, plump arms only from the elbow down—and her black headdress only added to the impression of frail innocence.

She looked, Athos thought, like a postulant in a strict convent—all youth and innocence submerged in darkness and discipline. Though he could tell on second glance, by the light of day coming through a thick-paned window, that she had faint wrinkles at the corners of her eyes and lips, none of this detracted from the impression that she'd just moments ago left her playfellows to come pray in front of grim saint statues.

And now Athos looked at the saint statue and his mind stopped working altogether, because the statue showed a female saint holding her severed head in her hands. From the intent expression in the face, it was clear the head was alive and the lips speaking.

The oddness of it confused him long enough that he was barely aware of D'Artagnan's performing the introductions, though he bowed when his name was mentioned. And he hoped, in a flash, that Aramis wouldn't find it necessary to exert his usual fatal charm upon his friend's mother. He did not think D'Artagnan would accept that very well.

And then he realized that D'Artagnan was talking of his father.

"*Maman*, how did it happen? How could it happen? He was the best duelist ever."

"Everyone has a bad day, my son," she said with a resigned expression.

"But, *Maman*, my Father!"

"Well, well...then, Henri, you know, your father was getting old. He was no longer the man you remember."

"But I've only been gone six months!" D'Artagnan protested, heatedly.

"Six months are a long time when one is as old as your father was," his mother said, soothingly. And as she spoke, her eyes turned towards Athos, as if in silent appeal.

Athos wasn't sure why he was being appealed to, and felt his cheeks color. Why did the woman keep emphasizing how old her husband had been?

A horrible thought crossed his mind that Marie D'Artagnan, still beautiful and clearly far younger than her husband, had seen it fit to get rid of the husband she disparaged. And was now making excuses.

Did they know there had truly been a duel, beyond her witness? Did anyone know?

Athos bit his lip and tried to banish these ridiculous fears. He could not and he would not allow himself to suspect D'Artagnan's mother of being a murderess.

## D'Artagnan's Fears; The Office of Monsieur D'Artagnan Père; D'Artagnan's Secret

**D'ARTAGNAN** could not convince his mother that his father would not have died in a fair duel. At least he could get no more than that from her in front of his friends.

Instead, he submitted to her motherly concern, as she had a light meal of roast chicken and bread served to them, and then endured with good grace as *Maman* made her domestic arrangements, assigning each of the visitors to a room in the older part of the house—the south wing.

D'Artagnan himself, of course, was given his childhood room. Or perhaps there was no "of course" about it. Perhaps he should have been given his father's room. But D'Artagnan could no more imagine sleeping in a chamber so recently vacated by his parent than he could imagine flying. And therefore, followed by the tottering but determined Angel, he took his saddlebags to his childhood room which looked exactly as he had left it.

This was not exactly difficult, as the whole room contained no more than a curtained bed and a trunk in which he stored whatever belongings he prized. The hooks on the wall, which normally held his clothes, were now notably devoid of them, since he'd taken all his possessions to Paris with him. In the trunk there would be books and interesting rocks he'd picked up on his walks through the fields when he'd been very young.

On the wall hung his most prized possession, given to him by his father when D'Artagnan had first held his father at bay in a duel—at fifteen. It was a sword, so old that it would be no use at all in a duel. This was the reason D'Artagnan had left it behind, rather than risking it on the road to Paris or in uncertain lodgings in the capital.

Normally he looked at the sword—which had belonged to some de Bigorre of almost forgotten memory—with great pride. Pride at his achievement in winning such a trophy from his father and pride too at the ancestors who had once wielded that sword in war. An ancestry as old, if perhaps not as noble, as Athos's.

But now he stared at it and frowned. The emblem blazed upon the sword's guard was that of the de Bigorre family. Two lions, mouths open, roaring at each other upon a field of azure.

What did it mean? How could a dagger with that same emblem have been in the hands of the dishonorable assassins who'd tried to kill D'Artagnan just days ago?

He shook his head at his own folly. It couldn't mean anything. The men had been murderers, probably robbers, as well. Surely they had stolen that dagger from a member of D'Artagnan's extended family. And yet...

And yet, the thought worked at D'Artagnan's mind as the sort of nagging pain that issues from a wound that should be healed and yet continues to flare.

Thinking of all his cousins—his two male cousins, Edmond and Bertrand, and his one female cousin, Irene, he tried to imagine why any of them might want him out of the way. None of them had any reason for it, not that he could tell, he thought as he undressed and washed away the travel dust perfunctorily with the water provided beside the wash basin.

Bertrand would inherit D'Artagnan's uncle's domains, a land so vast that D'Artagnan's modest keep could fit in it twenty times over. There would be no reason for him to kill D'Artagnan's father. At least no monetary reason. And then there was Edmond. Last D'Artagnan had seen him, before leaving for the capital, Edmond was well dressed and well spoken. Though the family had, initially, spoken of Edmond's entering into orders and making his career in the church, by the time D'Artagnan had left for Paris, this seemed to be wholly abandoned.

Instead, it was almost sure that well-spoken, handsome Edmond was on his way to marrying the heiress of some domains that bordered his parents' lands. These domains were large enough and prosperous enough that Edmond would never want for money or finery. And he too lacked a reason to attack his relatives—in the open or by stealth.

D'Artagnan put on a clean shirt and doublet, and laced it, thoughtfully. He was grateful he no longer needed to bind his wound. In fact, all that remained of that troublesome injury was a very little scab on his otherwise unblemished skin.

As for his cousin Irene...He flinched from the thought. Irene had been his first love, long ago, when he'd first become aware that women were different. He prided himself in its having been returned. Or, at least, Irene had allowed D'Artagnan to kiss her behind a hay bale, at five years of age.

D'Artagnan remembered too, all too well, the scolding that had ensued when they'd been discovered at their pastime. Irene was, after all, an heiress, and destined for better things than marrying the penniless heir of a second son.

In fact, spurred by their indiscretion, Monsieur de Bigorre had immediately contracted his daughter to Sever, the heir of Monsieur de Comminges—the lord of the largest domains in the region.

Though D'Artagnan wasn't sure why, exactly, that marriage had been delayed and she was still single when D'Artagnan had left for the capital. He doubted very much that would still be the case, but even if it were...

What danger could D'Artagnan be for the fair Irene? Was she afraid he would reveal to her fiancé or husband that he'd kissed her behind the hay bales when both were less than six?

Even in his current somber mood, D'Artagnan couldn't imagine this to be true. He smiled sadly at his reflection in the mirror.

No. It couldn't be any of his cousins who'd sent a man to kill him. And his uncle, frankly, didn't even seem to be aware of D'Artagnan's existence. He was that sort of man, blood proud, who'd prefer to pretend the less pecunious side of the family did not exist at all.

The dagger must be a coincidence. Nothing more. And he would not allow it to get in the way of the real investigation.

No. Instead of thinking anymore on that ill-fated weapon, he would go to the room his father had called his office—the small room in which he had done his accounting and other necessary pen-and-ink tasks. And there he would look for enlightenment on his mother's statement that his father had worked for the Cardinal. And perhaps he would find a clue to it all.

Outside his bedroom door, he ran into Porthos's servant, Mousqueton—who had, before Porthos took him into his service, been a larcenous street urchin by the name of Boniface.

Though Mousqueton would proudly tell one and all that he had abandoned his thieving ways when he'd become a musketeer's servant, D'Artagnan was all too well aware of many chickens that seemed to get run over by carriages when Mousqueton was around—leaving the servant no other option than wringing their necks to put them out of their misery. He was even more aware of the peculiar way in which bottles of wine and loaves of bread and the occasional leg of mutton seemed to get run over by carriages around Mousqueton.

Given that, he had to start a little at finding Mousqueton here, so far from the room assigned to his master and any sleeping space that might be allotted to a servant.

"Mousqueton," he said, betraying his surprise.

"Monsieur D'Artagnan," Mousqueton said, and bowed slightly with something very akin to military discipline. "I am come to tell you that my master has decided he needed a ride among the fields to clear his head."

"And he didn't need you?" D'Artagnan asked, wondering how much Porthos might be in need of a ride to clear his head, when they had arrived from a days-long ride just hours ago.

"Monsieur Aramis has accompanied him," Mousqueton said. "And Bazin with them. So, you see, I am quite unnecessary."

D'Artagnan nodded, frowning a little, because he could not determine whether Porthos or Aramis might be following a trail or hunch of their own, or whether they'd simply gone in search of the nearest tavern with good wine and agreeable wenches. Knowing the two of them, it could be either. Or both.

Instead, he said, "Very well. Thank you for letting me know."

Though it was clearly a dismissal, Mousqueton gave no indication of knowing he'd been dismissed. Instead, he bowed again, a small, controlled gesture of respect. "My master said I was not to leave you, monsieur. Your own Planchet is very busy looking at all of your family's horses, this, apparently, having taken him quite back to his childhood in his father's place. Grimaud is attending Monsieur Athos. Bazin is away with Monsieur Aramis. This leaves me, I'm afraid, to make sure that nothing happens to you."

He said the last in an embarrassed tone, as well he might have. D'Artagnan couldn't help a snort of derisive impatience. "Mousqueton! I am a guard of Monsieur des Essarts. I can scarcely need anyone to protect me in my own house."

But Mousqueton only set his lips, and gave every impression of becoming as mulish as Porthos himself could be in this type of dispute. "Monsieur," he said, in an injured tone. "While this might be your own house, I'd like to remind you someone attempted twice against your life on the way here. Also, while you might be a guard of Monsieur des Essarts, and while that noble regiment is often treated as a cadet regiment to the incomparable musketeers, yet I would like to remind you that this post—no matter what its honor—does not have the ability to confer eyes on the back of one's head." He bowed again. "Do not mistake me. I have seen you fighting and I know no one can equal you in fair duel. But this does not mean you can't be killed by a dagger slipped by stealth in between your shoulder blades."

D'Artagnan started and would have protested, except that Mousqueton's words were so patently true. He thought of the dagger in his luggage, which had fallen from the hands of the ruffians. A dagger with the emblem of his own relatives. It was all he could do not to shiver.

"My master told me to guard you and stay beside you, whether or not Planchet was on hand to perform the like service," Mousqueton said. "And, as you know, it is not prudent to disobey Monsieur Porthos."

D'Artagnan nodded. "Very well, then. But I am only going to my father's office, to look at his papers."

Without a second glance at Mousqueton, he hastened down the long stony corridor, with its curved ceiling, that had probably once been part of some much grander building, before the D'Artagnans had taken possession of the site. The windows to the left, also elegantly curved, gave out on a panorama of fields, just above the city walls. D'Artagnan remembered those fields in spring, filled with singing women helping in the planting.

For just a moment, he felt regret that he had come back in the beginning of winter, with the fields denuded and his beloved land covered in frost. And then he remembered he wouldn't be leaving these domains again. There would be springs and springs and springs, and winters too, stretching to the end of D'Artagnan's life.

He turned from the windows and hurried through the hallway and up a flight of stairs whose stone steps were so worn as to show an indentation in the center. He didn't turn, but he knew Mousqueton was following him.

D'Artagnan's father's office was one floor above, in a jutting observation tower that protruded from the roof of the otherwise relatively modest house. At one time it had been a guard tower, ready to warn the owners of incoming attack. His mother said his father had made his offices up there because—a man of action and always reluctant to undertake accounts or correspondence, or indeed anything that required him to put pen to paper—he had needed the silence and the isolation to force himself to work upon the dreaded tasks.

D'Artagnan, however, who had often gone up there to consult with his father on horses or swords, or other urgent issues of his early youth, suspected what drove his father to his isolated aerie was less of a desire for solitude and more of a desire to see all around him—the open vistas of fields and vineyards. As a man of action, a man who had traveled, the elder D'Artagnan must have found Gascony and the walled precincts of Tournon sur l'Adour terribly confining.

And his son, sighing, arrived by means of a winding staircase to the door to his father's office which, to his dismay, proved to be locked.

He rattled it in some impatience. His father had kept the keys on his own key ring, which would now be in possession of D'Artagnan's mother. D'Artagnan didn't anticipate his mother's barring him access to his father's papers, but first he must perforce go and find her in whatever dim recesses of the house she might be, doubtless supervising preparations for supper.

He made a sound of impatience, and found Mousqueton at his elbow.

"Monsieur," he said. "If you'll allow me, I can open the door for you." In his hand he had what looked like a key ring, except the "keys" depending from it were not like any that D'Artagnan had ever seen. They were, in fact, no more than a curious collection of various metal wands twisted this way and that.

D'Artagnan stepped aside, curious as to what Mousqueton proposed to do. He flattened himself against the wall while the young man, who was almost as tall and powerful as his master, stepped forward and worked on the lock with his metal implements.

For a moment it seemed to D'Artagnan as though he weren't sure what to do. He used now this implement, and now the other, and they made curious sounds as he inserted them in the keyhole, but nothing happened.

"*Bon,*" D'Artagnan said, ready to declare it a lost cause and go in search of his mother and the right keys.

But just then, there was the unmistakable sound of a lock turning and opening.

Mousqueton stepped back. "There it is," he said.

D'Artagnan pushed at the door and it opened. Over his shoulder, he told Mousqueton, "I thought you were done with illegality and larceny now that you work for Monsieur Porthos."

Mousqueton smiled. "Why, monsieur. Of course I am. How could you think otherwise? It's only that having learned the art of breaking in early enough, I hated to part with such a skill. So I keep my implements. But I assure you, I only use them for entertainment and emergencies and, occasionally, you know...to do someone a favor, as for instance, if one should need to go into a room that happens to be locked, due to some oversight. The Duchess my lord has befriended," he said, with the slightest of smiles betraying that he knew very well that Porthos's lover was, in fact, an attorney's wife, "often has need to get into rooms that her husband has accidentally locked, you see."

"I see. And I'd wager your services are invaluable in such capacity," D'Artagnan said as he walked into the room.

It was a tidy room, as it would be, Monsieur D'Artagnan père having been a soldier and one who had engaged in long campaigns. He had got used to taking care of his possessions and keeping them in order.

Order, in this room—which was scarcely larger than the sort of small chamber normally used to keep clothes or implements—meant that rolls of paper and stacks of books were on a long, narrow table by the window. A larger table was set in the middle of the room. This one, D'Artagnan's father had used as a writing table. There were stacks of unused paper on it, as well as inkwells and a couple of trimmed quills. A stool was pulled up to it, D'Artagnan's father having disdained more fanciful seating.

There were also two low trunks, under the table—one of them bearing scuff marks and a shiny spot on top, where D'Artagnan's father was accustomed to resting his feet.

The cutthroats in the hostelry had said something about D'Artagnan needing to be killed so papers would never be found. If there was a document that could enlighten him on their motives, it would be here.

Without a word, aware that Mousqueton had come in, closed the door and leaned against it, thereby protecting D'Artagnan from a stealth attack, D'Artagnan started examining the papers on the long table.

None of them seemed important. Most of the papers, folded or rolled, were letters—a lot of them from old comrades at arms, though one or two of them, written in the querulous tone of elderly people who suspect that someone, somewhere, might still be amusing themselves, were clearly from old and distant relatives.

D'Artagnan noted, curiously, that more than one of those letters made disapproving reference to his mother. At least, D'Artagnan could not interpret "that woman you married" in any other light. He frowned, realizing that even his near relatives, the de Bigorres, avoided contact with his mother in every possible way, and he wondered why.

There was nothing in his mother's history that could justify this. Though she'd never given him an account of her childhood, and her only reference to her family was to say they were all dead, D'Artagnan had gleaned enough from her stories to gather that she came from no-ble-enough people—that she'd trained in a convent as a young woman and that she'd come from the convent almost immediately to his fa-ther's arms.

He couldn't imagine what, in such a biography, could excite the dis-like of relatives who signed themselves with three surnames and sealed their letters with enough wax to keep a royal proclamation safe. But the de Bigorres were so proud they probably resented any of them—even a second son—marrying less than a great heiress.

D'Artagnan looked up and through the three windows, one on each side of the little tower. Through the windows he could see the fields and the vineyards and to the west a cluster of riders that he judged to be his two friends and Bazin, amid the fields.

From this tower he could see almost the full extent of his hereditary domains. He smiled at the idea that his mother hadn't been noble enough for the holder of such land.

But if his extended family so despised Madame D'Artagnan it was all the more reason for D'Artagnan to stay and protect her. He'd never see Paris again. No. He must stay and protect his mother, who would otherwise be devoid of protection.

He sighed and glanced at Mousqueton, who looked somber, as though he understood D'Artagnan's thoughts.

Putting the correspondence down, D'Artagnan skimmed the books, one of which appeared to be on the art of account and the other two mere ledger books. He'd have to look through the figures more carefully in the future, to determine whether his father had put the instructional tract to good use. He would also have to go over the figures, he sup-posed, to determine the financial shape of his domain.

If his father had been killed—if it hadn't been just a proper duel—then the reason for it would probably lie in those figures. It was D'Artagnan's experience most such reasons normally came back to money. And perhaps it would even explain why someone had attempt-ed to kill him too. And who that might be.

Leaving the stacks of papers aside, he knelt and pulled one of the trunks towards him, to look at its contents. The first one was unlocked and contained nothing more than more receipts and bills and accounts.

While the information in them might be very interesting, or even, perhaps, vital to the understanding of his father's death, D'Artagnan could not look through it all right now, much less absorb its import.

Instead, he closed the trunk and pushed it aside. He pulled the one with the scuff marks atop towards him, and was surprised to find it locked. How much security could it need? The office had already been locked. How much more did the trunk need to be secured?

"Permit me, Monsieur," Mousqueton said, and, kneeling, unlocked the trunk with worrisome efficiency.

D'Artagnan waited, his heart beating a little faster than he'd like to admit, until Mousqueton had turned his back, before he opened the lid.

Inside the trunk was...fabric. D'Artagnan frowned at it, as the fabric resolved itself into a military tunic and a plumed hat, and then he smiled to himself, realizing that what this trunk held were souvenirs of his father's life before he'd come back to his domains and settled down.

He moved the plumed hat aside, and lifted the tunic. Underneath the uniform was a dress. Silk, in a brilliant blue. D'Artagnan exclaimed to himself, wondering whether in his father's life, long before D'Artagnan had been born, there had been a young woman like D'Artagnan's own Madame Bonacieux. Driven by this curiosity, he uncovered the dress, which appeared to have been stained by water, long ago, but to have been of the best fabric and tailoring.

He pulled it up and out of the trunk, curiously. As he did so, a paper fell out of the trunk and fluttered to the floorboards.

It was a note, written in an aristocratic hand, with brown ink—and both the paper and the ink looked far too fresh to have been put in this trunk at the same time as the old clothing.

It read: "It was at my command and for the good of the kingdom that the bearer of this note did what he had to do."

# The Saints of Gascony; Feuds of Blood; Monsieur Aramis's Philosophy of Life

"**THAT** was a very strange saint, back there, in the praying room," Porthos said as they rode, apace, into the fields of D'Artagnan's domain.

Aramis looked at him, amused. He had been expecting the question since he'd first seen his friend stare, openmouthed, at the holy statue. "It is a Gascon saint," he said, keeping his voice even. "Saint Quitterie. She was the daughter of a prince, who wished her to renounce Christianity to marry a local chieftain. When she ran away to escape such fate, her father pursued her and beheaded her not far from here, in Aire sur Adour. It is said, by a great miracle of God, she then picked up her severed head and walked, holding it, to the place at which she wished to be buried, and where her shrine is to this day."

He allowed his words to fade into silence, while Porthos stared at him. Though Aramis had his reasons to doubt the veracity of the account—for one it was an echo of many other accounts he had heard attributed to very many different saints—he didn't judge it prudent to make Porthos privy to his doubts.

After all—as one of Aramis's Jesuit masters had instructed—just because as a learned churchman you might have reason to doubt many of the local traditions or miracle accounts, and though, as a theologian, you knew these were not an essential part of the gospels, yet it was true that a lot of popular faith rested on them. And as a learned believer, it was not part of your duty, nor indeed recommended, that you use your knowledge to tear down the innocent faith of the simple people.

Aramis thought on the gospel passage that stated it would be better not to be born than to give scandal to an innocent, and felt justified in his actions. Besides, surely a Saint Quitterie had lived and whether or not she had carried her head in her hands was a thing of very little importance beside the truly ineffable miracle of sainthood.

"Well," Porthos said. "With all the pagan chieftains these women are forever expected to marry, there must have been a shortage of Christian men. I wonder why. And besides, why couldn't she have married the chieftain and then converted him? It seems very foolish to me to run away just because you are expected to marry. Surely as the daughter of a king—"

"We can't judge the ineffable lives of those preserved for sainthood," Aramis said, half absently. Truth was, his mind was working at something quite different than Porthos's usual—or rather, as normal, unusual—ramblings.

The praying room had surprised him, and yet he hadn't quite known why. Now that he thought about it, it was because he realized that statue had been quite old, but the room it was set in was not, like a normal praying room, adorned with other marks of devotion. There was just the window, and the bare walls. None of the reliquaries or sacred bits of cloth of this saint or others that normally reposed in such rooms.

And besides, there was a small church just a few steps from the house. Few houses were so devoutly Catholic as to have a room for praying—unless they were also large enough and wealthy enough to have rooms for every other imaginable purpose.

The Queen had her own praying room, of course, as did other great noblewomen, simply because it was not practical to leave the house every time you wanted to spend the day at your devotions. But why did Madame D'Artagnan need a praying room of her own? And if the house was equipped with one from time immemorial, then why was the room so unadorned?

And then how devoutly Catholic could D'Artagnan's father be? Hadn't D'Artagnan's father fought for Henri IV, the Protestant King?

Oh, of course, Henri IV had converted to Catholicism that he might wear the crown of France, and a lot of his lieutenants, commanders and normal soldiers had converted with him. But most of those men had converted for the same reasons Henri IV had. Because Paris—or whatever reward they could hope for in Paris—was worth a Mass. They had not converted out of any great devotion or the hope for paradise from the Church of Rome.

Aramis, of course, disapproved of people who made such a travesty of his faith. Or at least, he didn't exactly approve of them. Though he had not read Protestant apologetics as part of his education—his masters did not believe in exposing their charges to the works of the devil—he had read about the Protestant doctrines. Enough, at any rate, to consider them grave error and not to be pardoned, much less embraced.

However, the other part of Aramis, the part that lived in the world and not in theology books, knew that many good men—and men of good mind and conscience too—had picked the other side in the wars of religion. Which meant however in error, that they held that conviction according to their reason.

He also knew that a lot of people had changed and far be it from him to doubt the sincerity of their conversions, but it was known a lot of them changed only so they could have a place in the new kingdom.

However, if D'Artagnan's father had converted out of ambition, where had that very old statue come from? And why a praying room in his own house?

Perhaps he had converted, but out of conviction.

He realized he'd been lost in his own thoughts and that Porthos had dismounted and was walking around what appeared to be a paved threshing floor. It was a vast space, encompassed by a low wall, and though Aramis knew next to nothing of agricultural work, he had a vague memory of seeing men threshing the grain in such places.

He also knew, from the directions they'd received at the beginning of their ride, that this was the place where D'Artagnan's father had fought his last and fatal duel. He looked cautiously around the area, feeling as though it should be inhabited by an unquiet spirit.

Porthos, on the other hand, was pacing the perimeter, staring at the ground and looking as if he were measuring the ground by steps.

Aramis didn't think this expedition—which Porthos had insisted on taking based on a stable boy's mention of Monsieur D'Artagnan's death—could lead to anything. What, exactly, could Porthos expect to find out from looking at the place where a duel had been fought two weeks before? Even if it hadn't rained, he was sure other people had crossed through here in the meantime. There would be nothing. Not even footprints.

"Porthos," he said.

The large redhead, now on his knees, stared at something on the ground. *What* God only knew, and even He might be at a loss to understand *why*. He grunted at Aramis.

"Porthos, attend to me," Aramis said. "Did D'Artagnan ever tell you what his father's religion was?"

Porthos looked up. "No. But D'Artagnan is Catholic."

"I know that," Aramis said, barely containing a snort of impatience. "And his mother clearly is Catholic, given the statue of St. Quitterie in her praying room."

Porthos shrugged. "Well, then," he said. "At any rate, what else would they be? They're good loyal subjects of the King."

"The King has good subjects who are Protestant," Aramis said. "Some of them noblemen living in the capital."

Porthos didn't answer to that. He was now, on his knees, following some trail on the ground. What could it possibly be? From atop his horse, Aramis could see no footprints, and nothing clearly defined. And then, given the way that Porthos thought...well...it could be anything at all.

Aramis had been friends with Porthos long enough to know that the tall man was not stupid. Oh, certainly, he was not the most able to manipulate language, and this often led those who didn't know him very well to think he was less than intelligent. But Aramis knew better. He had seen Porthos, in the past, solve puzzles the rest of them couldn't, by the application of an odd form of thought that seemed to be three parts composed of his senses and only one of his thought.

But intelligent or not, Porthos had a very odd turn of mind. And whatever he was following might be crucial, or might mean nothing at all. Still, Aramis dismounted.

"Porthos, attend."

"I am attending. You just don't seem to be saying anything of any import," Porthos answered, looking closer at something on the flagstones.

Aramis resisted an impulse to argue. While he and Porthos argued more or less continuously—long, involved disagreements that in no way affected their friendship—right then Aramis wanted answers, not a pastime. "Only because you don't attend," he said. "Look, D'Artagnan's father fought for Henri IV."

"Of course he did. Henri IV was the King of Navarre before he was the King of France, and Navarre is around here somewhere. His soldiers were almost all Gascons. That might have been why he had such success. Crazy men, Gascons. And fearless fighters too."

"No," Aramis said. And before Porthos protested, "What you say is true, but that is not what I mean. What I mean is that Henri of Navarre was a Protestant."

"He converted before he became King of France," Porthos said. "As it's only fair."

Aramis sighed in exasperation. "All this I know, but did Monsieur D'Artagnan père also convert? Or was he always Catholic? And if he was always—"

"It's unlikely he was, you know," Porthos said. "At least the noblemen in Henri IV's army were all Protestant. And Monsieur D'Artagnan père, no matter if he was a second son, was a nobleman."

"That is my point," Aramis said. "And frankly, that praying room has the look of a Calvinist chapel—all empty and bare and unadorned. No reliquaries, no paintings on the wall itself, not even crosses as part of the architecture. It seems to me that the praying room was a Protestant chapel or meeting room, later converted to a praying room, perhaps by Madame D'Artagnan."

Porthos grunted. He got up off his knees and followed something to the wall, then looked up at the flat top of the wall—built of rocks so thick it was probably, in Roman times or earlier medieval times, the foundation of a building. "I don't see what it matters. So perhaps the D'Artagnans—or whoever lived in the house before them—were Protestant. And they're now Catholic. I don't understand why this should exercise your mind, Aramis." Porthos snorted and shrugged. "Oh, sure, you worry about everyone's soul. But our friend's soul is safe in the arms of the mother church. So, why worry?"

"Because that statue is far older than Madame D'Artagnan," Aramis said. "Why, just from the proportions of the body...the head is much bigger than it should be. You know...I'd think that statue was created five or six hundred years ago."

"Didn't look that old."

"Well, I'm sure the paint has been touched up, and the gilding added, but I'm sure it's that old. And my question is, how did a Protestant family come by that kind of ancient image?"

Porthos looked up and blinked at him. "God's Blood, Aramis, sometimes I wonder if you're mad." Before Aramis could protest, Porthos laughed. "Statues! Why, my friend, statues can be bought and sold, no matter what their age. Perhaps D'Artagnan's mother heard that the statue had miraculous powers or such and spent a great deal of money on it. Or perhaps the statue was always theirs but forgotten somewhere, in the main house of D'Artagnan's relatives...what's their name again? Oh, yes, de Bigorre. Or perhaps it came from the side of D'Artagnan's mother's family.

"Or perhaps," he said, shrugging emphatically, "the de Bigorres were always Catholic, and only their son, D'Artagnan's father, converted to Protestantism. Or perhaps this is all your mare's nest and D'Artagnan's father was as good a Catholic as could be hoped for and only fought for Henri IV out of Gascon pride. Who are we to guess?"

"But—" Aramis started.

"No buts. Look, look here. *This* is solid, and I wonder what it means."

As he spoke, Porthos was touching the wall, and Aramis wondered what he expected the wall to be if not solid. But because there would be no talking to Porthos until he found out what was going on in Porthos's mind, Aramis obliged him by coming close and taking a look.

There, by Porthos's large hand, were stains on the rock—minute, dark stains. Aramis frowned on them, for a while, then said, "Blood?"

Porthos nodded enthusiastically. "Blood. You see, it comes from there, where the duel took place and where D'Artagnan's father was killed...to here."

"I see. So he was stabbed and backed this way?" Aramis said, wondering why Porthos was so interested in this.

Porthos looked up, frowning slightly. "No, no, no. His father was run through here. Through the throat. I asked." He got up and paced to the center of the threshing floor, where Aramis could see there was, indeed, a bloodstain. "He stumbled this way"—he stepped the opposite way from the bloodstains on the wall—"and fell here." Another spot with a large bloodstain.

Porthos scratched at his beard. "So, the question is, where did the other trail of blood come from? It comes all the way from there." He pointed to the wall. "And though the light is failing too much for me to determine whether it continues in the grass beyond, I suspect it does. If D'Artagnan's father was run through here—" He stepped towards the spot again. "And died here." Ten steps the other way. "Then how could he have bled all the way there, up the wall and onto the fields beyond?"

Aramis sighed. He knew that Porthos was not stupid. He valued his friend. But sometimes it was very trying how Porthos thought himself into these cul-de-sacs and didn't seem to glimpse the most obvious of paths out.

"Porthos," he said, his voice sounding as tired as he felt. "Perhaps the other man was slightly injured. Those drops of blood are very small. Perhaps he was slightly injured and went that way, to his own house, after the duel."

Porthos looked at him, with brow furrowed, a long time. "You know...that never occurred to me," he said. And he gave every appearance of trying to come up with some reason to doubt Aramis's logical explanation of events.

Aramis bit his lip, hoping Porthos wouldn't say something too strange. And meanwhile, he wondered what the D'Artagnan family's religion had been. And what it meant for this region of France that had so long been ripped apart by wars of religion.

Could it be reason enough for a murder, these many years after?

# The Wisdom of the Stables; Monsieur Athos's Refusal to Suspect a Woman; Where Men Are More Than Their Families

**ATHOS** had washed and dressed in clean clothes, after his travel, only to find his friends seemed all to be engaged in some sort of pursuit.

He understood well enough the weight that must suddenly have come to rest on D'Artagnan's shoulders. There was the house to take over, the mass of accounts and papers to go through. Athos knew very well what he would face, should the unlikely day ever come in which he returned to his position as Comte de la Fere.

Just the thought of it gave him a pang of longing for his comfortable office, with its lighted fire, his paperwork, the life he'd been trained for.

But he was better aware than anyone could be to know that the path home was barred to him. He'd dishonored his family, his name and himself, by killing a defenseless woman. At least, at the time, he'd thought himself to be executing a judgment upon an escaped criminal who had lied her way into marrying him. Now he wasn't so sure. And while he wasn't sure—while, in fact, he held himself guilty of murder—he refused to stain the home of his ancestors with his presence.

Could he have gone home—or rather, had his life not entered this strange byway—he'd have sons. And his son would be a lot like D'Artagnan. At least he would if Athos had anything to say to it.

Since he could never go home and never resume his ancestral duties, D'Artagnan was the closest he would ever have to a son. As such, it behooved Athos to find out in what circumstances D'Artagnan's father had died.

At first, when reading of the duel, he'd thought that the man had simply fallen victim to a not unusual fate. After all, men dueled and when men dueled some of them died. Athos had killed his own share of adversaries.

D'Artagnan's father had been old. In fact, if he had fought with Henri IV, he had probably been in his fifth or sixth decade. Men that age who had always dueled often forgot that their reflexes had changed and their footing could no longer be depended on.

Athos would be more than ready to consider that Monsieur D'Artagnan père had fallen victim to the combined misfortunes of age and pride, except for one thing. Or rather, except for two things—the two attacks on D'Artagnan on the road here.

Those attacks were enough to make it almost sure someone had killed Monsieur D'Artagnan on purpose and if someone had, then his son was in danger from the same people.

When it came to suspects, it was more complex. There was the dagger with the Bigorre coat of arms in the paid assassin's hand. How had it come to be there? It would be something from the de Bigorre house. Or this one, since D'Artagnan's father had been born to the de Bigorre family.

Athos did not want to think of the still-young Madame D'Artagnan. Not that her undeniable beauty aroused any tender feelings in him, but because he wondered if she'd had a reason to wish her husband dead.

But surely, no woman would be unnatural enough to hire assassins to kill her son? Athos, who had read the mythologies of Greece and Rome, grinned at the naive recesses of his mind. Of course some women did just that. His only doubt; his only rational reason to think it couldn't be so was that note, undeniably signed by Richelieu.

He clutched to that one reason like a drowning man holding onto the proverbial straw.

What could Madame D'Artagnan in her provincial home in Gascony have to do with the Cardinal who ran France from behind the King's throne?

And yet...

Her letter announcing her husband's death had said that her husband worked for the Cardinal. What if she'd only said that because she herself worked for his eminence, and wished to attribute such to her husband? What if she'd been trying to muddy the waters so her guilt would be less obvious?

What if, in fact, D'Artagnan's father had been working for the King and died due to one of those confrontations that daily took place in this kingdom between the devotees of the true King of France and those of the shadow power?

Then surely the attempts against D'Artagnan were explained? If Madame D'Artagnan were the Cardinal's agent, then her son, who was devoted to the King and his musketeers, was likely to thwart her plans when he arrived. And if that was the case, there was not even any need for Madame D'Artagnan to have attempted to kill her son.

It sufficed for her to have sent a note to her master in Paris. He would then of his own accord have hired assassins and tried to stop D'Artagnan from reaching his domains.

Athos sighed. After all, most of his suspicions were founded on very little beyond her anxious insistence that her husband was very old, an odd glint in her eye and her age and beauty. Not enough. Too well did Athos know that he was likely to condemn a woman unjustly.

"Grimaud," he said, calling to his servant, who emerged from the shadows where he'd waited since he'd laid his master's clothing out on the bed. "Tell me, what is the name of the live-in servant? The one who was Monsieur D'Artagnan père's servant in the war?"

"Bayard," Grimaud said.

"And did he seem to you talkative?"

Grimaud shrugged. "On the subject of horses and battles, as garrulous as you could hope, Monsieur le Comte."

Athos nodded. "Well, then, we'll start with horses and battles. And we'll see what else he has to say."

Grimaud didn't ask or argue further. It was one of his admirable qualities—and one in which Athos had carefully trained him—that he could go for days without talking at all, and had learned to obey his master's gestures, when Athos himself found that words were unnecessary.

"Where is he?" Athos asked.

"In the stables, last I saw him," Grimaud answered.

Athos allowed Grimaud to lead him to the stables, a vast space under one of the wings of the house. Well aware that D'Artagnan had come to Paris on one of the funniest horses God had ever created—ill-proportioned, all knees, and covered in the most horrible of yellow orange pelts—Athos was surprised to find several horses in the stable, besides five of the ones they'd brought with them.

There were at least ten very beautiful Arabians, with nervous legs and shining hides. Bayard was brushing one of these, talking to it in an undertone in that Gascon language to which natives seemed to revert when they thought no one from outside the region could hear them.

He looked up at Athos's entrance and bowed slightly. "Monsieur," he said.

"Hello, Bayard," Athos said. "What a very beautiful mare you have there. Was she born and bred in this house?"

Bayard shook his head. "Not her. We've only owned her for about four months." He looked around, slightly bewildered. "All of these horses, in fact. Before that we had only my master's old horse, which, as they say, has joined the battle eternal. And that horse's grandson, a fine mount but of a strange color most closely approaching orange, and all odd looking, if you know what I mean."

Athos nodded. Having seen the horse, he unfortunately knew. "So you bought all these just recently? Was your master intending to go into the horse breeding business?"

Bayard shrugged. "Not business as such, you know. He was a nobleman. Not a man of business. But he liked horses, and his father used to breed them, and he thought he could...breed a few of them. Keep the house in mounts and perhaps generate a little income.

"He used to tell me, the way Monsieur D'Artagnan was with the girls, there was but no telling that he would find some woman to marry while in Paris, and come back here to raise a passel of brats, and we might as well have some way of ensuring they would not all starve." He looked stricken. "My poor master."

"You served him long," Athos said, finding a place to lean against one of the stall doors.

"Oh, yes. He first hired me here, and I stayed with him through all the wars of religion and all. Even in Paris. Only then we came here, and we both married, and you see how it was."

"I suppose your wife served with Madame D'Artagnan," Athos said.

Bayard sniffed. "With Madame D'Artagnan sure. But not this one."

"Oh? There was another?"

"Oh, yes, there was another, much superior to the present. A real Madame D'Artagnan. She died, poor thing, in childbirth. And the babe with her. And then, but ten years later, my master he up and gets this one. Well, I hope he liked the bargain he made. Not, but I'm sure she led him to an early grave. And she didn't even go to his funeral. Says that funeral services just make her ill. Fact is, she never cared for him."

Athos did not want to suspect D'Artagnan's mother. But neither could he stop himself from asking, "How so?"

"Well...I'm not one to talk." Another sniffle. "And that's women's gossip, anyway, but with one thing and another, I'd not be surprised if she worried him half out of his mind."

"He did not die of worrying," Athos said.

"No. He died of a duel. And it was all her fault."

This was far more interesting, and besides, while Athos was trying hard not to suspect Madame D'Artagnan, it didn't mean he couldn't suspect some man who pined for her affections and who might have killed her husband—and attempted to kill her son—in order to achieve her hand in marriage.

"How was the duel because of her?"

"Well, then," Bayard said, and brushed the horse with a will. "Did the lord not die fighting with that Monsieur de Bilh? And did I not see Monsieur de Bilh, more than once, at our gates, talking to madam? Ah, it's all very well for him to tell us that he comes over because he has some boundary dispute with my master." He made a sound like spitting. "Boundary dispute. I ask you. How many men with a boundary dispute find it necessary to come to the house when the master isn't there?" He shook his head. "My wife says that I am imagining things, but I say...I say she doesn't know. Other women gossip, you see, but my wife doesn't. She's a good woman. But I tell you, there's no smoke without fire."

He finished brushing the horse and led her to a stall. "What I say," he said, turning around, "is that whether she meant it or not, that woman has a lot to do with her husband lying—such as he was—in the crypt. Because, you see, even if she didn't mean nothing by it, she smiled at him a lot. And men like that de Bilh are likely to take that the wrong way." He sniffed. "My master never had no dispute with Monsieur de Bilh, boundary or not, and if he'd challenged him for a duel, he'd have told me and taken me with him. No. That was too sudden. And no one who'd seen Monsieur D'Artagnan duel would believe that a stripling like de Bilh could run him through either. He's killed a dozen men better than de Bilh. I tell you, monsieur, it was treason and done as treason. They came at him, when he was not expecting it, I'm sure of it, and killed him before he knew it."

Athos inclined his head. Was it possible that someone had taken a fancy to beautiful, young-looking Madame D'Artagnan, and for her sake killed her husband and attempted to kill her son? It was possible, but it left unexplained the letter from the Cardinal found on the first set of attackers.

"So he'd never fought with this Monsieur de Bilh."

"Boundary disputes," Bayard said and snorted. "As if Monsieur D'Artagnan could ever have cared about his land's boundaries. He always said as they weren't much to look on, and that a man couldn't properly stretch in them without putting his foot on the neighbor's land. And he told Monsieur Henri, he told him, 'Son go to Paris and make your fortune there. Forget these lands. If you ever inherit them, they're barely worth the trouble. Unless you make a fortune to add to your inheritance.'" Another snort.

"So your master expected my friend to make his fortune in war?"

"In war or in the city. To do something, he said, that would get him noticed by the King, and get him some great boon. Many is the times he told me—very proud of that boy he was, and with good reason—that Monsieur Henri would make us bigger than de Bigorre, and that he'd rather have that one son than his brother's inheritance. Now, does that sound like a man who would duel another over boundary disputes?"

Athos shook his head. It seemed interesting to him that Bayard approved of D'Artagnan, even if he disapproved of his mother. A thought flashed in his mind, and he said, "Is Monsieur...uh...Henri the son of this Madame D'Artagnan?"

Bayard compressed his lips and nodded. "You wouldn't believe it, would you? But he is, and that much more worthy than her, that it almost makes up for the trouble she causes. Except bringing on my master's death of course."

"Of course," Athos said. He didn't think he'd get anything more out of the cantankerous old man—or at least nothing else with any value. At any rate, he had much to think about. He wondered if it was all venom, or if there was anything in the relationship between Madame D'Artagnan and the man who had killed her husband. "I suppose I should go within and ready for supper."

At the door to the stables, he thought of something else—something that had been nagging at the back of his mind. "Oh," he said. "I meant to ask. How did your master buy all these horses all of a sudden? Why not before Monsieur Henri left?"

The servant looked at him as if he had taken leave of his senses. "He didn't buy the horses, Monsieur. The Cardinal and the King sent them to him as a gift."

# The Lord of the Domain; Talking to Women; The Rules of Dueling

**IT** had taken D'Artagnan a good while to be able to pick up the note signed by the Cardinal. It seemed to him such a strange, incongruous thing to find in his father's papers that he half expected it to vanish like smoke before his eyes.

Perhaps he was still feverish. It was possible. Perhaps he hadn't realized it, but his wound had become infected again.

It was impossible that his father kept a safe-conduct from the Cardinal, and one worded in the exact same terms as the one that had been found in the pockets of the henchmen who'd attacked D'Artagnan.

Yet the note didn't vanish. It persisted in being impossibly solid and improbably signed by Richelieu. At long last, D'Artagnan folded it and put it within his sleeve. He stole a quick look at Mousqueton, who was, mercifully, looking out the window.

"Ah," D'Artagnan said, rising from his knees. "I see they are returning, and, indeed, supper will be soon enough. Perhaps I'll have the time for an interview with my mother before dinner. You see…accounts and…such."

Mousqueton nodded without asking anything—which in D'Artagnan's experience, he wouldn't anyway. The man had a way of guessing things and knowing them without ever asking as such. Not so very different, in fact, from his way of finding the chickens—and bottles of wine, and legs of lamb—that a carriage had just run over and which needed to be put out of their misery.

He followed D'Artagnan out of the room and, at D'Artagnan's instruction, locked the door with his improvised tools. He smiled then, and said, "I normally don't have to do this."

They climbed down the staircase to the floor below, where they parted ways, Mousqueton saying he needed to help his master dress for supper. For all D'Artagnan knew, it was true. Porthos had brought twice as much luggage as the rest of them and, knowing his habits of sartorial splendor, might very well require a servant to fit his clothes or outfit him with jewels or whatever he deemed necessary to present himself in proper style.

As for D'Artagnan, he walked slowly, pensively, to the door of his mother's bedroom, where he knocked.

"Come in," his mother said, and in he went.

His mother's room was the largest in the house—a vast expanse surrounded by whitewashed walls and taken up with a confusion of furniture. There was the large, curtained bed, some clothes trunks, a large wardrobe, a small, amusing set of shelves, several lavishly uphol-stered chairs and, finally, a dressing table with a vast mirror that his father had once told him came from Venice.

His mother sat in her dressing gown at her vanity, while Marguerite pinned her hair up in some complex style that appeared to be designed to look like she'd just carelessly pulled her hair up, allowing a curl or two to escape.

Something in D'Artagnan protested that she took too much care of her appearance for a woman so recently widowed, but another part—the saner part—told him it was all nonsense. His earliest mem-ories were of sitting on the floor in this room watching his beautiful mother prepare for supper in her own house and making herself beau-tiful as though she were appearing at court.

He remembered how proud his father had been of his mother's beau-ty and her youth, and he smiled at his mother as he sat down on the floor beside her dressing table.

She smiled at him, in turn, as though she knew the memories in his mind, then sobered, suddenly. "I am sorry, son, that you had to come all this way, and over such distressing news too. But I am sure once you have had time to look over your father's accounts, and once all the rights of inheritance are established, you can leave again."

D'Artagnan started. "Leave again? Leave my domains and my duty behind?"

She smiled at him, but the smile lingered a little too long, like some-one posing for a painting. "Of course. How big are your domains that they need you here the whole time? Son, I believe I know how to oversee the harvest and how to receive the rents from your tenants. This is not a duchy that you need to be here at all times, ready to defend it or take your people to war."

D'Artagnan frowned, "But in your letter, you said..."

She shrugged. "In my letter I said a lot of nonsense, I am sure," she said. "I was in shock you see." For a moment, for just a moment, her face mirrored that shock, in suddenly raised eyebrows and an aston-ished expression. D'Artagnan could not doubt he was seeing her as she'd looked when she'd got the news of her husband's death. "I didn't expect it. It was the most extraordinary thing. He never told me he'd challenged anyone for a duel, and Monsieur de Bilh, yet. I mean, you remember how they were, always joking about their boundary dispute in the south vineyard, and drinking unending bottles of wine together on the strength of it."

D'Artagnan frowned. His memories of Monsieur de Bilh, who was his father's contemporary and friend, were slightly different. Oh, he did drop by the house and spend long afternoons drinking with Monsieur D'Artagnan père. But he and D'Artagnan's father also carried on long, incomprehensible feuds over a few feet on that south vineyard.

The only thing that could be said about the two men was that they were either the best of friends or the bitterest of enemies. No one else seemed to be able to predict who would be what, or in what way or when. Sometimes D'Artagnan thought even the two of them weren't always sure if they were on good terms with each other or not.

He inclined his head. "It was a sudden duel then? Without provocation?"

His mother shrugged. "I don't know. I know he didn't tell me any of it. But he was getting very strange, Henri. He was spending most of his days up in that tower of his. He said he was doing paperwork, but what paperwork could he have to do all of a sudden? So he might have decided to duel de Bilh and not to tell me. Besides..." She shrugged and blushed a little. "He knew that I would tell him he was an old fool and that there was no reason at all to duel the poor man who'd never done anything to him."

D'Artagnan frowned. He'd often heard his mother chastise his father in just exactly those terms. What he'd never seen was his father making any effort to avoid being chastised. He'd kept on dueling and drinking. But then again, it had been a long time since he'd been home. And he knew, from observing other people—Bayard and Marguerite among them—that sometimes people changed when their children left the parental abode. Perhaps that had happened with his parents.

"Or perhaps my father just seemed strange because of his dealings with Richelieu?"

His mother jumped a little. He would swear to it. Just the slightest jerk of the body, and the curl of her blond hair escaped between Marguerite's fingers, and fell, causing the servant to exclaim.

But it was all in a moment, and when D'Artagnan looked again his mother was composed and showing only surprise. "Richelieu?" she said, in some alarm. "The Cardinal? Why do you think your father was working for the Cardinal?"

"*Maman.* You know you told me in your note that he was working for the Cardinal."

She dismissed her note with a wave of her hand. "I told you before," she said, her voice sounding distressed. "I don't know what I wrote in that note. I was so shocked and confused, and scared, you know, of...everything. Did I truly tell you he was working for the Cardinal?"

D'Artagnan nodded.

"Oh, what a very silly thing to do," she said. And managed a very creditable peal of musical laughter. "Why would your father be working for the Cardinal? What would his eminence want from the depths of Gascony? What interest could he have here?"

"I don't know," D'Artagnan said, while he tried to think over the situation. His mother was not only lying to him, she was giving the most creditable theatrical performance he'd seen from anyone in a long time, cunning Aramis included. In fact, the only reason he suspected her was that slight jerk of the body that he might or might not have seen. That and the note rustling inside his sleeve every time he moved his arm. "Perhaps being so near to Spain he thought my father could get him information on Spanish noblemen. How am I to know? In Paris they say even the owls and the rats spy for the Cardinal. So why not here?"

His mother frowned. "Well, I assure you...that is...I don't know of any work your father was doing for the Cardinal, nor of any reason for him to be doing so."

D'Artagnan realized she had worded her answer carefully enough so as not to lie openly to him. He didn't know whether to laugh or cry.

If he'd not spent six months in Paris and there been exposed to the guile of the masters in perfidy—Richelieu included—would he even have suspected his mother's careful prevarication?

"So, I assume you wouldn't know what this is about," he said, and, reaching into his sleeve, pinched the small piece of paper in between his fingers, and showed it to his mother at a distance.

She squinted at it. "No," she said. "I can't read it from this far, but I've never seen it." She blushed faintly and, D'Artagnan realized, was probably lying. Why else had she kept her husband's study locked and not given the key to D'Artagnan as soon as he arrived? "What does it say?"

"It says," D'Artagnan said. "'It was by my order and for the good of the state that the bearer of this note did what he had to do.'"

His mother looked in the mirror at D'Artagnan's reflection a long time, then she turned to her maid. "That's well enough, Marguerite, you may go. I'll dress myself."

Marguerite bowed and retreated, and D'Artagnan wondered if his mother was about to be frank.

But instead, his mother turned around in her chair, to face him. She waited till she heard the door to her room close, then turned to D'Artagnan. "What was it that someone did, Henri? What does all that 'for the good of the state' mean?"

"*Maman,*" he said. "You're not a fool. Don't pretend to be one."

She raised her eyebrows at him. "I am not being a fool. I simply don't know of what you speak. Who has signed that letter, Henri?"

"The Cardinal."

"Are you sure? It looked like it was signed with a single R. How could you tell from a single R that it was the Cardinal?"

"I understand from my friends that this is how he often signs letters of this nature," D'Artagnan said, now curious about how much his mother knew, and how much she would let slip. "How could you read the R from that far?"

"Well, it was a single letter, and that was the only one it could be," his mother said. "But son, where did you find it? And what could it possibly mean?"

"I found it amid my father's effects," he said. "In his tower study."

His mother looked more agitated than ever. "In your father's effects. Are you sure?"

"*Maman.* How could I not be sure? I found it in that trunk on which he always rested his feet."

"But...how did you..."

"Get into his study?" D'Artagnan asked, and smiled slightly. "I have my ways." He got up and stepped closer to his mother. "*Maman,* you know I'd never believe you guilty of any crime, but you must understand you're not making it easy for me to believe in your innocence. You knew about this note, did you not? Did you always know about it, or did you find it after his death?"

"My innocence?" She looked at him, her eyes round and blank like the eyes of a statue. Put a mantel on her and she would pass for an image of a virgin saint. "What do you mean my innocence? What crime are you speaking of? Even if your father worked for the Cardinal, surely that would not be a crime. He is one of the most powerful men in France and he—"

D'Artagnan shook his head. "No, not working for the Cardinal, though you must know there are many French noblemen and people close to the corridors of power who would consider it a crime. But we're not about to argue that. No. It's just that...what you say about my father's duel makes me wonder..."

His mother looked at him, agitated, a small pulse working at her white throat. "Makes you wonder if I walked up to him and ran him through the throat with a dueling sword?"

D'Artagnan shook his head again, as much to free it of the image his mother had evoked as to deny her accusation. "No. But I wonder if it was quite above board, or if my father might have been murdered. If he was working for the Cardinal, he was enmeshed into politics where—trust me, mother—men often die."

His mother shrugged. "The worst that could be said about your father's death was that it might not have been a fair duel. And that only because the two witnesses were both talking to Monsieur de Bilh moments before."

"Both seconds were for the other man?" D'Artagnan asked, shocked. This was a complete violation of the laws of duels. He was about to say that was enough to make it murder, when he remembered his very first duel in Paris, the one that had turned into a fight between musketeers and guards of the Cardinal.

For that duel, he had challenged Athos, Porthos and Aramis, who were all seconds for each other, and he had brought no second of his own. He hadn't known anyone in Paris. And though his father had known enough people in Gascony, if he had suddenly turned on Monsieur de Bilh for no reason any of his neighbors could understand, it was possible he couldn't find a second, either.

His mother shrugged. "They weren't seconds. I don't think it was planned, or else, if it was, Monsieur de Bilh had forgotten all about it. Which would explain why your father was so furious."

"My father was furious?"

"Indeed. Or at least that's what your cousin Edmond said."

"My cousin?" D'Artagnan asked in shock. "What had my cousin to do with it all?"

"Well, he was one of the witnesses. The other one was our priest. Both of them said that your father appeared suddenly and that he was obviously drunk."

"How did they know he was drunk?" D'Artagnan asked, frowning. The idea of his father drunk was as unlikely as the idea of his father losing a duel. Oh, the older man drank. Everyone in this region drank, and when it was your own wine and your own brandy, made from your own grapes, it was very hard not to drink, at least to sample it. But his father could drink most men under the table, and D'Artagnan, in his seventeen years under his parents' roof, had never seen his father lose control of his mouth or his movement.

His mother only nodded. "They all three say he was very drunk. He came stumbling over the wall of the threshing floor, and he walked right up to where de Bilh was standing, and he drew his sword and called de Bilh a damnable coward and proceeded to attack him."

"My father? He attacked de Bilh like that?" Even in the men's worst breaks of friendship, they'd never gone beyond exchanging curt words. "Why?"

His mother shook her head and shrugged. "Who knows? None of us does. De Bilh didn't even seem to know. And, oh, Henri, he was so sorry about your father's death. I understand it happened in the rush of combat, but he was as shocked as I was, if not more. The poor man looked one step from the tomb, himself. 'He wouldn't stop attacking me, Marie,' he said. 'He kept attacking me, and I was only trying to parry, but instead, I struck him. I never meant it.'"

"He called you Marie?" D'Artagnan asked, shocked. While de Bilh had been in and out of the house ever since D'Artagnan remembered, it was not done for men to call women to whom they were neither related nor married by their baptismal name.

His mother colored, then shrugged. "No, I don't think he did. I misspoke." She got up. "I'm sorry, son. I'm still confused and shocked, and

I should never have made you come back and get involved in this. You see, I'm just a foolish woman."

Looking him in the eyes, steadily unblinking, she said, "I need to dress, if I don't want to be late for supper with your friends. I will speak to you later and answer any questions you might have. But now you must leave and let me dress."

D'Artagnan left the room, his mind whirling. He very much doubted that his mother could or would answer any questions he might have.

His entire life, he'd seen his mother as a sweet innocent, relying on his father to keep her safe and steady. Had he been wrong all along?

# Porthos's Mind; Blood in the Fields; The End of the Trail

**SOMETIMES** Porthos despised his own mind. It wasn't just that it would not work like the minds of his friends and those men who were generally accounted very smart at court. That was it too, of course. He could understand neither Latin nor Greek, and some of the conversations between Athos and Aramis made his head hurt.

But it was not his mind's insufficiency of words that galled him. No. The worst of how his mind worked was the things it got hold of and wouldn't let go.

All through that dismal dinner, with all of them very quiet—and D'Artagnan looking at his mother now and then, as though she had personally betrayed him—Porthos had thought of the blood drops.

He didn't know what D'Artagnan's shock and indignation was all about. If he had to hazard a guess, he would suspect it was because his mother had dressed well and arranged her hair for supper with three nearly strange men so shortly after her husband had died.

Why this should upset D'Artagnan, Porthos could not imagine. After all, it was an honor his mother did them in dressing up for them as though they were important guests, above her in social station. And besides, however grieved she must be, D'Artagnan couldn't possibly imagine that a woman like her, as beautiful as she was, would spend the rest of her life in mourning her husband without finding another.

He couldn't understand it, and so he'd isolated himself from all the conversation around him and instead concentrated only on those drops of blood. It could be as Aramis had said. In fact, Aramis was a wise man and far more intelligent than Porthos, so it probably was as Aramis said. It could be that those small drops of blood had been shed by Monsieur D'Artagnan's opponent as he returned home.

But it seemed to Porthos that until they knew if the man had even been wounded in the fight, or whether he lived in the direction those drops had gone, he couldn't be sure. And then...and then there was something else, something about the path of those drops that bothered him.

If he was remembering correctly—and he thought he was, because his memory rarely played him tricks—then those drops didn't mill around on the threshing ground, and finally head that way. No. They were straight that way and to the place where D'Artagnan's father had been run through.

Surely if his opponent had run him through and immediately taken off running in the other direction, this would be known and would have been talked about?

Even in Paris, where the edicts against dueling were enforced—as Porthos knew they weren't in the provinces, or not yet—one did not kill an opponent in a duel and then run immediately away, without so much as checking to make sure the other man was dead. At the very least, Porthos would expect the drops to loop from the duel area to the place where D'Artagnan's father had fallen, and then go the other way and over the wall.

But instead there was nothing—nothing but that straight retreat or advance the other way.

It didn't seem right. And because it didn't seem right, Porthos's mind wouldn't let it be. He could tell himself it didn't matter. He could tell himself he was a fool for thinking on it nonstop. And yet, his foolish mind would not let go of it, and it would keep on worrying at it like a starving dog at a juicy bone.

In bed, he woke up in the night, again and again, thinking he'd seen the logical explanation of those blood drops in a dream, but just could not remember it. He stared at his ceiling and tried to understand it, and he could not.

At last, as dawn tinged the horizon a light pink, he'd got up, put on his clothes, and left the house as silently as he could and got his horse from the stable, to retrace his way to the threshing floor.

The bastide was very quiet early dawn, but by the time he'd left it behind and found himself amid the fields, the sun was up in the cloudless sky and the day was a warm one for November. Birds sang hesitantly in the nearby trees.

The pale, unblinking light illuminated the threshing floor unforgivingly. The blood stains were more visible than ever. There was the pool of blood that had doubtless come from the duelist's thrust into D'Artagnan's father's throat, and from his withdrawing his sword.

The still-pumping heart of Monsieur D'Artagnan père would have propelled blood out, along with the sword's withdrawal. And it would have jetted out like so, making exactly the pattern of blood on the smooth stones that Porthos saw just there.

And then he would stagger back, once, twice, his own feet leaving bloodstained footmarks on the stones. Back, and back, as his heart struggled to keep pumping, despite the severing of one of the body's arteries. Back and back, till his heart lost its battle—or at least his consciousness did—and he collapsed on the floor, there, where the rest of his blood had drained away until he was dead.

That explained the bigger stain there, indicative of a bigger puddle accumulated over a longer time.

There was no other blood, no indication of his adversary having received a wound—except the trail of very small drops going the other way along the threshing floor to the edge of the wall.

Again Porthos retraced his steps to that wall, saw the blood that crossed it and, leaning over the wall, saw the same blood drops in the hard packed dirt and stunted shrubs around the threshing floor.

Aramis said it was the adversary retreating, but when had the adversary gotten wounded, then?

If Monsieur D'Artagnan had wounded the other man in the fight, it had to have been before the man's final thrust, right? Or at least, it was most likely to be like that. However, it wouldn't be the first time that Porthos had seen a man come back at his slayer after being run through.

There was this duel he'd fought, back when he was young and foolish, where, after running the other man through, Porthos had assumed he had won the fray and turned his back on the enemy who was staggering and had, in fact, gone down on one knee.

Porthos had turned his back to ask the second if he would require satisfaction. If it hadn't been for the look of shock in the second's eye, as he looked over Porthos's shoulder, Porthos would never have turned. And he would never have jumped out of the way of the sword his mortally wounded adversary had lifted and was bringing down to cleave Porthos's head.

So, he wasn't such a fool as to assume it was impossible for a mortally wounded man to inflict injury. No. But the thing was, there was the puddle of the wounding, and there, clearly marked by back-stepping footprints of the dying man in his own blood, ten steps away, the puddle of the dying. Nowhere was there the faltering step forward, the attempt at attack.

So it was more than sure—almost absolutely sure—that Monsieur D'Artagnan had not rallied from his fatal injury for long enough to wound his foe. It being so, that meant that any injury from which the other man could have bled must, perforce, have been inflicted before Monsieur D'Artagnan had been run through.

But, in that case, there would be more drops of blood, as the adversary jumped around and parried and thrust—all activities likely to cause the blood to loosen from a recent wound. There would be increasing blood, as the fighting made the man bleed more.

None of this was there.

And in the unlikely event the man had been wounded, say, by Monsieur D'Artagnan's sword as he collapsed...or that the man had nicked himself on his own sword in retrieving it, surely there would be drops of blood as he approached the falling man to determine if he was alive or dead.

Regardless of the reason for the duel, even in case of mortal offense, the winner of a contest would verify that his adversary had died—or else if he was alive and needed assistance.

A gentleman, and Porthos had heard no rumblings that the slayer of Monsieur D'Artagnan was not one, would never abandon a wounded opponent without seeking help for him. If the hatred between them were such that it demanded more satisfaction, then the man would arrange for them to meet again and to settle anything that hadn't, so far, been settled between them. He would not, however, leave an enemy to bleed to death alone and without even the benefit of the sacraments.

That was done in war but not in a duel.

For a moment he wondered if that was what Aramis was pursuing as well; whether that was why he was so obsessed about the religion of the combatants. But Porthos had heard enough to surmise that Protestants too sought the blessing of the clergy before they died. And besides, chances were that Aramis was thinking of religion because he was Aramis. He was like that. He even read the lives of saints to likely females.

Dismissing Aramis with a shrug of his massive shoulders, Porthos frowned at the drops of blood. It made no sense at all, but the only way he could think of for the trail of drops to add up to something was if Monsieur D'Artagnan had been wounded before and had arrived, bleeding, from that direction where the drops started on the wall. He'd jumped down from the wall—and there was a spatter of drops there, as though the movement had increased the bleeding—and challenged and attacked his adversary, suddenly.

There were drops leading to the smaller puddle of blood. If the duel had been brief and intense, with Monsieur D'Artagnan attacking and the other man defending and neither of them moving much, any spatters of blood from Monsieur D'Artagnan would be lost in that bigger spurt when the sword that had sliced into his throat was pulled out.

And then there was the pouring of blood at his dying.

It wasn't perfect, as far as explanations went. Though Porthos couldn't find any facts that didn't fit in it, it didn't satisfy him completely. He didn't like to come up with explanations like that, one on the other and not know for sure.

However, the only way to know for sure was to interview the witnesses of the duel. He would do that too, later. At least if his friends didn't. He had no idea what Athos and D'Artagnan might be doing. He'd been so absorbed in thinking about the bloodstains that he didn't even remember if they'd discussed it at dinner.

But until he could interview those who'd been there, Porthos would assume that Monsieur D'Artagnan had arrived wounded and that events had taken place as he thought now.

Which meant, of course, that Monsieur D'Artagnan had been wounded elsewhere.

Porthos bounded to the low wall, and, following the drops of blood, over the wall and down on the other side. There was a sort of path there. Not a real one and probably not an official path of any kind. Just the sort of path beaten by boys running between fields, or by women carrying water. It was not a straight path—they rarely were—but wound around taller scrub, and it turned aside from stones too big to jump onto or from heels too steep to climb.

But the drops of blood followed its meandering, clear and black against the yellowish beaten dirt.

Porthos followed it, like a hound on the scent of a hare. Leaving his horse behind, tied near the threshing floor, he followed the small footpath, this way and that, up and down small hillocks.

It ended in a field and there—Porthos stopped—at the edge of the field, the scrub brush had been trampled and stomped and the field—left bare by harvest, save for a stubble of grass that looked much like the stubble on the face of an unshaven man—had been stepped on and kicked.

It looked, Porthos thought, as though a great fight had taken place here. A fight too intense and strong for him to be able to tell whether there were two men or six, or ten.

That there had been a fight, Porthos would swear to. He'd seen plenty of fields after duels. And this was a field where a duel had happened.

He looked around himself and it was all fields and, in the distance, a straggle of protruding trees, like the tongue of the forest extending onto the fields. No houses. No place where some urchin might have lingered and seen something. Nothing.

There was nothing for it. No obvious witness.

But, on his way back to his horse, Porthos reasoned that just because there was no obvious witness it didn't mean there were no witnesses.

The place was wide open and not hidden. If he remembered rightly, the duel had taken place in the light of day, and there was no reason that someone might not have seen the fight that preceded it.

Porthos had grown up in a rural area much like this—fields and woods and the occasional peasant house. He knew well enough how hard it was to hide anything at all without someone, somewhere, seeing it, commenting on it, and—if one were unlucky enough—carrying news of it to one's father.

So he would simply have to look further and spend more time at it. He would have to talk to the peasants hereabouts, in and out of the bastide.

He remembered the sight of the area they'd had from the higher ground. He remembered that in addition to the bastide there was a straggle of peasant houses, here and there.

In those houses, somewhere, there might very well be someone who'd seen people fighting in this field. They'd be able to tell Porthos whether the wounded man was Monsieur D'Artagnan père, and whether he'd been wounded fairly or by stealth. Somewhere in those houses, there might very well be someone who knew who had sounded whom, and whether the men were the same who'd fought a duel later on, at the threshing floor.

Porthos would be able to find the reason for those blood drops. And then he could stop thinking about them.

# *A Musketeer's Piety; Witness to Death; Where Some Truths Are Harder Than Others*

**IT** was at the moment of the elevation of the Host that D'Artagnan noticed Aramis.

He should have seen him earlier. After all, early Mass in the small church near D'Artagnan's house was usually attended only by those retainers of the house—Bayard and Marguerite and one or two of the men and women who came for the day—who felt particularly religious that early in the morning.

Even Mass at the larger church, in the center of the town, was sparsely attended, early morning on a weekday. For one, this was Gascony, where enough people remained who weren't exactly good Catholics. And tired of the continuous fighting over the last century, their Catholic neighbors often pretended not to notice that they didn't attend church. As long as a man didn't cause trouble, his neighbors tried not to notice what faith he believed in.

So the churches were sparsely attended, and at that, attended mostly by local peasants: a short, stocky, dark-haired breed. All of which should have made the tall, slim, blond Aramis very visible.

But the church was dark in the early morning. A Roman church, with its small, arched windows far up enough on the walls to allow the church to be turned into a fortress, it was dark at the best of times. Early morning it was darker than that, the dim light scarcely enough to see the pews, and the vague shadows of the other people at Mass—and the figure of the priest at the altar.

And then, D'Artagnan had been preoccupied with what brought him here—not a startle of sudden piety, but the need to ask the priest how his father had died.

His mother's behavior was so odd that D'Artagnan had spent half the night running away in his own mind from unfilial thoughts that his mother had engineered the death of his father.

And now he was here, hoping to lay the matter to rest.

So, when the priest lifted the Host, and people knelt for the adoration, was the first time he caught sight of Aramis in the front pew. The light had glinted briefly on the musketeer's hair as he knelt.

What was Aramis doing here? Was he here on the same errand D'Artagnan was? And if so, why had he come? Had he—also—suspected D'Artagnan's mother? And if he did, why? Could his mother be truly culpable?

In a worry that mimicked the effects of fever to an amazing extent, D'Artagnan had gone through the movements of the rest of the Mass in a confusion of suspicion and fear—and guilt at suspecting his own mother.

And after the Mass, as he got up to follow the priest into the sacristy, he found himself a step behind Aramis. "Father, please," he said, just echoing Aramis.

The priest was old. He'd been old ever since D'Artagnan remembered. In fact, D'Artagnan couldn't approach him without feeling as though he were again a small boy coming to him for lessons on the first letters or for instruction in doctrine.

Small, bent over, the priest had skin the color of old clay—the sort of skin of someone who started out olive skinned and then spent most of his life outdoors, in all weather. He'd seen the priest, often enough, cross the fields in the full heat of day to take the last sacraments to some peasant that lie dying in some hovel far from the bastide.

The younger priest who ministered at the larger church was not so devoted. But this man was. His name was Father Ustou, and the peasants hereabouts whispered that he was a saint.

He now turned his heavily lined face to them, looking first at Aramis, and then at D'Artagnan, with small, dark eyes that shone from amid the wrinkles. "Ah, my sons," he said, clearly confused. "How may I help you?"

Aramis started to open his mouth, but then bowed slightly to D'Artagnan as if to indicate that the younger man had a greater right to ask questions.

D'Artagnan bowed in turn, to thank him for the courtesy, all the while wondering if Aramis suspected D'Artagnan's mother, and if so, why. Of course, Aramis knew a lot about women. He could read their minds and hearts like other men could read books.

"Father," D'Artagnan said, rushing, afraid of losing his courage if he waited. "My mother says you were one of the witnesses at my father's duel, and I wanted to know...I wanted to know what you remembered."

The priest squinted, "Henri? Is that you? I didn't recognize you in those clothes." He smiled a little, vaguely. "So sad that you had to come back for such a reason." He sighed. "Yes, yes, your father...I was there, when your father died." Another sigh. "Such a strong man, you know, and in general a very good man. So sad for him to die like that, over such a foolish thing."

"What foolish thing?" D'Artagnan asked. "Why did they fight?"

The priest made his way fully into the sacristy and put away the vessels of the Mass in a cabinet, which he locked. "No one knows that, my son. Not even Monsieur de Bilh, who I think would give something to know it."

"How is it possible then," D'Artagnan asked, "for two men to fight to the death without any idea of the reason for fighting?"

The priest shook his head. "It wasn't a fight to the death. Not from where I was standing. It was more...well...Monsieur de Bilh was defending himself from your father's mad attack. The poor man laments every day that an unlucky thrust killed his friend."

"But—Why was my father attacking him?"

"We don't know. This is what happened." The priest, his cleanup after Mass done, turned around to face them. "I was talking with Monsieur de Bilh and your cousin, Edmond de Bigorre. Edmond was telling me the story of a saint, that he heard from his fiancée, and asking if I'd ever heard the like, and Monsieur de Bilh was waiting nearby. He wanted to speak to me of some of the poor I've been helping. He proposed to give employment to the man, if your father would consent to let him take it outside his lands. And as this was going on, I heard your father roar.

"We all turned to see him running through the fields towards the threshing floor where we were..." The priest frowned. "He ran...erratically. As if he'd had too much to drink. Not straight, you know, but stumbling a little and veering now this way and now that way. I remember thinking it very odd, because here we were, and not noon yet, and I'd never seen your father drunk, you know."

"No," D'Artagnan said, and his voice echoed hollow in his own ears. "Nor have I."

The priest nodded and his bald head shone like cured leather under the light from the sad single candle in front of the sacrarium. "But he was drunk, Henri. Drunk or..." The priest crossed himself hastily. "In the grip of an unholy spirit." He looked up at D'Artagnan as though afraid of the response. When that didn't come he continued. "He didn't seem to recognize any of us who were before him—not one of us—and he came charging at Monsieur de Bilh, sword in hand, and called him a villain." From the depths of his sleeve, the priest extracted a handkerchief, with which he mopped his glistening forehead. "It was a close-in fight, Monsieur Henri. Close fought. And then, while de Bilh tried to fend him off, your father charged blindly. He impaled himself on that sword, Monsieur Henri, and that's the truth. So much so that I was not sure I was within the rights of the church to give him a Christian burial."

"You mean..." D'Artagnan said, his legs going weak, his knees losing their steadiness. "That my father committed suicide? That he killed himself?"

The priest sighed. Again the hand with the kerchief mopped at his brow. "I don't know. I don't think so—or not on purpose. Had I thought so, I'd never have given him Christian burial on consecrated land. I do not mock the rules of the holy church."

"No," D'Artagnan said, but in his mind he could see it all too well—the bright sunlight on the threshing floor, and his father running into a sword. He thought of that dress and the uniform under the table, on the chest his father used to rest his feet upon. If a man had left behind everything he prized, and love besides...

Perhaps his father had held onto life and forged on so long as he had to bring up an heir to the name. But now D'Artagnan was grown, and had gone to Paris to seek his fortune. Perhaps his father thought himself exonerated of the duty to keep going now.

But no. D'Artagnan thought of his father as he'd last seen him. He thought of his father having a mock duel with him in the broad yard of their house, just the day before D'Artagnan had left for Paris.

His father had danced and jumped, and laughed with delight both at outwitting D'Artagnan and when D'Artagnan outwitted him. He'd been happy. Very happy. And it was hard to think of it as the happiness of a man who had finally discharged his duty and who could now put a period to his life.

Besides, his father had been ever mindful of how what he did affected others. He'd been the most attentive of fathers, the most considerate of husbands. Had he indeed been so pained at having to leave his Parisian life and perhaps his Parisian love behind, he wouldn't have forced his son to do the same.

And he would never use Monsieur de Bilh to put an end to himself. The two of them were friends when they weren't raging enemies, but on the whole the friends had lasted longer than the enemies. And besides...And besides even had Monsieur de Bilh been his father's heart-felt foe, it would be an injustice to implicate him in a death he hadn't intended. And D'Artagnan's father wasn't an unjust man.

"I think he was drunk, Monsieur Henri," the priest said, as though reading D'Artagnan's mind. "Or...not himself."

"There is an illness..." Aramis said. "That sometimes comes on men, particularly older men. Something happens in the brain. One of my teachers, who was learned in such things said that something burst in their brain. It made them...strange. Like a man who's been hit a blow to the head."

"Of course that might be it too," the priest said. "Perhaps his horse tossed him. They found his horse, you know, much later. It had run free. He didn't look..." He looked at D'Artagnan. "Your father didn't look as though he had fallen from the horse, but you never know. Perhaps he had. That would explain his behavior.

"But you need not be afraid he died a suicide. I'm sure in his heart of hearts your father could never have meant such a thing; could never have done it. I'm sure of it, Monsieur Henri. So sure that I have said all the Masses I can for his soul. And he was a good man, you know?" The priest's old, shriveled hand rested on D'Artagnan's arm, like a claw, but a benevolent claw. "He had his foibles, as who doesn't, all of us being fallen men. But in all that, and for all that, he was a good man and I'm sure when you and I, at last, come to the heavenly mansion, we'll find him there waiting for us."

D'Artagnan nodded, but his heart felt tight, tight, as though deep inside a hand were squeezing it. Yes, yes, he'd suspected something wrong with his father's death since he'd first heard of it. But now he could not doubt that something untoward and underhanded had happened. He could not doubt his father had met with foul play of some sort.

Either that…Either that or he'd gone mad.

And it fell to his son—his only son—and heir to find out exactly what that untoward something might be. It fell to his son, his only heir, to find out the reasons for his death, and who might have caused it.

"I'm sorry to pain you with the description of what happened, my son," the priest said in an almost whisper. "But I thought it best if you knew the truth."

"It is," D'Artagnan said. "And I thank you, Father." He bent to kiss the man's ring, then walked out into the sunlight.

He'd been so absorbed in his own misery he didn't realize Aramis had walked out with him till he heard the musketeer say, "I'm sure it wasn't a suicide, D'Artagnan. I wouldn't worry on it. Pere Ustou impressed me as a most careful man, and if there had been the slightest chance—"

D'Artagnan shook his head. "I never thought there was. Not of suicide," he said. He sighed deeply. "If it were…while I would worry about his eternal fate, I would no longer need to worry about how he died. No, Aramis. What I'm worried about is that I'm sure—almost absolutely sure—someone murdered him."

Aramis seemed taken aback. He leaned backwards a little, managing somehow to make himself appear more detached and superior. "What mean you? How can you be sure of such a thing, when Father Ustou just told us—"

"That my father acted drunk—which I know he could not be. Or in the grip of demons—which you know few of us are bad enough to warrant. Or had gone mad. You say it is possible to go mad from a blow to the head. And there's poison, you know." He shook his head. "I'm not doubting that my father attacked Monsieur de Bilh or instigated the duel. I'm not even doubting that he ran himself into a sword. But what I'm wondering is what happened before to cause him to act that way. And who brought it about."

Aramis frowned at him. Not with displeasure, but more as though D'Artagnan were the obscure text of a forgotten book, which Aramis was having trouble reading. "Perhaps," he said at very long last. "And if that's the case, who can it be? What enemies did your father have?"

"True enemies?" D'Artagnan asked. "Very few. Those he fought with, and made up with to fight with again? Almost everyone in the neighborhood. But he was not less than friendly with anyone, most of the time. The only family in the region with whom we did not speak was de Comminges, and, frankly, they are so far above us that..." He shrugged and permitted himself a small smile. "Not all high noblemen are like you and Athos, who will speak even to plebeians and associate with people like me, only one step above commoners."

Aramis smiled a little, in turn, a wan smile, embarrassed and indulgent in one. "Athos perhaps," he said. "Myself, I'm not that far above anyone. But I know what you mean. There are those who are...more blood proud."

"Yes."

Silence fell for a little while. D'Artagnan tried to order in his mind what he must do next. He did not doubt Father Urtou. In fact, he could not. The old man who'd taught him his first letters and his religion might have some price—some way by which someone could buy his testimony and with it his soul. But if so, D'Artagnan could not imagine it, much less name it.

But a man was just a man and, as Aramis and Pere Urtou would say, a fallen creature. Many was the time, in Paris and here, even, when D'Artagnan had heard someone give witness to an event which he had also seen. The differences in accounts were often so marked—even from honest people and where nothing could be gained by lying—that it seemed to have taken place in a different world altogether.

So, first, D'Artagnan would go see his cousin, Edmond de Bigorre, and Monsieur de Bilh. From them he would collect accounts to corroborate—or not—Father Urtou's.

And then...And then he would try to find out what had happened before the duel. And what enemies his father might had.

"Are the de Comminges very religious?" Aramis asked.

"I beg your pardon?" D'Artagnan said, confused. Aramis's voice seemed to come from somewhere else altogether and his words were at best incongruous.

"The de Comminges. This wealthy and noble family you spoke of. Are they very religious? And if so, what religion?"

D'Artagnan shrugged. "You know, I have no idea. I'm sure they're very religious, one way or another." He looked around at his native land, feeling for the first time out of place here, and yet loving it as never before. "In these forsaken mountains, to grow anything but rocks you need a miracle. We're all religious. But whether they're Catholic or not..." He shrugged. He tried to think, but of course the two families wouldn't attend the same church or frequent the same places. He shook his head. "I couldn't tell you. Why should it matter?"

"I simply wondered," Aramis said, and smiled one of his innocent smiles, that could be truly innocent or else the very center of guile. "I simply wondered if perhaps Athos and I owe them a visit."

This made sense, as much as anything else. At least Athos, the scion of one of the oldest and noblest families in the kingdom, probably should visit the greatest house in the region. At least if not divided by issues of religion.

D'Artagnan sighed. "Probably." Then shook his head. "I'm going to see my cousin, de Bigorre, to...to find out if he knows where my father had been before the duel." He knew better than to even hint to Aramis that he needed to corroborate the priest's testimony. Doubtless the blond musketeer would take it as an insult on the church, if not an insult on all of Christendom. "If you wish to come with me..."

Aramis hesitated. Then he shook his head. "No. When I think about it, Father Urtou probably would know if they're Catholic. I'll go within and ask him."

## Another Way Not to Wake a Musketeer; A Woman's Singular Lack of Intuition; The Perversity of a Man's Heart

**ATHOS** woke up with someone in his room. Without moving, he opened his eyes just enough to look between his eyelashes. He knew that it was not Grimaud. The rhythms of this breath were lighter and faster than Grimaud's ever were.

He didn't know whether it might be Planchet. The boy had broken into Athos's room once and, having broken into Athos's room and lived, who knows what crazy bravery he might be tempted to? But then, Athos had not locked his door, and he was in a strange house. It might very well be the pot boy, or an overzealous house maid. Who knew?

It was probably an innocent intruder, but then there had been at least one person killed in mysterious circumstances, and there were the attacks on D'Artagnan to consider. Athos would hold himself back, but he wouldn't be so foolhardy as to assume he was in no danger at all.

He reached under his pillow for the dagger he kept there, and half opened his eyes—enough that it wouldn't show beneath his long, black lashes. Through this opening, he looked around—seemingly tossing his head aimlessly—at a darkened room.

The only light came around his shuttered window, and it was enough to show him that the room was untouched—the clothing trunk remained where it was, with the clothes he'd tossed on it the night before. And there was no one immediately near his bed, so it was unlikely someone was about to attack him.

His nose picked up a delicate fragrance of roses, intruding on the stale air of the room, just before he caught sight of a billowing, black gown, the flash of long blond hair by the door.

A woman.

"*Sangre Dieu,*" he said, sitting up, his hand still on his dagger.

The woman by the door jumped and covered her mouth. "Oh, no, monsieur. Oh, no. I don't mean...Oh, monsieur."

He recognized Madame D'Artagnan, properly attired for the day.

It was, perhaps, not unusual, perhaps not even strange that a hostess should come into a guest's room. Perhaps she wanted to verify that all was as it might be. But when the guest was a man, the hostess a recent widow and when, besides, the guest had reason to suspect the widow of, at very least, immoral behavior...

Athos held the dagger, visible, on his lap. "Madame D'Artagnan," he said. "To what do I owe the honor of your visit?"

She shook, as though he had threatened her. She was holding, he noticed, a handkerchief between her hands, and this handkerchief she wrung, like a laundress removing excess water from clothing. Even in the shuttered twilight of the room, it was clear she had been crying—her very white skin marred by the tracks of tears and by red puffiness around her eyes.

Athos wished very much that he was still the sort of man whom this display would move; the sort of man who would assume a woman was innocent because she was beautiful and in distress; the sort of man he'd once been.

Out of this wish, though he could no longer be that man, he bowed his head and spoke with gruff almost kindness, "Madam," he said. "What do you wish?"

She walked in the room. One step, two, her skirts rustling, the scent of roses heavier in the stale air. Then she stopped. Whether from natural shyness or from having seen his dagger, he could not hazard.

"Monsieur...Monsieur...Athos? How odd that name? Isn't that a mountain in Greece?"

"Armenia," Athos said. And nothing more, since he didn't view it as his duty to educate her on geography. He viewed it even less as his duty to educate her on the subterfuges of men who, having left heart and honor behind, changed their honored name to another one, to keep that name safe, like a false sleeve will keep the expensive fabric beneath free of dirt.

She looked up, her blue eyes wide and full of incomprehension. Her gaze looked a little wounded, perhaps, as though she thought he was mocking her with his laconic answer. "Monsieur Athos," she said, and swallowed. "I come...I come as a mother in distress, to beg you...enfin, to beg you to take my son away as fast as it may be. Take him back to Paris and to his haunts there. Take him, as soon as you may. He is not safe here."

Athos looked at her consideringly, frowning a little. "Not safe? Why do you say that?"

She shook her head. "To tell you would only increase his danger and...and yours. And it would...it would injure Henri, should he find out. Oh, monsieur, please, take him back to Paris that he may be safe."

Athos heard himself laugh. He couldn't help it. "Madam, do you know how very few people—indeed, how no one else—would advise the taking of their offspring to Paris and the company of musketeers in order to keep him *safe*?"

She tossed her head, an impatient gesture so reminiscent of D'Artagnan when he thought he was being put on that it made Athos startle.

"I don't care," she said. "I don't care what other people will do or not. I just know my only son is in danger—real danger, monsieur."

"What type of danger?" Athos asked.

She walked over to the shuttered window and pulled the shutter wide, staying back just enough that no one would see her at the window of his room. It was, he thought, as though she'd practiced this art in the past, of opening a window without showing herself.

This was the old part of the house, and the window wasn't glazed. When the shutter opened wide, sunlight and the thin, brisk air of winter poured into the room together.

The light revealed Madame D'Artagnan as paler than Athos had seen her last, her eyes redder. She looked not only like she'd spent the entire night crying, but as though she'd managed to be tormented by horrible dreams the while.

"All danger. All of it attends him here. If he remains, I'm sure he'll lose his honor, his heart and perhaps his life."

Athos shook his head. "Why did you call him back, then, if you knew he would be in danger?"

She shook her head. "I was foolish. I am, monsieur, but a woman."

He laughed again, despite himself, the sound of it an almost hollow cackle in the air. "Ah, madam. I am old enough to know that when a woman professes to be weak she is, in fact, exercising her greatest strength, which is that of having men think her weak and mild and powerless."

"But I am weak and mild and powerless," she said, with real feeling.

He refrained from laughing again. "Madam. I know your son."

"My son...ah, my son is all his father. It has very little to do with me, at all. Or perhaps...not exactly like his father. Henri has a kind heart."

"Are you telling me Monsieur D'Artagnan lacked a kind heart?" Athos said.

She started. "Oh, no. Oh, no. My husband...my husband was the kindest man I ever met. Never would a stray come to the door that he didn't find it a place, feed it, care for it. It didn't matter if it was man or beast, my husband was ever ready to help all. Oh, he blustered and yelled, and could be quite terrifying in a temper." She shrugged. "Gasconades. All the men here—or at least the good ones—are like that. It means nothing."

"But—" Athos frowned. He didn't attempt to point out her contradiction to her. Doubtless, if he tried, she would tell him she was nothing but a poor woman, once more. It didn't make any difference, and it certainly didn't change anything, and he didn't care to cross the rapier of wit with this woman that was less open about her motives and thoughts than Aramis. "Enfin, Madame D'Artagnan, I must tell you that your son has a mind of his own. Having written to him—I don't know nor do I care from what motives—and told him that you needed his presence, you cannot now dismiss him. I cannot now convince him to leave."

"But he must," she said. It was almost a wail. "He must go back to Paris."

He permitted himself to raise a skeptical eyebrow. "Madam. I don't think you could make D'Artagnan leave from the moment he found out his father had died. Why, even our coming with him was an imposition. He wanted to travel alone. He was sure—and probably still is—that it is his bound duty to remain in Gascony and to take over his father's duties here at the estate."

"Oh, but he doesn't need to," she said. "I can do it. I am here."

"Alas," he said, bobbing a little bow from his sitting position. "Your son believes it is his duty, and his right, to look after you and protect you."

The handkerchief was out in her hands again—a thin little scrap of linen bordered in lace. "Oh, but he must not. I'm in no danger, so long as he's not here. With him here, we're both of us in danger. In fact, if you hadn't traveled with him..." She stopped, shook her head.

"He would never have arrived," Athos said, completing the sentence that she had started. "How do you know that, madam?" He tightened his grip on the dagger. "I'd dearly like to know."

She startled, and her eyes opened yet wider, showing more guileless innocence than ever. He would not believe it.

"Oh, but I don't know it," she said. "I don't know it at all. But...but it would make sense. I knew he'd be in danger as soon as he started towards Gascony. Or at least...I had good reason to suspect as much, since shortly after I sent that letter, and, monsieur, I was in fear till he arrived. I spent the days in my praying room, crying and begging God for the life of my only son. As you see, he heard me. And now you must hear me as well. You must take him out of here, that he may continue to be safe. And that I too can rest."

Athos looked at her. Everything she said was either a clear and a blatant lie or a twisted mass of contradictions. And yet...

And yet, his perverse heart insisted in believing she was truthful about some of the things she said—that she hadn't known upon writing the letter that it would be dangerous for D'Artagnan to come to Gascony; that she'd realized it shortly after; and that she was sincere in her wish to get him out of here—that she believed this was the only way to keep him safe.

Tangled with it, and even more confusing, was the tone of voice in which she'd spoken of her deceased husband. After witnessing the almost cold way in which she referred to him in public, Athos couldn't help but feel startled at the tenderness in her voice when she spoke of his kindness to what she termed strays coming to the door unannounced.

Athos wondered if the coldness she'd shown in public was her attempt to get her son to leave, and to leave quickly.

And yet, even realizing how sincere she was, and that she was well-intentioned towards his friend—that she was, in fact, a natural mother seeking to protect her offspring—Athos couldn't help but mistrust her.

Part of this was that he mistrusted all of womankind. Once having been betrayed by the most innocent seeming and purest looking of them all, he could not bring himself to trust any other. Purity and seeming innocence only made them more unreliable. It had been his experience that those who looked more like innocent flowers were the most likely to harbor venom in their hearts.

But beyond that...Beyond that, he didn't trust Madame D'Artagnan's reasoning. She might be D'Artagnan's mother, and he the most cunning of all Gascons who'd ever come to Paris in search of his fortune, but the pale blue eyes held none of the quick intelligence of D'Artagnan's dark ones.

He sighed and shook his head at her. "Madam, when you tell me to take your son to Paris, you overestimate my influence—indeed, anyone's influence—over him. Your son, madam, is the most stubborn man who ever wore a uniform. If you think I can tell him to go to Paris and that he will meekly go..."

She smiled a little, even as tears started in her eyes and her voice, curiously, mingled despair and pride as she said, "Oh, he was always like that. Always from a babe. It was never, 'Henri, do this' and he would do it. Oh, no. He needed to be tricked, cajoled and pushed into doing what he must do. Not that he was..." Her lips trembled. "You must understand, monsieur. He was neither ill-intentioned nor malicious. You must not think that. And he was not disobedient as such. Rather he had a way of finding out how to seem to obey your order exactly while doing exactly the opposite of what you wished." Now the tears poured down her cheeks, even as her smile enlarged. "My husband, Charles, he often said that the boy was just like him, though I don't know...He said that Henri was the son of his heart and his soul, and he delighted in his spirit, and his little rebellions."

"Unfortunately, madam, that same spirit means my ability to turn him away from what he views as his duty is very small indeed. He wishes to stay here and look after you and his domains, and I think to turn him away from it is beyond my influence."

"Oh, but you could trick him. We used to trick him into doing things..."

"Madam! What trick could I use to make him leave you and his household?"

"You could send a note to his commander in Paris, and get him to send him an urgent note requesting his presence."

"Indeed, I could," Athos said. "But your son resigned his commission before coming home."

"Oh," D'Artagnan's mother said, and put her hand in front of her mouth. "Oh no. It is impossible, then?"

Athos nodded, his features dour. And then, before he could anticipate what she was about to do, this madwoman fell to her knees beside his bed and inclined her head. "Monsieur Athos, as you are an honorable man, then, and as you are the oldest and most respectable of this band of friends my son brought with him, I beg of you that you will keep my son safe. Please, monsieur. I am a poor woman begging you for the life of the only real family she has left in all the world. Please, protect my Henri."

Flushing, Athos nodded and shook his head, and grunted. "Madam," he said, in some heat. "Get up madam. Never go on your knees, except to God and king. Never. I would protect your son with my life, anyway. He is my friend. He is almost my son. I will keep him as safe as I can. There is no need for you to beg me."

And like that she got up, and flashed him a smile through her tears, and grabbed his hand, and kissed it—before he could withdraw it—and said, "Thank you, monsieur, thank you."

And like that she was out of the room's door, leaving Athos sitting on the bed, bewildered, the warmth of her lips still on the back of his hand, a dagger in his other hand, and her words like a riddle marching through his brain and turning it into a labyrinth.

"Bah," he said, at last. "Women!"

Getting up, he locked his door and set about washing and dressing for the day.

# The Richer Branch; Nothing Is Quite as Dead as a Dead Love; The Familiar Binds

**STRANGELY,** D'Artagnan's memories of early childhood were devoid of any contact with this family so closely related to him by blood and whose lands bordered his father's along the eastern edge of their property.

The first he remembered going to the house, he was four, and his father had dressed him in his best clothes and mounted him ahead of himself on his horse, and taken him around to introduce him to his uncle, his aunt, his three cousins.

Of all his cousins, only Irene, who was his age, had regarded him or treated him with any kind of friendliness. The older boys, Bertrand and Edmond, had acted as though D'Artagnan were an interloper, and his uncle and aunt seemed scarcely to look on him any more warmly than that.

In fact, even though his relationship with his cousins had improved—particularly his relationship with Irene—he had never become a favorite with his uncle and aunt. Instead, they had a way of looking at him with disdain, as though he were too baseborn to darken their threshold.

Riding his horse across the fields, in the brisk autumn morning warming up to midday, D'Artagnan thought perhaps it was just his inconsiderate kissing of Irene when both of them were little more than babes. Perhaps they were afraid that Irene would forget herself and throw off her brilliant arranged match for the sake of her penniless cousin.

He had to snort with laughter at the thought. If they truly thought that, they didn't know their own daughter.

Despite himself, the mild morning cheered him. He rode across a path between the fields that separated their properties, then took the main road—the one that the peasants used to go to the fair at the bastide every week. The road was paved, which was easier on the horse, and besides, after his absence and given that he was now Monsieur D'Artagnan, the lord of his own domains such as they were, he thought he should approach the house via the front door. He should not come around the back like little Henri had, once, looking for playfellows and company.

He crossed over a creek on a little whitewashed bridge and found himself in his uncle's lands. Even here, at the periphery of the domain, it was obvious that the de Bigorres were the wealthy branch of the family. For one, on either side of the road, bordering it, were carefully planted bushes that were verdant in winter and flowered in spring and summer. This made the roadside pleasant, but was more refinement than the D'Artagnans could afford, in either material or the effort of their vassals.

Farther on, D'Artagnan veered from the public road into the path that led to the gates of the de Bigorre house. The gates were eight feet tall, made of iron, and creaked when the porter opened them for him. Inside, they disclosed a meandering path amid impeccably manicured gardens—the whole ending in a huge...palace—there was no other word for it—of golden stone. He'd once accompanied Athos to the home of a duke, Athos's childhood friend. The de Bigorre house, though a little smaller, did not look more humble than the duke's palace. It sprawled, golden and carefully designed—balconies and glazed windows giving it an air of being, by far, above the common herd and as though in an entirely different world from peasant hovels or comfortable farmers' houses, even.

Despite his mind knowing better, D'Artagnan found it hard to believe his father—once soldier of fortune, scapegrace, teller of great tales and peerless duelist—had grown up in this house. When he thought back on his father as a young man, he always imagined him living in the D'Artagnan's house which was little more than a glorified farmhouse.

It was nonsense, of course. His father had not inherited his home, and his junior title from his grandmother's family, till well after he'd become a man. In fact, he had been living less than ten years in that house when D'Artagnan was born. Until then he had been the younger son of de Bigorre, living in this house, surrounded by a battalion of servants. D'Artagnan could not picture it.

He gave his horse to a servant who came to meet him and hastened up the front steps of the house, to the entrance hall—a vast room, in the Roman manner, or at least what someone in D'Artagnan's family had once believed to be the Roman manner. The room was crisscrossed by utterly unneeded columns; busts of deceased classical somebodies sat on pedestals here and there; and the floor had been done in an elaborate mosaic showing what D'Artagnan suspected was supposed to be the war of Troy—horses and men and a whole lot of blood; though the men wore the French attire of a hundred years ago.

He looked about him for one of the ubiquitous servants, ready to request an audience with his younger cousin, Edmond.

Oh, he knew all too well that he was supposed to visit his uncle and aunt and pay his respects. But then, neither of them had come to visit him, on his arrival, or to present condolences on the death of his father. Head of the family or no, he was the grieving party, here.

So he would simply talk to Edmond and confirm the truth of the priest's description of his father's last duel, and then he would leave. He still had to see Monsieur de Bilh for complete understanding of what had happened.

"Henri!" a female voice called. And then, half swallowed, as though she were correcting herself, "D'Artagnan!"

He turned towards the voice, and saw his cousin Irene. There was a time, in fact just before he left for Paris, when the sight of his cousin was enough to set D'Artagnan's heart aflutter.

Irene was tall for a woman and more so for a Gascon woman. It was said her mother had English blood and it was probably true, because Irene was taller than D'Artagnan by a full three fingers. With all that height, she was slim and straight.

This she used to full effect by standing very upright, to display her long, clean length, broken only by the very appropriate curve of her bosom. This was displayed to further advantage by being more cradled than covered in a peach-colored gown of daring design. Even her neck rose like a white column to support a more than uncommonly pretty face: oval in shape, it had a small but straight nose, shining blue eyes, and the sort of lips that always seemed to be on the verge of a sigh.

D'Artagnan had spent a considerable portion of his adolescence dreaming of kissing that white throat and meeting those lips with his. It was clear from the way Irene stood watching him—blushes and confusion mingling with the certainty of being admired and desired—that she thought she retained her hold on him.

But the truth was that though D'Artagnan could look at her and judge her as being very pretty indeed, his eyes hastened to uncover flaws—at least when he compared her to his Parisian lover, Madame Bonacieux.

Irene's blond hair had a brassy tone that seemed to indicate that she'd used some wash or tint to make it golden. Its natural color might very well be closer to D'Artagnan's own black hair, or to Irene's brothers' dark brown locks. And her half-parted lips gave the impression of a studied pose, and of her having bitten them to bring up their color. In fact, in her whole pose, with hands lifting the sides of her skirts to display admirably small feet in embroidered slippers, there was the feeling of one who knew she was worthy of admiration, and who set herself to be admired.

This in itself was enough, in D'Artagnan's mind, to make her inferior to his Constance, who never considered how she would look to him, but only showed how pleased she was in seeing him.

"Oh, hullo, Irene. I came to find Edmond. I don't suppose you know where he is?"

"Oh," she said. Surprise was obvious. But then the playacting reasserted itself. She crossed the space between them, anxiously. "Edmond? Why do you wish to see Edmond, Henri?"

"I must ask him some questions," he said. "About my father's death."

"Oh," Irene said again, and this time the sound was pure playacting. She put her hand in front of her mouth and said the "oh" echoingly, in the most becoming manner she could find. "Oh, your father, Henri, how terrible for you. How sad we all were when he heard he had died."

"Yes," D'Artagnan said, thinking of his own revelation—of his mother's letter in his hands, of the thought that he would have to give up everything: friends and lover and his newfound independence. He realized he still hadn't gone to the grave; couldn't bear to think of it. He'd go, he thought, when he'd found out who his father's murderer was. "Yes, it was a great shock to all of us," he said. "But Edmond saw the final duel and I want to ask Edmond how it happened."

Irene frowned at him. "Why? I mean, your father is dead. Surely..." And then with sudden animation, she let a little gasp escape through the carefully half-parted lips. "Oh. You mean to challenge de Bilh for a duel and avenge your father. I know it."

"Don't talk nonsense," D'Artagnan said, impatiently, before he could stop himself. "From all I hear it was not de Bilh's fault in the least."

Irene stared. D'Artagnan realized he might very well be the first person in her life who had ever told her anything to remotely curb her playacting. She stammered, "But...but...why else..."

"It is nothing, really." D'Artagnan embarked on a detailed examination of his lace cuff, a gesture he'd often seen Aramis engage in. He now wondered if Aramis did this when he didn't wish to laugh out loud in someone's face. "It's just that I feel it to be my duty as a son to know how he met his end. I've talked to Father Urtou and I simply wish to speak to Edmond for some details that might have escaped the good Father's eyes."

Irene looked at him, her gaze for once reflecting genuine curiosity. D'Artagnan wondered if she had never before met anyone who displayed genuine filial piety. Or if she simply found herself shocked that his attention wasn't wholly focused on her.

Frankly, seeing her again after his six months in Paris, D'Artagnan felt like a fool for ever having regretted that she was above his station. He had met—though fortunately not been involved with—her type at court. It seemed to him as though Irene never did anything without watching herself on a mirror, real and imaginary. If the mirror were wholly removed, if she didn't think on the effect she was causing in others, Irene would not know how to behave at all.

"Edmond isn't here," she said, at last, as though this were a reluctant admission, torn from her lips. "He has gone to Bordeaux this last week, to meet with some friends of his for a gaming party of some sort,

Edmond gambles to an appalling extent. In fact, I'm surprised he has enough money left to dress in creditable fashion."

"So Edmond is in Bordeaux?" D'Artagnan asked, wondering if his cousin had found it necessary to leave the region when his uncle had died. And if so, why? What was he afraid might come to light?

In his mind was the image of Edmond hitting his father on the back of the head, and then hastening to the threshing floor to talk to the priest and de Bilh. Perhaps his father had attacked not because de Bilh was there, but because Edmond was. And perhaps it had just been poor luck that had put de Bilh and his sword in his way.

"Well...he went to Bordeaux," Irene said, giving him a very odd look. "But he's meant to return any moment. Father said he would be back today." She tilted her head a little, in what, doubtless, she thought was an endearing and fetching way. "You could walk with me in the garden and see if Edmond arrives in the meanwhile."

D'Artagnan's immediate impulse was to reject the suggestion. After all, everything considered, his being found alone with Irene would only make his uncle and aunt uncomfortable, and it might, in fact, cause some sort of rift. But the truth was, he had no interest in Irene, and if his family forbade him the house, then he would simply have to find another place to meet Edmond. From what he remembered of his male cousin's habits this shouldn't be hard, as Edmond was known to attend the village tavern when other opportunities for entertainment failed.

And D'Artagnan remembered that Irene knew everything that was taking place everywhere in the surrounding area. She knew everyone's dirty secrets and whatever each family was trying to keep quiet. If those attempts on him had come from here, Irene was likely to know from whom. Or at least, she would be likely to know something that would illuminate the situation. And she was very likely too, to be able to give him some idea of what work his father might have been doing for Richelieu.

Thinking this, he bowed slightly to her, and led her, or allowed her to lead him, out a side door and into a garden that was magnificent in spring and merely coldly beautiful in autumn.

In spring, when he'd taken his last stroll with Irene, the rose bushes now denuded of leaf had exploded in a riot of color amid the statues of fauns and ancient goddesses whose patina proclaimed them to be almost certainly the real thing, plundered from some ancient temple.

Now the only green was evergreen, clipped into fantastic shapes of horses with riders and birds taking flight. They walked along a pebbled path, Irene's hand resting on his arm, as she said, "There can be no harm in it. We are cousins."

They strolled in silence a few steps and D'Artagnan could almost hear the rearranging of thoughts in his cousin's head, as she tried—he thought—to work out how to restore her old influence over him.

"Did you know," she said at long last, "that I'm not married yet?"

D'Artagnan chuckled. "Considering that you are still here in your father's house, I'd surmised as much," he said.

"Well...I might have been visiting," she said. And then, again after a pause, "You know, I'm not even sure I want to marry him."

"Your fiancé?" D'Artagnan asked.

"Yes," she said. "Sever de Comminges is so..." She shrugged as though she had run out of words.

"You've been engaged to Sever since you were six," D'Artagnan said. "I don't think your wishes have much to do with the plans of your families."

"Oh," Irene said. Her hand squeezed his arm a little, if in surprise or to punish him, he did not know. "You are so cruel. You're still exactly like you were when you were a little boy and you used to pull my kitten's tail."

"I never pulled your kitten's tail, my dear. You're mistaking me for Bertrand."

"No. I'm sure I'm not. You used to pull his tail to make the poor creature cry."

D'Artagnan, who had never wished to make anyone or anything cry in his whole life, had to content himself with being silent. Against Irene's memory, no matter how erroneous, there was no defense.

"Sever is cruel too. He rides his horses till they fall, and he whips his hunting dogs," she said. "He is a horrible man." And suddenly, with an unexpected tone of urgency and truthfulness in her voice, "I don't want to marry him." She stopped and looked at D'Artagnan, her gaze intense. "Henri, don't make me marry him."

D'Artagnan stopped too, and turned to her, bewildered. "I don't know what you think I can do in the matter," he said.

She reached for his hands and took them in hers. He was wearing gloves and she was not. Even through his gloves he could feel the hard, very cold tips of her fingers. "Marry me," she said. And, in response to what must have been his genuine look of surprise, "Marry me, Henri. You used to love me. We can ride together, tonight or tomorrow, to Spain, where no one will know us, and we can find a priest to marry us. Against that, what can Sever do? What can my father?"

"A lot, Irene. For one, they can separate us, demand that the marriage be annulled, or say it never happened. And if they don't..." He looked up, searching her eyes, wondering where the sincerity came from suddenly. He would wager she was not in love with him any more than he was in love with her. They had both playacted at love when they were very young, but now they both knew better, and he could not imagine why she was so determined to tie their fortunes together. "If they don't, you'll have to live the rest of your life married to me."

She nodded eagerly. "Gladly, cousin. Gladly."

"Irene," he said, seriously. "Don't be a fool. This is no time to playact. I don't love you, and I know you do not love me. What we had was no more than a plaything, the way boys play at being kings and fighting great battles. We played at being in love."

Her lips trembled, "Oh, no, no. It's not true, you know, I…"

"You're not going to say you love me, because you can't. You couldn't bring yourself to utter it, and you know it."

She sighed. Again it was a genuine sigh, with no trace of the overwrought or dramatic. "Perhaps not love," she said. "But I do like you a lot. You know marriages are made on less. The church says that all you need is a strong friendship, a holy bond, which the Lord…"

"Irene, please. I do not wish to learn my catechism from you." D'Artagnan felt he was on the verge of bursting into laughter, and he didn't wish to insult her that much. He could too well imagine what the effect of laughter would be. Irene would exclaim and cry and then run.

Knowing Irene there were good odds she would then try to exert her revenge by denouncing him to her father—telling him that D'Artagnan had offered her insult or attempted to kiss her or who knew what. And her father was quite likely to then become unpleasant, perhaps even challenging D'Artagnan to a duel.

There had been enough dueling done in this family and besides…and besides, D'Artagnan desperately wanted to know what Irene found so enticing about his small house and his barely recognizable name.

"Let's sit," he said, and led her, studiously, to a place where the ground rose ever so slightly and a stone bench stood where they both could sit down. And where he could see eavesdroppers approach long before they were close enough to overhear them. "Now suppose you tell me why you'd ever wish to marry me. Wait." He raised his hand. "Before you protest undying friendship, or that you ever had a marked partiality for me, or any of that, let me remind you that I know better. In spring when you said your farewells to me, you explained that as much as you liked me, you didn't believe you could live within the income my title could provide; and that you didn't wish to take second place to my mother in a house that was, at any rate, too small for you.

"My house has not grown, nor has my title. While I intended to go to Paris to make my fortune, I was called back far before I could attempt it. In fact, I was not even yet a musketeer, but merely served in the corps of Monsieur des Essarts, which is sort of a cadet or training corps for the musketeers. So, you see, though I've been to Paris, I have no great name to give you and the entire fortune I acquired in my sojourn near the royal court is a few new tunics, a couple of new pairs of breeches and this hat, with a new plume." He touched it as he spoke. "None of which is enough to pay for your clothes or keep you in the style due to your birth station and beauty."

"Oh, it matters not," she said, and burst in sudden tears, while fumbling blindly at her sleeve for a handkerchief. "It matters not. You don't know. You don't understand."

He found his own handkerchief and gave it to her. "I am willing to learn and understand," he said. "If only you will tell me."

"It's Sever. Henri, I'm *afraid* of him."

"Oh, nonsense," D'Artagnan said, as he thought back on his few encounters with de Comminges. There weren't many, since they moved in quite different circles. But over seventeen years of living in the same region, he'd crossed paths with Sever de Comminges, the de Comminges heir, half a dozen times. He was a dark-haired, dark-eyed man with olive skin, and uncommonly tall. Though he never went out of his way to be sociable, usually sitting slightly apart at any feast or meeting to show he knew what was due to his birth, he had piercing eyes that seemed to catch on every nuance and turn of the conversation, every expression of those around him. He limped a little, on his left leg, from some injury sustained at his birth. D'Artagnan didn't know if that was why he always acted—playacted. As much as Irene—like the hero in a tragic play, or if he was perhaps shy and the act bolstered his confidence.

He tended to dress in black, and kept such a dignified and private persona that, though he was only D'Artagnan's age—in fact a few months younger—D'Artagnan could understand why locals would think he was sinister, or at least unapproachable. But he could not understand why Irene would feel that way.

But she shook her head to his exclamation, brassy blond hair flying. "Not nonsense. Oh, no, Henri. It is not nonsense. His father, the old Monsieur Adrien de Comminges died, did you know that? Just a week before your father. He died suddenly, and people say..." She lowered her voice, though patently there was no one around to overhear them. "People say that he died of poison, and that he was poisoned by his son, who couldn't wait to come into his inheritance."

She looked at D'Artagnan with huge, tragic eyes. "What if he marries me and then decides he doesn't want me around either? What if he uses the same poison on me?"

Her white hand, with its long, cold fingers, touched her own throat, as though she already felt, there, the constriction caused by the poison. "I don't want to die."

He didn't laugh. He knew all too well that around here this type of rumor attached to anyone who held himself aloof from the common society. Also, frankly, it would probably attach to Sever de Comminges, with his dark hair, his dark clothes. A man who didn't speak much and left others to imagine what might move him.

Instead, he very gently took Irene's hand away from her throat and held it in his. "Irene, is Sever pressing his engagement to you now?"

"Yes," she said. "Oh, yes. After all these years, when his parents were content to let him wait and me, until we were of a proper age to marry, he's come into his domain and he wants to marry this coming summer's eve. He says it's the only thing we can do, the only thing we must do to..." Her lips trembled. "To give heirs to his house."

D'Artagnan squeezed Irene's hand in his. "I think you are scared," he said, softly.

"What?" she asked, surprised. "Of course I'm scared. I've been telling you I am scared. I—"

"No," he said. "Not of that. Though you might have persuaded yourself of it, allowed yourself to believe that you are scared of Sever, and of his intentions towards you...I think you know as well as I do a man doesn't press a suit on his intended wife and attempt to speed their marriage if he truly doesn't wish to marry her."

"But what if he marries me and then changes his mind?" she asked, her hand pulling away from his and flying to her throat again. "What if I don't give him the heir he wants? What if something happens and he decides I'm not the bride he wants, after all?"

He frowned at her. "I don't think that's your fear, Irene. I think you fear changing. For all these years, you've lived in your father's house and been protected. And now you must take your place as the lady of your own house—in fact the lady of the largest house in this region, and you don't wish to. You're afraid of the change it will wreak in your life."

"How dare you?" she asked, indignation flying. "How dare you? If I were afraid of marriage by itself, why would I wish to marry you?"

"Because my house is nothing like that of de Comminges. Because you know while my mother lives, she would never let you have control of anything, from the kitchen to the yard. Because you know you'd still be a child, just in a different house."

She shook her head. "Oh, you wrong me," she said. "It is not that at all. If I were marrying anyone else, anyone else at all—even Sever's younger brother, Geoffroi—I would not mind it. I would be happy, rather, to be moving out, to have my own place. But Sever scares me, Henri. And I believe I have cause."

"And I believe you only think you'd be more willing to marry anyone else because there's no danger of that. In fact, if I had a house of my own and if I were to agree to your scheme, you'd soon find reason enough to be scared of me, as well."

Irene looked like she couldn't decide whether to be insulted or saddened. She bit her lip, then sighed deeply. "You won't help me, then?" she asked.

"Not if helping you means marrying you, no," D'Artagnan said.

"Well, then," she said, and stood up, and bobbed a small and correct curtsey. "Well, then, I hope you'll think of me and of this conversation when you receive news of my death."

And on that, she turned and ran, through the garden path towards the house, leaving D'Artagnan more bewildered than ever.

# Religion and Fighting; Pastoral Care; A Burden to Keep

**ARAMIS** watched D'Artagnan ride away, then turned back towards the sacristy. The priest was still there, apparently lost in prayer, or at least in thought.

"Father," Aramis said. "I would like to ask you a few questions, without my friend listening to them."

The priest inclined his head. "I thought as much," he said. "I noticed you came to the Mass separately, Monsieur..."

"Aramis," he said. "Just Aramis."

Father Urtou shook his head, in a slightly disapproving manner. "Not a man's name."

"No," Aramis said. "But the name a man would take, having killed a man in a duel when he was yet in seminary and on his way to the priesthood. After the killing, and with dueling being banned and therefore a crime, how could he present himself to any worthy bishop and ask for ordination? And if he had a bend for communal life, how could he, in clean conscience, ask any congregation to accept him?"

"So you relinquished your name as penance?" the priest asked and ran a jaundiced gaze across Aramis's elegant figure in his tunic which, despite embellishments of lace and ribbon, was unmistakably a musketeer's uniform. "And entered the musketeers? What kind of penance was that last?"

"The sort of penance that the King said would earn me pardon," he said, and opened his hands palm out, in the sort of gesture that meant he couldn't help himself. "Or at least, the King never said it, but it is known..."

The priest shook his head again. "One wonders at the sort of penance that consists of more killing."

"You sound like my servant, Bazin," Aramis said, and stopped, immediately, afraid he had insulted the priest. "I'm sorry. I am usually more polite."

The priest shook his head. "I do not take it as impolite to compare me to someone who is, obviously, a pious and worthy man. Do not fret." He looked at Aramis again, consideringly. "You were a seminarian once? Do you still intend to take orders?"

"I was intended for the church from the earliest childhood," Aramis said.

"Ah, but that doesn't answer my question."

Aramis inclined his head. "You are correct. It doesn't. For many years, my mother said I was meant for the church, and I followed the course set for me because I thought that would be for the best, and because I did not wish to do anything else. And then..." He shrugged. "And then a few months ago I was faced with the reason my mother had intended me for the church—"[5]

"What was it?" the priest asked, with real curiosity.

Aramis shrugged. "It doesn't matter. It does not apply. She wanted me for the church for a reason that isn't even...for fear of something that didn't come to pass."

"And so you've decided to give it up," Father Urtou said, crossing his hands in his lap.

"Oh, no," Aramis said. "Suddenly, faced with the fact that my mother no longer cared if I went into the church or not, I found that I truly wanted to become a priest. I'm not sure it's a vocation." He hesitated. "I've never heard a voice calling in the night."

The priest laughed. "Very few of us do." His eyes shone, as though he were privy to a good joke. "And yet we manage, somehow."

"That's what I thought," Aramis said. "Unworthy though I am, I am willing to lend my hands to the work in the...in the vineyard. If He will have me."

The priest looked at him again, once more, from head to toe. "Oh, I imagine He will. He's taken worse. So, my son," he lifted his hand, as if in a position of absolution. "Why did you come back without your friend? If you wish to confess we can go and..."

Aramis shook his head. "It's not a confession," he said. "It's...I'd like to ask you some questions, about the death of my friend's father."

The priest nodded. "I see. Well, then, pull up that stool there, and sit, and we shall talk like civilized people. It makes my neck hurt to sit here and look up to talk to you, but I'm too old to stand for a long interview."

Aramis nodded and pulled up a three-legged stool from the corner. It looked rickety, the wood blackened, but as he sat down on it, he found it would take his weight, even though it shrieked madly every time he moved.

"It's the children," the priest said, at the shrieking. "They sit in it for their catechism lessons, and they find nothing better to do when they get bored than to rock back and forth. It wears at the wood and makes the whole shriek. But it's sturdy enough, never you fear." His eyes shone, with sudden amusement. "Provided you don't rock back and forth on it."

Aramis smiled a little and shook his head to signify his willingness to not do any such thing. "I wanted to ask you about the wars of religion."

"Ask me?" the priest said. "Why me? You're a musketeer. You know as much about it as I do. Why, if I read the signs aright, before much more time passes you and your comrades will be laying siege to that Protestant stronghold, La Rochelle."

"Yes, but..." Aramis shook his head. "No. What I want to know is about the wars of religion in this place—around this region. Hereabouts. Who was on which side, and why, and what...what bad feelings there might be."

The priest frowned. "Why? What can this mean to you?"

"My friend's father was killed. He fought for Henry IV. It is hard to believe that there wouldn't be some religion wrapped up in that."

The priest tilted his head sideways, a little. "Hard to believe, perhaps, but I don't think it was true. You see, both de Bilh and D'Artagnan were good Catholics, and besides, you forgot I saw the fight. As I told your friend, I was there all along, and I saw everything that transpired. There was nothing covert, or murderous to it..."

"Except that the way you said D'Artagnan was acting...often comes from a blow to the head." As he spoke, Aramis remembered that other blood that Porthos had talked about. What if it had come from just such a blow? What if someone had hit Monsieur D'Artagnan hard upon the head, and caused him to bleed just a little?

"Often it comes from nothing, my son," the priest said, compassionately. "You see, we, human creatures, are more frail than we think ourselves to be, and as we get older...things happen, within and around us. Our inner works decay—like a beautiful machine, once wound, will over time lose force. And sometimes, men of Charles D'Artagnan's age...Something breaks in the brain and has much the same effect as a blow to the head."

"Perhaps," Aramis said. "And then again, perhaps not."

"Why are you and your friends so sure that there was foul play?" he asked, looking intently at Aramis.

"There are...reasons."

"If you forgive me saying so," the old priest said. "I don't know of any reasons that would be..."

"Father, on the way here we were attacked twice."

"Unfortunately in these sad times we live in..." The priest shrugged. "That's neither rare nor unexpected. Gascony...and all of France are sadly fraught with evildoers."

Aramis sighed. "Yes, Father, but these evildoers were intent on avoiding the rest of us and did not seem interested in money or valuables, but only in killing D'Artagnan." He hesitated, considering whether he should tell him that there were other complications, like the note from the Cardinal found on the highwayman. He decided to avoid it, so he didn't have to tell him, also, about Monsieur D'Artagnan working for the Cardinal, at least according to his wife's letter.

The priest was looking at him, anxiously, as though trying to gage the truth of his words by look alone. "I see," he said, but his look showed plainly that he did not, in fact, see. "That is grave indeed, that someone would try to kill young Henri, but...my son, it might have nothing to do with his father's death. Or at least...You must know there is bad blood there. His parents' marriage..."

"His parents' marriage was opposed?" D'Artagnan asked. "By his family? Or hers?"

The priest shrugged. "By both I imagine. She...well...with the irregularity of your friend's birth..." He shook his head, perhaps at the surprise he read in Aramis's eyes. "But forgive me, about that I'd best be still. Others have sinned in larger ways. It doesn't matter anymore, and he's dead at any rate. And she's a good woman and a good mother."

Puzzled, Aramis could instinctively tell that there would be no prodding there. But what could be irregular about D'Artagnan's birth? Save perhaps that he had anticipated the marriage by a few months, he couldn't imagine what it would be. D'Artagnan's parents were married, and he was their recognized son. So it would be that. D'Artagnan's parents would have married while she was expecting D'Artagnan. Or perhaps D'Artagnan was already born and a babe in arms.

It had to be that, and that would explain the comment about others having committed greater sins. In fact, to own the truth, France was full of bastards, some of them from the greatest families in the kingdom.

But what about that kind of birth could justify someone's trying to kill D'Artagnan on the way to claim his inheritance?

"Did you marry them?" he asked. "Did they marry here?"

The priest nodded. "I found it odd that they didn't go to Paris, since her family was there, but—"

"Paris?" Aramis asked.

"Well, it's where she was raised."

"Were both of my friend's parents from Catholic families?" he asked, sure that this was the crux of the matter.

The man frowned at him. "Yes, yes. The de Bigorres have always been Catholic, though Monsieur D'Artagnan's mother, Henri's grandmother, came from a Protestant family. But she converted before marriage. Indeed I baptized her myself."

"So, I was right," Aramis said. "That house was, once upon a time, Protestant and that was a Calvinist chapel, devoid of all ornament."

The priest smiled. "Indeed. Do they still have the chapel, then?"

"It is madam's praying room, with a fine old statue of Saint Quitterie, holding her head in her hands. It must have come from the de Bigorre house." He paused a moment. "Would the rest of my friend's grandmother's family oppose, those who gave them the title of D'Artagnan, having a Catholic like my friend inherit it?"

The priest shook his head. "There's no one left of that family. She was an only daughter...or the only surviving one. Her brothers died in the war, you see. Only she was left, and the title and lands were all hers. There is no one to dispute it."

"Not even a hidden heir?"

"Son," the priest answered gravely. "Such things exist only in fables."

"But...if she was from a Protestant family, and her brothers died in the war against the Catholics, surely there must be some relative, no matter how distant, who would resent her marrying into a Catholic family."

The priest looked at the musketeer and something very like a shadow passed before his eyes. It was as though he were remembering things he wished to forget, the sort of things no one's memory should be burdened with. "Ah. But the war wasn't that clear cut in Gascony, you see. There were enough armies, trampling the land and fighting each other, each of them in the proper uniforms, and all that you think of as war. The kind of war you and your friends would wage."

He sighed. "In these small towns, though, the small towns and cities of Gascony, the war was both more confusing and more personal. Like the gospel says about families where one will be taken and one will be left, it was the same thing, in this land. Half of a family would be Protestant and half Catholic, and in the families where they were well disposed towards each other, they continued well disposed, while in the ones where they wanted an excuse to fight and kill, then they seized on religion as an excuse. Take de Comminges. The father was a Protestant who converted to Catholicism but who might have reverted to Protestantism at his death. However, his sons are both good Catholics. So, you see...they might say it was religious if anyone wanted to take issue with the marriage of Henri's grandmother. But no one would resent her marriage just because her new husband was a Catholic."

"Oh," Aramis said. "You are telling me, then, that religion had no bearing in this? That they were trying to kill my friend for reasons not related to religion? But then, you must see, it must mean that it is related to his father's death. That someone is afraid of what he might discover about his father's death."

The priest frowned. "Well, I don't know what about Charles D'Artagnan's death there was to warrant killing anyone else for it, much less his son, Henri. But...this is a sad land, my son. A very sad land. And once men start shedding blood, they tend to forget what the beginning of it all was."

He shook his head, sadly, and shortly thereafter dismissed Aramis, who left feeling like he'd discovered more questions, but no more answers.

What if, despite what the priest said, there was a hidden heir to the D'Artagnan fortune? He would want both D'Artagnan and his father out of the way.

# The Useful Lord; The Fine Art of Talking to Village Maidens; A Man in the Noonday Sun

**"MONSIEUR,** you really should not be working like this," the farmer said, while Porthos, pitchfork in hand, helped load a cart high with hay.

"Why not?" Porthos asked with a smile. "What else are these muscles good for, I ask you, but to make the work light for others?"

The farmer looked up at him, squinting. He was a short man and though powerfully built nowhere near as powerfully built as Porthos. He spoke with a noticeable lilt and sometimes corrected himself after slipping into a whole sentence in Gascon. "It is not right," he said. "For quality to work in the fields."

Porthos let out with a peal of laughter. He'd been up since dawn and in the course of the day—still before noon—had helped a shepherd boy find a missing goat; had carried a load of wood for an old lady; had collected eggs from a henhouse; had helped a farmer chop a fallen tree. At each of these occasions, people had given him confused looks, but none had boldly stated their problem as this man had.

"I'm from Normandy," he said. "My friend Athos says that my ancestors came over as invaders, in longships. I'm not sure how he knows that, but I'm not going to ask. A great one for learning, Athos is, and he'll talk your ear off for hours at a time, about history or theology or what have you. And—I tell you—it gets really confused when he starts explaining all about the Philistines and the Sardinian. But the thing is, you see, my people were hardly better than just wealthy farmers with a lot of land. Oh, my father said we were. Descended from kings and all that." He shrugged and threw another pitchfork of hay onto the cart. "Never set much store by it myself. When I was little, I used to play with the other children nearby, which means I often helped them at their chores. My favorite friend was the miller's son."

The farmer shook his head. "Still doesn't seem right. You are a lord, and one of the King's Musketeers."

"Yes, and I can fork hay."

Since the man could not deny this, he stopped protesting, and allowed Porthos to go on working. After a long time, when he judged the moment right, Porthos sprang the question, "By the by," he said. "I'm here with my friend D'Artagnan."

"Oh, yes," the man said. "Monsieur Henri, who went to Paris. Very sad about his father."

"Yes. Particularly that he should go to that duel already injured."

"He went injured?" the farmer asked, and his pitchfork stopped, in turn. "To the duel?"

"Oh, you didn't know that?" Porthos asked, managing to look surprised, as if such a fact had to be common knowledge.

The man shook his head. "Not as such. I mean, we've heard that he was drunk or something, and that this was why he challenged Monsieur de Bilh to a duel, but I never thought...Injured you say?"

"Oh, yes. Judging by the blood track on the threshing floor and beyond, someone wounded him, there, near that great big oak, at the end of the field, where the path starts that leads to the threshing floor."

"What? By old Jacques' field?"

"Right there, yes. Someone wounded him, and he bled all the way to the duel."

"But...who would do such a thing?" the farmer asked. "Did he perhaps have another duel before that one?"

"That I don't know," Porthos said. "I was wondering if anyone was likely to have seen it, its taking place there, in the middle of the fields."

The farmer looked at him so long, and with such a lengthy, absorbed look that Porthos wondered if he'd forgotten the question. But at long last, he shrugged. Pointing behind him, at a small hill, atop which there was a stone house, he said, "My sister might have."

"Your sister?"

"She lives in that farmhouse at the top of the hill. It's an old house, and it has...attics." He spoke as though attics were the latest innovation in building or perhaps something of such class and standing that he barely dared mention it in conjunction with his own family. "And I swear she does nothing all day but go up and down those stairs and look out those windows. Her mother-in-law lives in the attic, like, and she's an invalid, so my sister spends a lot of time there, looking after her. Unless I'm mistaken, from the attic she would have a view of Jacques' field, and she might very well have seen something." He paused. "I confess I'm now curious about who else old Monsieur D'Artagnan could have had a fight with."

"He wasn't a man for fighting then?" Porthos asked.

The man cackled. "Ah, that he was. A great one for fighting. But he was not such a devil as to fight two duels in a day. Most of his fighting, i' truth, were no more than talk. He would call someone a villain or a dog's pizzle, but it all meant nothing, you know? It was just words. Like he and that Monsieur de Bilh, they did argue once a week, regular, but then you'd see them in the tavern of a night buying wine for each other."

He shook his head, suddenly sad. "I never thought it would end in a duel and blood. Never, monsieur. Not in a hundred years."

Porthos agreed with him about the sadness and lack of sense of it, and helped him finish loading his wagon, after which the man walked him up a pathway to the house he'd pointed to.

"It is better," he said, confidentially, "if I introduce you. My sister Louise, she gets strange ideas, and this way she will know that you know me, and that everything is safe."

In fact, when the door was presently opened by a remarkably pretty woman in a white apron, the farmer said briskly, "Louise, this is Monsieur Porthos, and he is a big lord, with lands and everything, so mind your manners. But he helped me load my hay wagon, and he is as good a fellow as you'll ever meet, so I'd be obliged if you'd oblige him in whatever he wants to know."

Louise curtseyed enthusiastically, causing her loose curls to fall against her pink cheek, and she lowered her eyes modestly. "Monsieur," she said. "Anything you want to know. You do me a great honor, monsieur. If you'd come in and have some wine and cheese, monsieur."

Porthos felt a fleeting attraction and thought that she would probably be as much fun as his own beloved Athenais, who was, after all, an accountant's wife. But then he thought that Athenais, who was in her mid-thirties, would resent his admiring this woman. Oh, she wouldn't be angry with him. Or perhaps she would. She was a woman of very little patience and she'd once put Aramis in a green dress—which Porthos was sure was the result of Aramis looking at her disparagingly. But whether she was angry with him or not, she would be hurt. And since Porthos found all women beautiful but only one woman worthy of his love, he disciplined his thoughts away from the rosy-cheeked Louise.

She led them both into her kitchen—warmed by a large fire and smelling of stew and fresh bread. There she gave them each a mug of wine and a large slice of cheese with fresh bread to go with it. "We make our own cheese," she said. "And our own bread. And our own wine too."

As they started eating, she sat across from them at the well-scrubbed table. "Very well, monsieur," she said. "What did you need to know that I can tell you?"

"It is about that old Monsieur D'Artagnan," the farmer said, before Porthos could open his mouth.

"What, the one that died?"

"That one," her brother said. "Monsieur here says that he was wounded by the time he got to the duel with Monsieur de Bilh."

"He was? Poor man. No wonder he was taken mortal."

"Yes. At least monsieur here says he was, and I see no reason to doubt him. He says there was blood, right there at the edge of old Jacques' field, and he wonders...well...he doesn't know who done it, and he doesn't know if it was a duel, you see?"

She frowned intently, as though trying to follow her brother's reasoning, and Porthos felt less regret at having to stop thinking of her, for Athenais's sake. His Athenais never needed things explained twice.

Oftentimes she didn't need them explained once, as her very acute intellect penetrated what had not been said and discovered what no one had told her. But then, this one did make good cheese, he admitted as he took another bite and savored the sharp flavor.

"When was that?" she said, at last. "That he was killed?"

"Why..." Her brother thought, as he counted upon his fingers. "It wasn't last week, or the week before. I think the funeral was on the day after Pierre's goat ran into the Cazou's farmyard, remember, and their dog set upon it. I remember because that wasn't half a to-do and it came on the day after the duel. So it was...Monday three weeks ago. I remember because I'd seen Monsieur D'Artagnan at Mass just the day before, and he seemed so happy and cheerful, and little did he know that he would lie there in a coffin in the next week."

She nodded, as if all this made perfect sense, and frowned a little.

"You wouldn't happen to have seen whoever it was that he fought with at the edge of Jacques' field on that day, would you?"

She made a face. "Well, then, I did, but I wouldn't call it fighting. Not as such. Because, you see, he put a knife into him."

"Monsieur D'Artagnan put a knife into someone?" the farmer asked, slamming his empty mug of wine down.

"No, no. The other man put a knife into Monsieur D'Artagnan. At the time, I thought he touched him with a stick or something, because, you know, I was looking from my attic. But now I'm not so sure. Not if it was in that same day, and if he bled from there to the threshing floor. It had to be a knife. But the funny thing..."

"There was something funny?"

"Yes. The funny thing is that Monsieur D'Artagnan didn't fall. And he didn't fight back. He just staggered a little, then he turned around, and it was as if he had nothing against the man, you know, which is why I thought he'd only touched him with a stick or something. But he staggered a little, and then he continued, towards that threshing floor." She crossed herself. "Where he met his death, poor man."

# Where Cousins Rarely Are Highwaymen; Surprises and Shocks; At Monsieur de Bilh's

**HAVING** eaten at home and answered half a dozen questions from Bayard, who wanted to know what fodder to buy for the horses, and had a dozen other questions that baffled the mind, D'Artagnan found himself in a very bad mood.

The more time he spent at home the more he became convinced that, much as he loved Gascony, he wasn't ready to settle into the life of a provincial lord and do what his father had done for years. Now, more than a week away from Paris, he ached for it with an almost physical longing. He wanted to walk the crowded streets. He wanted to return to his lodging, in the Rue des Fossoyers, climb the stairs and find everything as it was when he'd left. He wanted to stand guard at Monsieur des Essarts—and at the Palais Royale with his friends.

He wanted to go drinking with Athos; he wanted to go riding with Porthos; he wanted to attend Mass with Aramis. Though he'd done the last just this morning, it wasn't right. Even his friends weren't right in Gascony. They'd been going one each way, and D'Artagnan saw less of them now than he did when they all fulfilled guard duty.

So it was in a very bad mood that he set off on his horse, across the countryside to Monsieur de Bilh's house.

There was no way to cross where their lands met. For one, they met only at a place where they shared a boundary for the space of maybe twenty steps—which was why his father's insistence that they had a disputed boundary had been taken as a joke by all, including Monsieur de Bilh and, presumably, by D'Artagnan's father, himself.

So, instead, D'Artagnan took himself toward de Bilh's house by road, which involved taking a long circle around both houses and the woods between them.

It was in crossing those woods that D'Artagnan found his way—a narrow path amid the tall, thickly planted trees—barred by a man on horseback. The man wore a cloak, pulled up and over his face, and D'Artagnan had no idea who it might be, but his first thought, as he drew his sword, was that he was out of patience for this.

"Remove from the road, monsieur," he yelled. "Or I shall remove you."

The man threw his hood back to glare at him, and D'Artagnan recognized the dark brown hair and the sharp features of his cousin Edmond. "Is that all you have to say, Henri? That you will remove me?"

D'Artagnan sighed and returned his sword to its scabbard, as his horse moved restlessly beneath him. There was still a chance Edmond would move quickly and kill him before he could draw. But—having known Edmond his whole life—D'Artagnan knew there was about as much chance of that as of Edmond's suddenly growing wings and flying.

"What do you want, Edmond?" he said. "And I must tell you right now that whatever Irene told you is the greatest of falsehoods."

Edmond scowled. As the younger son of a very wealthy family, he was excellent at scowling, and he practiced the skill several times a day. "She told me you were looking for me."

"Oh, well, that wasn't a falsehood, then. But I'd have come to meet you, by the by, without the need for you to block my way, by the road."

"Stop, Henri. I don't know what you wish of me, but I'm not willing to do it."

"Pray?" D'Artagnan said, confused.

"Go and tell your master that if he doesn't wish me to marry Jeanne de Laduch, he'll have to make it worth my while not to marry her. As a second son, it's either marrying the de Laduch heiress or entering orders—and some of us take our orders more seriously than he does."

"What?" D'Artagnan would have liked to ask something more to the point, but all he could extract from the confusion of his mind was that one word.

"Go tell your master, Richelieu, that I will not give up my engagement, no matter how much he wishes the de Laduch fortune for one of his tame protégés; he'll have to come and fight me for it."

D'Artagnan felt his hand fly to the pommel of his sword at the accusation of his working for the Cardinal. It was only by an effort of will that he kept his voice relatively calm as he said, "What makes you think I work for the Cardinal?"

"Why! Why else would you be coming around to my house and questioning Irene about my whereabouts? Your father worked for the Cardinal, and clearly you do too."

"Is that what Irene told you?" D'Artagnan shouted, and laughed. "That I questioned her about your whereabouts?"

Edmond looked confused. This wasn't exactly hard, in general, but it normally took longer to achieve. He looked at D'Artagnan, his blue eyes, just like his sister's, filled with utter confusion. "You didn't ask Irene where I was?"

"No. It means nothing to me where you were. I just wanted to speak to you about the duel that killed my father."

"Oh," Edmond said, sounding so much like Irene that it was all D'Artagnan could do not to laugh. "You don't care, then, that I went to Bordeaux?"

"No, should I care that you went to Bordeaux?"

Edmond frowned at him, then dismounted, slowly. "Dismount," he said, looking up at D'Artagnan. "We can speak better on foot with the certainty that no one hears us."

Given that the man couldn't use a sword any more than he could fly, Edmond was not stupid. At least, he had been brilliant at his letters and his catechism, which had, initially, given his parents the idea of sending him into the church, until the possibility of a marriage with Jeanne de Laduch had presented itself.

He was two years older than D'Artagnan and a palm taller, a well-built man and accounted the toast of society wherever he graced with his presence. He now looked at D'Artagnan and said, "Shall we begin again? Why did you wish to see me?"

"I wanted an account of my father's last duel," D'Artagnan said.

Edmond shrugged. "There isn't much to tell. He was...drunk, I think. Or perhaps feverish. I was talking to the priest, and Monsieur de Bilh was waiting to talk to him."

"Had you met on purpose, or..."

Edmond shook his head. "No. By accident. We all happened to be crossing the field at the same time, and we ran into each other, and I remembered there was something I must speak to the priest about, and so I was, while Monsieur de Bilh waited his turn.

"All of a sudden, your father emerged from the path, huffing and puffing as though he'd been chased by the devil himself. I said '*Hola* Uncle, what's here?' And the others didn't speak at all. Sometimes I wonder if he was drunk, and if—had I stayed quiet—he might not have passed us by, without even noticing we were there. But, alas, I spoke up, and he turned."

Edmond paused and shivered in so noticeable a way that D'Artagnan could see it out of the corner of his eye. "He looked at us, but it was really odd. As though he couldn't see us, but something else. Like...like he was following a panorama of his own mind, if that makes any sense."

D'Artagnan nodded. Once or twice, he'd seen men like that. The drunk, the mad, the terminally wounded all had a look that stared beyond the present at the unimaginable future.

"So, he looked at us," Edmond said. "And then he focused on de Bilh, though I'd swear on the holy book that he wasn't seeing him. He stumbled across the distance between them, though, pulling his sword out of its sheath and saying...in this odd tone, not quite a whisper, 'Ah, you villain. I will teach you to attack a man by stealth.'

"De Bilh was so shocked you know? Speechless. At first he looked to smile, as though he thought your father was joking—and very well he might have been, since just the night before the two of them were talking together in the tavern. And then your father came at him, sword in hand..."

"Yes," D'Artagnan said, more to encourage him to continue than in agreement.

"You know what your father was," Edmond said.

"Yes."

"He came at de Bilh with his sword raised. It was all the poor devil could do to draw his own sword. And he was parrying, and saying 'Stop, Charles, you don't know what you're about.'"

"Did my father talk, also?"

Edmond shook his head. "No, not at all. Just huffing and puffing and giving these weird little grunts, almost whimpers, but with it all, still coming at him, in a dead heat. It took no time at all for the fight to get really close at hand, with them standing practically together, and de Bilh was still trying to defend himself, just using his sword to parry your father's thrusts. And he'd raised his sword thus"—he lifted his arm beside his own neck as if to demonstrate.

"And then your father said, 'You're my undoing but I'll be yours.' And charged towards the sword. It went into his neck, where the great vein runs, and there was blood everywhere." He swallowed. "And that was that. De Bilh was horrified and pulled the sword out as fast as he could, and called for me or the priest to send for a surgeon. But one look at that injury and I knew a surgeon couldn't do anything. The blood was pouring out of your father like water out of the fountain in the main plaza.

"Your father took ten steps back, and then he collapsed, and then he died. And that was it." He gave D'Artagnan an appraising glance. "So if you were intending to do something supremely foolish, like challenge de Bilh for a duel, stay your hand."

"Why does everyone think I want to challenge people for duels on the flimsiest of excuses?" D'Artagnan asked.

Edmond merely looked at him a long time.

D'Artagnan sighed. "And about what you said earlier? You say my father was working for Richelieu?"

"I don't wish to discuss it," Edmond said.

"Well, and I regret the necessity to ask you to do so," D'Artagnan said. "But it is necessary, nonetheless."

"Why is it necessary?" Edmond asked. "I have told you what my involvement in your father's death was, and exactly what happened. If you can find some way in which the guilt of this can be laid at my door..."

D'Artagnan thought of telling him about the ambushes on the way to Gascony. Or perhaps of telling him about the letter from the Cardinal in his father's trunk. But he could not. For one, it was possible that Edmond had something to do with one or both of those events. He thought of the dagger with the de Bigorre shield now in his luggage.

"It is not a matter of laying anything at your door. Only my mother told me in her letter that my father was working for the Cardinal. In Paris, I've thrown my lot in with the musketeers who, whatever you have heard in the provinces...," D'Artagnan said realizing how insufferably smug he sounded, but not knowing what else to do. "Whatever you've heard, the musketeers do not support the Cardinal. Rather they're for the King, in spite of and beyond his eminence's machinations."

"So it was a shock to find your father worked for the Cardinal?"

"Not...a shock as such," D'Artagnan said. "But a sharp reminder that when I left home my father told me to respect Cardinal and King alike. Advice I don't think I know how to keep, as my preference for his Majesty's camp is very decided. But...enfin, I'd like to know what my father was doing for his eminence."

"I don't know what else he was doing," Edmond said heavily. "But as it pertained to me, he told me they knew of my gambling debts, and that his eminence had purchased some of them. And if I should not break my engagement to Jeanne de Laduch and allow a protégé of the Cardinal to win her hand, I'd be made to pay those debts, with money I do not have."

"I see," D'Artagnan said.

"No. I don't believe you do. This is why I went to Bordeaux, trying to gamble what I have in exchange for what I don't." He frowned. "I broke even, but I did not win."

"But...what was the Cardinal's interest in your marriage?"

"None but to allow someone he favors to take Jeanne's hand and her fortune."

"Are you in love with Jeanne, then?"

"In love..." Edmond made a sound. "D'Artagnan, she is ten years older than I and cross-eyed. But if I don't marry her, I'll have to go into the church, and I don't think I'm suited to being a priest."

"I see..." He took a deep breath, seeking to gain courage. His cousin had motive—more than motive enough—to rid himself of D'Artagnan's father. While his cousin had not said it, D'Artagnan could well imagine what kind of pressure his father would bring to bear on behalf of the Cardinal. *Give in, or we'll tell your father about your debts,* was part of it, as was *Give in or we'll tell Jeanne's family.* Instead, D'Artagnan said, "You said you don't know what else he was doing. What makes you think he was doing anything else at the Cardinal's behest?"

"Well..." Edmond looked at him a while. "I don't know what, and I'm not sure why, but I am sure that your father was meaning to ensnare de Comminges."

"Ensnare...?"

"Well, there was much muttering about how now de Comminges would finally pay for the evil he'd done. And about how your father had them under eye and they could not escape."

*Oh, Father, how could you be so foolish?* D'Artagnan thought.

"I tell you, it worried me most of all when old de Comminges died. Only a week before your father, but at the time I wondered if your father had done it. Sometimes, I still wonder."

# A Musketeer's Conscience; Religion and the Cardinal; A Matter of Horses

**ARAMIS** found Athos in the stables. A shrugging Bayard pointed him that way, with a good deal of babble in Gascon to the extent that he wasn't sure why monsieur had gone that way but that—at least from what Aramis could make out of the utterly alien tongue—all non-Gascons were crazy anyway.

Going into the stables, Aramis was tempted to agree with the man. Athos, for no reason Aramis could understand, seemed to have acquired a maddening interest in horses. In fact, he was going from stall to stall and from horse to horse, examining hooves and manes, and seemingly studying the creatures as though he intended to buy one.

"Athos," he said, squinting into the dim stable, trying to see if one or more of the D'Artagnans' hirelings might lurk in the shadows. What he had to say didn't bear discussing in front of the servants, not the least because Aramis wasn't wholly sure of where the servants fell, on which side of the religious divide.

Athos looked up from what he was doing—which looked uncommonly like examining one of the horse's mouths—to give Aramis his coolest look. "Yes?"

"I must speak to you," Aramis said, coming fully into the stable, and looking around into its cool, darkened depths to confirm that, indeed, his friend seemed to be alone here. "Listen—I've been thinking about religion."

Athos frowned up at him; a puzzled look that seemed to ask when Aramis *wasn't* in fact thinking about religion.

Aramis let out a deep breath at this, allowing air to hiss out between his teeth. "It is not funny, Athos. I did not mean that I was thinking about my own religion, or about my relationship to God, or yet about the way in which I might earn salvation. All these are right and proper to concern oneself with and indeed should occupy any right-thinking man's time, who is concerned for his salvation and who yearns, as all fallen humans must, for that time when he must shed his external, mortal coil and embrace—"

"Aramis, have done," Athos said, as he moved to look at a bank of saddles against the wall. "What has put you in such a muddle?"

"I am not muddled. I am merely saying that—"

"Yes, yes, that I should be looking forward to the day when I will finally shuffle off my endless mortal coil and face my maker." Athos permitted himself one of his infuriating smiles that seemed to slide across his lips and vanish leaving only bitterness behind. "Forgive me, my friend, if some of us are not quite that anxious to meet with judgement for what we've done." He lifted a hand before Aramis could protest that Athos underestimated God's forgiveness. "No, please. You and I have gone the full rounds on it, and it doesn't befit us any more than a playground discussion. I've told you often enough that I would not forgive any divinity willing to forgive *me*."

"But—"

"No. I will discuss this, or what you wish with you, at another time, but not now, in Gascony, while our friend D'Artagnan might be in danger of his life. And I assume it is something about this, and not about my immortal soul's longing for forgiveness, that has put you in this state. Please, leave my immortal soul alone, and speak to my mortal body. I presume you mean you were thinking of religion in Gascony?"

Aramis swallowed back unpronounced words and tried to straighten in his mind what he meant to say and what it signified. It was characteristic of Athos to be able to throw Aramis into complete and muddled confusion, far from the strict rules of thought and logic he'd learned back in his seminary days. And Athos had also a way of bringing up near-blasphemous, and yet fascinating, thoughts, such as whether one had the right to refuse forgiveness from God. And then he expected Aramis not to pursue it.

Aramis let out breath again, this time in a great explosion. "I was thinking about the wars of religion," he said, and as he spoke, he backed up onto a straw pile behind him, and sat on it full force. "And how they wracked this region. And I thought perhaps the whole thing—the Cardinal's interest in Monsieur D'Artagnan, or yet someone's wishing to kill D'Artagnan—might not have its origin in just such a time. That it might be, in fact, the wars of religion by other means."

"You think Monsieur D'Artagnan père was killed because of his religion?" Athos asked, frowning.

"Well, not for sure, but I do think that it might have something to do with that. That it might have something to do with the wars, in some way. That this is why he was working for the Cardinal."

Athos continued to look over the saddle for a moment, and Aramis thought that the older musketeer was dismissing his idea out of hand, which worried him. If Athos didn't listen, who would? Porthos was likely to not believe that anyone could kill for a motive as philosophical and distant as beliefs. And D'Artagnan...He had grown up in this region, rifted with religion and war. He probably would not even think of religion as a motive.

But Athos turned around, from looking at the saddle and, dusting his hands together as though some contaminant might have come from the saddle to them, said, "What did you do about this suspicion of yours, Aramis?"

"I—" Aramis said, and frowned at the saddle. "Why were you looking at the horses and the saddles?"

Athos shrugged. "It matters not. We'll just say that Bayard says the King and the Cardinal sent these to Monsieur D'Artagnan less than a month ago."

"The King and the Cardinal?" Aramis said, looking at Athos in shock, while he tried to imagine the exact conjunction of circumstances that could bring such an unlikely gift from such unlikely quarters. "Surely..."

"No, surely not. Or at least," Athos said, shrugging, "it is possible, of course, that his eminence sent them and said they were from him and the King. This far in the provinces, you know, people often don't know that the King and the Cardinal are not of one and the same mind." Another shrug. "For that matter, even in the capital, this is not often absolutely sure."

"No," Aramis admitted, thinking of the many times when they'd fought for the King only to find that he had united with the Cardinal to reproach them. "But..." He started, feeling that Athos had other suspicions, that he thought something else that he was not saying. Else, why the careful examination of the horses?

"Just an idea I had," Athos said. "If it were possible, I would send Grimaud to Paris to get word on exactly how these horses got here. To find out, at the very least, if any gift of horses was sent to Monsieur D'Artagnan from the capital. Surely, these many horses, traveling across the mountains," he shrugged again.

Aramis understood what he meant. Those many horses, traveling over the mountains would be sure to be remarked. And someone in the capital would know too. "But why is it not possible?" he asked. "We could send Grimaud. We have the money."

Athos sighed heavily. "We were attacked twice on our way here, Aramis. Surely you don't think D'Artagnan is safe now."

"Well, we haven't been attacked since we got here."

Athos waved a dismissive hand. "D'Artagnan has been watched or in our company all the time, has he not?"

"Well, at night he sleeps in another..."

Athos shook his head. "Wing of the house. Yes, but Aramis, I have taken the liberty of recommending Planchet to sleep across the door of his master's bedroom. And our excellent Mousqueton has stood in front of that same door, in a very prominent way. Surely, any malefactor would be afraid of attacking D'Artagnan in his own house when he was thus guarded? It could, at the very least, rouse alarm. And here..." He gestured to include the house in his words. "Someone would be bound to know the attackers, or know whence they came."

"So, you're saying he hasn't been attacked because there hasn't been opportunity."

"To an extent. I've made sure he has at least one of our more bellicose servants with him, or is under their eye, somehow. The one thing I'm sure of, though," Athos said, "is that the longer we stay here, the more likely he will be attacked. Well. The longer we stay here without finding out who the murderer is. As soon as we find out the real killer, the danger should pass. But that means I don't have the week to send Grimaud to Paris, and the week to wait for him to come back. And that's if everything goes well."

Aramis nodded, understanding. "But then, how can we know where the horses came from? And why should it matter?"

"Well, it should matter," Athos said, "because we know Monsieur D'Artagnan said he was working for his eminence, and this is the first possible reward we've seen around here. If we trace it, we can confirm that he was working for the Cardinal or...Or not."

"Of course," Aramis said, finding the flaw in the reasoning. "He might have received his reward from one of the Cardinal's minions, not from the Cardinal himself, you know?"

"Doubtless," Athos said. He leaned against the piled-up saddles, comfortably. "But Aramis, I didn't say my whole goal was to prove they didn't come from Paris. If we establish where they came from, then we can find out if the master of the house was in his eminence's pay or not."

"Oh," Aramis said. "And you were examining the horses because..."

"I wish to be able to describe them by identifiable characteristics to Porthos, to whom I will give the unpleasant chore—or perhaps he finds it pleasant—of speaking to hostelers and farmers hereabouts, and to stable boys too. And finding out where the horses came from." He made a face. "One thing I tell you. I took myself this morning, soon as I was wakened, to that pleasant village we were at last, on the way here. The place we had dinner. And no one recalls these many horses coming through. Save some horses from Monsieur de Comminges, which seem to have been sent from his other estate, where, I am to understand, he breeds a few of these sort of cattle."

"De Comminges," Aramis said, hearing his own voice echo hollow, like a sermon preached in an ancient and deserted church.

"De Comminges," Athos said. "Why? Did the name come up in your investigations?"

"I went to the priest this morning," Aramis said. "Or rather, I went to Mass early morning, at the little church around the corner. I thought perhaps afterwards I could approach the priest and ask questions."

"And did it work?"

"Well, to an extent, though not immediately." He frowned. "You see, D'Artagnan turned up at the Mass too."

"D'Artagnan? By the Blood. Why?"

"When I first saw him," Aramis said, "I thought he was there for the same reason I was. Or at least, I thought he might have discovered something or read something, perhaps in his father's papers, which had led him to believe that his father had been involved in religious strife. And therefore, I thought, was there to talk to the priest and find out how the religious situation was in the region."

"I take it you were wrong in his motives?" Athos said.

"Yes. It turned out he was there simply because Madame D'Artagnan had informed him that his father was killed in front of some witnesses, one of them being the priest. And he was there to check the priest's account."

"And how did that...relate?"

"His father seems to have been drunk or irate, or perhaps mad when he came onto the threshing floor," Aramis said and made a dismissive gesture. "But that is not the whole of it. The thing is, the priest seemed bewildered by Monsieur D'Artagnan's behavior. Oh, he told us it meant nothing, what with the age of the man and all, but...I wondered..."

He sighed. "At any rate, you see, I could not ask the priest about D'Artagnan's father's religion. I told you before—or perhaps I only told Athos—that the praying room Madame D'Artagnan uses has the marks, the spareness of a Protestant meeting room. Which would also explain its existing here, what with the chapel and the church so nearby. But then, if it was a Protestant praying room, why the statue of Saint Quitterie, which is clearly an old statue? And don't tell me statues can be sold and bought. Porthos did. And I know that. But such praying rooms, for such women, are usually...private and close, and they surround themselves with relics and saints that remind them of childhood."

"You know a lot of women and saints," Athos said, in a completely serious manner.

Aramis refused to pursue the bait. "But I couldn't ask any of that in front of D'Artagnan. So I stayed with him and heard the whole description of the duel, as I've told you, and then I left with him, only to backtrack."

"And what did you find in backtracking?" Athos asked.

Aramis frowned. "That is the problem and why I sought you. I scarce knew what I learned. The man, it seemed, was talking around secrets he could not tell, perhaps secrets he learned in confession. Or...or merely gossip, which he was afraid would hurt someone if revealed."

"It can happen," Athos said.

"Undoubtedly. But...oh, it was all maddening."

Another smile slid across Athos's lips. "Let's speak of it, from the beginning. What did he say when you asked him of the D'Artagnans' religion?"

"That Monsieur D'Artagnan's mother, from whom the name D'Artagnan comes, was indeed Protestant, and the last of her line.

She married into the family, bringing her patrimony and, incidentally, converting. And that way, she made D'Artagnan the junior title of the de Bigorres."

"Perhaps she had some cousin, or someone, who thought themselves more entitled to the name and who—"

Aramis nodded. "The priest said no. That all her brothers died in the wars, but..."

"But one cannot be sure, no," Athos said. "It might be worth looking into. But you said it was maddening."

"There were...other..." He looked over his shoulder to determine there was no one close to the door of the stable, and lowered his voice, nonetheless. "Athos, the priest seemed to imply that our friend was perhaps not of...well...that Madame D'Artagnan might have been with child when she got married."

As he heard the words leave his lips, he was horrified at pronouncing them, and even more horrified to hear Athos laugh at them. "Come, come, Aramis," Athos said. "You're not as naive as you look. Certainly, she might very well have been...with child. These things happen."

"No, I know they happen." He smiled a little. "Though it's odd to think of them happening to one's friends, if...if I may say so. I mean, we think of the women with whom we...associate, but not..."

"Not of our friends' mothers, no," Athos said, and made a face that Aramis couldn't quite interpret. "Though you realize that Madame D'Artagnan is probably not much older than I, if she's older at all."

"Well...and there's the other thing. I don't know how to...Well...Madame D'Artagnan seems to be a mystery."

"All women are mysteries," Athos said. "Mysteries that the sane man leaves unsolved."

Aramis permitted himself a smile. Athos's misogyny was too well known to be worthy of more than a smile. "Perhaps so, my friend. But Madame D'Artagnan is more of a mystery than most. She was raised in Paris, the priest said. I don't know how she came by Monsieur D'Artagnan at all. With their age difference, you'd think..."

Athos shrugged. "How does anyone come by anyone else? A cross-country journey, a trip into the provinces, and two traveling parties that meet. Or else, we know that Monsieur D'Artagnan spent sometime in the capital, in the service of the King. Perhaps one of his old army friends had a likely daughter."

"Of course," Aramis said. He let out breath, in frustration. "Oh, I don't know. That is not how it felt to me. There was something more...I can't even begin to explain it. Just the feeling that there was something about her living in Paris that the priest did not wish to discuss."

"It could be nothing but the child on the way, Aramis. You know better than most that many men of the church feel very shy about such things."

Aramis nodded. "But all the same...It left me feeling uneasy. Only you say we don't have time to go to Paris and investigate."

"No," Athos said. "Or at least, that is our last resort, and I would have to somehow take D'Artagnan with us." He frowned again, as if remembering something. "So what was there about de Comminges?"

"Nothing. Or nothing that I can put my finger on, except..." He again exhaled in frustration. He was beginning to understand some of his friend Porthos's problems with words. Now he, who was normally so fluent and quick, seemed to be searching in vain for words and coming up wanting. "Except the priest made it such a point of bringing him into the discussion...as though he expected me to glean something from the mention. He said that Monsieur de Comminges, like the D'Artagnans of old, was Protestant, then Catholic, and then maybe at last Protestant again, and yet his heirs—whom I understand ascended just very recently—were good Catholics." He heard his own voice taper at the end of the sentence, and realized how irrelevant it sounded, said aloud. "I'm perhaps making too much of it," he said, defensively. "But he just made it such a point of bringing the matter up."

He looked up at Athos, expecting his friend to shrug or to look like Aramis had taken leave of his senses. But instead Athos was looking at him, with just the slightest of frowns, like a man concentrating on an object that's not quite visible.

"Perhaps we should speak to the priest again," he said. "Perhaps tomorrow morning."

"You don't think, then," Aramis said, feeling an absurd amount of relief, "that it's all a mare's nest."

"Oh, it might very well be a mare's nest," Athos said. "But I trust your intuition. You've looked into murders before. If you feel that the priest brought de Comminges up in an unwarranted manner, then he probably did. Perhaps it is nothing but the drifting mind of an old man. Or perhaps..."

"Or perhaps...?"

"Or perhaps it is much more."

# Dead Man's Clothes; The Blood Speaks

"**LISTEN** here, Bayard," Porthos said, coming into the courtyard, under the noonday sun, and finding the old servant busy, as it seemed, putting wooden handles onto agricultural implements.

The old man looked up at the redheaded giant's approach. "Monsieur?" he asked with that curious Gascon lilt to the word that Porthos always thought was part accent and part defiance.

"Your master's clothes. Was he buried in them?"

The man stared, dropping the handle he'd been holding in his hand—a polished bit of wood. "My master's clothes? Well...certes we didn't bury him naked."

Porthos, dismayed, realized he had, yet again, let his treacherous tongue betray his meaning. "No, no, man. I don't mean you'd have him buried naked." He crossed himself at the thought. "Forbid the idea. No. I know you buried him dressed as a Christian. The question is, did you bury him in the clothes in which he died?"

"Oh," the old man said, comprehension dawning. "No, monsieur. Only because, you know, the clothes were all over blood and you can just imagine the yelling at I'd get when my master rose for the final judgment, all dressed in his bloody clothes.

"'Bayard,' he'd tell me, in that tone of voice he used when he was young and I forgot something he needed for the campaigns. 'Bayard,' he'd say, 'what could you have been thinking?'" He shook his head, while his lips twisted in the slightest of smiles, as though remembering his master's ill temper gave him comfort now. "And besides, monsieur, this is the thing, that my master lain for the wake, you know, visible to all, and we'd not want him to make a sad spectacle of himself. So, no. Madame D'Artagnan," he said, pronouncing the name with distinct disapproval, "and Marguerite, themselves, washed him, and I brought him his best suit of clothes."

Porthos nodded, not knowing what else to do and suspecting there were tears just waiting to let loose from the old man's eyes. "Look, Bayard, the thing is...Did you dispose of the clothes he wore when he got wounded?"

"Dispose of...?" The man shook his head. "Well, no, monsieur. I did not. You see, there's some good patches there, and besides, Marguerite thinks that she can wash the blood away. Not, but I think that's foolish, but you see, just because he died in them, doesn't make the clothes unusable. Stained, surely, but the master was always very close with his money and his things, and he would be the last to want us to waste money. So..."

"Has she washed them, yet?"

"No. She says she means to, but the thing is, I don't think she's quite able to yet. Not over her own grief for the master, you know."

"I understand," Porthos said, and indeed, composed his face to the most understanding expression he could manage. "And could you perhaps show me the clothes, Bayard?"

"Why?" Bayard asked, looking straight at him.

Porthos shook his head. "I don't think I can explain it to you, as such. I'm not very good with words. But there's something...strange about your master's death. I think those clothes—the blood on them might help me understand what it might be."

Bayard frowned at him. "But, monsieur. The clothes are all over blood. Thick with it. He was wounded on the neck, where the great vein runs..." And now the tears did come, a shimmer in the man's dark eyes. "My poor master. What a terrible thing. One moment there, and fighting, and the next...well...Monsieur de Bilh and that de Bigorre sent for help, but by the time people got there, he was dead, and no wonder, with a cut to the throat. And his clothes were that soaked."

Porthos nodded patiently. The last thing he wanted to do, in fact, the last thing he thought could help him attain his objective of looking at the clothes, was to get in an argument with the old servant. In his experience such old servitors, attached to ancient houses, were very much dictators when it came to protecting the family from strangers. And this one, clearly, was very attached to his dead master.

"I understand, but, Bayard, both the priest and all...all of them, say he was acting funny when he approached the threshing floor. And I think I found a trail of blood through the fields, approaching the threshing floor. From the...from old Jacques' field," he said, proudly remembering the name the locals had given it.

Bayard stared at him a while, as though trying to figure what game Porthos was playing. Porthos could not entirely blame him. After all, most noblemen were like Aramis or even Athos, quite capable of duplicity, and of having two or three plans, one within the other, in anything they did. But for himself, he'd just confessed the truth, save for involving the peasant woman who might have seen Monsieur D'Artagnan's first fight. And that only because he did not want to expose the woman to any revenge, if any were coming, or even to any gossip.

So he stood his ground and tried to look as guileless as he was. Truth be told, he suspected that he only managed to look as though he had a very severe toothache. But with that, it must have succeeded.

Bayard nodded to him and sighed. "Very well, monsieur," he said. He looked at the sky. "It doesn't look like rain, at any rate, so these tools can stay here without peril of getting wet. If you will come with me."

Turning, he entered the house through a door close by and opposite the one that D'Artagnan had taken into the house the night before. This door led to a lower passage, such that Porthos needed to bow considerably to follow without hitting his head.

The passage was like a dark tunnel with doors opening from it. From what Porthos could see of those doors, he thought that Bayard and Marguerite lived here, in this part of the house, which might very well, at some time, have been storage for grain or provisions. Perhaps the much more abundant provisions, which had doubtless been needed by the house at any time that the bastide was under siege by enemy troops.

Now it was furnished in simple but comfortable style with straightforward furniture probably homemade of pine planks. It reminded Porthos of the homes of his peasant friends when he'd been a boy in his father's domains.

The smell of something savory boiling only added to the hominess. But at the end of the passage, Bayard took a sudden right turn into a tiny room whose walls were covered in shelves. On the shelves, in disarray, lay what seemed to be a broken sword, a couple of broken plates, a leather harness that Porthos suspected would also be found in need of mending, and, neatly folded at the top, a suit of clothes. The smell in the air was thick with sickly sweet odor of rot and old blood.

"I keep things here as I mean to mend," Bayard said. "Plates and such, you know, that I do for my wife. But I put Monsieur D'Artagnan's suit here too, because Marguerite says she won't get to wash it, or not properly, till she can wash outside in the river. She said blood mostly takes soaking, and lot of running water, so I..."

He continued speaking, but Porthos wasn't attending. In front of the shelves there was a battered table, made of little more than planks of pine lashed together.

Porthos reached up for the suit of clothes, unfolded it, laid it on the table. It was very much like the suit that D'Artagnan had worn into Paris six months ago. Faded by much washing, both breeches and doublet showed an ugly russet color that Porthos was willing to bet bore no resemblance to its original color.

Over that color, black splattered—black that had once been blood. And though Bayard had said it was all soaked through, this was not true. Only about a third of it was stained, all over the right side of the body and the right sleeve.

The cut of the doublet itself was like Athos's—in the Spanish manner that had been fashionable in France ten years ago—the type that was tightly laced and molded to the body.

More fashionable, now, was the German sort of doublet, where the fabric flowed more freely and the lacing was less restrictive. But all that meant nothing—not even how up to date Monsieur D'Artagnan might be.

Porthos, who was quite interested in fashion, had been looking around him as they progressed deeper into Gascony. And the deeper they got, the more the Spanish doublets were favored over any other style. Which Porthos supposed made perfect sense, considering how close they were to Spain.

He spread the doublet carefully, and then the breeches. Inside the breeches—there the blood was pooled in patches, as though most of it had come when Monsieur D'Artagnan had fallen down on his own shed blood—was a shirt, where the blood was the same obvious pattern as on the doublet...save for one thing.

On the shirt, in the back, a little to the left side, it was obvious that there was a tiny rip and a small flourishing of blood. Well, small as a way of speaking, as it could not be covered by Porthos's spread out hand. But that flow was quite independent of the other, and the cut in the middle of it could not be denied, thin though it was.

Porthos realized he must have made some sound at the discovery, as Bayard said, "What is it, monsieur?"

"Here," Porthos said, and showed him the small hole.

"It could be the moth," Bayard said, thoughtfully, looking up at Porthos, as though trying to gage how this excuse would be received.

"Well, then, assuredly it's not the moth, for I've looked around this shirt everywhere and there's no other signs of weakness or age, so why would there be a moth hole? In fact, the shirt looks quite new."

"It is. It is, at that, but...but you know, sometimes the moth."

"Leave off with the moth, man," Porthos said, irritably. "Look here." He showed him the stain again. "See how that stain does not touch any of the other stained portions, and how that hole is right in the center of it? I will bet you it speaks of another wound, an earlier one, that made your master bleed all across the fields to that threshing floor."

He picked up the doublet, and examined it in the same area that the shirt had the hole and the stain. There too, against the russet fabric, there was the much darker stain of the blood, and in the center of it a small rent that exactly matched the rent in the shirt. "And then, what are you going to tell me, uh, Bayard," Porthos said, showing him the newly discovered hole. "That the moth with great ability pierced both the shirt and the doublet at the same spot?"

Bayard stared at the doublet a long time. "It does seem as though..." He said. "But what kind of blade would cause that rent? It is so narrow."

"A stiletto," Porthos said, proud to remember the word he'd heard from Athos and Aramis a long time ago. "At least it looks like it to me. There's these three-sided Italian blades, you see, very thin. And they cut on all three sides. And it looks like something like that."

"But why would Italians want to wound my master?" Bayard asked, in shock. "We never fought against Italians. Well, there might have been Italian mercenaries in some armies we fought, but it was all so long ago."

"I don't know," Porthos said. "But the way this blade went in, I'd say there's a good chance it pierced your master's heart. And doubtless made him lose enough blood that he was already dying as he came onto Monsieur de Bilh on the threshing floor."

"But..." Bayard protested. "If it pierced his heart, would it not have killed him?"

Porthos shrugged. "Not always. There's times when you put a sword, even, through someone's heart and they still have it in them to turn and come at you." He shook his head. "I used to teach fencing, see, and I always told my students not to ignore the adversary when he had fallen. There are people capable of such stamina, that, even though they are already dying, they will turn and kill the adversary with their last breath. So...you see..."

"Monsieur was very strong," Bayard said. "Very strong. They used to call him the horse of Gascony, you know, when we were young and in the King's service. Because he was like one of those horses who keep moving and fighting long after they should have collapsed."

He looked at Porthos, miserably. "But that means...my master was murdered, does it not? Or does anyone duel with these...still..."

"Stilettos," Porthos said. "And not to my knowledge. Besides, look here, the cut is at the back of your master's suit."

"So it is," Bayard said, disconsolately. "Mark my words, it was at that woman's orders."

## An Unexpected Fight; The Eyes of Adulthood; What Man Knows His Own Mother

**I'M** *going to see the man who killed my father,* D'Artagnan thought. And the thought so consumed him that he barely paid attention to anything. Having left his cousin Edmond behind, he rode down a country path in de Bilh land. The path wound amid denuded vineyards till it came to a small pine woods, which encased the packed dirt ribbon as if it were a green tunnel.

Alone with the sound of his horse's hooves and his own thoughts, D'Artagnan thought mostly on how many times he had seen de Bilh drinking with his father, and how unlikely he'd have thought it, had anyone told him his father would die at the tip of de Bilh's sword.

It seemed senseless. It seemed insane. But then he thought of the note in his father's drawer, *It was by my order and for the good of the kingdom.* Could whatever his father had been doing have involved de Bilh? And if not...what could it have been?

And then he thought of his mother saying de Bilh called her Marie. He didn't want to think about it, and looked at the ground under his horse's hooves, there, in the darkest part of the little woods, where only a thin yellow light filtered through the overarching branches of the palm trees above him.

It was a lucky thing his thoughts led him to look down just then. Had he not done so, he would have missed the movement of shadows on the ground of the path. There were three shadows, all armed. And all moving. Towards him.

He jumped from his horse—not wanting it injured—and took his sword out of its scabbard in a fluid motion.

The men were on him before he could see what they looked like. He had an impression of blurred motion—of cloaks and plumed hats and swords. The swords were the most immediate impression, one that intruded glaringly on his attention, as a blade thrust close barely allowed him the time to turn and parry. And then there was the one on the other side, aiming for his heart.

All the while he was aware of the third man, maneuvering at the edge of trees to get behind D'Artagnan.

D'Artagnan had neither illusions that these people would follow honorable duel rules, nor an extra hand with which to stop an attack by ambush.

*It's de Bilh,* he thought. *He will kill me as he killed my father.*

Aloud, he screamed, "To me, musketeers! To me of the King!" His voice echoed strangled and desperate in his own ears and it was foolish to even call out, of course. Who would hear him here? Who would come to his help here?

His friends were at the house, having no idea where he'd gone. He'd not even brought Planchet with him. He would die here, alone, and add the mystery of his death to that of his father's death.

And no doubt perfectly respectable people would swear he'd come upon de Bilh and drawn his sword and challenged the man to a duel without provocation. It would go down in town legend as the curse of the D'Artagnans.

All while these thoughts ran through his head, he turned and parried and fought. All the while in his mind, he gazed on his own death. And the man was still sneaking around behind him, and there was nothing he could do. Nothing.

There was a sound of wood hitting something to his left where the man had been when he'd last glimpsed him. Dancing back from a thrust, D'Artagnan risked a look. Where the enemy had been there was now an amiable giant holding a three branch.

"Mousqueton!" D'Artagnan shouted. "You here?"

"Yes, monsieur," Mousqueton said. "Monsieur Athos said I should guard you. At a distance."

"Ah, well, then," D'Artagnan said, not absolutely sure what he meant by it, as he turned his attention to the two men coming at him with swords. Mousqueton still could not help him here, or not without running too much of a risk. Tree branches were not the nimblest tool to defend oneself from swords, and if he wadded in with just that, Mousqueton was likely to get hurt.

At least he wouldn't be stabbed in the back, D'Artagnan thought, and there would be a witness of sorts.

And then running through the trees came a third man, sword drawn. D'Artagnan could see Mousqueton lift his branch, and he himself thought, *not another one!*

Only the man coming in screamed, "To me, villains," and fell on one of the men attacking D'Artagnan, forcing the man to turn and give him his full attention—and leaving D'Artagnan with only one adversary.

It wasn't till D'Artagnan had dispatched that one adversary that he looked at the man calmly pulling his sword out of a fallen foe and recognized the man he'd come to see.

"Monsieur de Bilh!" he said, surprised.

The older man, perhaps a finger's width shorter than D'Artagnan and with white threads in his black hair, sheathed his sword and, taking off his hat, bowed to D'Artagnan. "At your service, Henri. I beg your pardon about this ambush on my own lands." He looked down at the face of the man he'd killed. "Is it anyone you know, Henri? Because they don't seem to me to be locals."

D'Artagnan looked down at the face of the man he'd killed. It had a brutish quality beneath the wide open eyes with the expression of incredulity stamped on them. And it was no one he knew. Not from his homeland and not from Paris either.

"No one I know," he said.

"Well, there it is," de Bilh said. "We'd best talk about it inside. We'll tell your servant—"

"He's not my servant. He's my friend, Porthos's servant."

"Is that so? And where did he get to?"

Just then there was the sound of a horse behind D'Artagnan, and he turned to see Mousqueton, leading his horse and another, that he'd presumably ridden. "He'd run a little. Got spooked," Mousqueton said. "But I've got him back."

"Thank you, Mousqueton."

"Give the reins of his horse to Monsieur D'Artagnan, then," de Bilh said. "And then bring these corpses to the house on yours. I'll tell my people to dispose of them. Your master—Monsieur D'Artagnan and I shall be in the house."

And with that announcement, he turned and led D'Artagnan, who led the horse, down the rest of the path, till it opened into a large yard. A stable boy came running from the stable to the left side of it, and took D'Artagnan's horse.

And though there was no reason for it—de Bilh had, after all, helped him, possibly saved his life—D'Artagnan thought that this would be an easy way to dispose of him; that this was all that de Bilh meant to do.

"Come," de Bilh said. And led him into the house through a nearby door then up a flight of stairs to a room comfortably appointed with tables, chairs and sofas.

"I heard you'd come to town," de Bilh said, sinking into one of the yellow upholstered chairs and gesturing D'Artagnan to take the other, across a broad, low table. "And I did wonder if you meant to visit or..." He looked up at D'Artagnan, vaguely alarmed, as though an idea had just occurred to him. "By the Mass," he said. "You don't mean to challenge me for a duel, do you now?"

D'Artagnan shook his head, then sighed. "I came...to ask you about that last duel with my father. And then they attacked me."

"I'm sorry again. It was in my lands. I had no idea such things happened in my lands, or I'd have..." He shook his head. "I beg your pardon most earnestly."

D'Artagnan mumbled something—even he was not sure what.

"And no idea who they might be," de Bilh said. "It's come to that, then? Unknown men attacking people on my land..."

He seemed to be speaking to himself more than to D'Artagnan. A servant came in bearing a tray with a bottle of wine and two cups. De Bilh looked at the bottle for a long time. "Are you fond, then, of our local wine, boy? Your father never said."

D'Artagnan nodded. "My father...I meant to ask you...my father..."

Monsieur de Bilh stopped, mid opening the bottle, and sighed. "Ah, your father. You know, I've been wondering all along what to tell you about that, and more than a little afraid you'd challenge me to a duel. Not that I don't hold my own with a sword, but i' faith, boy, I have no wish to fight you."

"No," D'Artagnan said, his voice sounding hollow and as though echoing from a long way off. "No. Everyone tells me not to duel for it, from the priest to my cousin Edmond. But I confess...I never had any intention to duel you." He looked up. "I don't know why everyone seems to think I'm such a hothead, forever in search of people to challenge to a duel."

De Bilh looked up and a reminiscent look crossed his eyes. "D'Artagnan...your father, he said that in your first day in Paris you challenged three musketeers to a duel and you won too."

"Well, I—" D'Artagnan started, feeling as though he should explain that he hadn't exactly won so much as taken the musketeers' side against the guards of the Cardinal. But he couldn't quite remember what he'd told his father in that first letter from Paris. It seemed like years ago since the young, naive D'Artagnan had written to tell his father of the wonders of the capital. And it didn't seem worth explaining.

"He told that story over and over again," de Bilh said, offering D'Artagnan the mug, and smiling at him. "You'd never seen anyone so proud as he was of you."

D'Artagnan nodded and took a sip of the wine, only afterwards thinking that it might very well be poisoned. But if that were the fact, it was an odd poison that left no trace of flavor in the beverage. He took another sip. "My father..." he said. "The duel..."

"Oh, it wasn't a duel," de Bilh said. "I know what people call it, but it wasn't that. It was more of an accident. Henri, I swear on my own life I was just trying to stop him attacking me. And I'm still not sure that he wasn't attacking me in jest."

"In jest?" D'Artagnan asked.

"Well, surely, in jest. You remember the times he would pursue you or me, or one of the servants, three times around the yard, with his sword, only to sheathe his sword and laugh like a loon when at last he had us cornered."

D'Artagnan nodded. He remembered. He remembered his father laughing and joking. He could not believe he would never again play that game with any of them.

"But then your father was attacking blindly," de Bilh said. "And he threw himself at my sword, Henri. Threw himself. And that's more than any of his playing."

"Yes," D'Artagnan said, and, again, his voice echoed hollow. "The priest thinks that perhaps he had something go wrong with his brain. Fell and hit it or simply...something went wrong."

De Bilh looked surprised. "I'd give something to know that it was so," he said. "Else I'll have to carry the remorse of his death with me my whole life, without even understanding why he felt the need to attack me, or why..." He shrugged.

There didn't seem to be anything else to say. Little though he'd said, de Bilh had confirmed what both the priest and Edmond had said. There was only so much that D'Artagnan could doubt the memories of all who'd been present.

And yet...and yet..."On the way here," he said, taking another swig of the wine, "I was attacked twice, by parties of ruffians. Do you have the slightest idea why?"

De Bilh shook a little and looked stunned. "Attacked?" he said. "Well, there are bandits—"

D'Artagnan shook his head. "Not like that. These people were after me, personally and particularly. They wanted to kill me. They ignored my friends, unless my friends attacked them. And in the last hostelry in which we stayed, they drugged my friends and would have drugged me but for an accident of circumstance. And they said they were sent to cut the throat of the dark-haired one—which was almost certainly myself."

"The devil," Monsieur de Bilh said, staring at D'Artagnan not so much in disbelief but as though he couldn't think of an explanation for what D'Artagnan was relating. "Are you sure then?"

"As sure as I am of breathing. That, by itself, almost makes me wonder if my father...Well. At the time I thought my father had been murdered and the whole simply disguised as a duel."

De Bilh looked shocked. He opened his mouth, then closed it, only to open it again. No sound emerged. He shook his head. "The devil," he said again, at last. "You thought I'd murdered your father? Murdered my oldest...almost my only friend?"

D'Artagnan sighed. "I don't know what I thought. But it was possible, you know, that you hadn't murdered him, that he'd been murdered by someone else who, somehow, convinced you to take responsibility and my cousin and Father Urtou to attest to it."

"But no," de Bilh said, his voice still echoing of shock and surprise. "No, Henri. In a way I wish it were so. It would be easier, truly, to know I'd nothing to do with his death, even if I had to lie over it. But no. He threw himself at my sword. It went in his neck, before I had the time to avert the blow."

"Could he have been poisoned?" D'Artagnan said. "I mean, on that hostelry they gave us a sleeping potion. Perhaps they gave my father some herb or something that caused him to—"

"Attack me? Possible. You'll have to ask your mother what he ate that day, and perhaps where he went before he came upon me on that threshing floor. If he stopped at the tavern in the morning and had something to eat, perhaps..." His voice trailed off. "At least that would explain it, D'Artagnan, if he'd been poisoned and was half out of his mind."

D'Artagnan nodded. It was possible. It was possible this would be the sort of poison that made people see things and attack people without knowing who they were attacking. "Who...My mother says that my father was working for his eminence."

De Bilh ran his fingers through his well-trimmed, salt-and-pepper beard. "Yes, Marie told me that too. I'll be damned if I know of what she could be talking though."

"Marie..." D'Artagnan said, and to de Bilh's uncomprehending stare. "You called my mother Marie!"

"Oh...er?" Monsieur de Bilh looked surprised for a moment, only to laugh, suddenly. "But, Henri," he said, his blue eyes sparkling with mirth, "I've always called your mother Marie. Why, I knew her when she was just a little girl, just like I knew you."

His laugh echoed perhaps just a little false. Or at least D'Artagnan could have convinced himself of that. On the other hand..."Where did my mother grow up?" he asked, in sudden urgency.

"Where? Why, Paris of course."

"Paris?" D'Artagnan asked, in confusion. He'd never asked his mother, but she spoke with a Gascon accent and, in fact, spoke the local dialect with the best of them. He knew she'd spent some time in a convent as a young woman, but he didn't know where, nor why. He'd assumed she'd been boarded, as girls often were, to learn some letters and sewing, before she was married. "And her people...?"

"All dead now," de Bilh said, and nodded, perhaps a little too enthusiastically. "All dead. That's why she never told you of when she was young, I'd wager. But yes, I knew her. Her father..." And here, he hesitated, as he had hesitated when he'd mentioned D'Artagnan's father. "I was very young, you see, and her father was...a very good friend of mine."

It all made no sense. D'Artagnan shook his head ruefully. Until now, he'd never had any curiosity about his mother's people—parents, or other relatives. In a Gascony crisscrossed by wars and treasons, it wasn't so unusual for a still-young woman to have no living relatives. He'd thought—if he thought about it at all—that his mother had been an orphan and raised in a convent, perhaps. And that her marriage to his father had been arranged in some way. "How did she come to meet my father?" he asked suddenly. "Was it while he was in Paris?"

He'd asked it before he realized that would be impossible. His father was that much older than his mother. A good twenty years at least. Though D'Artagnan wasn't absolutely sure—his father didn't like talking about it—he thought his father must have been over sixty. And he'd left the capital and settled down long before Marie D'Artagnan could even had been walking on her own, much less of marriageable age. She might very well not even have been born by then.

"No," de Bilh said, his words following as confirmation on D'Artagnan's thoughts. "No. Your father was married for a long time to...a lady his parents had arranged for him to marry." He smiled distantly. "We married at around the same time, in fact. Married women that our parents had arranged for us to marry."

"And he was unhappy?" D'Artagnan asked.

"Uh?" de Bilh shook his head. "I don't believe so. Amelie was a good woman. Perhaps a little insipid, but...enfin. One doesn't marry a woman to be entertained. And she was a good wife to him, just like my Jeanne was to me. Neither of us had children. Well, at least not for a very long time. And then Amelie died giving birth, when she finally did conceive." He looked into his wine a long time. "It was all..." He shrugged. "But your father and I stayed friends for a long time, and that was how..." Here he looked at D'Artagnan, and his gaze for a moment looked as though a brilliant idea had just occurred to him. "That was how I came to arrange his marriage to your mother."

"You arranged their marriage?" D'Artagnan asked, surprised. "But..."

"Well, nothing for it, you know. She was a young and penniless woman, who'd just lost both her parents. And he was a widower and direly in need of descendants and an heir to take over his lands on his death...though death was very far from both our thoughts, then, of course."

"Of course," D'Artagnan said, as he finished his cup of wine. He wouldn't say it. He couldn't say it without courting that duel that he'd promised several people he would not undertake. But, in that moment, he was sure as he hoped to be sure of salvation that de Bilh was lying to him.

Why would he be lying about D'Artagnan's mother? Why would he be lying about having arranged her marriage to his old friend?

D'Artagnan didn't know. The thought crossed his mind that his mother might be involved with de Bilh. The idea, monstrous and horrifying, hung over D'Artagnan's mind, not quite expressing itself.

He drank his wine and wished he could wake; prayed that all this, from his father's death on, was just a nightmare.

# The Tale of the Blood; Where D'Artagnan Ponders Unknown Relatives; The Cardinal's Methods

**"SO,** you see," Porthos's voice said, earnestly from within the recesses of Bayard's quarters. "He was wounded before he was wounded."

"Porthos, you make no manner of sense," Aramis's voice echoed, after his. "What can you mean by that?"

"I mean, see..."

D'Artagnan hesitated a moment, outside the door into the rooms that Bayard and his wife used as their more or less private residence. It wasn't, properly speaking, his home. Or at least, his father and mother were always scrupulous about respecting the servants' privacy. But then, D'Artagnan, from his youngest years, had been in and out of their rooms as though he were their own. And he couldn't imagine Bayard's reaction to his invasion being more than a mild surprise.

And besides all that, his friends were in there. And they were talking...D'Artagnan shook his head. They were talking of someone being wounded before he was wounded—which sounded much like what D'Artagnan had talked about with de Bilh. His father...

D'Artagnan hastened down the long, dark corridor.

"This blood stain?" Aramis said. "Couldn't it have been from his mortal wound?"

And on those words, D'Artagnan walked in on them and, for a moment, they all stopped talking and stood, as though caught at fault.

They were in Bayard's *officine* at the back of his lodgings—a small windowless room with a table and some shelves that were usually full with things to mend or modify for his wife or D'Artagnan's parents.

Right now, there was a suit of clothes on the table. Bayard was holding a lantern over it. And around the table, clustered as though they were surgeons examining a dead body, were his three friends.

"Ah, D'Artagnan," Porthos said, recovering first. "You see, we were examining—"

Athos stepped in front of the table. "It is nothing, D'Artagnan. There's no reason to distress yourself with—"

"I want him to see it," Porthos said, sounding mulish. "D'Artagnan has a good mind, and you'll see he'll agree that—"

"Porthos, my friend," Aramis interrupted. "I've told you this before, but you have all the natural sensibility of a donkey."

"Bah, sensibility," Porthos said. "All I say is if D'Artagnan sees the bloodstains, he will see that—"

"And at that I might have overestimated it," Aramis said, softly.

Meanwhile, D'Artagnan's mind had worked. Porthos wanted him to see something pertaining to blood. There was a suit of clothes on the table. And he'd heard Porthos say his father had been wounded before he was wounded. From which D'Artagnan would deduce that his father had come wounded to the fatal duel—which, just as well as an issue of the brain or poison, could explain his behavior on that threshing floor.

While his friends argued and protested, D'Artagnan stepped forward, feeling as though he were in a dream, and, gently, pushed Athos aside.

"D'Artagnan!" Aramis said.

"Are you sure?" Athos asked.

But D'Artagnan, faced with one of his father's familiar suits, covered in what was presumably his father's blood, turned mute, questioning eyes to Porthos. "Porthos," he said. "What do you mean he was wounded before he was wounded?"

"Oh, you heard that?" Porthos said, immensely pleased. "Yes, look here—see that bloodstain? It's wholly unconnected to the others."

"But the blood might have...poured that way, somehow," D'Artagnan said, numbly. "Deflected...somehow."

"Well, then, it didn't," Porthos said. "Couldn't have. Look here." He lifted the suit.

Though the smell of old blood was overpowering, there was another smell. It was a smell for which D'Artagnan had no name, but which was as familiar to him as the smell of burning fire; the smell of food cooking; or any of the smells that he'd known from childhood. It was his father's smell.

He could remember being very young—he couldn't have been much more than two—and his father traveling somewhere. D'Artagnan didn't remember any of the details, if indeed he'd ever known them. But he remembered—fully in the charge of his mother and Marguerite—desperately missing his father. He remembered sneaking into his father's room and putting his face on his father's suit. The smell from that suit was the same smell that now came from this suit—the echoes still clear even through the stench of old blood.

His eyes swimming with tears, he tried to concentrate on what Porthos was showing him, in the center of the bloodstain. And there was, as Porthos spread the fabric with his hand, just a tiny cut, there.

"There's the like in the doublet," Porthos said. "In the exact same place, so don't tell me it's moth."

It didn't look like moth. "No," D'Artagnan said. "It is not moth."

"What is more," Porthos said, with a hasty look at Bayard, "I went around here, and talked to the peasants, you know. And there's a woman, Louise, in the farmhouse that way"—he pointed. "Outside the walls—"

"Louise Boulanger?" Bayard said. "In the new farm?"

"Might be," Porthos said, as usual not resenting that a servant introduced himself in the conversation, though D'Artagnan noted that Athos raised his eyebrows.

Porthos shrugged and went on, "She told me that she can see the fields from her attic, and, on the day of the duel, she saw a man come and...come up behind your father and touch him with something. She said at the time she couldn't understand, and thought the man had just touched your father with a stick...But I'm sure that wasn't it. You see, this cut and the blood...are on his back."

"But that would be right through his heart," D'Artagnan said. "How could—"

"Men do, sometimes, if they're very strong," Porthos said. "Survive even that type of injury."

"And your father was strong, monsieur," Bayard said.

D'Artagnan put his hand out to support himself on the edge of the table. "You...certainly you can't possibly...Who...Murdered? My father? Who would want to murder him?"

To his mind came the voice of de Bilh calling his mother Marie and saying he'd known her from a child. But he couldn't believe that his mother was guilty. He'd rather suspect himself.

Oh, his mother was not an angel, and not perfect. And she and his father argued—mostly because everyone, sooner or later, argued with Charles D'Artagnan. His very best friends said he derived more pleasure from a good argument than from just about anything else. But D'Artagnan remembered the looks they traded—by the fireside in the evening, or when his father walked in on his mother suddenly. He remembered the way their eyes softened and widened when they looked at each other.

No. She could not have harmed him. She could not have betrayed him.

"I don't know," Porthos said, softly, his words penetrating through the fog of what seemed to be a raging argument in D'Artagnan's own mind.

"The priest said your mother's people came from Paris?" Athos said. "Perhaps someone...perhaps..."

"One of my mother's relatives?" D'Artagnan said, looking up. "Why would he want to kill me? Or my father?"

"Well, you know..." Athos said. "If they live in Paris, it is possible they work for the Cardinal. And if they work for the Cardinal..." He shrugged. "Killing your father might be a way to get you to leave the city and come to Gascony." He smiled a little. "And leave the four inseparables reduced by one."

Even if D'Artagnan could—which he couldn't—believe he was so essential as to inspire the Cardinal to plot that way, it made no sense. "But...but my father had a...one of those notes from the Cardinal."

He realized from the looks on their faces that it was the first time they heard of this.

"A safe-conduct?" Athos asked.

"In his locked trunk, in his office," D'Artagnan said. "With...a lot of other things."

"Monsieur D'Artagnan worked for the Cardinal," Bayard said, as though he suspected them all of being less than sane. "I've told Monsieur Athos that the Cardinal and the King have sent horses for him. Why would you think the Cardinal would want to murder my master?"

"It wouldn't be the first time his eminence disposed of his own agents that way," Porthos said.

Before Bayard could speak—though he had opened his mouth and was obviously intent in defending the man whom D'Artagnan's own father had called a great man—Aramis said, "But it's not even necessarily so. I mean, just because you found a safe-conduct, D'Artagnan, it doesn't follow that it was given to your father. Those all are addressed to the bearer. Perhaps your father found it. Or perhaps he got it from someone in a duel. I know your mother believed that he worked for the Cardinal." He pronounced it as though he were saying he worked for Satan. "And I know Bayard here thinks he was paid in horses, but there are other explanations for all of it. And your mother and Bayard might have misunderstood his intent too."

"I didn't miss—"

"Or he might have been making a jest," Aramis said. And this time Bayard was silent. "The thing is, D'Artagnan, of the two times you were attacked, the first one was indisputably by guards of his eminence. And the second it was, without doubt, the kind of riffraff that his eminence is likely to hire."

"Three times," D'Artagnan said. "I was attacked three times." He told them of the attackers outside de Bilh's home, all the while feeling as though his head were swimming and this weren't quite real. Couldn't be quite real. "But those too..." he said. "Might very well be the type of men that his eminence is likely to hire. They weren't locals, and they were...Well...I don't think they would have scrupled to kill me by ambush or in secret. If I hadn't seen their shadows as they approached...I think they would have killed my horse, and then me, while I was stunned." He shook his head. "As it was...One of them was sneaking around towards my back when Mousqueton—who says you sent him, Athos—killed him with a blow from a tree branch."

"Very handy that way, Mousqueton," Porthos said.

D'Artagnan nodded. "So yes, they could have been sent by his emi-nence." In his heart of hearts he wanted to believe that. Richelieu had been his sworn enemy since his first day in the capital. He'd tried to kill or capture D'Artagnan's friends by various methods, the latest one being to send those totally hapless guards after them.

He could have no love lost for D'Artagnan. But it made no sense. Try as D'Artagnan might, a lot of it still made no sense.

His mother was either the last one of her line or she wasn't. If she was, what relatives, near or far, could have been convinced to serve the Cardinal? And if she wasn't, what family did she have? What was their station?

It came to him, almost as a flash, that perhaps his mother was the last heiress to some great fortune. Sometimes, the way the noble houses tangled and twisted and—suddenly—died off, it was possible to have relatives you'd never heard of.

Perhaps his mother had rich and powerful relatives who'd died leav-ing her a fortune of which she was quite unawares.

From all D'Artagnan had heard about the Cardinal's methods in the capital, it would not be unheard of for his eminence to dispose of an heiress before she knew she was such and to claim her estate as his own.

"I must talk to my mother," he said. And stumbled out of the room, towards sunlight and air. And from there, into the main house, in search of answers.

# Madame D'Artagnan's Confusion; Where Relatives Aren't Exactly Relatives; The Impossibility of Making Women Speak

**"MAMAN,"** D'Artagnan said, coming upon his mother in one of the upstairs hallways. She was sitting on one of the stone window seats that protruded from the wall on either side of the broad window—allowing someone to sit with a view of the outside or plenty of light.

Light was the material consideration in this case. His mother was working at white fabric, embroidering it in light colors. She looked up from her work and for a moment, for just a moment, D'Artagnan would have sworn she was on the verge of tears.

But she blinked, and smiled dazzlingly at him. "Ah, son," she said. "Come sit." And pointed on the other seat beside the broad window.

D'Artagnan sat. The window was glazed in tiny panes set in a lead frame. Through the uneven, thick glass he could see the fields outside, and villages, all of it looking like it was underwater.

"You left very early," his mother said. "Before I was up."

"I went to Mass," he said, impatiently.

"Ah, that must be a new habit from Paris," she said. "Going to the early Mass and on a weekday yet."

He didn't rise to the bait. True, he'd never been afflicted with an excess of piety and was rarely known to make an effort to attend more than the Sunday Mass—and that one often midmorning at the larger church.

But this was not the time to allow his mother to tease him about the lazy habits he'd left behind when he'd left the house. And it was not the time to allow her to indulge in motherly reminiscences of his stubbornness either. Instead, D'Artagnan spoke quickly, before he could lose his courage, "*Maman*, did you grow up in Paris?"

She startled, then laughed a little—a laughter that seemed out of place in someone who was pale from crying; wearing all black; and in whose eyes, tears shone, still. "Yes, Henri, I did. Remember I used to tell you stories when you were very little?"

"No, you told me stories of the convent," he said.

"That too," she said. "But surely I told you stories of the capital, as well, and of what it was like to grow up in a big city."

He shook his head impatiently. "No. Not that I remember. I don't remember your mentioning your mother or father, ever."

"Oh." She shook her head. "No, I wouldn't have mentioned them. You see...I never knew either of them."

"How not? Not know your own parents?"

"My mother died at my birth and my father...And my father shortly after, Henri. So, you see, there was not much to know. I grew up with some distant cousins, who brought me up as if I were their own."

"And are they still alive?" he asked.

Marie D'Artagnan shrugged. "I don't know. It's been a long time, and, you know, the parents died there too, and I haven't kept up my acquaintance with their children."

"Acquaintance? They raised you!"

She laughed a little again, as though his outrage amused her. "Well, it is not that simple, you know. They raised me, it is true, when I was very little. But at six, I was sent to the convent as a boarder."

"So you could learn your letters?" D'Artagnan asked.

"That," she said, in tones of great patience. "And I think they hoped I would have a religious vocation, since I didn't have any other relatives or..." She shrugged. "They always said it was what my father wished me to do."

"But your father was dead," D'Artagnan said. And remembered de Bilh saying her parents had only died just before her wedding.

She frowned a little. "Well, yes, but they said it was his last wish, and who was I to deny his last wish? But you know, I never professed. A lot of the other girls professed at twelve or so, but I never did. I felt it wasn't quite right and that I'd prefer marrying and having children." She smiled at him. "Which, as you see, is what I've done."

"But you speak Gascon!"

"Oh, yes. My parents were from Gascony. As were my distant cousins. And so, you see, I speak Gascon, though I had to become familiar with it again after I married your father."

"And how did you marry my father?"

"I met him and fell in love with him and he offered for my hand," Marie D'Artagnan said. She looked confused. "And then we married."

"No, but how did you come to meet him, if you were in a convent, I presume in Paris?"

"Oh...some...some friends of his had mentioned me and he came to meet me."

D'Artagnan chewed the corner of his lip. There were already enough contradictions between his mother's stories and Monsieur de Bilh's. And she didn't seem to remember that de Bilh had arranged the marriage.

And yet, it was all capable of a very simple explanation. Perhaps de Bilh had forgotten that she lived with guardians and not parents. Or perhaps because she was in the convent then, and he was talking to guardians, he wasn't sure exactly of the relationship between them. And it was possible his mother truly didn't remember how she'd come to meet her future husband. Perhaps the dazzle of meeting Charles D'Artagnan had driven every other thought from her mind. Perhaps. He'd been that much bigger than life, a man who attracted attention wherever he went.

Or perhaps she'd been Monsieur de Bilh's sweetheart before settling for Monsieur D'Artagnan. Perhaps that had been her big romance. And perhaps it had been through his agency—intentional or not—that they met. In which case it made perfect sense for her to refuse to tell the story to her son. It would also account for the sudden flame of blush putting roses in her otherwise mortally pale cheeks.

And yet...

"What was your cousins' name?" D'Artagnan asked.

She started to open her mouth, then closed it. "It was so long ago," she said softly. "What can it all matter, Henri?"

"It can matter enough," D'Artagnan said. "There might be an inheritance on that side, something the Cardinal wants?"

Madame D'Artagnan smiled, a rueful smile. "There is no inheritance, Henri. These are fairy tales."

"If you don't tell me their name, why should I believe you?"

"I can't tell you their name. It is not my secret."

"Secret what? That they harbored an orphan?"

"No," she said, her voice strangled. "No. You don't know. I can't tell you. It is not my secret."

"Well, madam," D'Artagnan said, standing up and disciplining himself to speak coldly, as though this were not his mother and as if her eyes were not trembling and full of tears. "Then you may congratulate yourself on keeping your secrets, even if your secrets caused your husband's death and may very well cause mine."

"My husband's death? They never did. And yours?"

"I've now been attacked three times since my father died," D'Artagnan said.

And now her confusion became alarm. Madame D'Artagnan rose, putting her embroidery down on the seat. She rose and she put her hands on D'Artagnan's shoulders. "You must go, son. You must leave. I tried to tell you before, but it is not safe for you in Gascony. You must leave. Now. This moment. Don't wait. Take your friends and go, back to Paris."

"Why should I go back to Paris, madam? Why don't you tell me that?"

"I can't tell you," she said.

"Yes, I see," he said, struggling to keep his hot temper in check and managing to sound—or at least he hoped so—controlled and indifferent. Truth be told, he was copying Athos's manners. "It is someone else's secret and you can't reveal it?"

"Yes. Oh yes." She pressed her hands into his shoulders, slightly. "But you must go. You must go as soon as can be." And turning from him, she took a step away. "I'll tell Marguerite to pack dinner for the four of you and your servants, and I—"

"Don't bother," D'Artagnan said. "I'm not going."

"But you must go. As long as you're in Gascony you'll be in danger."

"Well, in Paris I will be in danger too," he said. "I was attacked first not a day out of Paris."

"You were?" she asked. Then shook her head. "It doesn't matter. If you leave Gascony, no one will have a reason to kill you."

"Why would they have a reason while I am in Gascony? Tell me mother."

But she only shook her head and cried.

"*Maman!* Are you...Is Monsieur de Bilh your lover?"

She looked up, so startled that the tears stopped. Something very much like a gurgle of laughter escaped her lips. "Monsieur de Bilh? Oh, no, that is monstrous."

"Is it?" he asked. "Why? He calls you Marie. He says he knew you from childhood. He says he arranged your marriage with Father. What do you have to say to that?" He stepped forward towards her as he spoke. "Why don't you tell me what's happening? Must you keep me in the dark till I die?"

But she only looked at him, and it was as though her eyes suddenly focused. She nodded to him. "No, of course," she said. "Listen, son, believe I had an affair with no one and that this secret, in which you place so much anxiety, is nothing shameful and nothing pertaining to me. Not truly, at least. If it did have to do with me alone, I'd have told you and be done with it."

"But...But then why do you think I need to leave Gascony lest someone kill me?"

"I think they're confused," she said, as if talking to herself. "Yes, I think it's all confusion." And then, with a sudden, dazzling smile. "Don't worry son. I shall arrange everything."

Looking into her beautiful blue eyes, remembering the tenderness with which she'd gazed at her late husband; remembering her devotion to himself, D'Artagnan could not imagine her as a murderess. And yet, what else could he think?

"Mother, you must explain!" he said. It was almost a wail.

But all she did was shake her head and say, "It would still be safer if you left. But if you insist on not leaving, then I must just take care of correcting the misunderstanding. I must think how." And with those words, she picked up her embroidery and ran down the hallway and into her room.

D'Artagnan, left alone in the hallway, wondered what she meant, exactly, and in what kind of trouble she was still going to get him.

Guilty or not, it was clear to him his mother knew something. And it was equally clear nothing short of a miracle would convince her to tell him.

# The Impossibility of Women; Secrets and Their Keepers; An Unexpected Meeting

**"WOMEN** are impossible," D'Artagnan announced, coming upon his friends in the great salon of the house, where the good Bayard had served them sausage and bread and wine.

Athos only smiled at this statement. It had been his opinion for a long time now that most men would live happier, or at least more tranquil, lives if only they could stay away from feminine wiles.

Looking up at his young friend, whose lips were tightly set in a line, and whose feet moved with the rigidity of someone carefully controlling his legs lest he start kicking things in sheer fury, he waited till Bayard had left the room.

"Your *maman* didn't tell you what you wanted to know, did she?" he asked, when the servant had closed the door behind himself.

D'Artagnan approached the table. "No. She says it's not her secret, but someone else's, and she cannot betray this someone else's secret. She also told me I should go back to Paris because I would be safe there."

Athos thought of Madame D'Artagnan imploring him to take her son back to Paris. He didn't want to share that with D'Artagnan. Instead, he asked, "What did you tell her?"

"That I'd been attacked a day out of Paris and that therefore I hardly thought of the capital as a safe place." He helped himself to the sausage and bread and ate with the appetite of one who was not yet fully grown.

"And yet," he said, between bites of sausage. "I don't believe she meant it, you know, as...I mean...I don't think she's guilty or knows anything about my father's death or...or the people that attacked me. You see...I remember her with my father. She and he were always...Oh." He shrugged, and stuffed a piece of bread into his mouth and chewed it as though it had personally done him harm. "You see...It wasn't like they were in love, you know, like...like young people are in love, but they...they had a great friendship, an underlying understanding and...and their eyes grew soft as they looked at each other."

Athos didn't feel equal to telling his young friend that women could be great actresses. Oh, he'd told him that any number of times, and in many circumstances—but it was too much to expect that he could tell him that about his own mother and not suffer any resentment.

"It's just…" D'Artagnan said, as he took a drink of wine and fell upon the bread again as a wolf upon a deer, midwinter. "It's just that I know she knows something she doesn't think important. And she says…she says she will take care of it, so no one will attack me anymore."

"Well," Aramis said. "You must understand that all women are like children. This is why the church hands them to the stronger hand of men to—"

"I would like to hear you say that to Athenais," Porthos said with a chuckle.

"Porthos, you can't deny that men fell through women. Men fell through the sin of Eve, who…"

And Athos, who had also fallen perhaps through the sin of a woman, but definitely through his own sin also, could not sit there and listen to Aramis's sermonizing Porthos. Instead, he got up and walked towards the fireplace, with no great thought in mind beyond getting away for a while. But there, by the side of the fireplace, hung the portrait of a man in full military uniform of two generations ago. He was tall and blond and blue-eyed and, save for the hair color, looked, in fact, like no one so much as Porthos. Oh, it was not the type of resemblance that denoted a blood relation. Rather, it was just belonging to the same type of man. Tall, blond, bluff. He'd probably—Athos smiled a little—had duchesses and princesses hidden under the homely guises of accountants' wives and maids. And he'd probably enjoyed his food and drink as much as Porthos did.

Porthos and Aramis were well away in a big, rambling argument. Athos heard steps behind him, and then D'Artagnan's voice saying, "Oh. I'd forgotten about that. They must have moved it from upstairs. I wonder why."

"The portrait?" Athos asked. "Whose is it?"

"Oh, my father's. He had it done when he lived in Paris, you know. When he must have been about Aramis's age or thereabouts."

"Your father?" Athos asked, turning around in astonishment, to look at his short, dark, lean friend.

D'Artagnan smiled. "I don't look a thing like him, I know. Or like my mother, either, I suppose. I must take after someone on her side of the family. Perhaps my maternal grandfather. You know…until now I never had any curiosity about her people? But now…"

"When it might be a matter of life and death."

"Yes. I apologize for being so angry when I came in, but it was so frustrating not being able to make her understand that…That no matter what value she put on the secret she's keeping, I would, perforce know more…or at least know if it related to me."

He told Athos of his frustrating conversation with his mother, who corroborated de Bilh's words—or at least close enough to it—and yet with enough discrepancies to be a problem. "But," he said, "I couldn't even get her to tell me the name of the cousins who raised her. What can she think is such a great secret about their family name?"

"Perhaps it is Richelieu," Athos said, with a small smile.

D'Artagnan smiled too, taking the joke as it was intended, then shook his head. "I can't understand any of it."

"Attend, D'Artagnan. Perhaps she doesn't know their name anymore?"

"Why? How would she forget it, if they raised her?"

"No, listen—if they sent her to live in a convent at six, as you said, she might very well not remember their surnames. She would remember perhaps the names she called them by—and it might never have been more than aunt and uncle and cousins."

"But surely..." D'Artagnan said, at a loss. "There would be letters and...and..."

Athos shook his head. Sometimes he forgot how young the boy was. And sometimes he was forcibly reminded. "People who raise an orphan, even one of their own blood, often consider providing for her welfare charity enough and feel no need to keep contact."

"But...why wouldn't she tell me that, then?"

"Perhaps trying to spare you?" he said.

D'Artagnan shook his head, not as though denying it, but more as though expressing confusion. "But if she is...if *maman* is determined to protect me, how am I to find out...I mean, let's suppose the danger does come from her family with or without the Cardinal's intervention—how am I to find out who they are? And how am I to protect myself?"

"We'll need to talk to the priest," Athos said.

"He wouldn't tell me anything before," Aramis said, and Athos realized that Aramis and Porthos too had been listening to the conversation.

"No," he said. "But then, Aramis, it is not your secret nor does it involve you in any way."

"It is possible he doesn't know any more than what he told me," he said.

"And what did he tell you, Aramis?" D'Artagnan asked, his voice pleasant and his dark eyes showing a sparring sort of intensity.

Aramis looked up, his green eyes meeting his friend's for a moment, then looked away. "I went back, as you know...and I asked...well...I wasn't asking about your mother, but she came into the conversation, and he said that your mother came from Paris."

"Paris," D'Artagnan said. "It all accords then."

Aramis inclined his head. "Except that..." He blushed. "He seemed to think there was something irregular about the marriage."

"Irregular?" D'Artagnan asked. "What in the devil can you mean by that? My parents were married. His first wife was dead. I can't—"

Aramis shook his head, but seemed unable to speak.

Seeing D'Artagnan's hand stray to his sword, Athos said, "D'Artagnan, our friend got the impression that your mother was already with child...with you, when the marriage took place."

For a moment, D'Artagnan's hand continued hovering near his sword hilt, while he looked up at Athos with a truculent expression. But then at last he said, "Oh."

"We are all human," Aramis said, piously.

D'Artagnan nodded to the sentiment, without turning. "It doesn't sound like an arranged marriage to me," he said. "But then...perhaps...Monsieur de Bilh only meant that he'd introduced them and thereby arranged their marriage."

"Perhaps," Athos said. But something about all of it bothered him. Something gnawed at the back of his mind, as though he should know it—as though there was some important fact he already knew but was neglecting. He couldn't put his finger on it. It receded before his thought like a rainbow before those who chase it. He shook his head. "At any rate, I thought the priest might know something of her family name—or her relatives before marriage...since she thinks it important not to tell you other's secrets."

"How would he know, if she came from Paris?" Porthos asked.

"You know, the bans will have to have been read here, as well as in Paris," Aramis said.

"Very well," D'Artagnan said, with sudden decision. We'll go see Father Urtou. Perhaps he will consent to tell me what he wouldn't tell either of you."

"There is a good chance," Athos said. "At least if we tell him the...circumstances. And that your father was probably murdered and you stand in danger."

"Very well," D'Artagnan said.

As his friends left the room, Athos lingered behind. He took one more look at the portrait of D'Artagnan's father.

Something about it bothered him, and he couldn't quite put his finger on what. It wasn't that Charles D'Artagnan was a completely different type from Henri D'Artagnan. Lots of fathers did not look like their sons and vice versa. Even the fact that D'Artagnan didn't at all look like his mother made no difference.

Athos knew—would have needed no more than the perusal of his own family's portrait gallery to inform him—how often children looked like an ancestor four or five generations back. And yet, something was not quite right. Perhaps he remembered Monsieur D'Artagnan from somewhere?

He frowned at the big bluff blond in the portrait, with his carefully trimmed blond beard, his luxurious hair, his blue eyes that seemed to dance with sheer joy of living.

He could not pinpoint anything specifically wrong with the portrait. It would come to him, doubtless. And it probably would strike him in the middle of the night, when he would sit up in bed, gasping at the sudden realization.

And it probably would have nothing to do with Monsieur D'Artagnan's murder or with the attacks on young D'Artagnan.

# On Horses and Roads; Neighbors in Gascony; A Great Lord's Hospitality

**RIDING** through the broad, straight roads of the bastide, Porthos thought it a great improvement on Paris. The smiling girls ogling him from the side of the road didn't hurt either.

"I think if you end up staying here, D'Artagnan, I'll have to visit you very often."

They were on horseback, riding slowly through the street, two abreast, Porthos and Athos at the back and Aramis and D'Artagnan in front.

From behind, Athos could see D'Artagnan's shoulders shake. "You will be very welcome to, Porthos," he called out, in such a tone that Athos felt sure the shake had been laughter.

And Athos thought it a good time to talk to Porthos, casting his voice lower than he would if he wished for D'Artagnan and Aramis to hear it. "Porthos," he said.

The redhead turned. Athos half expected him to boom a demand that Athos speak, but Porthos's face held polite enquiry.

"Porthos, I'd like you to...look around and ask at the stables around here. I have a description of some horses. I want you to find from where they might have come. Do you think you could do that?"

"Assuredly, I can do it, but why?"

"They are in Monsieur D'Artagnan's stables and..."

"Ah, the ones that Bayard thinks the Cardinal sent to him?"

"Exactly so. I have a feeling this is not quite right. I'm not absolutely sure, mind you, but I have reason to suspect it."

"Reasons?"

"The way the horses are shod seems local work, but beyond that, no one remembers a caravan of horses passing through."

"Oh. I'll ask then."

"Thank you, Porthos. I'll be glad to give you the list of the horses. I wrote it down." He saw Porthos make a face. Reading was not one of his favorite pastimes. But he could read, and well enough. Particularly when it was only a list of horse characteristics.

"Ah, well met, D'Artagnan," a sonorous voice with a strong Gascon accent called from in front of them.

Athos looked that way to see the dark man they'd first glimpsed when arriving in the region. In contrast to then, when he'd ridden by them as though they'd been the dirt under his horse's hooves, he now looked at them—or at least at D'Artagnan—with something very close to affability.

"Well met. You did not pay us a visit when you first arrived."

"I only arrived yesterday," D'Artagnan called out. "I've had little enough time to visit."

His voice sounded bewildered. Athos had gathered from his conversations with D'Artagnan before that de Comminges was not exactly on visiting terms with any of the neighborhood.

"Are you on an urgent errand, then?" he asked. Just like the time they'd seen him before, the dark-haired man was dressed entirely in black from head to toe. Even his horse was a well brushed, glossy black mare.

"I was going to see Father Urtou," D'Artagnan said. And then, as though realizing that this might not be the most common of errands, "He was present when my father died and there're some details I don't quite understand."

De Comminges lowered his head, not quite a nod, just acknowledgment. "Surely Father Urtou can wait?" he asked. "You can come to my house and drink a glass of wine with me, and tell me the news of the capital. We're both bereaved, you know, for my father died just a week before yours."

"Yes...I've heard," D'Artagnan said. "But..."

"Come, do me the honor. You know that your cousin and I will be getting married soon, and then we'll be as good as family." He made what, in another man, might be an expansive gesture with his black-gloved hand.

Athos, behind D'Artagnan, could not tell him that they might as well comply with this invitation. There was always the chance they'd hear something—some scrap of local gossip—which would help with the crime. But more than that, he had a strong feeling if they didn't go with de Comminges now, de Comminges would insist on accompanying them to Father Urtou's. And then, surely, the good priest would not say anything of any consequence.

As though his thought had struck the wrong person, de Comminges said, "Perhaps I'll accompany you to the priest's, and then you'll consent to come to my house for a glass of wine?"

"No," D'Artagnan said.

It was almost a shout, and he must have realized the impropriety of it, because immediately after, he controlled his voice. "No. We'll come with you now. There is no reason to drag you with us to Father Urtou's or to scare the poor creature halfway to death with the visit of the greatest lord in this region." The way he said it, it was part concession and part praise.

"Ah," de Comminges said, and smiled, a smile that seemed to be part joy and part relief. "Ah, very well, then. If you'll make me known to your friends?"

D'Artagnan, turning his horse sideways, on the street, so he could face both sides at once, said, "Le Comte Sever de Comminges, I'd like to make known to you my friends, Athos, Porthos and Aramis."

Each of the musketeers touched his hat in turn. If de Comminges found their names strange he didn't say anything. His eyes did linger on Athos for a moment, but Athos was used to that reaction. It wasn't that every nobleman knew each other by look—or even by name—but Athos knew his family was old and respected enough that something about his appearance told people he was a nobleman.

"A pleasure, sirs," Sever de Comminges said. "And now, if you will follow me." And, having thus spoken, he turned and set an easy pace, out of the bastide and along the roads of the surrounding countryside.

The day was mild for the winter, a yellow sun beating down warmly upon the denuded fields and the backs of the musketeers, as they left the bastide well behind, crossed a small river, and then rounded one of the ubiquitous local hillocks.

Athos thought the way was too long by far, certainly for a simple drink, but D'Artagnan didn't look alarmed, and therefore Athos held his peace. Presently they came in sight of a vast, sprawling and untidy stone palace.

That it was a palace there could be no argument. It was proclaimed by the vastness of the place, whose outbuildings, from stables to other various dependencies, were far more extensive than all of D'Artagnan's house. In fact it was so vast that Athos, who had recently visited his childhood friend, the Duke de Dreux, at his seat, had to admit this palace was larger than de Dreux's.

On the other hand, it was also more untidy. De Dreux's palace had been built and maintained according to the best educated taste of the time and conforming to the artistic dictates of Greece and Rome.

The de Comminges home conformed to no dictates whatsoever, of good or bad taste, save perhaps the dictates of their consciences or, more likely, the internal drive of their emotions and minds. Low slung, made of stone of varying corners, it had a broad staircase leading to the front door, but it was longer on the south than on the north side, and it was made of stones of different colors.

The owner of the house rode resolutely to the extreme south of the house, where he dismounted and called out something that might be someone's name. Five liveried servants came running out of the stables—wearing black uniforms which looked too clean to ever have been near a stable, much less in it.

However, the five boys took charge of their horses with expert motions, and Athos felt reassured they weren't merely decorative.

"If you'll accompany me, monsieurs," de Comminges said, as he led them up along the side of the building, pointing casually at the part that was a different color. "This is the oldest part of the house. We think it has been here since the time of the Romans. In fact, from some mosaic work on the floor, we believe it was once upon a time part of a Roman villa. It probably belonged to my family, since we've been here ever since the Romans displaced the native Novempopuli. We use this part for storage." He hurried along the house, which Athos could now see represented probably close to two thousand years of building styles.

When they started up the broad staircase to the front entrance, someone opened the oak door and stepped aside, to allow them to pass within.

Inside, the hall was all marble and columns, if not in the best taste of Greece and Rome, at least definitely acknowledging Greece and Rome in its lines and appearance.

De Comminges crossed it, and admitted them into a broad room scattered with chairs upholstered in delicately peach colored silk. "Have a seat," he said. "I will have refreshments brought in."

All along, since they'd entered the house, Athos had the feeling of shadows, scurrying just out of sight, moving this and arranging that. He had a feeling servitors had rushed into this room, just ahead of them, to make sure everything was according to the master's orders.

Now, he noted a shadow detaching from the thicker shadows near the walls to listen to the lord's orders for refreshments.

He could not imagine living like that. In fact, in his most patriarchal moments, in his own domain, he would have been very alarmed had any of his servants lurked in the shadows, waiting to hear his orders.

But Monsieur de Comminges was clearly satisfied with himself and his arrangements, as he seated himself and leaned against his chair, and started talking to them.

Talking to them was the appropriate term, or perhaps talking at them. For someone who'd been so anxious to hear about D'Artagnan's experience in the capital and his news from Paris, he seemed more interested in telling them what the situation was.

"Richelieu is a great man," he said, unselfconsciously branding himself with the mark of their enemies. "He is making France the most powerful country in the world."

Porthos squirmed in his chair like a child having trouble sitting still at church. "And himself the most powerful man in it," he grumbled.

"Perhaps," de Comminges said. "But surely his diligence bears reward. Of course, I do not approve of his jumping ahead of so many men of higher rank, but sometimes sheer intelligence and bravery must be acknowledged."

"Or at least intelligence and effrontery," Aramis said, between his teeth, just loud enough to be heard, just low enough that it couldn't be acknowledged.

De Comminges didn't seem to take offense—he also didn't appear to see any humor in their comments—instead, he allowed his dark, penetrating eyes to sweep to Aramis. "Well, perhaps, but you must admit he did put an end to the wars of religion, and he's doing remarkably sound work in clearing off the last few pockets of dissent.

"You surprise me," Athos said, spying his chance to move the conversation away from the Cardinal and the gauche and provoking comments his friends were quite capable of making.

"I do?" de Comminges asked, looking at him surprised.

"Yes, with your talk about his putting down the religious dissent. Surely you must know, his eminence has practically eradicated the last Protestant nobility."

De Comminges looked at him puzzled. "And why should I object to that?"

"I was under the impression your lordship's father had been Protestant?"

De Comminges laughed, a curt bark. "Oh, no. At least, I suppose his father was, the same way that King Henri IV was Protestant. But like him, my grandfather thought that Paris was worth a Mass, and he converted before they took Paris. My father, as indeed my brother and I were brought up in the Catholic religion."

"Indeed?" Aramis asked. "Father Urtou seemed to think otherwise."

Athos could have kicked Aramis on the instant—for why would he want to discuss his talk to the priest with this man who seemed so strangely sympathetic to the Cardinal? To own the truth, Aramis also looked, immediately, like he would like to have swallowed his own tongue.

"You discussed my family's religion with the priest?" Monsieur de Comminges asked, smoothly. And though his hand didn't go to hilt of his sword, it nonetheless gave the impression of wishing to.

"Not your family in particular," Aramis said. "I beg your pardon if I fostered that impression. You see, I was once a seminarian and I'm only sojourning in the musketeers till I deem the time right for me to take orders. So, you see...I am interested in religion. And as such, I talked to the priest about what the wars of religion were like in this part of the country which suffered so much from them."

"Ah, yes," Monsieur de Comminges said, and appeared somewhere between relieved and suspicious. "It was a terrible scourge in Gascony."

At that moment several servants entered, one carrying a tray of dainties, and the other a tray of bottles and cups. Athos decided that no matter how cumbersome the social situation might be, at least they would get good wine.

And good wine it was, which he sipped as he listened to Aramis and de Comminges each trying to impress the other with how much he knew of the various Protestant sects, and how well he understood the various guerrillas and vendettas which had crisscrossed the Gascon countryside.

They sat and drank for hours and listened to de Comminges talk and—sometimes—argue with Aramis. If they'd spent this long drinking with anyone else, Athos thought they'd be well on their way to friendship or at least cordiality. But there was no such with de Comminges.

For all his insistence on bringing them here and giving them refreshments, he remained about as cordial and warm as a lizard. Athos wondered why. Had he no social feelings? And if not, why bring them here?

# The Dangers of the Gascon Countryside; Lovers and Fools

"I think," D'Artagnan said, when he judged they were far enough from the de Comminges palace that they would not be heard by either lord or retainer, "that he wanted to see me and evaluate me as a rival."

"A rival?" Aramis asked, sounding bewildered. He was very flushed, which looked odd with his pale skin and hair. "Why a rival?"

"He is engaged to my cousin Irene," D'Artagnan explained. "And she and I...Well, I used to think I was in love with her."

"I see," Aramis said, with not a little of amusement in his voice. "And was she in love with you?"

"Well, she never thought so," D'Artagnan said. "Though the last time I saw her, just this morning, she seemed to have changed her mind and been ready to throw everything over, including her chances at being a countess, for the chance of being Madame D'Artagnan."

He didn't know whether to be offended or amused that Aramis went from looking mocking to looking shocked. "Indeed?" he asked. "And why does she crave such an honor?"

D'Artagnan shrugged. For a moment—for the briefest of thoughts—he considered telling Aramis that of course any woman would give up on wealth and a title for the sake of marrying him, but he decided against it. Either Aramis would laugh at his joke—which would make him feel badly—or he wouldn't, which would be worse because then he would know that Aramis had decided to humor a madman.

"I don't think she had any real interest in marrying me," he said, simply. "But that, for whatever reason, she seems to be terrified of marrying Sever de Comminges."

"Ah. Has he done anything in particular to terrify her?" Aramis asked.

"Except perhaps discussed theology with her," Porthos said.

D'Artagnan turned to smile at Porthos, but then answered Aramis. "I don't know," he said, frowning. "Nothing that she would admit to me, except to tell me she feels uneasy and that she would rather marry anyone at all, even Sever's younger brother, Geoffroi."

Athos, on the other side of Aramis, was frowning. "I wonder why. I will grant you he is no sparkling conversationalist, but then again few noblemen are, at any level. And surely..."

D'Artagnan smiled. "I don't think that's it at all. You see, she's been engaged to Sever ever since she was six years old. We're all of an age, Sever, Irene and myself."

"Truly?" Aramis asked. "He's only your age? I would have taken him for being older than I, myself."

D'Artagnan shook his head. "He always looked older than his years," he said. "But he is only my age. And his parents engaged him to Irene when they were both still small children. Being engaged feels normal to Irene. It has ever been a part of her childhood. It's marrying that scares her. And since it is Sever she's engaged to..."

"She's scared of Sever," Athos finished, with one of his half smiles.

"Yes. And since she must be behaving very strangely, Sever wanted to look me over and see what his rival was. Even though," he added, with a mock sigh, "the last time I was in Irene's high favor was when I kissed her behind a hay bale just before her parents got her engaged."

"I see," Athos said.

"That is quite likely the explanation," Aramis said.

"Shouldn't we hurry home, though?" Porthos said, looking at the red-tinged sky. "Surely your mother will have supper ready and we don't want to keep her waiting. It wouldn't be courteous."

D'Artagnan smiled at Porthos, and spurred his horse on.

They rode for quite a while, at speeds that made it too difficult to keep up any type of conversation. And then, as they approached the bastide, two people ran in front of them, on the road, with no warning.

Athos and Aramis who had the lead twisted their horses suddenly sideways to avoid running the two people over, while Porthos and D'Artagnan pulled their horses up short, suddenly.

When everyone was stopped and the horses had quieted, Athos dismounted and started going over his mount, carefully. "Fools," he threw at the two people who, shocked, still stood in the middle of the road, holding on to each other. "You could have caused me to lame my horse."

He returned to his inspection, while D'Artagnan looked at the two. It was a man and a girl, both enveloped in heavy winter cloaks. But from beneath the hood of the girl's cloak peeked a lock of brassy blond hair. "Irene," he said.

There was a sound of fear from within the hood, and then the male in the other cloak stepped forward, pulling back his hood to reveal an unexceptional olive-skinned face, with dark eyes and lank black hair delineating it.

"If you take offense at your cousin's company," he said, "I take full responsibility. Call me out, only leave her out of this and do not tell her parents."

It was all D'Artagnan could do not to laugh. In the countenance of the young man facing him, he recognized Geoffroi de Comminges who must be all of fifteen if that much, and who looked almost exactly like his brother, or at least he would look like his brother if his brother were capable of human expressions.

He was looking at D'Artagnan, all solemn eyes and responsible-looking face, waiting, D'Artagnan was sure of it, for a call to duel.

"Easy, de Comminges, I don't duel babies."

The young man colored deeply, as D'Artagnan himself would have done at his age. And, as D'Artagnan at his age, he put his hand on the hilt of his sword, and said, "If you want to see how much of a baby I am, do me the honor of crossing swords with me."

"Can't be done," D'Artagnan said. "It is my honor at stake. If I killed you, they would accuse me of having despoiled youth and innocence. No, you must wait. In two years, if you're still hot to duel me, I'll accept your challenge, but not now."

"And besides," Porthos rumbled from beside D'Artagnan, "we just came from your brother's house and it would be a very poor return for his hospitality."

"You just came from my brother's house?" the boy asked, dropping his hand from his sword and looking at them, stricken, as if they'd announced they were about to execute him.

"Indeed. He invited us for refreshments."

"Did he...did he say anything about me?" Geoffroi asked.

Puzzled, D'Artagnan shook his head.

"Did he ask if you'd seen me?"

"Not at all," D'Artagnan said. "Though when we met him it was on the streets of town, so perhaps he meant to look for you there."

The young man nodded earnestly. And suddenly, Irene tossed back her hood and came to hold his arm, as if to give him strength or to hold him up. "We went to the priest," she said. "But he wouldn't marry us. He said a deal of nonsense about bans and all that."

"Oh, so you found a likely prospect," D'Artagnan said. "I congratulate you. Though I regret to say they won't marry you, anyway, as your groom is underage."

And here Geoffroi shook his head. "I won't be underage if we go where we're not known and—"

"Oh an elopement," D'Artagnan said shaking his head at the folly of the pair. "How very pretty. You'd find my cousin pretty hot at hand, de Comminges, once she realized being married to you was still being married and that she won't be able to live with no responsibilities at her parents' house, after all. Irene," he called imperiously. "Do mount on my horse. My friends and I will escort you home."

They were going to be late for supper after all. And there was not a hope of doing any more investigation tonight. They would have to start again tomorrow.

In the confused welter of D'Artagnan's mind there opened so many avenues for searching out the murderer that he was not sure where to begin. He spent the ride to de Bigorres' in silence, trying to find how to even start looking.

# Four Cloaked Men Conspiring; The Many Paths of Enquiry

AT dawn the next day, by mutual, undiscussed agreement, they went outside, on horseback, to the nearest hill. There, they assumed they could speak without interruption, without being overheard and with ease of seeing who approached from any side.

There, on top of the hill, they dismounted to talk, while their servants held their horses nearby. It was cold—a cutting wind blowing and biting at the cheeks that their cloaks and hoods left exposed. And Aramis wondered what they looked like, there, atop a hill, four men in dark cloaks. In the more superstitious regions of the country such a sight would probably be enough for rumors of ghosts and demons.

Here, it would doubtless be assumed they were plotting. Which they were, but not against any authority nor to overthrow any order.

"I was thinking," D'Artagnan said. "Yesterday. One of us must go see the priest, of course, but I think it might be best if I go on my own."

"Never," Athos said. "You shouldn't go anywhere on your own. Remember what almost happened when you went to visit de Bilh?"

"But what can happen to me in the middle of town and in a sanctuary?" he asked.

Athos shook his head. So did Porthos. And Aramis felt himself joining in. "D'Artagnan," he said. "The chapel is dark and isolated. How hard would it be for anyone to slip in after you and put a dagger in your back before anyone—even Father Urtou—noticed? Surely you don't want that?"

"No. I'm no more suicidal than any of you," he said. And sighed. "We'll do it that way then. I shall go with..."

"Me," Athos said.

"Right. Provided Athos stays outside the sacristy when I go in to see the priest in private, as I think it far more likely he will confide in me alone than in me accompanied by anyone else."

"Very well," Athos said. "And as for Porthos, I've already discussed with him what he must do. He must go to the various houses hereabouts and see what he can find about the horses."

"The horses?" D'Artagnan asked.

"Yes, the horses your father said the King and the Cardinal had given him. Or at least that's what your good Bayard understood, though how much of it your father said, and how much Bayard allowed his partiality for your house to deceive him..."

"Quite possibly a lot," D'Artagnan said, with a thin smile. "He is—was very loyal to my father." He frowned a little. "Aramis, I'd like you to search something for me. It is really imperative that we find out what, if anything, my father was doing for the Cardinal. I found that safe-conduct but nothing else."

"And it could be all or nothing," Aramis said. "Very well. Where did you find the safe-conduct and where do you think it would be most fruitful for me to search?"

"My father's study," D'Artagnan said, and proceeded to give his friend close instructions. "Oh, and take Mousqueton with you. He knows how to open the door and the box under the desk, and anything else that might be locked." He gave other instructions about what the trunks were likely to contain.

"And take Planchet also," Athos rumbled. "If you're going through papers and books, the boy is invaluable, should there happen to be a secret code on any paper."

"*Hola*, Planchet and Mousqueton," Aramis said, turning. "It appears I have need of you. Let's get on our horses and go back to the D'Artagnan house."

It was only as they were about to leave that he stopped and asked D'Artagnan, "What do I tell your mother, if she should ask?"

D'Artagnan smiled, an impish smile that made him look very much seventeen. "Tell her it was by my order and for the good of the family that you did what you had to do."

# A Sacrifice of Blood; Death and Asking; The Search

**THEY** approached the chapel just before Mass should have started. It was Athos's devout hope that they could talk to the priest before anyone arrived for the Mass and that, this early in the morning, he would be pliable and disposed to answer their questions.

He entered the chapel, crossing himself reverentially. For years now, he hadn't been sure that there was a God at all. Or, more exactly, he hadn't been sure that, if there was a God, he could be counted on to be a gentleman. This, however, did not excuse him from showing reverence—in the same way that the fact that Louis XIII was undeniably a weak king did not excuse Athos from showing reverence and loyalty to the monarchy.

He slid into the shadows of a pew, while D'Artagnan forged ahead, step by step, stopping to genuflect in front of the altar before going to the little door to the side that led to the sacristy. "Father Urtou," he called. "Father? It is I, D'Artagnan."

Athos slid to his knees on the pew, joined his hands and rested his forehead on them. Not praying exactly, but thinking of everything they were facing and asking Him, if He should chance, indeed, to have a hint of noblesse oblige, to take a hand in it. To keep D'Artagnan safe and, if possible, to arrange for a way for the boy to return to Paris, as it was obvious he would be miserable if forced to stay behind in Gascony.

His eyes were covered, so he didn't see D'Artagnan come out of the sacristy. But he heard his disordered breath, fast and with an odd edge almost of sobbing.

He had opened his eyes and turned before D'Artagnan said, "Athos."

The boy stood in the door to the sacristy, looking pale as death and seeming to totter on his feet.

Athos's first thought was that the boy was wounded—that, somehow, the priest had been bought by their mysterious enemy and, forgetting church, vows and loyalty, he'd plunged a knife into the boy.

Carried by his concern, Athos found himself out of the pew and halfway across the chapel, stretching out supportive hands to hold the boy should his legs give out altogether. "D'Artagnan," he said. "D'Artagnan, my friend, what is wrong? Are you wounded?"

D'Artagnan shook his head. He drew in a breath, noisily. "Not wounded," he managed.

Athos was by his side by now, holding onto his elbow, looking him over for any sign of blood, in the dim light. Relaxing a little when there didn't seem to be any obvious wound.

But the boy was still as white as curds as he turned his face towards Athos and said, with some impatience, "I'm well, Athos. I'm well. It is...Father Urtou."

"What? Did he say anything?"

"No, Athos," D'Artagnan said and stepped out of the door to the sacristy.

Athos surged forward, entered the sacristy. It was quiet, very quiet. Slightly brighter than the chapel, since there was a long, narrow window on the wall and the space was small. It was furnished with various locked cupboards, what looked like a pole on which someone—or various someones—had hung a confusing welter of vestments, and a tall, narrow writing desk with shelves beneath it. Presumably the shelves had contained several heavy black notebooks.

Presumably that is, because Athos had seen other arrangements of the kind. And the top book was still there, opened, on the top of the multitiered furniture piece. On it the priest would write marriages and baptisms and funerals. For most people these were the only records of their lives—the only marks they made in an otherwise indifferent world.

In Gascony, because of church burnings and Catholic and Protestant enmity to record keeping of any sort by the enemy, Athos suspected the records in most churches didn't go back all that far. But this one looked to have enough records. Enough that each book, its covers and pages torn out and strewn wildly about, had furnished enough paper to form a mound that took up half of the sacristy.

At first Athos thought it was all it was, and that D'Artagnan's exclamation about the priest related to how much work the poor man would have, to restore his records to any semblance of order. But then he caught sight of a wrinkled, yellowed hand protruding from the pile of paper. It lay, palm up, as though begging for an alms that Athos could not give it.

A second look revealed, peeking out of the papers at another place, a small wrinkled face and beneath it, stretching and staining the paper, a dark red puddle. The smell in the air, thick, mingled dust and blood.

"Someone hit him on the back of the head," D'Artagnan said, sounding on the verge of nausea. "I almost stepped on him, covered in papers as he was. What—Who do you think did this? And why? Who would have any interest in hurting him?" And then, in the plaintive voice of a child, "People hereabouts said he was a saint."

Athos didn't believe in God—or at least not the way he was painted—but he did believe in saints. Saints were those who, under difficult circumstances, strived to bear more of a burden than they were made to carry. By that definition, perhaps Father Urtou was a saint.

Certainly in this region, where the last fifty years had provided more than enough martyrdom for everyone of every possible denomination, no one would be a priest just for the glory or the power of belonging to the church. Not when death was on the line.

"It was probably church robbers," Athos said. "In search of the platter."

D'Artagnan inhaled with a sound that might have been bitter laugh. "Then it couldn't be anyone local," he said. "Because no one—no one—here would think there was platter worth selling. It was stolen years ago, in the wars. Father Urtou made do with a clay plate and a few cups, no better than those at a peasant house."

Athos was examining the bank of doors on the wall behind the priest's corpse. "Every one of those doors has been opened," he said. "And not by someone of Mousqueton's ability." Each of the doors, at least the nearest ones that he could see clearest, were broken, the wood wrenched till the metal had come free of it, and the door had opened.

"Oh," D'Artagnan said and, stepping carefully over the priest, opened the nearest door, to reveal several altar clothes of the finest linen, roiled and thrown about as if a small and exceedingly vicious wind had scattered them. "Oh," again, in a different tone and then, "I don't think this was done by robbers, Athos. I don't think they killed Father Urtou to steal what he had. Buy why do it, otherwise? Who could have a vendetta against the poor man?"

Athos opened a couple more doors, to find the contents—holy books, missals, and what looked like a pile of schoolboy exercises in catechism and letters—tossed about just like the linen and the pages on the floor.

"I don't think it was a vendetta," he told D'Artagnan. "I think whoever did it was looking for something." He looked around at the pages torn from the registry books. "I'd guess they were looking for a birth, death or marriage record."

D'Artagnan made a sound of disbelief, followed by a bitter chuckle. "Couldn't they have asked?"

"I don't think they could. I don't know why not—but it is obvious they'd rather kill than ask, and that's not the usual choice."

"No," D'Artagnan said, and then soberly, "We should go call his housekeeper. She lives next door. I'll tell my mother too. I don't know if he has family, but someone will have to take charge of the corpse and prepare it for burial and—"

"Not just yet, D'Artagnan," Athos said. "First let us look at these papers, one by one, shall we? Let's make sure there's nothing here that the murderers left behind that might incriminate them."

Again the laugh-sigh echoed from D'Artagnan. "I don't think they left anything at all of any use behind. Look how thoroughly they looked."

"Yes," Athos said. "But the fact they rent the record books page from page and only searched the other areas perfunctorily tells me they were looking for a record. And the fact that the other areas were searched at all tells me they didn't find what they needed in that book—and probably ran away at the sound of our approach. Which, in turn, tells us they expected us to recognize them on sight—so that even if they managed to escape, we'd be able to point a finger at them."

D'Artagnan had calmed down. At least his breath was slower and more regular. "I think I understand what you mean," he said. "You mean for us to search page by page of this." He gestured at the floor. "And to go through those cupboards, also, if we fail to find something here."

Athos nodded and, kneeling down, started to pick up pages, look at them, and stack them, roughly by date. Birth, marriage, death. Birth, marriage, death. What a senseless round.

"But Athos, what I don't understand is why you want to do this. How could this possibly relate to my father's death or to the attacks on me?"

"I don't know," Athos said. "I only know this. There are crimes happening in Gascony, from your father's murder to the attacks against you. They seem wholly unrelated. And they might very well be. But if they are, D'Artagnan, with these many attacks happening in the last few weeks, Gascony is worse than it was when it was at war."

D'Artagnan looked at him a moment, then knelt down at the other end of the pile. "What if he's alive still?" he asked, looking at the priest. "What if we allow him to die by not calling for help?"

Athos could have told him that no one with their head bashed in like that could possibly be alive, but it would require too much explanation and argument. Instead of arguing, he reached for the priest's neck, to feel for a pulse he knew wouldn't be there. Aloud, he announced his results, "He's cold, D'Artagnan. The Mass will start in just a few minutes. Let's gather the papers."

"The Mass can't start," D'Artagnan protested, his normal quickness of mind overwhelmed by shock. "He's dead."

"Yes," Athos said. "But the people don't know that, and they'll be arriving. If they find us here, they might be so delusional as to think we murdered him. Let's collect the papers quickly and then call for help at his house."

This seemed to jolt the young man into action as nothing else might have managed to. Together, the two friends sifted through the documents—some so old they were written on stray pieces of parchment and some, more recent, loose and charred—setting them by order of the date they'd occurred.

"I still don't think we'll find anything," D'Artagnan said.

But Athos, looking at a document with familiar names, was very much afraid he already had.

# Between Musketeer and Servants; Dead Man's Accounts; Letters

**ARAMIS** waited while Mousqueton unlocked the door. He felt, somehow, that he should stop it. It was after all not exactly moral of him to allow someone to break into someone else's locked space under his watch.

But Aramis the musketeer took Aramis the would-be-priest severely in hand. After all, he told himself, he was working here for the greater good. Finding who had killed Monsieur D'Artagnan and who was trying to kill his son was a good on its own. It would prevent the loss of life. That it had to be done by less than orthodox methods only came from the fact that criminals, also, tended to use less than orthodox methods.

*And it's no use whatsoever telling me what Augustin said of righteous men condoning sin*, he told himself. *Monsieur D'Artagnan is dead. Whom does it help to keep his study locked?*

Inside the study, he found everything as D'Artagnan had described. The two servants stood by the door.

"Planchet," Aramis said. "You look through the record books, there; it is all figures and the like, and I daresay you're better than I at seeing it through." He pointed at the long shelf. "And you, Mousqueton, could you open this trunk for me?" He pulled forth the one with the shiny top, upon which—D'Artagnan said—his father had been in the habit of resting his feet.

The servant knelt and, his tongue caught between his teeth, the tip of it just protruding between his lips, he worked with his various tools until the trunk sprang open, in a disquietingly short period of time.

Mousqueton bowed to him slightly and Aramis nodded to him. "How good is your reading?"

The servant gave him an elusive smile, of the sort that might mean he'd taken offense and on the other hand, might mean that Aramis amused him. With Mousqueton it was harder to know and hazardous to ask. "Oh, I read fairly well, monsieur," he said, with the sort of eager, half-simpering tone that made him sound like the stereotypical peasant in awe of the musketeer.

Aramis bit his lip. Sometimes he wondered that Porthos was so fond of Mousqueton and, in fact, never seemed to have the sudden need to beat his servant. But Aramis, who in general disapproved of beating servants, knew he wouldn't hold his temper half so well if he had to deal with the man very often.

"Look through that trunk, would you?" he said, pointing at the trunk that didn't have the polished surface on top, and which he judged to mean was the trunk that D'Artagnan said had contained a "never end of bills and correspondence, none of it, probably, much to the purpose."

"What am I to look for?" Mousqueton asked.

Aramis sighed. Definitely, more time spent in the company of Mousqueton would be enough to wholly turn his ideas on the liberal treatment of servants. But he managed to say aloud and in very civil form, "Anything that might pertain to the current affair. I trust a man like you, so skilled in rescuing chickens and even wine bottles that have got run over by carriages, is doubtlessly equally skilled in knowing what might pertain to this case and what might not." And anticipating that Mousqueton would come back and ask for more explicit instructions, he said, "Anything having to do with Monsieur D'Artagnan's and Madame D'Artagnan's marriage, or else anything pertaining to his work for the Cardinal. Anything he might have done for the Cardinal. Anyone he might be investigating for his eminence."

He expected an argument, but he got none. Instead, Mousqueton knelt down and pulled his allotted trunk to him.

As for Aramis, he pulled the remaining trunk to him and looked, in some confusion, at the contents. There was what appeared to be an antiquated guard uniform of some sort, complete with hat, with its plume. It would seem to him, considering the horrible state of the plume and hat D'Artagnan had worn to Paris the first time, that his father would have passed this hat down to his son.

But as he uncovered, farther in the trunk, a very fine sword and an even finer dagger, each in its scabbard, and beneath this a dress which, though water stained, had once been made of the finest material, he thought that he was almost surely looking at a man's souvenirs of youth and, gently, he removed the objects, one by one, from the trunk and set them aside atop the slightly dusty floor.

Being Aramis and, as such, a cunning man and a man of the world accustomed to the oddness of men—and women—in Paris, which was, rightfully, the capital of the world, he didn't scruple to go through the sleeves of the uniform as well as to inspect it all for hidden pouches or recesses.

In the sleeve of the uniform he found a note, addressed in neat handwriting, asking Monsieur D'Artagnan to meet the undersigned at such and such a time outside the convent of the Barefoot Carmelites, on an affair of honor that must be settled. He smiled a little at it thinking that the father was not so unlike the son. But the name of the signatory was quite unknown to him, and as such Aramis set it aside without regret

The woman's dress was wholly devoid of any paper or anything that might have given an indication as to its wearer, save a single, crumpled handkerchief, within its right sleeve. It looked very much like it might have been cried upon, and the embroidery on the fine linen said "M. R."

He frowned at it a moment, before restoring it to its sleeve. Folding the gown carefully, he turned his attention to the other objects in the trunk. At the bottom, doubtless thrown there by his careless pulling of the garments, there was the famous Richelieu note. And next to that, covered in a brown leather binding, flaking with age, a sheaf of paper that had once been blank, and upon which someone had made a confusion of notes in a tight handwriting, in brown ink.

All together, the notes, as far as Aramis could tell, came to very little. It was all appointments and notes about appointments. A noted battle of the wars of religion was written down simply with the name of the region and the single word, afterwards—survived, which of course was wholly unnecessary since there were many notes made afterwards.

All in all, the writing, such as it was, gave Monsieur Aramis a pretty good view of Monsieur D'Artagnan père. He had doubtless been, just as his son, a noted duelist and much involved in those essential parts of the life of a young guard in Paris—drinking, dueling, dining out with friends.

What Aramis saw no evidence of was his friend's quick wit or his facility with words. Instead, Monsieur D'Artagnan père expressed himself with all the lack of elegance Porthos might employ.

Tapping his teeth with his tongue, Aramis thought such awkwardness with the language could be dangerous. At least, when a man set himself to wading through the deep waters of intrigue, and through anything at all that involved his eminence, if he had no facility with meanings and words, and no friends to make up that defect for him, he would find himself very rapidly in trouble. As Monsieur D'Artagnan doubtless had found himself.

The last entry in the notebook was "Marriage arranged. Father wrote to hurry me home. It's farewell Paris."

Certain that the letter his friend said he had left for them in Paris contained more grief and better expressed chagrin, Aramis set the little book back in its place and was about to search the sheathes of the swords, when an exclamation from Mousqueton made him look up.

The young man had gone about the business very meticulously and was now surrounded by small piles of paper. In his hands, he was holding what looked like a creased and bent note.

"What have you found, Mousqueton?" Aramis asked.

"It is a duel challenge, monsieur."

"From de Bilh?" Aramis hazarded.

"No, monsieur, but from another name that has come up a few times." Thus speaking, he handed Aramis the note.

THE MUSKETEER'S INHERITANCE

Aramis unfolded the age-brittle paper. A stain in the corner seemed to indicate that there was a mark of blood upon it.

Inside the paper read, in terse terms, "To Monsieur Adrien de Comminges, if you'd do me the honor of meeting me at the threshing yard near old Jacques' field tomorrow at sunset, I'll seek satisfaction for the offense of which both of us are aware and which cannot be erased in any way but in blood."

For a moment, for just a moment, Aramis thought that he had found the thread to the whole thing, the duel that Monsieur D'Artagnan must have fought before he fought his last one. But then he looked at the date hastily penned in the corner. As it was over eighteen years past, it was unlikely that it was blood loss from that event that had made Monsieur D'Artagnan confused enough to attack de Bilh.

"I don't see how this is to the purpose," Aramis said.

"Well, we now know that they were not on good terms, Monsieur D'Artagnan and Monsieur de Comminges."

Aramis had to agree this was so, but pointed out that it had all been a long time since and clearly neither of them had died from the encounter.

"The only puzzle," he said, "is how Monsieur D'Artagnan came to keep that note, or why he bothered. However, since it's marred with blood, perhaps he took it from the body of his fallen—if not dead—adversary. Not sure why, since the edicts against dueling were not in force then, but he must have had a reason to hide the encounter. Perhaps no more though," he said, sententiously, "than the desire to hide that they didn't quite get along. After all, in a region so riven by strife, he probably didn't want anyone else to suspect they didn't get quite well along."

Mousqueton looked dubious but nodded, and took the letter, and put it, gently, atop a stack. Aramis wondered if the entire stack was challenges to duels.

He returned to his own work, searching out the sheathes of the blades, which proved to be fruitless. He was about to return the various contents to the trunk and ask Mousqueton to lock it yet again, when he noticed, caught in the leather lining, and almost hidden, a letter, which he picked up.

There were bits of sealing wax adhering to the paper, which was unequivocally addressed to Monsieur Charles D'Artagnan.

Inside...

Aramis drew in a sudden and deep breath, as he discovered at least one of the answers to his many questions.

The letter lacked a heading, and from the slanted handwriting, had been written in some haste.

The contents read:

*I have conveyed your last letter to his eminence, and he is gratified you are making progress on his behalf.*

*In the matter of Edmond de Bigorre, it is certain that he is a most dissipated gambler and that something might perhaps be worked upon to get him to break off his engagement. In point of fact, other agents, closer to that matter, have long since informed us that he is on the verge of being wholly bankrupt. Perhaps you should approach him and offer him money on behalf of his eminence if he should beg off his engagement. This would please his eminence and his eminence's friend very much.*

*On the other matter, we're glad to hear de Comminges had indeed been in correspondence with the rebels at the Bastille. We have long since suspected his conversion to Catholicism was less than sincere and there is proof. We shall take steps to prevent his raising an army to come to their aid. And we will move to intercept further correspondence between him and Buckingham. The attached will give you an idea how to proceed.*

*Yours as ever, Rochefort.*

There was nothing attached.

# A Priest's Doubts; A Musketeer's Fears

**ATHOS** stared down at the paper between his fingers. It was about the marriage of de Comminges and for a moment—for a blinding, half-laughing, half-confusing moment—he thought it was D'Artagnan's cousin who'd gone and got herself married to the boy he had started calling, in his mind, the hapless Geoffroi.

But then he realized it was the marriage record of the Lord de Comminges, which, certainly, the young Geoffroi wasn't, and some woman referred to as Lady D'Entragnes.

The record itself was unremarkable, and dated over eighteen years ago—certainly the marriage of the Lord Adrien that was the father of the present lord.

He was about to put the page back in the midst of the other pages and turn his attention to the rest of the book, when he found a note at the bottom of the page, in what appeared to be the same hand that had recorded the marriage.

Spidery and so faint that it must mean the person pressed not at all with the quill, the hand was devilishly hard to read, but squinting and turning the paper to the light, he saw at the bottom an entry dated a month or two after the marriage, "Sent an enquiry to Paris regarding his previous marriage to Marie R. My messenger brought me back word that the priest, whom she'd said had performed the ceremony, could not be found. It must be assumed the paper Marie has is a hoax and that this marriage is valid and proper."

Athos darted a look at D'Artagnan, afraid the youth would look his way and ask what he had found. It seemed thoroughly useless to tell the boy about this document now. Marie might be his mother, then again she might not. There were a lot of women named Marie and there was no telling what the R might signify. And at any rate, if there had been a pretense of marriage with de Comminges, it had been a hoax and there was nothing to tell.

All the same, he stared at the page in great unease. Something about this was trying to form into a thought—a feeling—Athos didn't know what to call it, except he could feel it rising, like a dark thing from the layers of the unthought. And he was afraid of allowing it to fully emerge. He felt as though once that feeling that now troubled him, like a nagging pain within his mind, had coalesced nothing would be the same.

D'Artagnan was collecting papers together and putting them away. He stopped suddenly. "Athos?"

"Yes?" Athos asked, hoping that the boy had not found any note referring to the events he'd just read about.

"I...This is my parents marriage record."

"And?" Athos asked. The boy's voice had trembled. "Anything shocking?"

D'Artagnan shook his head, then shrugged. "My mother's name was Ravelet," he said, frowning a little. "Doesn't sound like a Gascon name."

"Perhaps it is only the name of the family who fostered her?" Athos asked. He was trying very hard not to think that she'd been Marie R. There must be many more Maries with a surname starting with R. Surely it wouldn't mean anything.

"Perhaps," D'Artagnan said, but he still looked worried.

"What is wrong, my friend?" Athos asked.

"It's...the marriage was three months before my birth."

"Oh," Athos said. And sighed. "But you knew we had reason to suspect it, did you not? What is so shocking about it? They did marry."

"Yes," D'Artagnan said. He laughed, uneasily, and shook his head. "It's ridiculous, I know. It's just...there is a difference between suspecting it and knowing it." He blushed. "I mean...it is my mother. It is hard to think that she..."

"That she is human?" Athos asked.

D'Artagnan sighed. "I suppose." He shrugged. "When it's one's mother, it's easy to get foolish."

Athos nodded. "My mother died at my birth, but I can picture what it must be like. Yet..." He shrugged. "It is what it is, and many years have passed. We know nothing of the attendant circumstances. Perhaps it was the only way they could...I don't know...and you don't know how it came about. But you are legitimate nonetheless and...it can't mean anything."

D'Artagnan opened his mouth as though to answer, but at that moment there was a voice from the church. "Father Urtou?"

Athos held his finger in front of his lips, commanding silence, and pulled D'Artagnan towards the door out of the sacristy.

Reaching for the handle, he started opening it, slowly, slowly, to avoid its creaking, while from outside the voice called again, "Father, are you there?"

He managed to get the door open and ran out, into the morning light, with D'Artagnan after him.

It wasn't until they were some streets away that they checked each other and themselves for bloodstains. There were none.

From the area of the church came loud screams.

"We couldn't let them think we'd done it," Athos said. "It would only make apprehending the real killer that much more difficult."

D'Artagnan nodded, agreeing. "And now," he said, with a deep intake of breath. "What do we do now? Father Urtou can't talk to us, poor man..."

Athos was trying to collect his thoughts. And more than everything, he was trying to keep at bay that one thought—that one image, feeling, whatever it was—that was attempting to surface. "We go back home," he said. "We see what our friends have found."

# Horses and Men; Monsieur Porthos Engages in Philosophy; The Odd Relationships of Provincial Gentlemen

**PORTHOS** had spent the whole morning riding around; hit up all the taverns around there. In most places his probably not too subtle questions about horses had been dismissed with the sort of shrug that meant they thought the big man from Paris was less than sane.

It was Porthos belief—and he philosophized on this a moment—that if anyone knew where the horses had originated, and if indeed there was any secret or shame attaching to their origin, the people would either hotly deny any knowledge of them or else—of course—innocently tell him what they knew.

The shrug, on the other hand, and the shake of head of the provincial damsels he'd queried on the matter, he thought, meant that neither did they know of any horses having come that way, nor could they imagine any harm in a movement of horses between noble houses. Therefore, he presumed, these were not the people he was looking for.

A visit to the de Bigorre house proved no more fruitful. Though there he met with more than a shrug, a smile and a head shake. The laughter, with which the groom told him that while de Bigorre was selling his horses it was piecemeal, not all at once, told him he was on the wrong track.

Besides, he judged, with the proximity by blood of the two houses—de Bigorre and D'Artagnan—the grooms and stable boys were quite likely to know each other. Had the horses come from the de Bigorre house, then Bayard was likely as not to know where they'd come from. And while he might want to hold on to the fantasy that they came from Cardinal and King, he would not so blithely repeat it, because if he did he was likely to be uncovered in a lie and he would know it.

As the sun climbed towards noon, Porthos found himself mounted upon his horse by the side of a bare field, while the weak sun of winter beat upon his broad shoulders and back. He was trying to accomplish something he did not very often attempt.

Porthos, a huge man, good with his hands and with the physical movements of dancing and dueling, and an expert at noticing anything awry in a picture or a room, was slow and awkward with his words, and thinking of what other people's words—or indeed their actions—meant was bound to confuse him.

He sat on his horse, while his complaining stomach told him that he should head back to the D'Artagnan home for food. But the thing was—he tallied it on his fingers—the horses didn't seem to have come to the D'Artagnan home through any of the surrounding villages, or any of the approaches from Paris.

Even supposing that they'd come from one of the neighboring villages—supposing Athos was right about such details as how the horses were shod in a different manner from the Parisian work—they didn't seem to have passed any of the roads they must have passed on their way to the bastide.

And they'd not come from the de Bigorre house. Of that Porthos was sure.

He frowned at the pale blue sky. "The devil," he said, to himself. "Unless Gascons have found a way to make their cattle fly, they must have come from somewhere around here."

It was then that he realized he had not yet checked de Comminges. There didn't seem any reason to. He would own he didn't like the fellow, despite his very hospitable behavior to them. In fact, he didn't like him so much that he'd been inclined to forego the wine he'd served, because, truth be told, he wasn't sure such a creature as that, dressed all in black and thinking himself so above anyone else, wouldn't believe it incumbent upon himself to poison them.

But he'd drunk the wine and come to no harm, and still he couldn't like Monsieur de Comminges. A great part of that might be that he'd spent such a large time fluently discussing religion with Aramis.

It was Porthos's belief that anyone who could argue religion or philosophy at any length, turning one end against the other and back again, must perforce be someone that could not be trusted. But then again, he was a fair enough man to admit this might be his prejudice alone.

And knowing he was prejudiced against the man caused him to hesitate to go and question his servants. Priding himself on his fairness, Porthos suspected that if he went in to speak to them, he would be likely—too likely—to interpret any dubious pronouncement as indicting de Comminges.

But then again—he owned a very large house. It had many horses and some might easily have disappeared, without causing any alarm. What was more, he had farms and horses in the country, and in one of the villages both Athos and he had heard of horses being sent from the farm to the de Comminges house recently.

Nothing for it but to go and check that last possible source for the cattle, before heading to the D'Artagnan home for a bit of food.

Sighing, he set his horse on the road to the de Comminges house, which he approached the back way and through a gate which, he'd noticed, led to the stables. Approaching the stables, he'd smelled cooking sausage, and, his stomach rumbling, he'd approached, while frantically making up an excuse in his mind for his presence here.

But as it turned out, all the men and boys who worked in the stables were gathered around the fire, cooking sausages, and didn't take it as at all remarkable that he'd first visited the lord and now came and ate sausage with them in the stables.

On the contrary, Porthos recognized in them what he'd seen before from men in the capital—it was a twin reaction to his presence which never ceased to amuse him. On the one hand these people—common born—felt themselves honored to have a lord in their midst and would say nothing to remind him he was outside his proper sphere. On the other hand, noting his difficulty with words, they would sometimes trade smiles among themselves, as though to signify that he might be a lord, but he was not, in any way, better than them.

Here, in the de Comminges household, was added, as it hadn't been in Paris, the fact that most of the servants spoke the Gascon tongue and seemed to amuse themselves trading comments about him when he could not possibly understand them.

Porthos, used to people thinking him far dumber than he was, didn't mind. Instead, he settled to play the part of the amiable dunce—it being his experience that people were far more likely to speak unconsidered truths to people they considered their inferiors in wit than to those they judged their superiors.

"Monsieur D'Artagnan bought some fine horses from your master," he said at last, in the tone of a man who's run out of conversation and turns to horses because these people work with them.

"The young master, aye," one of the stable boys said. "Because the old devil wouldn't sell anything to him, not even for breath if he were starving for it."

"Ah," Porthos had said, as if this meant a lot, and had taken a bite out of the sausage. It was spicy with garlic and sage and he had no trouble at all pretending to be too busy with it to attend. "So the young master sold him the horses?"

"Aye," the older stable boy said. "And must have made him pay dearly for it, because he had no need to sell the horses otherwise. Prime ones, too, brought in from his farm and taken to the D'Artagnan house forthwith."

"They are very fine horses," Porthos said. "Better than most I've seen."

At that one of the stable boys made a comment to the other in Gascon, and Porthos pretended he didn't notice it or hear it. He was sure it pertained to the fact that he must usually ride mules or worse.

But he didn't care. He'd found what he'd been sent to find, and he could now go back to his friends and bring them this fact for all it was worth.

# A War Council; Horses and Mothers; The Dangers of Cousins

**THEY** met at D'Artagnan's house, where Madame D'Artagnan more or less forced them to partake of a late midday dinner.

Athos observed that Porthos ate very little, and that D'Artagnan tended to blush when he looked at his mother. If Madame D'Artagnan noticed her son's unusual behavior though, she made no mention of it.

Instead, she was all full of news of poor Father Urtou's murder. "And the thieves must have thought we had better plate than we do," she said. "They must have been some of those dreadful highwaymen that move about the countryside, attacking churches and despoiling virgins," she said, and blushed a little. "They killed the poor man by hitting him over the head with the heavy crucifix from the altar. One wonders how it came about, for surely he wouldn't let some stranger take the cross from the altar and sneak around behind him. That sacristy is so small that there is not any possible way he would not have seen an intruder, or been conscious of his presence." She sighed. "I'll tell you how it had to be. Someone had to have broken into the church before the poor man arrived, and taken the cross. And then, armed with the cross, they must have gone into the sacristy." She shook her head. "But it makes no sense at all. Because if they'd taken the cross, that was probably what they wanted and why should they take it to the sacristy? And if they'd gone to the sacristy in search of plate, surely they would leave that cross alone, for it's plain to see that it's iron and made by our local blacksmith—a thing of no very great artistry." She paused and took a moment to take a bite of chicken and a bite of bread. "But none of it signifies, of course. Perhaps they took the cross with them to use as a weapon?" She looked up, puzzled. "Do such people not have weapons of their own? Knives and swords? I don't know anything of the breed, but surely..."

"Usually," D'Artagnan said. "Usually they have weapons of their own. In fact, most men carry either a sword or a knife. Mostly noblemen at least." He sounded as if he were deep in thought.

"Oh, you can't think this was a nobleman, son, can you? Surely it had to be some peasant? Perhaps not a highwayman, but a brutish peasant, full of wine and mirth, come to the church after having drunk all night."

She frowned. "The thing is, how could it be one of our local peasants? If it were such, surely he would know that we have no plate left to speak of. All stolen by some army or another during the wars." A look at D'Artagnan. "Your father told me all about it, of course, but I can't remember which army it was. It is so hard to keep these things straight in one's head."

After a silence, in which none of them ventured an answer, and in which Athos tried not to think—tried very hard not to think—that if it were a woman who'd killed the poor priest, it would be highly unlikely she would have a weapon, Madame D'Artagnan sighed. "At any rate, the Mass and funeral are tomorrow morning. Most of the village will be there, of course. Not I. Funerals do make me that ill that I cannot attend. Else, it would be my funeral as well. But Marguerite and Bayard will attend, doubtless, and perhaps you gentlemen..." She sighed again. "I know he was very old, and that he lived a long and good life, and is doubtless, even now, rejoicing in heaven, but truly—such a good man and so devoted to this land and our people, it is hard to believe that he is gone. And gone like that too, violently and at the hand of an unknown person." She shuddered. "You'll think me silly, Henri, but it seems to me a...a memento mori, as it were. First your father, then...No. First Monsieur de Comminges, then your father and then this poor priest. It makes you wonder if there will be more. But perhaps not, for they say disaster normally comes in threes."

Athos thought of de Comminges and the document he'd seen but refused to show D'Artagnan and he blushed dark red at the thought and turned his attention to the excellent wine in his glass.

This was when D'Artagnan rose and announced, "We must go for a ride, my friends. I feel I've eaten too much and I will be ill, at this late a dinner with no exercise."

Porthos looked as though he would argue, then flinched suddenly. A sure sign, Athos thought, that he'd been kicked under the table. As for himself, he rose quickly, concurring, "Oh, yes, all this food and being close confined will surely be unhealthy."

Madame D'Artagnan, still sitting, blinked up at them, her sparkling pale blue eyes filled with confusion. "But, monsieurs," she said, hesitating. "You were out only this morning."

"Ah, but not enough," D'Artagnan said. "I must survey some of the fields, perforce, and decide which farms need new planting."

His mother seemed to accept this without further ado, and they went on to the stable, where Bayard helped them onto horses, with no argument and very little conversation.

Save only, as Athos was leaving the stable, after the others, Bayard held his sleeve. "Monsieur," he said, in an almost soundless whisper. "Monsieur, I'm sure it was she that did it. It was she who killed that poor soul of a priest. She's a madwoman, I tell you, and that full of venom. I wouldn't be surprised if my poor master met his death by poison or...or other womanly arts," he added, as though not very sure what those womanly arts might be. "She was that thick with de Bilh. Still is. Why, he came by just this morning, while you were out. I'm sure she means to have him, and for that she disposed of my poor master."

Before Athos could ascertain if he meant Madame D'Artagnan, and, if so, how could she have killed the priest while she was entertaining de Bilh, D'Artagnan called from outside, "Athos? What delays you?"

"We'll talk later," Athos whispered to Bayard, just before letting out with a bellow of, "I'm coming."

And he rushed forth on his horse. They followed D'Artagnan's lead, which took them to the threshing floor.

Athos, all the while, tried to understand why Bayard had told him that. Was it only the dislike he bore Madame D'Artagnan? Or could there be another reason. Surely he wouldn't accuse her like that, with no reason. And if he would...How could he make sense of it? How could she have been entertaining de Bilh all the while attacking the priest? Of course, the priest had been killed very early, so perhaps she'd entertained de Bilh later, while Athos and D'Artagnan had been in their respective rooms—Athos trying not to let the thought emerge that was struggling to make its way up to his mind and D'Artagnan presumably being embarrassed about his parents' late marriage.

His parents' marriage. Athos saw in his mind Marie D'Artagnan's blue eyes, and the picture of the big, bluff gentleman in the great salon at the house. Was it possible that D'Artagnan had emerged like this, short and dark-haired, from such parents? Well, possible enough. Any noble house's portrait gallery contained more than enough throwbacks to make anyone believe in them. Centuries after the original, a child would be born who was the spitting image of some lost ancestor—more so than of the parents who'd given him life.

He wished very much that the D'Artagnan house had a portrait gallery, and he was furious at himself that he allowed it to work itself through his mind that long. It was like that with him, always. His wife's fleur-de-lis had triggered his certainty that she was an escaped criminal. He hadn't entertained any innocent explanation for it.

But the fact that even now, though he tried, he couldn't think of any way that anyone could get marked with a fleur-de-lis by accident irritated him. He concentrated on nothing but the fields, and their ride, until they stopped by the threshing floor. D'Artagnan dismounted, and the others followed suit. Arriving after them, he dismounted also, and the four of them gathered close in a war council, all the while looking around—to see if anyone might approach.

D'Artagnan told their story, of finding the priest dead and the papers ransacked.

Porthos was the first one to speak, afterwards. "What a very odd thing to do," he said. "Did they take anything, then?"

"Not that we could find," D'Artagnan said. "Not even papers—though that was hard to tell, since they tore them all one from the other and scattered them all over the floor."

"What, and you found nothing at all interesting?" Aramis said.

"No. My parents' marriage record," he said. And blushed. He didn't say anything else, and though Aramis's gaze met Athos's over the youth's head, and though it had a clear question in it, it wasn't as though Athos could tell him all about the questions the priest had about the validity of the marriage—much less about the date of the D'Artagnans' marriage. It was not his secret, but D'Artagnan's.

He found that, as the youth said, one thing was suspecting that he might have been conceived before marriage. Another was knowing it and having proof. He didn't feel it incumbent upon him to uncover his friend's shame.

Aramis shrugged at long last, and then spoke, "We found...several things...some of them very odd."

They all turned to him and it was Aramis's turn to blush, as though what he'd discovered embarrassed him. "Well..." he said. "Planchet went over the books for the estate, and he..." He shrugged. "You know how your servant is so quick with figures, D'Artagnan."

"Yes, of course. That's why I sent him with you," D'Artagnan answered, bewildered.

"Well...it's just...do you trust us with everything? Everything that might possibly be found about your parents? I mean..."

D'Artagnan's eyes opened wide. "How not?" he said. "You are my friends. But what can you possibly have discovered that..."

"Planchet says your father's books were...not right, that he was going into debt more and more...until about three weeks ago."

"What do you mean?" D'Artagnan asked. "I know about the debt, of course; that was part of the reason he sent me to Paris, you see, to try to make my fortune and to restore the house's fortunes in the process, but...How do you mean until then?"

"At that time...about the time the horses arrived in your stables, your father seems to have received a large influx of money," Aramis said, softly.

"From?"

"Well, I have reason to think from the Cardinal," Aramis said. "At least there was a letter from Rochefort in his papers, thanking him for information."

"Information!" D'Artagnan said, and then in a tone that might as well be a bell tolling death, "Rochefort."

"But yes, Rochefort. You could have anticipated that, my friend," Aramis said. "Since he's the éminence grise. He's the motor of all of the Cardinal's plans. Doubtless it was he who planned all. It is he, in general, who serves as a liaison with his eminence's operatives, you know."

"Yes, but..." D'Artagnan rubbed his hand over his face. "I wonder if he had already planned to find my father or someone in the region or if..." His voice dropped. "Or if it was my letter that he stole in Meung that gave him the idea of recruiting my father into his eminence's service."

"Does it matter?" Aramis asked.

"If my father died because of his association with the Cardinal, it matters," D'Artagnan said, and, before they had time to argue the point, he said, "What was my father doing for the Cardinal? What that would justify a payment in money? What?"

"Well..." Aramis said, softly. "The thing is that he seems to have investigated de Comminges—not sure how, but doubtless by watching the house, or getting Bayard to watch it—for correspondence with la Rochelle. And...he found it."

"Oh," D'Artagnan said.

"There was a letter dated from about a week before de Comminges's death saying that the Cardinal would take care of everything from there, and you see..."

"De Comminges died a week later!" D'Artagnan said, his voice terrible to hear. "Aramis, do you know what that suggests?"

"I know very well, but D'Artagnan, your father didn't know what the Cardinal was. That much was sure from the fact that he told you to always respect the Cardinal. He can't have known what methods his eminence would use to dispose of trouble. And besides, if de Comminges was truly communicating with la Rochelle and the English...well...he was a traitor and this once, perhaps the Cardinal's actions were justified."

"But..." D'Artagnan said. "The man's blood would be on my hands."

Aramis sighed. "Your father's hands, perhaps, never yours. Though there is reason to think..."

"What? To think what? Do not spare me!"

"Your father and de Comminges fought a duel of honor, the year before you were born. I believe your father injured de Comminges." He told D'Artagnan, rapidly, of finding a note inviting de Comminges for a duel, and of the stain in it that looked like blood. "So you see, there was old enmity there."

"Are you asking me to believe my father forged evidence of de Comminges's treason so as to get him killed?" D'Artagnan asked, his voice hard and brittle. "Aramis. You cannot know what you're saying."

"I'm not...No. What I'm saying is that perhaps the injury he'd done your father...perhaps there was bad blood between them and as such your father wouldn't scruple—"

"To use the might of the kingdom to kill his enemy?" D'Artagnan shook his head. "I know you've never met my father, Aramis, but, surely you would understand this is an insult. My father would be far more likely to invite him to another duel." He took a deep breath and exhaled in a deep, tremulous sigh. "No. No. You must allow me to think he didn't know what the Cardinal would do. It is the only true explanation."

Aramis nodded, though Athos thought he didn't look particularly convinced. Perhaps because Aramis, such as he was, would be able to both challenge someone for a duel and use whatever underhanded means were necessary to bring about their downfall, provided they had annoyed him enough. "The other thing the Cardinal had your father attempt was to get your cousin to break his engagement. I assume this never happened?"

D'Artagnan shook his head. "No, I talked to him and he said he can't break his engagement."

"Ah, nothing can stand in the way of true love," Porthos said.

"It is not love," D'Artagnan said. "He said he is practically penniless and so he needs to marry his wealthy heiress, you see?" He shrugged.

"Oh," Aramis said. "Indeed. The letter from your father said that your cousin is a gamester and because of it he was penniless and in need of money. The Cardinal suggested bribing him into breaking his engagement. I suppose it never happened."

"Either that," D'Artagnan said, "or when my father talked to him, Edmond realized that if he killed my father and me, he would stand to inherit the whole fortune that came from my father—and his father's—mother. And while the domains of D'Artagnan aren't much compared with those of de Bigorre, they are more than a second son's allowance, and they would permit him independence and the chance to marry whom he pleases."

"What makes you say this of your cousin?" Aramis said. "What would make you suspect him?"

"The dagger at the last hostelry," he said. "I told only Athos, because it didn't seem to fit with anything, but the dagger had the shield of the de Bigorres on the pommel."

"But...surely that doesn't mean anything?" Porthos said. "There must be people who have such weapons and who are not de Bigorres?"

D'Artagnan sighed. "That's the devil of it. I'm sure there are. For one, I, myself, have a sword with the coat of arms in my room. And I'm sure there are other descendants in this region that don't bear the name. It is not enough to condemn him. In fact, it's barely enough to suspect him of intent against me.

"However, both the attack on my father, by stealth as it was, and the attempts to kill me, making use of hired hands, would seem to point to Edmond, because he can't handle a sword any better than Irene, so you see...He could never seek revenge in a duel or in a fair fight."

"But there are many like him," Porthos said.

D'Artagnan nodded. "This is true and that is why I said there is barely enough evidence to even suspect Edmond, and yet I find myself suspecting him." He shook his head as though to clear it. "And you, Porthos, what did you find about the horses?"

"I found they came from the de Comminges' stables, right after the old lord died. The servants think your father bought them."

"I'm starting to think," D'Artagnan said, his voice bitter. "I never knew my father at all." And then, with sudden decision, "I'll go and ask Edmond what he knows of that dagger."

"Not alone," the others said. "Not alone. Should he be the murderer..."

D'Artagnan looked resigned. "Very well. You might as well come with me. Though I beg you to believe, I'm more than equal to fighting Edmond."

# A Warm Reception; The Matter of a Dagger; Where Monsieur Porthos Loses Patience

**THEY** rode in silence to the de Bigorre house, and entered, this time through the back, following D'Artagnan's lead.

In the stable yard, D'Artagnan handed off his horse and asked one of the servants, "Is Edmond at home?" He could feel his heart as though it were beating at his throat, and he wondered if he wanted Edmond to be home. Perhaps it would be better if his cousin had left for parts unknown. D'Artagnan would never know who had tried to kill him, and who had killed his father. But then, on the other hand, he wouldn't need to know his cousin had done it. He kept thinking of all the times, growing up, when he'd come to the de Bigorres in search of company.

Oh, Edmond had never been his friend as Irene had. And yet, they'd spent plenty of time hunting together, and D'Artagnan had tried to—unsuccessfully—teach his cousin to use a sword.

He had never been successful, but it could be said that despite their initial cold reception of each other, he and Edmond had warmed up to one another. When there were only so many young noblemen in the neighborhood—and the de Comminges didn't count since they didn't act as though they were part of the neighborhood—it was hard to avoid developing, at the very least, a form of camaraderie with them. And he couldn't believe Edmond would kill his father.

"Monsieur Edmond is in the back parlor. Or was, when I last saw him."

D'Artagnan nodded. So he was home. Nothing for it but to confront him. He started towards the house, up the big staircase, through the halls, seeing nothing, paying attention to nothing. His heart was beating so fast and loud that it seemed to deafen him. He knew his friends were right behind him, but it was scant comfort.

"Henri," a voice said. Irene's voice.

He blinked, to see his female cousin standing in front of him. "Ah, you villain," she said. "You have come to tell my father after all. After all your promises, you will undo me like this. And it is all for nothing, for you could have had me yourself, but you refused me and—"

"Irene," he said. The name sounded, even to him, as though he weren't sure of it and were pronouncing it tentatively, trying to get a handle on who this apparition might be. "Irene, don't be a fool, my girl. This does not concern you."

Perhaps it was the tone of his voice, perhaps his words were so unexpected that she stopped the script of her own personal drama to stare. "It...doesn't?" she asked.

He shook his head and walked past her, without turning to see if she stayed or ran off somewhere. He fancied he heard her steps, but through his heart beating, and the blood rushing through his veins, it was hard to tell where they were heading, or, indeed, if he could hear them at all.

Into the back parlor, in which through their growing up years they'd played many a game and spent hours talking—himself and Irene and her brothers—he erupted like something out of Greek myth, seeking revenge for blood spilled.

"Edmond," he said, his voice hollow sounding.

His cousin, fully attired for going out, had been sitting and reading something that looked uncommonly like a letter. He looked up startled at their entrance, and something to D'Artagnan's pale countenance made him drop the letter, jump up and take his hand to his sword.

"Oh, you'd serve me like that?" D'Artagnan asked. "You'd welcome me sword in hand? What have you done? Why does your conscience pain you so that you must receive me by drawing?"

"I've done nothing. Why do you invade my home and speak to me in accusing tones?"

"I'm not accusing you of anything yet. But if you wish me to, here it is. You lied to me."

"Lied? Are you calling me a liar?" Edmond said, and drew his sword.

Upon the same instant, D'Artagnan drew his sword. Somehow, part of him knew it would be murder to duel Edmond. How could it be otherwise? Edmond was the least efficient of fighters, the least proficient of duelists. He'd survived this long only by not dueling. And certainly he couldn't duel someone of D'Artagnan's prowess.

He came at D'Artagnan blindly, roaring, his sword held in a shaking hand.

D'Artagnan parried, hooking his cousin's sword so that it went flying.

In the next moment, the room erupted into pandemonium, in a way that D'Artagnan had never seen happen in the more serious duels he fought in the capital. As Edmond ran for the sword, there were fast steps the other way, and when Edmond got to the sword, Irene put her foot on top of it. "Stop you fool," she said. "I would be more man to defend myself with that than you are. And if D'Artagnan needs to duel with someone, he should duel with me."

Edmond, maddened, made as if to pick up the sword nonetheless and Irene hit him, an open-handed slap that echoed through the parlor.

"Stop, I said. What are you? A suicidal fool? Have we not had enough of death around here lately?"

And just as D'Artagnan started thinking she might not have been so bad to marry, after all, she turned to him, "Put away your sword, Henri. My brother will talk. Do not insult him though."

"Or you'll call me out?" D'Artagnan asked, faintly alarmed.

"Or he'll become too incoherent to speak to you," Irene said. "He's not very good, you see, at emotions, not having been disciplined enough as a child. So, instead of telling him he lied, I suggest you tell him what you came to tell him."

"I came to ask him if he sent assassins against me on my way to Gascony."

Another incoherent roar answered him, and he made for the sword, again, but Irene had hidden it behind her back and was leaning against the wall, keeping it secure. They were matched equally in size, and clearly in strength as not all of Edmond's efforts succeeded in getting hold of the sword.

Suddenly Porthos strode forward and took Edmond in hand. Their size difference was enough that Porthos could hold both his hands together behind his back while demanding, "Answer D'Artagnan, monsieur. If you're innocent you have no more than to say it."

Either Porthos's height or his strength or just the fact that he could hold him immobile seemed to work on Edmond. He glared at D'Artagnan. "Why would I kill you? What would be my interest in you?"

"So that you could inherit my father's domain," D'Artagnan said. "And wouldn't need to marry a woman you don't love."

"Even if that is true, and an advantage," Edmond said, "why would I kill you?" He seemed calmer, just genuinely confused. "You don't go about killing your relatives," he said, and added sulkily, "Well, at least I don't."

He seemed so thoroughly subdued that Porthos eased up his hold on him a little.

Edmond rubbed his wrists, where the giant redhead's hand had held it fast. He glowered at D'Artagnan. "And how can you accuse me of trying to kill you? We met in peace and we talked. What about that looked to you like I was trying to kill you, Henri? I think you've run mad."

D'Artagnan shook his head. He didn't put away his sword. He couldn't trust this cousin of his. Or at least he felt he couldn't trust him. And that was bad enough. "Twice on the way here and once since I arrived in Gascony, someone has tried to kill me," he said. "And in thinking, I realized you were the most likely candidate, because, attend." He sheathed his sword and started counting on his fingers. "On the first my father was spying on you on the Cardinal's behalf. You told me so yourself. And someone killed my father—"

"Yes, de Bilh!" Edmond said. "Do I perchance look like de Bilh to you?"

D'Artagnan shook his head and gritted his teeth. Would Edmond try to jest, now? "No. There are...reasons to believe he was wounded before, with a dagger or *poignard* through the back, wounding his heart, but not enough to kill him on the spot. This was why he attacked de Bilh erratically. And you must admit that you'd never be able to face my father in duel. Your only hope would be to hit him through the back with a dagger."

"But..." Edmond said, and raised his eyes to heaven as though in mute begging for help. "Surely you know that could not be, Henri. I was on the threshing floor at the time."

"Oh," D'Artagnan said. The thought had never occurred to him, and it did, indeed, seem to put a stop to any suspicion of Edmond being guilty. For how could he be guilty if he'd been elsewhere all the while? "Oh. So you were. And yet...perhaps you ran?"

"Ask de Bilh," Edmond said. "Poor Father Urtou can no longer be appealed to, but ask de Bilh. He was there with me a good few minutes, perhaps half an hour, before your father came up." And then, "But surely that isn't the only reason to accuse me? There are other men who would be as afraid to face your father in a duel as I am."

D'Artagnan sighed. In his confused mind, the thought ran that perhaps that was why Father Urtou had been killed. Because, being involved in a duel so shortly after, de Bilh's memory might be faultier or more inclined to being manipulated. Suspicious, he said, "The other reason is that twice on the way here we were attacked."

Edmond raised his eyebrows at him, "But the roads of Gascony—"

"No. The times we were attacked, it was clear the malefactors were making for me particularly and it was me they wished to kill. And I was attacked once more after I got to Gascony, just yesterday."

Edmond stared at him, then sighed in turn. "In truth, there is something smoky in that; something undeniably suspicious. But, cousin, why would it involve me? Surely there are others who might want your death. I can't think of any right now, but..."

D'Artagnan shook his head in turn, and unsheathed from its case a dagger. "Do you recognize this?" he asked, showing it to Edmond.

"My dagger," Edmond said. "My dagger."

D'Artagnan felt blood drain from his features, and his heartbeat increased again in volume till it threatened to deafen him. He had been right then. He had been right. "And yet you say you didn't try to kill me."

"Don't speak in riddles," Edmond said. "How came you by the dagger?"

"It was in the possession of one of those ruffians who tried to kill me on the way here," D'Artagnan said. "And now, will you deny that you armed them? That you hired them? That you sent them out to kill me?"

Edmond looked stricken. "Yes, I deny it. I lost that dagger six months since, at a dice game."

"A dice game?" D'Artagnan asked. Even in the hard and fast dicing and drinking world of the musketeers, he'd never seen anyone bet a dagger. Money, usually, less often jewelry. When Athos was drinking and playing—and when he played he invariably lost—D'Artagnan had seen him remove a ring from his finger or a jewel from his hat to bet upon the table. But never a dagger.

"A dice game with de Comminges, if you must know. He asked me to play, and as he usually never gambles, I thought it would make capital sport."

"You thought, in point of fact, that he'd not play well and, therefore, lose," D'Artagnan said.

Edmond looked sheepish. "Well...perhaps. But he had the devil of a luck, and after taking all my money and jewelry, I bet my dagger, trying to recover it all."

"And you lost."

"And I lost." Edmond said, then rallied. "But you should not for that think that de Comminges has sent someone to kill you!"

D'Artagnan was thinking of what his friends had said, of de Comminges being an old enemy of his father's. And yet, whatever the offenses of D'Artagnan's father against de Comminges, he could not possibly imagine they would continue with his son. To try to kill D'Artagnan before he even arrived in Gascony was unwarranted, and something that could not be countenanced as logical.

"He would have given the dagger to one of his servants," Edmond said. "It was of little value to him."

D'Artagnan nodded. He felt suddenly very tired. He could imagine de Comminges giving the dagger to a servant who, doubtless, had then in turn lost it in a dice game with some anonymous ruffian. Nothing meant anything. Everywhere he looked he was in danger, and he'd never find the person responsible for it.

He'd die in the dark, with a dagger between his shoulder blades, and no one would even ever know why.

Immersed in gloom, he didn't remember leaving the house, much less getting his horse and riding out, but as they were dismounting, in his own home, something occurred to him. "And yet," he told Athos, as the thought appeared, "I find it hard to believe that there is no connection at all between Father Urtou's death and this. I...It misgives me that he should die like that, when he was one of the three people present when my father died. I just wish I knew what secret he took with him to his grave."

# Ghosts; A Musketeer's Sleeplessness; Eyes Only

**IN** the middle of the night, Monsieur Athos woke up—starkly awake, he sat up in his bed, staring.

It took him more than a moment to realize it was neither a sound nor movement in his room that had awakened him, and that there was nothing besides his bed, not even that ghost that he sometimes believed he could see out of the corner of his eye, in the dead of night.

No, he was simply and unavoidably awake, in this room, in Gascony, in D'Artagnan's house, in the night.

Perhaps it was, he told himself, no more than that his friend's life appeared to be threatened and there was nothing at all he could do for it, nothing he could do to protect D'Artagnan. After all, in the last six months since he'd met D'Artagnan, they'd all faced down terrible threats and emerged victorious. But, alas, one thing it was to face a threat you could understand and another—altogether different—to face this danger, here, in Gascony, where murder seemed to flash from every corner and yet the murderer remained hidden.

Athos groaned, thinking to himself that he was too old for this and, furthermore, that he'd been a fool to ever come to Gascony. What could he do but uncover more mysteries to keep him awake? And if D'Artagnan were killed, what would it have availed him, all of Athos's friendship, save that Athos—and Porthos and Aramis—should he escape with his life, would forever carry in his mind and heart the sense of having failed once again at his responsibilities.

Now, when Monsieur Athos woke like this, in the middle of the night, there was a sure treatment for his melancholy. Well, perhaps treatment was not the best name for it, for it did not cure his sadness and guilt and his endless replaying of what might have been. But it did, in the silence and darkness in which he didn't dare ask another human being's help, give him a palliative and, if nothing else, allow him to sleep.

He now got up and stumbled to the corner where Grimaud had stowed the two saddle bags Athos had brought with him. Most of their contents were changes of clothes, his razor, a small book with Suetonius's life of Augustus, which he would read to while away idle hours. And at the bottom of all this, a dozen bottles of his best wine, sent to him from his own domains by a cousin who knew he was alive but chose to pretend he was dead or at least missing.

Athos found the bottle by touch and pulled it out, its cool exterior seeming to calm his nerves. He would drink and then he would sleep. Though drinking seemed to increase his grief, it did, at long last, bring him calm and relief.

Normally the relief he required was to forget his past and his own misdeeds. Now...Now he wanted to forget the danger he was in. And if death came for them all, let it come and at last welcome.

Holding the bottle, he collected his dagger and went to the window to use the light of the moon to better see the string that held the glass stopper in. But as he applied himself to cutting the string with his dagger, he heard clearly in his mind—as though they were repeated in front of him that minute—D'Artagnan's words on their arrival home: *I find it hard to believe that there is no connection at all between Father Urtou's death and this.*

Athos frowned down at the wine bottle, as though it were somehow guilty of that thought, then carefully set it on the windowsill, illuminated by the light coming in through the shutter slats, and backed all the way to his bed, where he fell to sitting more than sat down.

It was hard to believe, indeed, that Father Urtou just chanced to be killed at the same time that another spate of deaths seemed to have overtaken the countryside. In fact...He bit at the inside of his cheek...It was very strange that there had been so many seemingly unrelated deaths. The elder Monsieur de Comminges; D'Artagnan's father; Father Urtou; the attempts against D'Artagnan's life itself.

Seemingly, all of these had clear explanations. Seemingly, none of them involved any of the others. But between the seeming and the truth, there had to be a gulf in this case. There had to be, else they were all fools and Gascony was, in fact, a much more dangerous location than could be supposed. Either all these murders and attempted murders were connected, or one must believe that there were, loose in the Gascon countryside, many people intent on killing someone else, without it much mattering who.

Oh, old people and spinsters and children frightened by their nurses would believe the countryside a vast trap populated by homicidal maniacs. But Athos was neither aged and infirm, nor a spinster lady, nor a child. No. These deaths must be all related.

To start with Monsieur de Comminges, it would seem that the Cardinal had disposed of him—or perhaps ordered D'Artagnan père to dispose of him. The matter of the safe-conduct found in D'Artagnan's father's trunk came to mind and Athos frowned. That he knew, the man hadn't killed anyone. Not even in duel, much less by those means that would make it harder to escape punishment.

He frowned, and his temples throbbed, at the thought that there might be yet more deaths they had not discovered.

But he wouldn't allow himself to think on that. It seemed to be so much foolishness as speculating on what constituted virtue or saint-hood, much the type of silliness that Aramis would engage in, and not at all a profitable exercise for the mind.

Instead, Athos went back to the beginning. Supposing that the first death that mattered had been that of Monsieur de Comminges, who would benefit from it?

The Cardinal, he supposed. He frowned at this, as it was quite pos-sible the Cardinal had decided to rid himself of Monsieur D'Artagnan, an agent who had fulfilled his duty and who might have, at any rate, grown if not a conscience then greed. Hard to believe the whole matter of the horses hadn't been a bit of freelancing on Monsieur D'Artagnan's part.

But this brought on, then, that the Cardinal must have attempted to kill D'Artagnan. Athos couldn't quite conjure a motive for that. Oh, the Cardinal hated them all, Aramis perhaps a little more than the rest, but all of them with admirable inclusiveness. Still...

If the Cardinal had attempted to kill D'Artagnan—and at least the first set of bandits had carried one of those damned safe-conducts from his eminence—it must profit him some. This, Athos could imagine, would tie in with the inheritance of D'Artagnan's domain. Perhaps his eminence had decided that nothing would make the young de Bigorre give up on his engagement but the provision of another domain for his taking. Such a plot was ruthless enough for the Cardinal to undertake.

However...try as he might, Athos could not think of a reason for the Cardinal to order Father Urtou murdered. The priest was just a provin-cial priest, and, had the Cardinal wished him silenced, there were other means to accomplish this, including perhaps calling him to Paris and instigating in him a taste for honors and recognition.

So for now, and until he could discover a motive for the Cardinal to want the priest killed, he would consider Richelieu—if not innocent, because he clearly was deeply involved in the matter—at least not exactly involved in directing the deaths.

And then he came to the next suspect—the young de Bigorre. While it was true that Edmond was present at the duel and therefore couldn't, at the same time, be attacking Monsieur D'Artagnan by stealth, yet it was possible the wounding had taken place earlier than the peasant woman remembered. Perhaps D'Artagnan's father had lost conscious-ness a while and seemed dead, before reviving, with disturbed mind. If he had bled on the plowed field it would be quite invisible.

Edmond might very well have killed Monsieur D'Artagnan and at-tempted to kill young D'Artagnan, but here the mind beggared. How would he contrive to pay for mercenaries to kill Henri D'Artagnan? Surely a man who had ruined himself with unwise gambling would be in no position for so expensive an enterprise. And beyond that, why kill the priest? If the priest had seen something or known something, he would surely have talked about it.

Athos frowned at the darkness intercut by moonlight. No. Oh, it was possible that Edmond de Bigorre had contrived it. He certainly stood to gain by the death of both men who might have a claim to the title of D'Artagnan. As a second son of the de Bigorre house, if no other heir obtained from this line, the title would naturally devolve to him.

And while Athos was quite sure the young man would rapidly expend all his patrimony in gambling and soon be as penniless as he was now, he would also be sure that Edmond Bigorre did not think so. Gamblers never did.

Therefore, it must be someone else. Who else—always barring agents of the Cardinal—could have profited by the deaths of de Comminges, Monsieur D'Artagnan, the priest and young Henri D'Artagnan himself?

De Comminges's son, a creature that Athos did not find particularly pleasing, might very well have profited from the death of his father, who seemed to be of Monsieur D'Artagnan's generation and therefore sullied with all the splatter of the wars of religion.

Monsieur de Comminges the younger might even have profited from the death of Monsieur D'Artagnan. Unless Athos misread the situation with the horses—as he very much doubted he did—then Monsieur D'Artagnan had used blackmail to obtain horses from de Comminges, who was involved in treason.

So, getting rid of Monsieur D'Artagnan made perfect sense. But what use could it possibly be to get rid of young D'Artagnan, or the priest, yet?

Athos thought of the wedding record for the older de Comminges. Something about the wedding with Marie R. being a fake one. And then there was that gown that Aramis had found in the trunk, and the challenge to a duel, stained, presumably with de Comminges's blood.

What kind of events could have taken place at that time that would cast their shadow upon the present, like a tree that once cut down will return from the roots to occupy the space it occupied before? Something to do with Madame D'Artagnan. That much was sure.

There was much about Madame D'Artagnan that Athos could not like, and some of it, probably, had to do with the present situation. He just couldn't imagine what. He also couldn't imagine what attached her to de Bilh. Something was there, but he could not believe it was the infidelity that Bayard was so ready to impute upon her.

For one, from what D'Artagnan had said of how de Bilh referred to his mother, then certainly Monsieur D'Artagnan would know about it too. Any relationship, Monsieur D'Artagnan would have known about. And yet the one thing none of them had found evidence of was any true animosity between the two men. On the contrary. Despite the fact that de Bilh had killed D'Artagnan, even the witnesses to the death ascribed it to accident.

To imagine that de Bilh had faked friendship for D'Artagnan for so long only to kill him was something out of a crazed novel or Roman myth, something that even Athos's wild imagination, plaguing him with chimeras and monsters, would not countenance.

So, what could have happened those many years ago, before D'Artagnan's birth, that could have caused the younger de Comminges to want to exterminate the family, root and branch?

Athos thought of the note in the registry again. And he remembered, cloudily, from the days D'Artagnan had spent recovering at the last inn, the boy saying something about the ruffians wishing to kill him so papers wouldn't come out.

Papers. Marriage record. Suppose the note on the de Comminges marriage record had referred to Marie D'Artagnan. Suppose it had been wrong. Suppose...

Athos felt his hair stand on end at the back of his neck, but he forced himself to go on, ruthlessly. Suppose that in fact Marie D'Artagnan as she called herself had been truly married to de Comminges, who had, somehow, through some contrivance, and with who knew what intent, decided to repudiate her and remarry. And on remarrying, he had convinced Marie the marriage had been false.

Then that would make the de Comminges heir illegitimate—which gave him double the reason to kill D'Artagnan, and perhaps to kill the priest. At least if he believed the priest had the papers. That too would explain the ransacking of the sacristy, as no other of the ideas would have.

Athos sat up straighter. The only thing that remained and made no sense whatsoever was both the Cardinal and the younger de Comminges attempting against D'Artagnan's life.

If this scenario were true, then, perforce, D'Artagnan was himself a bastard. Whether he inherited the D'Artagnan domain or not in that case was much of a question, but not one that he could imagine would excite de Comminges' interest, though it might interest the Cardinal.

He thought of this drama he'd dreamed up, lost in the time before D'Artagnan's birth, and frowned. None of it made sense nonetheless. Perhaps he'd simply sat around dreaming of improbable tragedies well befitting a Greek playwright for no reason at all.

In his mind, Marie D'Artagnan's pale blue eyes looked out at him in wounded outrage. She'd trusted him. She'd begged him—as the oldest and most responsible of them all—to keep her son safe. And Athos, instead, had sat here thinking up calumnies about her.

He thought of the portrait of Monsieur D'Artagnan, downstairs, in the great salon, with its bluff appearance, and despite its blond hair, looking like nothing so much as like Porthos.

And then the monstrous idea he'd been keeping submerged in his thoughts for so long emerged. Like a beast, long forgotten, it rose from the depths of his consciousness.

He thought of the portrait again, and he was not sure of anything anymore. He'd looked at it, but not with the intent of deciding what had happened so long ago.

He must see it again.

Rising swiftly, he lit his candle wick upon the banked fireplace. With it in hand, dressed only in his shirt which, not being tucked into his breeches, covered him to the top of his thighs, he started out of the room and down the stairs.

He turned along shadowed corridors, forever afraid something or someone would jump out of the shadows, and all the while telling himself he was a fool.

The great salon was deserted, tables and chairs carefully arranged, probably by Marguerite. And the portrait on the wall was undisturbed and seemed to smile at him, by the twitching light of the candle, an ironical, mocking smile. Its dark blue eyes seemed to flicker and dance by the moonlight, just like D'Artagnan's dark brown ones did when he was most amused.

Athos felt his jaw drop open and disciplined it to close. No. This was not the time to stand around gaping and wondering what to do. He didn't know if there was anything he could do, but he had a feeling…

The murderer had, after all, killed three times, and had attempted over and over to kill again. He'd been responsible for at least two attempts on D'Artagnan's life, Athos would wager. And now, he knew they were questioning people. They'd alarmed him enough to have a close look at them himself. And since then, there had been Porthos questioning people about the horses, and there had been the scene with Edmond de Bigorre yesterday. If Edmond had not reported, Athos would have been much surprised.

The question was, when would the murderer ready himself to attack next? And whom? And would he do it himself, or send someone to do it?

Without warning, a picture formed in Athos's mind. D'Artagnan had proved hard enough to kill—and D'Artagnan was no threat, anyway. Having talked to the boy, doubtless the villain understood the boy had come to Gascony with no other aim than to settle down and administer the D'Artagnan lands. No threat in that.

But there was still one person who was a threat, one person who might, on purpose or by design speak of the events eighteen years ago. Athos could not imagine the murderer taking much more time than tomorrow to do it.

Tomorrow everyone would be at the priest's funeral in the morning, including the house's faithful servants. All but Marie D'Artagnan. And doubtless, in a place as small as this, everyone knew that someone hated funerals and didn't attend them. There had been reason enough recently to remember it.

So...The picture formed in Athos's mind. The deserted house and the murderer coming and executing his victim in bed. He was sure the murderer would come personally. After the failures with D'Artagnan, not to mention the fact that Monsieur D'Artagnan had got up from a supposedly fatal wound and fought again, the creature would be feeling insecure enough he'd want to be sure of things.

There was only one thing that Athos could do. And he would pray that if he was right the creature would indeed make an attempt.

Because, otherwise, he would have no proof at all.

# Invading Bedrooms Again; A Son's Duty; Dogs and Angels

**"INTO** my mother's room?" D'Artagnan asked, rubbing his eyes. "Why? What could it possibly serve? And..." He looked around, wild-eyed, sure that his friends had gone insane. "It is not proper."

Athos, a fully dressed, grave-looking Athos, shrugged imperiously. D'Artagnan had never thought of a shrug as a commanding gesture before, but Athos somehow managed to make it so—like a general, before battle, shrugging away all unnecessary impediments to his mission. "Never mind the propriety of it," he said. "It might be her life we're saving. And yours. We pretended to go out to the funeral Mass with all of the servants. In a big group, so I doubt they could tell you weren't among us. Once away, we doubled back one by one and secreted into the house. Hopefully no one saw us."

Behind Athos, Porthos and Aramis—also fully dressed and armed—nodded their resolution and agreement.

D'Artagnan was sure he was dreaming. He must be dreaming. Things like this didn't happen in real life. One's friends might come into one's bedroom and wake one—in fact, D'Artagnan was willing to admit this had happened before. But they didn't, then, lay forth a plan for invading one's mother's bedroom.

"Here," Athos said, and as he spoke, gathered D'Artagnan's clothes and threw them on the bed, beside him. "Dress yourself. We have not a minute to lose. Though it's still dark, it's already morning, and the bell has chimed for the priest's funeral. We can't be too late."

"To the funeral?" D'Artagnan asked, sleepily putting on the venetians that Aramis had persuaded him to buy in Paris, but which had got him some very odd looks here, in the provinces.

"Not the funeral," Aramis said, in a tone of great exasperation. "D'Artagnan, you're not attending, and you must. We must go to your mother's room. Athos has made it all perfectly clear."

"He has?" D'Artagnan asked.

Sleepily he put on his clothes, and strapped on his sword, when commanded. Sleepily he stumbled out of his room and down the long, still dark corridor to his mother's room.

The wind carried the sound of the chapel's bell ringing death, and D'Artagnan felt a shiver. What could Athos possibly mean with all this? Why wasn't anyone explaining things to him? And why did they want him along if they weren't willing to explain things?

Well, possibly because breaking into his mother's room without him would be quite a different plan from breaking into his mother's room with him. But in that case, why weren't they explaining to him the necessity of breaking into it at all?

Athos tried the door and whispered, "As I feared." Then made a gesture.

From the darker shadows of the hallway, the figure of Mousqueton detached. The man got his bits of metal from his sleeve, and did something. The door clicked open, and he nodded.

"Will you be needing my help inside?" he asked Athos.

"I would think not," Athos said. "I expect that the four of us should be more than equal to the task. But do you and your fellows stay alert, should the murderer try to escape."

Mousqueton nodded and melted back into the shadows, which D'Artagnan could now see contained, in addition to his quite respectable bulk, the slim figure of Planchet, the silent Grimaud, and the rotund and clerical Bazin—the latter recognizable because he was crossing himself as he stood there.

D'Artagnan cleared his throat. "Athos—" he whispered.

But Athos only put his finger on his lips commanding silence as, with the other hand, he slowly, slowly slid the bedroom door open.

To be greeted with a low canine growl.

"Angel," D'Artagnan whispered. The shape of the little dog darted towards him in the darkness, growling as he came, only to thump his tail upon catching scent of D'Artagnan.

D'Artagnan petted him absently, then followed Athos's stern gestures, to melt into the darker parts of the room, the corners where light would not reach, even were the blind open. Not until the sun was quite a bit brighter than it was now.

His mind was a whirlwind that would not stop. Why would his friends not tell him what the necessity was of going into his mother's room? Even as hurried and incomplete as their warnings normally were, they were more complete than this. There must be some very powerful reason not to have explained everything to him.

Unfortunately, D'Artagnan could only imagine one. And that one made his hair stand on end and sent a cold chill up his spine, as though a frigid finger were running the length of it.

Had his mother killed all these people, and commanded his death too? Did they expect her to rise from her bed and...

His mind beggared for thought. And what? Find him in his bed and kill him? What could they think? Surely if she wanted to murder him, she could have used poison? They'd all been at her mercy every day they'd eaten there.

"Athos," he started again, in a whisper.

Athos shook his head and again took his finger to his lips, and this time pointed towards the window.

At first D'Artagnan wasn't sure what the pointing towards the window meant. And then he could hear the scuffing of shoes against the stones of the wall. Someone was climbing the wall. Not a hard feat, since the D'Artagnan house was stone construction and quite old enough to have irregularities and fissures. But that D'Artagnan knew no one had ever climbed the wall. Why was someone doing it now?

Slowly, slowly, the blind creaked open, inward. Fully open, it revealed a man perched on the windowsill. That it was a man there could be no doubt. That he was about some no good pursuit no doubt also.

D'Artagnan thought, suddenly, it was de Bilh, come on a secret assignation with his mother. De Bilh was the murderer for the love of Marie D'Artagnan.

Angel started to stir, and D'Artagnan, kneeling, petted him silently. He subsided.

The shadow looked around and, seemingly, couldn't see them, knit as they were with the wall, behind a large wardrobe.

He turned to the bed, where Marie D'Artagnan slept. Though her bed was curtained, she had not closed the curtains. She never did. D'Artagnan could see her head on the pillow, the blond hair spread around it.

So could the intruder, who stepped forward, pulled a dagger from his belt, and raised it over her sleeping, unsuspecting form.

"Monsieur de Comminges," Athos said, his voice very calm and perfectly conversational from the shadows. "Do you often murder defenseless women? Can you also murder the four men who saw you do the deed?"

Sever de Comminges turned around, and D'Artagnan recognized him. Though the light was still scant, his face was so pale that it seemed to shine with its own light.

Madame D'Artagnan woke up and screamed. Sever turned towards her, dagger raised.

He was so lost to all that he would kill her and damn the witnesses. This wasn't quite a thought but a feeling that, as it formed in D'Artagnan's mind, grabbed hold of him and sent him, headlong, towards de Comminges, grabbing at his arm. He would have been a moment too late, hadn't Angel attacked the intruder's ankle, growling and biting.

That moment of confusion—of frantically trying to kick the dog away—was enough. Porthos was on him, holding his hand, and D'Artagnan and Athos and Aramis, swords drawn, had taken their places between the madman and Marie D'Artagnan's bed.

There was a frantic scurry, a scramble, and de Comminges bent and twisted like a heel, managing to draw his sword. Porthos jumped back, his sword in his hand.

De Comminges looked around, at all of them, with their drawn swords. His voice emerged from between his lips like a vicious growl. "What, it takes all four of you to duel me?"

D'Artagnan started to step forward, but felt Athos's hand on the back of his doublet, pulling him back.

"This is not a duel," Athos said. "No more than it was when you sent your assassins to dispatch my friend. It's a pity you were so badly informed you didn't know two of us were dark-haired. Your henchmen wasted time discussing which of us to murder, and murdered neither."

"More the fool I," de Comminges said. "I should have told them to kill you all."

"Indeed you should, monsieur," Aramis said. "For so it is always with us, one for all and all for one."

"Bah," de Comminges said. "Friendship and its softening ties." He spit onto the floor and glared at them. "I despise friendship. And I despise you. How do you propose to capture me, now?" he asked.

"There are four of us," Porthos said, in a low, perplexed tone. "Surely capturing you will not be the problem."

But he only laughed, a hollow laugh and, suddenly, turned and ran towards the window.

In a leap he was gone over the sill. D'Artagnan had a moment to wonder if they'd ever capture him again—and then he heard the noise of the fall against the stone patio. De Comminges wouldn't be getting up again.

Porthos looked out. "He broke his neck."

Athos sheathed his sword and nodded, as if to himself. "I thought he would prefer death to dishonor."

"Some of us won't get the choice," Marie D'Artagnan said in a voice full of tears.

"*Maman!*" D'Artagnan said in shock, now thinking that his mother must have been carrying on an affair with Sever de Comminges, but how was that possible?

But Athos, smiling slightly, said, "I don't think it will come to that, Madame D'Artagnan." He bowed slightly to her. "We will now leave you to dress yourself, and you can give us an explanation when you're more composed. We'll fetch Bayard to remove the body and send word to de Comminges's house. I pray, do not do anything foolish. I'm sure it is not your fault and you were most terribly imposed upon."

"Little that will matter to the world, should it all come out," Marie said, still lachrymose.

"But it won't madam. He is dead and with him the cause for his crimes. No one need find out."

# Old Secrets and New Grievances; Where a Father Is Lost and a Grandfather Found; A Name Worth More Than All Lands

"YOU see," Marie said, speaking almost in a whisper, as she sat at the table. "I was so young and so foolish."

Her cap was askew and her hair disheveled. She sat facing the four men, pale, as though they were her executioners. That one of them was her son seemed to make no difference. Or perhaps it made it all the worse. She looked at D'Artagnan and blenched more, and her lips half opened but nothing came out of them.

Even in this state of distress, she was a beautiful woman and Aramis could well imagine how much more beautiful she must have been in those days of her youth that she referred to in such pitying terms.

"My mother, you see..." She hesitated. "She died when I was very young. I didn't know my father, though of course I knew of him. And I knew he was a Gascon."

"Your mother wasn't then?" Athos asked.

She shook her head. "No. She was Parisian, born and bred. But I knew my father was Gascon. And he wrote to me sometimes."

From across the table, Aramis saw D'Artagnan starting to open his mouth, and creasing his forehead, but he must have thought better of speaking. "I was raised by some cousins of my mother's," she said. "Until I was six, when I was consigned to a convent with the idea that I would profess when I was old enough. My father was willing to proffer a handsome dowry for that purpose as in the eyes of the world it would be the best of all solutions."

She lowered her head and colored, then sighed. "Don't ask me how I met him. He was young and dashing, a Gascon Lord, one with a true patrimony, enjoying his time in the city. They...They let us go to Mass and..." She shook her head. "Oh, I was foolish beyond consent.

"I escaped to meet him, and I allowed him to kiss me and...But to allow him to make me his mistress I would not. I knew how my poor mother's life was blighted and I was not that foolish. So I told him he could only have me if we married...

"We married late at night in his townhouse. A priest came out and not only made a record of the marriage, but gave me a letter, certifying that I was married. That letter..." She shrugged. "I couldn't find it." She looked at D'Artagnan. "Your fath—Monsieur D'Artagnan had it and he...I don't know where he hid it. I've looked all over. And I'm sure Sever did too. It was why I locked your father's study against you, Henri. In case you should find it, where I'd failed."

She shook her head and took a deep breath. "I am making a great muddle of it. As I said, I married de Comminges and was installed in his townhouse as his wife, I thought, though I have reason to believe others thought I was only his mistress."

D'Artagnan across the table made a sound between a sigh and an exclamation of protest. His mother looked at him and shook her head again. "I was very foolish, Henri. I lived with him three months, I think. It took that long for the novelty to wear off. And besides, his mother—who was then still living—was putting pressure on him to marry well. It seems his finances were not, then, all that could be desired. His father was a famous...or perhaps infamous...gambler. He needed to marry an heiress, and his mother stood ready to make sure he did so."

She took a breath as though it hurt to breathe and looked down at her hands, entwined on the table, as she spoke. "He told me we were never married. Never in fact. That the priest was not a priest at all. That it was all a sham." She set her chin in a way oddly reminiscent of D'Artagnan. "I took a horse. One of the horses from his stable. It was spring and warm enough. I came towards Gascony on the horse. Slept by the wayside."

Aramis could easily see her doing that. It was foolish. No, more than foolish, it was insane. But she was D'Artagnan's mother, and he could easily imagine the very young Marie D'Artagnan galloping across the fields. "Dangerous for a woman," he said.

She shrugged. "I was just seventeen and I dressed as a boy, in one of de Comminges suits."

"But what did you expect to find in Gascony?" Athos asked.

"Well...for one thing I expected to find my father," she said. "Monsieur de Bilh."

She let that fall into the silence around the table and sighed. "That you didn't know, did you? Yes, he is my father. I am his daughter by his Parisian mistress. He never had any children by his wife, but I was born where he didn't want me.

"I said I was young. I had some idea of presenting myself to him and asking him to stand by my rights." She smiled a little. "Little did I know, his wife being yet living, then, that he would be more likely to turn me out into the cold. But as it chanced, the saints favor the foolish. I stopped in the hostelry outside the bastide, and I changed into my female attire, thinking it more likely I would earn my father's support that way. And then I rode...Only there was a storm, and I got soaked to the skin, and so confused I didn't know south from north...Instead of going to Monsieur de Bilh's, I ended up here, at my husban—At Monsieur D'Artagnan's doorstep."

She looked up, a light color tinging her cheeks. "I don't know why he took me in, but he did, and he was perfectly gentlemanly and protective. Marguerite, too, she fussed over me and took care of me. And Monsieur D'Artagnan and I fell in love. It turned out, you know, that when I went to the priest and he sent enquiries abroad, he could find no sign of the marriage being real. But I know just before his death my husband told me he had shown the marriage letter to the young de Comminges and that made him give my husband several horses. Oh, if only that wasn't what caused him to kill my husband and the priest and..."

"It wasn't," Athos said, kindly. "I have, I think, pieced together the whole as well as it could be pieced together. Seeing the letter might have caused him to kill your husband, but I think your husband only showed him the letter because he had already mentioned the marriage. You see, madam, if it were just your husband showing him the letter, he'd have sent enquiries to Paris, and it would have come back negative. If he'd talked to the priest—and perhaps he did—that too would have reassured him. He could have told your husband to divulge; the old intrigue would only have hurt you and not him. No. I think what happened...

"Is that his father, on his deathbed—and I don't know if his death was natural or not, but I would bet you it was a prolonged death."

"Oh yes," Madame D'Artagnan said. "The poor man lay in his deathbed for days and days and he refused to call the priest, having reverted, in his agony, to the Protestant faith of his youth."

"Ah," Athos said. "And yet in those conditions men want to confess. I will wager that he confessed to his older son. Told him the truth."

"He did," a voice said, from the doorway to the room. Looking up, they saw Geoffroi de Comminges on the threshold. "Your servant came to tell me my brother had met with an accident...I'm sorry, I did not mean to intrude, but I heard what you said."

Aramis looked up for a moment, but there didn't seem to be anything for it. All the others being silent, he said, "Well, the harm is done, then. You might as well come in and speak to us. How do you know your father told your brother about the marriage?"

Geoffroi approached, hesitantly, to sit at the table. "Because there is a secret passage, behind the room. I used to hide there when my father wanted to be alone with Sever. Sever was not...good. He was not even an honorable person. He killed dogs, you know...and...and cats and birds. Ever since he was a boy. His pleasure was to wound and kill. And I was afraid what he might do to our father, defenseless as our father was. So I heard. He told...Father told Sever that we were...bastards. That he'd married before he married our mother, and the lady, still living, was living as Madame D'Artagnan."

"What purpose can there be to having told him?" Porthos asked. "Seems a very foolish thing to do."

Geoffroi shook his head. "He wanted Sever to promise that he would look after his son...Henri D'Artagnan. That he would do what he could to advance the boy in his career."

"His son?" D'Artagnan asked, half shocked, half outraged.

"I am afraid so," Geoffroi said. "You are my father's son and my older brother." A bitter smile twisted his lips. "You are also the legitimate heir to de Comminges and I hope you will be kind to me."

"I don't think so," D'Artagnan said. "It can't be."

"Unfortunately," his mother said, "I must tell you it's true. I was with child before I ever lay with your fath—with Monsieur D'Artagnan."

"Don't be absurd," D'Artagnan said. "I'm a D'Artagnan."

"Indeed, D'Artagnan, you can't be," Athos said. "You see that your mother has blue eyes, and so did Monsieur D'Artagnan. Take it from one that has seen countless family galleries, two blue-eyed parents have had a dark-eyed son so rarely as to be almost never."

D'Artagnan looked from Athos to his mother, and finally to Geoffroi. "I say I'm Monsieur D'Artagnan's son." He raised his hand. "I understand all your protests, but these old intrigues are best left buried. I do not have proof that my mother was ever married to your father, and I choose instead to assume the identity her lawful husband endowed me with."

"I am sure," de Comminges said, miserably, "the letter will surface sooner or later, and if you looked through the various parishes in Paris, and if you were to exert enough force, you'd find the priest who performed the marriage or some record of it."

"I'm sure I would," D'Artagnan said. "If that letter wouldn't, unfortunately, fall in the fire as soon as it is found."

It took Geoffroi de Comminges a moment to realize what he was saying. "You mean it?" he asked, at last.

"Of course," D'Artagnan said. "I would not trade my honored name for yours. No offense meant."

"None taken," Geoffroi said. "But you must know there are lands and..."

"All the lands in the world are nothing next to a respected name," he said.

Athos cleared his throat. "So I assume," he asked the young de Comminges, "that it was your brother who killed the priest? And Monsieur D'Artagnan? And who sent ruffians to kill D'Artagnan?"

"Yes. I have no proof of it, but I am sure it was him. Once he knew he was not legitimate, his goal would be to eliminate everyone who could have testified to this. I'm sure to his feverish mind, the fact that Monsieur Henri D'Artagnan came to Gascony meant he was going to contest Sever's position. It's why he wanted to marry Irene as soon as possible, so that Monsieur Henri would scruple to overset his cousin of whom he was so fond."

"I realized the danger you must be in," Marie said. "It took me a while to remember it, in the confusion of the death. And even longer to feel uneasy about your father dying so soon after de Comminges. I've been looking over my shoulder this while," she said. "And looking for the letter."

"I'm sure the only thing that tempted him was the circumstances of your being, as he thought, alone in the house," Athos said. "And the fact that he had already killed twice, undetected. And I'm sure he only came because Edmond told him he'd confessed to losing the dagger to him."

"Poor Edmond," D'Artagnan said. "Now...the question is, how do I give him his true inheritance?"

"His true inheritance?" Aramis asked, in some confusion.

"Well," D'Artagnan said, and a bit of his old roguish self crept into his smile. "The thing is, if I'm not truly my father's blood son, then I have no right to the D'Artagnan house. Edmond should have it by rights, and I can go back to Paris and resume my life." He sounded like a man freed from jail.

"But...Henri," his mother said. "Far be it from me to hold you to a duty you find distasteful but...what's to become of me?"

D'Artagnan stopped for only a moment, then shrugged. "Well, since I can't tell Edmond the truth, I'll have to tell him I'm giving him the lands. I'll make it so on condition he provide for you."

## The Best Laid Plans

**BEFORE** leaving, D'Artagnan visited his father's grave, outside the main church of the bastide.

He stood silently a long time, looking at the stone slab that overlaid the tomb. He felt nothing.

His father was not here. Oh, his body was, surely, but not his spirit. The same way that his body might not be D'Artagnan's father, but the spirit certainly was.

That spirit, wild and free as always, would be drinking and dueling in some heavenly tavern.

"Good-bye, father," D'Artagnan whispered, putting his hat back on his head. "I've arranged for mother to be well looked after, and I'm on my way to Paris, again."

"But she won't be living with Edmond after all," D'Artagnan said, as he and his friends had dinner at a hostelry on the way to Paris. "Monsieur de Bilh's wife is dead, and it is now sure he won't have any other children, so he chose to take *Maman* in, and announce their relationship before the world. I believe he will make it sound so she will seem to be the daughter of an early and unequal marriage that he's kept hidden from the world since. As it was, he only married his wife after his mistress's death, so it matters not."

"And was he happy to have her?" Porthos asked, interested.

D'Artagnan shrugged. Who was he to judge his grandfather's moods? "He looked to be. And she also. She'll nag him halfway to the grave, but it will do her good to have someone to look after her. *Maman* never did very well without a man to support her."

"It remains to see," Porthos said, hoisting his flagon of wine, "why those men first wanted to kill you, and why they had a safe-conduct from the Cardinal."

"For that matter," D'Artagnan said, "it remains to find out why my father had one too."

"How do you propose to find out?" Aramis asked.

D'Artagnan grinned at his friend's worried face. "I intend to ask him."

But he did not feel nearly as sanguine, a week later, as he found himself in the antechamber to the Cardinal's office. Surrounded by guards of the Cardinal, he had the hardest time staying out of quarrels, and it was all he could do to wait until the Cardinal's secretary said, "His eminence will see you now."

# His Eminence's Displeasure; Where a Letter Falls in the Fire

**"WHAT** did Richelieu say, monsieur?" Planchet asked, as D'Artagnan returned home.

D'Artagnan supposed that he shouldn't have disclosed the whole to his servant, but given everything the servants observed in Gascony, secrecy was a lost hope. He looked at Planchet's cat eyes which showed decidedly feline curiosity, and grinned. "He said that I've done him a bad turn by killing Sever de Comminges, who bid fair to be a good ally for him."

"But you didn't kill him," Planchet protested.

"No. And I told him so. In what his eminence did not say, it transpired that he tried to have me killed so that I would not interfere with Sever de Comminges, who had proved to be of service to him."

"I see," Planchet said. And given the nature of his brain, he probably did. "So that was why he sent ruffians to kill you. But what about the safe-conduct your father had?"

"It seems," D'Artagnan said, "that he wanted my father to dispatch de Comminges père. That my father refused to commit murder says a lot for him. Of course there was the matter of blackmailing Sever, but I would say he did it more to even the score with the family."

"I am sure, monsieur," Planchet said. "I'm sure he thought only of you and your inheritance."

D'Artagnan nodded. He was sure of that too. "Ah, little did he know he'd already given me a father I could look up to. The best inheritance of all."

"What should we do, then, about this letter?" Planchet said. "It arrived, you see, while we were gone. It was sent consigned to the kind offices of some Gascon acquaintance who, upon entering town, was too busy with drinking and dueling to remember the letter for a few weeks. The landlord said it was delayed with much apology."

D'Artagnan picked up the letter. It was addressed to him in his father's hand. Once having broken the seal, though, he found two sheets of paper inside. One written by his father, saying, "Henri, keep this safe for me," and another. The other he opened.

After the date and the usual salutations, it said, "This testifies that I performed a marriage ceremony uniting Marie Ravelet and Adrien de Comminges." It was signed by Father Bellamie[6] and D'Artagnan sighed. No wonder they hadn't found the priest who had performed the ceremony. No one would think to look in such a humble parish for the man who had performed a lord's marriage. At any rate, Father Bellamie was now beyond the reach of their curiosity.

D'Artagnan turned towards the roaring fireplace and dropped the paper in, just as a soft voice called from the stairs, "Henri?"

Smiling, D'Artagnan called to Planchet. "*Hola*, Planchet, go visit Monsieur Porthos. And don't hurry back." He tossed the boy a coin so he could buy wine with his friend, Mousqueton, and turned to welcome his mistress.

He had come home.

# Footnotes

[1] Monsieur D'Artagnan père was referred to, exclusively, in the previous manuscripts as Françios, but in this one he is referred to, almost exclusively, as Charles. As a mere compiler/translator of these adventures, I chose to leave the seemingly contradictory appellation as given in the originals. This single line might hold the key to the difficulty and the dual name might well be the result of one name being the legal one and the other the preferred.

[2] *The Musketeer's Seamstress.*

[3] De Bigorre could not possibly be the real name of the elder branch of D'Artagnan's family. In fact, all the family and town names in this portion of the diaries of Monsieur D'Artagnan seem to be vague allusions to the geography of the area or to families long vanished from the annals of Gascon nobility.

We have long known that Dumas had used fictitious names for his heros and attributed fictitious domains to them. It is now apparent that this obfuscation dates back to the diaries of Monsieur D'Artagnan. Given the revelations about their families—and others—contained in this portion of the diaries one can hardly marvel at it.

[4] This too is clearly a made up name. In fact, this is perhaps as good a place as any to dismiss the now popular fantasy that D'Artagnan was based on Charles de Batz and his cousins who accompanied him into the musketeers.

Though those musketeers had some points in common with our heroes, it is clear to anyone who examines the records with a clear-eyed, dispassionate interest that they were in truth quite different people. For one, we are sure that Dumas's Athos could not possibly be a Gascon. We're equally sure that there are no blood ties between Dumas's musketeers.

While some of the exploits of Monsieur de Batz and his friends sound like those of D'Artagnan, one can't help suspecting that given the spirit of the times these were exploits common—more or less—to all musketeers.

The diaries found by the author of these chronicles show clearly that we are dealing with quite a different group of gallant musketeers.

[5]*The Musketeer's Seamstress.*
[6]*Death Of A Musketeer.*